Flying With Angels

Enjoy! ☺
bbparker

Library and Archives Canada Cataloguing in Publication

Parker, B. B., 1958-
Flying with angels / b.b. parker.

ISBN 0-9733469-6-5
I. Title.

PS8631.A753F59 2004 C813'.6 C2004-906115-1

Publisher/Distributor
Windshift Press
P O Box 1176
Ladysmith,
BC, Canada, V9G 1A8
E-mail: press@windshift.bc.ca

Printer
Printorium
911 Fort Street
Victoria
BC, Canada, V8V 3K3
www.printoriumbookworks.com

Cover Design: Trevor Cook
Layout: Loonbook,Nanaimo, www.loonbook.com

for my Stevie

Special thanks to Sandra Janssen, my publisher for believing enough in me that she created a new imprint Rooster Fish Press; to John Hellum for being such a great sounding board; and to Steve, my partner in life, for his support and love.

"Hi Rick, I'm going to be a couple more hours here at the office tonight," I say right after the beep from the answering machine, "so don't wait to have dinner and I'll see you around sevenish." As I hang up the phone I wonder if he is actually there listening to the call. I've been late every night this week, and it's Friday and I don't want to work over the weekend. I just want to kickback and relax and spend some quality time with him, but I'm afraid that isn't going to happen. It will be just like every other weekend. He'll want to go out to the bars and get all liquored upped, we'll fight about something stupid, and not talk until Monday evening after I get home from work. It's always the same, but maybe not this time.

"Andy? Are you still here?" a soft voice comes into my office over the desk phone.

"Yes, I'm still here."

"Are you trying to get me to make you a partner in this firm?" she asks.

"You know I wouldn't turn you down, Laurel. So what about it?"

"Didn't you have plans for tonight?" she says, avoiding the issue of partnership.

"You know it's already seven fifteen."

"Oh shit!" I sigh. "Okay, okay I'm on my way. You leavin' now?"

"Meet you at the elevator in five."

There is silence again in my office, but only for a moment. I quickly start my backup, turn off my computer and pick up the files and folders and disks I would need to finish this up at home. I figure I can skip my Sunday jog and get a couple of hours of work done, so much for not working at home this weekend.

I lock my office door, turn around and make my way down the hall to the elevator. There she is, standing there like some kind of movie goddess, wearing an emerald green skirt and blazer, briefcase in her right hand, umbrella and Trench coat hung neatly over her left forearm; her flaming red hair frames her face. It all comes together so perfectly, she knows it, but rightly so because she is beautiful.

"So what are you waiting for?" she asks.

I start down the hallway, trying hard to get myself into some sort of order, one arm in my overcoat, one clasp undone on my briefcase, tie loosened and twisted to the side, I look like something the cat drags in. Laurel giggles as I fumble my way towards her.

"What's so funny?"

"You," she smiles, "You look so damned cute when you've been working hard."

"A mess you mean." As I stop and take a quick look at myself. I can feel the smile break out on my face as we make our way to the elevator.

She pushes the buttons for the main lobby and the underground parking, and puts down her briefcase. She reaches up and starts to fix my tie.

"You know if you weren't gay..."

"If I wasn't gay, then we'd have probably made all the rumours in this building true."

"Yes and Daddy would have gone to his grave a very happy man. He liked you a lot, almost as much as I do, but he could never figure it out. He kept saying that I was too aggressive, or that you were just too afraid to get involved with the boss' daughter. If he'd only known." She giggles again. "There, much better."

The elevator dings, my stop. She doesn't move as the doors open, then stretches up and gives me a kiss on my cheek.

"Well good night." Her eyes sparkle.

"Night."

"Oh, let me know how the weekend goes, and say hi to Rick for me. We'll talk about that partnership soon, I promise."

The doors close before I can say anything, I know she really doesn't like Rick but she always acknowledges that he is a part of my life. She says that I deserve much better. I just smile and make my way out of the building into the New York rain.

Eight twenty, shit is going to hit the fan, I think to myself as I climb the subway stairs to the street. I have another fifteen minute walk before I'm home. Thank God the rain has stopped, I had forgotten my umbrella this morning, but I'm still soaked from the walk to the subway. I think about just taking my time, why put myself through a whole lot of shit, it's not like I had planned to be late or that I'm fooling around on him, and besides I have phoned to let him know that I was going to be late. I know I'm talking myself into thinking that there is no reason for anything to happen when I get home. Who am I trying to fool. As soon as I walk through the door it will start, some catty remarks about finally getting home and it'll go from there into the shouting match, oh well, been there done that, no point in putting it off.

Stairs or the elevator? I'll wait for the elevator it's already on it's way down, just a couple more floors. The doors open and a young man in his early twenties walks out, quite good looking, with a beautiful smile, blue eyes, he gives me the once over and walks past. In the elevator I turn and watch him as he walks through the doors and into the city street. Nice, I love this part of town, always a lot of good scenery.

The door to our apartment is right in front of me, I take a deep breath as I unlock the door and enter. I walk down the hallway and look in the dinning room, table set for two. In the kitchen I see the makings for a pasta dinner in progress, shit I'm really in for it tonight. The living room lights are low, my favourite CD is playing, I walk into the bedroom, the bed is a mess. I hear water running in the bathroom shower.

"Hi, I'm home," I call in.

"Be out in a minute," is the reply.

I feel puzzled, not quite sure what is going on.

As he gets out of the shower, the bathroom fills with steam. "Boy, you sure are late tonight. Still working on that one account from last week?"

"Yeah, got it almost done, I was hoping to have it finished today, but it's taking a little longer than I expected."

This is not the way things are supposed to be going, this is not the way they always go. I finish getting out of my suit and start to put on a pair of sweat pants.

"You can have a shower while I finish up dinner," he says, sticking his head out of the bathroom. "I had a nap while I was waiting for you to get home, I'll tidy up out there in a second."

"Sorry, I'm later than what I said I was going to be. I guess I lost track of time."

"Good thing you called otherwise you'd have spoiled dinner," Rick says as he comes out of the bathroom, naked but dry. He comes over and gives me a hug and kiss. He holds his body close to mine. I can feel his whole body, the muscles of his arms as he squeezes, his semi hard cock pushing into my crotch, his hands as he rubs my back. It feels so good.

"Mmmm," he moans. He gives me another kiss and slaps me on the butt.

"Go on have your shower, dinner will be ready in about twenty minutes."

"Okay," I say as I go into the bathroom. This doesn't feel right, this whole scene didn't just happen. We're supposed to be shouting at each other by now. I think I'm in shock. This whole situation doesn't jive, there is something I'm missing. I wipe the steam from the bathroom mirror and look at myself through the streaks. Maybe I'm making too much out of this, maybe I was right that this weekend was going to be different, maybe I should just go with the flow and not try to project too much. What have I got to lose? I walk back into the bedroom and scan the room again just to make sure that I'm in the right place. Yes everything is right, the room looks like a bomb has gone off in it, the bed is a mess, work clothes on the floor, a bit unusual, he's messy but not usually this bad. I return to the bathroom, strip down and get into the shower, turn on the hot water. I'm still confused, deep down I know I'm missing something. As the hot water splashes against me I lather up and take stock of myself, yes, I have been neglecting myself these last few weeks, but tax time is always tough. I'm in pretty good shape, not bad for someone almost twenty-nine, but I have to work hard to keep it. Rick on the other hand is naturally built; the body of a well put together construction worker, just big enough and solid everywhere. He's twenty-six, about an inch taller than me, blonde and blue eyed, a hundred and ninety pounds of solid man, and very well put together. He's got a butt to die for. I continue to lather myself and stroke myself.

I stop stroking myself and look at my own equipment, I'm not bad if I do say so myself, a bit longer and a little thicker. I think I'll save this for later seeing as though everything is going better than expected. I finish showering, dry myself, walk back out into the bedroom and start to dress. The room's been tidied. There it is, I knew I've missed something. By Rick's side of the bed stands the bottle of lube. No sex tonight. He's a once a night only kinda guy, he's been that way for the last year or so of our six year relationship, so I'm used to this. I put the lube in the night stand by his side of the bed. I'm sure that he prefers to do himself rather than have sex with me, I guess the only consolation is that he's not sleeping around and when we do have sex it's great sex, at least I think it's great, and anyway sex isn't everything in a relationship. I should confront him about it but he would deny that he would ever jerk himself off. It's not worth arguing about again, and so far tonight everything is going so well that things might just turn out different. I don't want to jinx it, so I'll leave it alone. I put on my sweats and go into the dining room.

"Hey, ten more minutes and dinner will be ready."

"Smells good."

"I hope you're hungry. I've made quite a bit," Rick says as he comes into the dining room. "I've poured you a glass of wine, here."

"Thanks."

I know that there is something up now. He never gets me a glass of wine. "So what's this all for tonight?"

"What do you mean?" he asks.

"Well you know, the dinner, the wine."

Rick looks at me with those gorgeous blue eyes like a puppy that has been caught peeing on the carpet.

"Nothing, I just thought it would be a nice change for you. You've been working late just about every night for the last three weeks and I thought I would make tonight a little more relaxing than it has been for you."

Now I feel like a heel. Don't go any farther with this, just leave it be. Say something appreciative.

"Thanks, do you want a glass of wine?"

"I've got a glass in the kitchen. You can top it off for

me," he says as if the last couple of minutes didn't happen.

Dinner was great. We talked and ate and drank, just like we had when we first started seeing each other. This is too good to be happening. It's the way I've wished my relationship was everyday. Not meaning that I wanted to be waited on hand and foot but share without feeling that it's a chore. You want to do things for him and he wants to do things for you. The spontaneity of being touched or hugged or just simply being together is enough. Maybe it's the wine that is making me feel this way or maybe I'm just really tired from work. Rick gets up and walks around the table to me and gives me a long kiss. I close my eyes and sigh. This is real good.

"I'll do the dishes," he says. " You go relax in the living room." He starts to clear the dishes from the table. I get up, refill my glass of wine and retire to the living room. I park myself in the big overstuffed love seat, leaving plenty of room for company. I stare out of the big windows of the room and notice that the rain has left small rivers of water on the glass. April has been extremely wet this year, but right this minute it doesn't matter how wet it is outside. I'm feeling very happy. Is it just the moment or the wine that is making me feel this way? The music in the room plays softly in the background. I close my eyes and tell myself that it is the moment and that all my earlier suspicions were unfounded and that I was right this weekend was going to different. I finish my wine and sit and listen to the rain and the small noises coming from the kitchen. I close my eyes and slowly drift off to sleep.

Next morning I wake with a start, Rick has covered me with a blanket and tidied up the living room. The sun is shining for the first time in weeks.

I've slept on the love seat all night. Oh well, nothing would have happened last night, sexually that is. But maybe this morning? I go into the bedroom and Rick isn't there. I walk back into the living room, then into the kitchen. Nobody. Except there is a note on the counter, it reads:

"Andy, gone to work today. The job foreman said if the weather is good he would have a shift on as the job is about two weeks behind because of the weather. Could use the OT too. I'll see you tonight, Rick."

PS: Gerry called yesterday and wants to get together with you today, so give him a call.

Damn, I've been planning to spend the weekend, just him and me. This is the first weekend in weeks that we could spend together and he has to take an overtime shift. He's never taken an overtime shift before, so why this weekend? I feel myself getting angry. I pick up the phone and just automatically dial Gerry's number.

"Hello," is the answer after the first ring.

"Hi Gerry."

"Well hello honey, how are you this fine morning?"

"Pissed."

"Ooh, trouble in paradise again? You two lovebirds quarrelling again?"

"No we're not fighting. It's just that I've had this whole weekend planned so that Rick and I spend time together but he's off doin' overtime at work."

"So honey is that all? Well, you know you've been doin' all this overtime stuff yourself lately, so why is it so bad that he does some of it himself? Mind you, I can't understand why anyone would want to work anyway. Yuk!"

I can feel myself lightening up.

"Gerry, not everyone is like you, independently wealthy, but why this weekend?"

"True enough honey, true enough. So enough of this dirty work talk. What's on your social calendar for today?"

"Well, looks like it's completely clear."

"Good. Then let's start with a nice healthy breakfast at Georgio's and then some good ol' shoppin' to get your mind off that Rick of yours."

"Gerry," I say sternly, "let's not get into this again."

"Well honey, if you ask me..."

"Gerry!" I cut in.

"Okay honey, I won't say another word, at least not now."

"Gerry!"

"Okay, okay! What say we meet at Georgio's in 'bout an hour and go from there?" He continues as if the past conversation never happened.

"Sure, but only if you promise not to trash Rick."

There is a silence from the other side of the phone.

"Gerry?"

"Well of course, for you Andy honey I'd do anything. So I'll see you in an hour. Bye."

There is a click of the phone and he's gone. Gerry is impossible. We have been friends for about twelve years. He's my oldest and dearest friend, the most flaming homo in New York City and probably the most fun person that I know. But when it comes to Rick, let's just say that neither of them really care for each other, and both have no problem in letting me know how they feel about the other. If the two of them just sat down and talked they both might see that they really like each other. That's not saying that I haven't tried and every time it's been worse than a hurricane. So I've pretty much given up on the two of them ever becoming friends.

I pull into the parking lot at Georgio's and luckily find a spot in the front parking lot. I'm sure that Gerry is here and has already ordered us up a fantastic breakfast spread, as he always does. I walk in and Georgio himself is working the door this morning.

"Morning, Georgio."

"Ah, Andrew. Gerry is already at your table. Let me take you there."

He ushers me past the other waiting patrons in the lobby. Some of them giving us that I was here first look.

"I sat you by the window on the second floor, I couldn't put you in Gerry's usual spot. I've got some restaurant reviewers from the Times in so I gave them the best spot in the house to impress them. Gerry was a little upset and started to put up a fuss until I told him that Alberto would be your waiter. Got to keep him happy. He's one of my best customers."

I chuckle. Gerry would be more worried about not having Alberto wait on us than anything else. And I'm sure that Alberto prefers to wait on Gerry only because of the size of the tips he leaves.

"Good morning, Gerry."

"Oh Good morning honey. I'm sure Georgio explained this terrible seating arrangement that he has for us this morning."

He makes it sound so dire that we've been relegated from the A list to the C list, when in fact the seating is as nice if not more private than our usual table. But I guess the whole idea is also to be seen and who you are seen with. There's just too much fuss with all this social stuff.

"Yes, he has, but all for good reason."

"No reason is quite good enough you know."

"But isn't Alberto waiting on us?"

"Yes, but only after I demanded."

I smile and start to laugh. I sit down across from him and survey the table. It is still impeccably set, the best china and silver, good linen and crystal.

"Gee, I don't think I notice anything different at this table than at the usual one."

"Now Andy don't you go startin' to try and tease me about this awful situation. Alberto will be by in a few with your coffee. And I've already ordered."

"I wouldn't expect anything less."

"Good."

Gerry is definitely thrown off by this change in seating. He's not usually one who doesn't get his way. His chubby face is flushed and I'm sure it all has to do with the table location. He's thirty-five and almost as big around as he is tall. But he looks good; I guess that's what money does for you, especially if you have a lot of it. He's very dapper this morning, wool suit for the weather and I'm sure he has his camel overcoat, which he would have made quite a production out of how it should be hung at the coat check in the lobby. His trademark fedora hat, which never leaves his head, tilted slightly to the right, gives him an Oscar Wilde sort of look. Gerry is also well taken care of financially. He was left a large fortune from a sugar daddy that had passed away about six years ago. They had been together for ten years. Gerry used to joke about the old guy and his money but when he actually passed away he was a mess. It took him two years to rejoin civilization. Now he's out and about with a vengeance. As I look at him now I can see that he still has moments, that he's not quite finished mourning the old guy. A big white-toothed smile breaks out on his face.

"Alberto," he says excitedly.

"Gerry," he says as he smiles at him.

"Andy, your coffee." He stares into my eyes and holds the look for a long moment.

"Thanks," I say as I fumble for the sugar.

"Your breakfast will be up in about ten minutes, gentlemen," he says as he's still looking into my eyes. He then turns around and returns downstairs to his regular section.

"My God!" Gerry exclaims. "That boy is just so absolutely gorgeous."

"Yes he is, but I think he's straight."

"Oh honey, the way he looked at you I don't think so."

"He is so. He was just doing that to get a bigger tip. He knows the game. The more you tease, the bigger the tip."

"Well, if he ain't gay then it would be so much fun convertin' him."

"All your money won't make a straight boy stop chasing women."

"But it would be fun to try."

"You maybe, but I'm taken."

"Oh, you two would make the perfect couple. You'd look just absolutely gorgeous together. By the way tell me, how is life in paradise with your Rick?"

"Gerry."

"I was just askin' a simple question, I didn't mean anything derogatory."

"The usual, I guess, except last night."

"Well, what about last night?"

"It was just different."

"God, this is like pullin' whales teeth, what do you mean different?"

Breakfast arrives and I proceed to relay the events of the previous evening with Rick

"Nothing seems to fit right, you know what I mean?"

"He's seeing someone," Gerry blurts out.

"Gerry!"

"Well he has to be, honey. Don't you see it?"

"No I don't. Anyway, he isn't seeing someone, he

couldn't be." I decide that I'm not going to let Gerry start in on me. "No, of course not, it's just not possible, we're committed to each other. Rick and I don't have the typical gay relationship, just based on sex. It's got more to do with respect and trust."

"Humph! When reality sets in honey, don't say I didn't tell you so." And with that Gerry stands up from the table. "If you'll excuse me for a moment while I go to the powder room to freshen up." He turns on his heels and waddles off to the washroom.

Just then Alberto returns to the table.

"Well, how's everything here?"

"Fine," I say, not really paying much attention. I'm a little distracted by what just has transpired between Gerry and I that I haven't really noticed Alberto. "Yes, everything is great, thanks Alberto." This time I look up at him. Gerry is right. He is gorgeous. He's Latino, with beautiful dark eyes and colouring, with a strong jaw, and lips you could kiss for hours. He's Greek godlike in physique, but not too perfect.

"Is there anything I can get for you, Andy?" The question is pointed and I'm not sure how I should be taking this. Is he making a pass at me? I'm not sure.

I hold his gaze. "I don't think so."

"Well, let me give you this then." He hands me the tab for breakfast and a small card. I check it out, to find that it's his phone number.

"Alberto, thanks but I'm seeing someone."

"Aren't we all?" he says.

"Well no, I guess what I mean is I'm committed to someone." He continues to stare into my eyes and I can feel my face getting flush. I'm not used to this kind of attention. It's usually Rick who gets it, but never me. I really don't know how to handle it. Rick knows just how to either play it or brush it off. I don't have the experience to know how to do it without making a scene, and I don't want to make a scene here. "Maybe what I meant is that right now in my life I'm satisfied with my partner." Boy am I searching. Can't I come up with anything better? I can feel my face getting redder by the second.

Alberto, our eyes still locked says, "Maybe, keep the

number. You may want to give me a call." He winks and leaves the table just as Gerry returns.

Gerry turns his head and watches Alberto walk away, his perfect butt moving snugly in the black slacks of his uniform. He looks at me, then back towards where Alberto has disappeared.

"Honey, what's goin' on here? Is there somethin' I should know?"

"Uh, no Gerry, he, uh just left the bill."

"Are you sure he just left the bill, honey?"

I tighten my grip around the card with Alberto's number on it and discretely slip it in my jacket pocket. "I'm sure that's all he left. See here it is."

Gerry sits down. "Hmmm. Well, I still say you two would make a great couple."

"Gerry!"

"All righty then, let's be off," he says, ignoring me. He leaves a fifty on the table. I can see why Alberto likes to serve Gerry. We get up and proceed down the staircase to the lower level. Gerry ushers me in front of him. I'm sure he does that just so that he can watch my butt. He retrieves his coat and we leave the restaurant. Alberto is serving a table near the entrance. He looks up, nods to Gerry, then smiles and winks at me.

Gerry, who is right behind me sees the whole thing, clears his throat and says, "I'm sure that's all, honey." He chuckles as we go out to the street.

"Gerry, really nothing happened in there. I'm sure he was just trying to get a larger tip."

"You wouldn't be tellin' me a story now would you?"

"Gerry, you know I don't have that kind of effect on men. It's Rick that usually does."

"Oh, but honey, Rick isn't here now is he. Did you bring that butch jeep thing of yours," he says avoiding any more conversation about Alberto. "I do so feel like being seen with a good lookin' guy and his jeep today. Makes a princess want to squeal you know," he says with a southern drawl.

We both break into smiles and start to laugh. Gerry can turn it on so much sometimes that one just can't help laughing. We get to my black YJ and Gerry goes to the passenger door and does a little curtsy thing and squeals. I unlock his door and bow to him as I open the door. He then makes as dramatic an entrance in as one can getting into a jeep.

"Off to the Village for some shoppin', my prince!" Gerry squeals.

"Oh, let's stop here and have a cappy, Andy. My feet are killing me. It's a good thing I don't wear heels," Gerry says as we walk into a trendy little cafe. We wait at the door to be seated.

"You've heard that Gordon is back in the hospital?"

"No," I say. "When did he go in?"

"Wednesday evening," Gerry replies.

"Hopefully nothing too serious?"

"I'm not so sure. Tom says that this time it's the worst he's ever been."

"How's Tom doing with this?"

"Seems okay, he hides it very well. He is trying hard to be strong for Gordon."

We both stop and just look at each other with nothing much else to say. Gordon and Tom have been lovers for almost twenty years. Unfortunately both are positive. Gordon hasn't fared well. The drugs don't seem to work very well for him. Tom, on the other hand, seems to be the exception to all the rules. It's like he's in remission, if one can be in remission. He just keeps on going. Finally, we are seated at a nice little table at the window.

"I'll have a cappuccino and my friend here will have a cafe mocha," Gerry says to the waiter.

"This is a nice little spot. I'm sure glad we found it, aren't you Andy?" says Gerry as he nods over towards the back of the room, where two very good-looking young men are sitting.

"Oh Gerry, they're much too young. How old do you think they are? Twenty?"

"Twenty would be just fine for me," he says.

"Well, they're a bit too young for me."

"Have you had one that's twenty?"

"No, it's been a long time."

"Well honey it might be just what you need..."

"Gerry!" I say in a scolding way.

"But honey just look."

"Gerry, you promised you wouldn't trash Rick today."

"Honey, I haven't said a single word about Rick, I was talkin' 'bout you." He is right. He hasn't said two words about Rick all afternoon.

"But now that you mention him..."

"Let's just talk about something else. We never seem to agree about anything when it comes to Rick."

Gerry sits silently for a second. "Well, okay honey, if that's what makes you happiest then we won't talk about him."

Silence comes over the two of us again. We sip our drinks and Gerry stares out the window onto the crowded street.

"Oh, my god!"

"What?" I ask.

"There he is!"

"There who is?"

"Rick, that's who!"

"Gerry, you're taking this a bit too far today. You know that Rick is at work."

"No, no, there he is. Look across the street, there," as he points towards the corner of the street.

"Gerry," I say looking at him square in the eyes, "I'm not going to play this silly little game. Rick is at work. Who ever you think you are looking at, it's not Rick."

"Oh honey please, I'm not trying to pull one over you. Quick, look before he goes around the building." Silence again. Hopefully, he has realized he has made a mistake.

"Oh my god, he's with another man."

"Gerry!"

"Quick, look they're goin' around the building, quick!"

"Gerry! If it'll keep you quiet I'll look." I turn my head and stare across the crowded street. Two men disappear around the corner. I can't tell who they are as they go around the corner too fast.

"There! You happy! I looked and that wasn't Rick."

"Oh yes it was, and we're goin' after him!" Gerry says as he starts to get up from the table.

"Gerry, please sit down, everyone is looking at us," as I grab his hand. Gerry, already standing, stops and looks around our table. More than a few sets of eyes are on us. He sits back down.

"I think you've embarrassed us enough don't you think? Us running out of here chasing trangers, I don't think so."

"Andy, I'm sorry but..."

"Gerry, please!"

"But I'm so sure it was Rick."

"He's at work, remember?"

Gerry sits quietly. I can't imagine what is going on inside his head and this obsession with Rick seeing someone. I know that Gerry has had a crush on me for a long time, but I'm not his type nor he mine and he knows that. We both just sort of stare at each other and finish our drinks. I'm sure that he's not doing this just so he can start seeing me. He must really not approve of Rick at all. This is really going to make our relationship difficult.

Out on the street he says, "Andy, I'm very sorry about what just transpired in there, I truly am. We've known each other for too long for these types of situations to come between us. So from this moment on I promise on a stack of bibles as high as the Empire State Building never ever to say anything about your man again."

"You've said that before and it's never happened."

"Oh honey, this time it's for real, but just let me say one thing..."

"Gerry, see you can't even go for ten seconds without saying something."

"Just let me finish. What I was going to say was that whatever you decide with your man it's okay with me. And if anything happens I want you to know that I will be there for you."

"That was two things!"

He gives me that yeah so what look.

"You're just so absolutely right. I guess that's the accountant in you!" He giggles and looks at me with his puppy dog eyes. We both smile.

"Okay, where to next?" I ask.

"Back to our chariot, my prince!"

Rick hangs up the phone and returns to the bedroom. He looks at Trevor sitting cross-legged on the bed. This one is different than the rest he thinks to himself. Young, handsome, somewhat naive and full of life. He doesn't know quite what it is about Trevor that keeps him with him, but it's something he's obviously missing in his everyday life. At first he thought it was just the thrill of having the affair, but this one is different than the rest. He just leans in the doorway and stares at him. Trevor makes him feel good.

"What're you looking at?"

"Nothin'."

Trevor leans over and picks up a shoe and throws it at him.

"Hey! Watch it your gonna hurt someone!"

"You've made your phone call?"

"Yup, he's not home yet, so I left a message on his machine." Rick is careful about the us, me, him stuff. He's had years to get it right, so that no one would ever figure it out that Andy and him are partners.

"I don't know why you have to keep your roommate informed as to what you're up to. Is he that insecure?" Trevor says as he sits on the bed in a pair of boxers.

"You know, we've already gone through all this about Andy before," Rick says as he sits down on the bed facing Trevor. "Since his lover died..."

"Yeah, yeah I know. I guess it's kinda nice he's got you as a friend. I know it sort of gives him a sense of security. But boy does he need to get a life so that we can get on with ours," Trevor says as he leans over and licks Rick on the cheek and then bites his earlobe.

"Ow!" Rick exclaims. He grabs Trevor by the shoulders and pushes him back onto the bed. "Now that wasn't very nice now was it?" He leans even closer and kisses him on the mouth.

"But that was."

It's five thirty as I pull away from Gerry's apartment. As soon as I get out of eyeshot I'll phone home. Hopefully Rick will be there. I dial our number on the cell phone and it starts to ring. Once, twice, three times, four, the answering machine picks up, "Hi, you've reached Andy and Rick. We can't get your call at the moment so leave your name and number after the beep and we'll get back to you as soon as possible." Beep!

"Hi, it's me. It's five thirty and I'll be home in ten, just dropped Gerry off. We'll make dinner plans when I get there."

I hang up. It's almost dark out; he must be on his way home. We'll probably be home within minutes of each other. And anyway they have lights at the construction sites; they can work in the dark these days so if he's a little late it can be explained. Could be anything keeping him from being home, traffic could be really heavy, that's probably it. I'm trying to make excuses as to why he isn't home yet. Why am I thinking like this? I must be getting paranoid. Oh Gerry, look what you've got me doing. I trust Rick. That's what relationships are based on. If you can't trust the one you love then you really can't love them all that much and I know I love him. He hasn't given me any reason to not trust him in the six years we've been together.

I pull into the underground parking at our building and park my jeep. We only have one parking stall, so Rick parks his truck street side. I haven't noticed it on the way in. So he's probably got held up in traffic. I hit the up button for the elevator and stand there waiting. I'm feeling a little antsy. The doors open, I walk in and push the ten. Today this elevator feels like it's taking forever. There, my floor. I hurry down the hall to our apartment, open the door and it's filled with darkness. "I'm sure he'll be home shortly," I try to comfort myself. I turn on the light in the hall and see that the apartment has been cleaned. It's maid day today, so Rosie has been here. You can always tell when Rosie's been here. She brings fresh flowers, even on the coldest days of winter. Today she's brought lilies. Their distinct fragrance fills the apartment. I move into the kitchen and see the lights flashing on the answering machine. Three messages. I peer into the dining room and at the centre of the dining room table is a vase of magnificent yellow daylilies. They are perfect. Rosie knows exactly what colour works. I hit the message button.

"Hi it's me. It's five..." My message, I hit the skip button.

"Hi Andy, just finished work and am heading out for a beer with the guys. Shouldn't be too long. Don't know how long I can put up with all these straight guys and their pussy talk. See you later. Oh yeah another shift tomorrow if the weather holds."

"Hello, no one home yet, my, my. Anyways, this is for Andy." It is Gerry. "Honey give me a call when you get in. It's about Gordon. Bye."

Damn! He's gone out tonight. I hit the play button again, and skip the first two messages. I haven't been paying attention to Gerry's message. The message replays. I hope that everything is okay; I don't want any bad news. I pick up the phone and dial Gerry's number.

"Hello."

"Hi, Gerry."

"Oh Andy, I'm glad you call. It's Gordon. I've had a message from Tom. The doctors don't think he's going to make it this time. They give him a few days at most."

There is silence on both ends of the phone.

"Andy honey are you still there? Did you hear me?"

"Yeah, I heard you. This is not good."

"No, it sure as hell ain't." Gerry usually doesn't use any foul language, but it slips out when he's upset. "Your man not home yet?"

Gerry's probably not ever going to use his name again after this afternoon.

"No, he's left a message. He's at a service station getting a flat fixed and should be home anytime now."

Why am I lying to Gerry? Rick's message about going for a beer with his work buddies should have been okay to tell him. Maybe I'm just trying to avoid getting into another trash Rick conversation with him.

"Sure honey. Anyway, I think we should go to the hospital to see Gordon. What do you think?"

"Sure, I guess we should. Is it all right with Tom?"

"Tom suggested it. He said that Gordon wants to say his good-byes. That's if he's there. You know what I mean? Tom says he's been slipping in and out of a coma."

I can hear his voice crack. We all know that this day would come for both Gordon and Tom but I don't think that one can really plan for that day to happen.

"Gerry? You okay?"

"Oh, I'll be fine. I think I'll just have me a glass of wine and order in tonight. Why don't you give me a call in the morning and we'll set up a time. Not that there seems to be much of that. Is tomorrow okay, to go and see Gord?"

"Yeah, sure, I can probably fit it in. We have no concrete plans and this is important. So tomorrow then. I'll call you around nine?" Again, I avoid telling Gerry the truth, namely, that I really have no plans as Rick is going to go to work again tomorrow.

"Nine will be fine. Thanks Andy."

"No problem. Are you sure you're okay? I can come over if you want?"

"Yeah, I'm fine, I'll be okay. It's just, you know..." Silence again. "We'll talk in the morning, okay?"

"Sure, tomorrow then. Bye." I hang up the phone. Gerry doesn't seem to be doing so well. He has lost a lot of his long time friends to AIDS in the last few years. I know he tries hard to be strong but each time he loses someone else, he breaks down a little bit more. He always says that for every friend he loses he loses a bit of himself. And these losses are taking their toll on him.

I go to the refrigerator and get out a bottle of wine, a wine glass from the cupboard, corkscrew from the drawer and walk into the dark living room. I pour myself a glass, turn on the CD player and sit and stare out of the window into the night. Tomorrow is going to be rough. The situation with Rick not being here seems trivial right now. My mind is running wild with what the next week or so is going to be like if Gordon dies, the funeral, the wake afterwards, Gerry, this is going to be tough on him. I pour myself another glass of wine, put my head back on the loveseat and try and force myself to think of something else but it's hard not to drift back to thoughts of Gordon. I've gotten to be good friends with Tom and Gordon over the last couple of years, through Gerry of course, but nevertheless I think of them as close friends. I finish my second glass of wine and look at the bottle.

"Oh hell, why not. I'll probably need some help sleeping tonight." I say out loud, as if there is someone else sitting in the dark with me. I pour myself another glass of wine and continue staring out the window.

Well that's it, second bottle of wine gone as I pour the last into my glass. Still no sign of Rick. My thoughts of Gordon and Tom are starting to get fuzzy. I'll deal with them in the morning and probably with a major headache. Where in the hell is Rick? It's almost eleven. I just can't believe he'd spend the whole night with those straight construction guys that he works with talking about pussy.

Just then the door closes and Rick walks into the living room.

"Oh!" he says startled. "I, ah, didn't expect to see you up. You, uh, got my message?"

"Yeah." I slur.

"So I guess I owe you an apology for being a bit late..."

"No, it's okay." I interrupt him. "I don't think I would have been much fun tonight anyway." I'm sure he can tell that I've been drinking, alone at that. Two empty bottles on the table and one half filled wine glass.

"Why?" he asks. "Is there something wrong?"

"Of course there is something wrong!" I say angrily.

"I said I owe you..."

"No, it's Gordon. He's in the hospital."

"Look Andy, I don't want to sound unsympathetic but Gordon's' been in and out of the hospital a lot lately and..."

"This time it's different."

"Andy, every time is different and every time he comes out and this time it'll probably be no different."

"This time is different, because the doctors say that this time he won't be coming out. He's been in and out of a coma so this is it."

There is silence as we just stand and stare at each other. The space between anything happening or being said seems an eternity.

I know what he is thinking, that this is probably a good thing. He never really liked Gordon or Tom. He would avoid having anything to do with them. I've told him it's his fear of them being HIV positive. He always denied it, saying that he really didn't have much in common with either of them. Deep down inside I know it's his fear of the disease.

"Andy, I'm sorry." Rick breaks the silence.

"Should you be telling me or them that?" I snap. "Rick, I'm sorry, I'm just angry with the situation. I just don't think it's fair."

"And I guess the wine hasn't helped much either?" He says motioning to the bottles on the table.

"No, I thought it would just help me not think about it I guess."

The distance in the room between us hasn't gotten any smaller and neither of us seems to want to get any closer.

"I've, ah, got to work tomorrow."

"Yeah, I know," I say as I look at the answering machine.

"So I guess I'll head off to bed." Rick stares at me. "I think I'll sleep in my room tonight, 'kay?"

"Sure." I say as I turn and start to clean up my bottles. "Why not." I mumble under my breath.

"You gonna be all right, Andy?"

"Yeah, I'll be fine." I can't look at him as he leaves the room for his bedroom. I can feel the tears in my eyes start to well up and I can sense that he really doesn't care.

"Yeah, I'll be just fine," I mumble to myself.

"Hello?" I say groggily into the phone.

"Morning honey."

It was Gerry. I roll over and look at the clock, nine twenty, I'm late.

"Sleep in this morning? Well that's' okay at least someone got some sleep last night. I don't think I slept at all last night," he says. "So how you doin' this morning?"

"Oh fine, bit of a headache."

"Uh huh, you two go out last night?" he asks.

"No, just got into a couple bottles of wine, thought they would help me keep my mind off things, you know, drown my thoughts."

"Oh honey, alcohol isn't the way to go."

"Yeah, I know, but I guess it helped me get some sleep. So, how are you doing?"

"Okay, I guess." He sounds tired. "So is Rick going to the hospital with us today?" Gerry asks.

"Ah, no, he's got another overtime shift today."

"Oh well," he says.

You can tell just by the tone of his voice and by how quickly he answers that he is quite relieved that Rick would not be with us today.

"I hope he doesn't get too wet today, the weather man is calling for rain later this morning."

There is something in his voice that hints that he doesn't believe that Rick is at work at all.

"Well, maybe that'll mean he'll be home early today."

Even I sound a little doubtful to myself but I put it off to the headache that seems to be getting worse.

"So, what time do you think we should go?" Gerry sounds a little unsure of himself, which really isn't like him. He is always so definite and positive especially when making decisions.

"I don't know. I guess we'll have to check and see when visiting hours are."

"I don't think it'll matter, we'll just tell them..."

He falters, his voice trembles a bit. There is silence on the line. I can sense that Gerry is collecting himself.

"You know we'll just tell them we're family," I finish for him.

"Of course, we are you know."

"Yeah, I know. So you want me to pick you up?" I ask.

"Okay. I was hoping you would. It'll make me feel better being in that Jeep thing of yours."

"How about I pick you up at ten thirty?"

"I'll be waiting with bated breath. See you in a bit," he says, and then hangs up.

I hang up the phone and lay in bed thinking about Gerry. He is really not doing well with this. He's known Gordon and Tom for years. As a matter of fact he and Tom went to high school together. The three of them are very close, so it's no wonder he's having a hard time.

Our visit to the hospital is short. Gerry's sister has arrived from Chicago, which causes a lot of tension, as she and Gord are not close. We have just enough time to say our last goodbyes before Father O'Brien arrives to administer last rights, before returning to Gerry's apartment for the afternoon.

Gerry's apartment is one floor down from the penthouse and there is only one other apartment on this floor, owned by a little old Jewish widow who spends most of her time in Miami. He unlocks the door and we walk in.

"Juanita!" he calls out. Nothing. "Juanita dear, are you here?" He knows that she is.

"Oh jes I am here," she calls back in her broken English.

He leans over to me. "Isn't she the sweetest," he says to me quietly, and then says to the rotund olive skinned woman coming down the hall, "I've brought over a friend for lunch. Is that okay?"

"Oh shure Mester Gerry." She says as she comes into the entrance foyer. "I well make you somethin' spechal, hokay?"

"That would be just great," he says still smiling. "You remember Andy?"

"Oh jes I do. Hello Mester Andy," she says with a little bow of her head.

"Hello Juanita."

"Thanks Juanita for making lunch on such short notice," Gerry says.

"You are so welcome Mester Gerry." She turns and heads off towards the kitchen. "It is no problems to make you a lunch," she says still talking away as she disappears around the corner.

Before Gerry's lover Paul had died, they had hired Juanita. She is a short, rotund, plump, Puerto Rican, about to be sent back because she couldn't find a job, when she ran into Gerry at the local A&P and from then on, she's been employed by Gerry. They take care of each other. She keeps house and cooks for him and he gives her money.

She actually lives there with him in one of the four bedrooms of his apartment. What more could they ask for. And they trust each other implicitly; Gerry has even given her a credit card to do the household shopping. I don't think Gerry would ever say anything if she did buy herself something, but I don't think she would ever do it. I guess she feels indebted to him for helping her to stay in New York. They've been working at getting her citizenship, which Gerry will say has been a little trying at times but she'll get it eventually. It's her 'inglich' as she says that's not helping.

I look at Gerry as we walk down the hallway into the large living room. His face is aglow and there is a twinkle in his eyes. She makes him happy.

"You know if I didn't know you were gay I just might get the idea that you and Juanita..."

"Andy just get that thought out of your head right this minute," he says with a grin as large as Long Island. "Mind you if I was straight she'd be the woman for me. She cooks and cleans."

We both start laughing. It feels good to laugh.

"So after lunch why don't I put on a movie and we can spend the afternoon just hanging around?"

"Sure I've no plans." I know he just doesn't want to be alone today so why not, I really don't have any plans. If I was at home I'd probably just work on that account I was going to finish, but in my frame of mind I'd probably just get cozy with another bottle of wine or two and I don't need another headache.

I pull into the underground parking and notice that Rick's truck isn't in its usual parking spot on the street again. Oh well, I guess I deserve this. I did take out my anger on him last night. He really didn't deserve it, so I guess he's making me pay for it by being out late again. This time I won't put it on him again. I'll apologize for how I treated him last night and then hey you never know, maybe a little sex before bed. I unlock the door to the apartment and walk in. I leave the hall light off and walk into the kitchen where the telephone is. The answering machine light is flashing. I hit the button.

"Hi Andy, hope everything is okay." Rick's voice sounds sincere, "There was some trouble at the construction site last night. Someone broke in and let's just say it's a mess. I've gone with the site foreman to my Dad's to get this sorted out so I'll be late but if it's too late I think I'll just stay at his place till tomorrow. If I do, I'll call. Bye. Oh yeah, Andy, I really am sorry about Gordon." I hit the erase button.

Odd, going to his Dad's. I guess it must've been pretty bad to actually have to see his Dad about it. Rick's father owns the company he works for, but him and his father had a falling out when Rick told his father that he didn't want to have anything to do with the management of the company. At least that's what Rick said happened. His father couldn't understand why he only wanted to be just one of the workers on site. Sure he'd always have work but at the same time he is in a position to learn how to run a large construction company. But I think the real problem is Rick's sexuality. The falling out was not because of him not wanting to take over the family business as Rick would have me believe, but that he's gay. And since he came out to his parents there has been little contact between them. I base my assumptions on a time three years ago. Rick and I had been living together for almost a year and it was Christmas and I thought that it would be a nice gesture if I invited his parents in for a bit of Christmas cheer. When I phoned to offer the invitation and told his father who I was, he told me I was to stay out of his and his wife's life and that I was the cause of their son's abnormality and he hung up on me. I never told Rick of this conversation. He'd be angry if he ever found out. I'm sure that he is upset that his parents don't accept him for who he is. So when it comes to his parents I just let him give me his story. It must be awful not to be loved by those that brought you into this world. I feel sorry for him. It's got to hurt. So what ever happened at the site last night must have been pretty serious for him to actually have to go up and see his father. This situation might be just what's needed to get their relationship kick started. I can only hope for Rick's sake. I won't expect to get a call from that household tonight. I'll just hunker down and see if I can get that account finished off tonight.

I roll over and turn off the alarm on the clock. Six o'clock came too quickly this morning, and no phone calls from either Rick or Gerry. If Rick has made it home last night he would have slept in his own bedroom, so he wouldn't have bothered me. I walk to his room and quietly open the door. No, he's not there. Hopefully this is a good thing, Rick and his father will get a chance to work things out. Sometimes it takes a disaster to get things back to the way they are meant to be. I'm sure Rick will call me when he gets back into town.

"Morning, Mr. McTavich."

"Morning Trish, any messages?" I ask.

"Just Miss Pickford. She wants to see you in her office as soon as you get in."

"Thanks Trish," I say as I walk down the corridor to her corner office.

"Morning Andy," her personal secretary says as I approach her desk. "Go right in, she's expecting you."

As I enter the room, I find her sitting at her desk in her father's swivel chair staring out of the large plate glass windows that face 42nd Street. She hears the door close behind me and she swivels around to face me. She's been crying. She gets up and comes to me, puts her arms around my neck and places her head on my shoulder.

"Gerry called?" I ask.

She nods, "Yes, half-hour ago. I knew you'd be on your way and so did Gerry so he wanted me to tell you." Her voice cracks. I squeeze her and hold her tight. There is silence for a few minutes.

"How's Gerry doing?"

"He sounded fine, said he had no more tears. He said he'd call later to let us know about the funeral arrangements." She has stopped crying and moves to lean on her desk. "Well, this is going to be a tough day to get through."

"So why don't you go home?"

"No, I've got a few things to do this morning like get

ready for the partners' meeting on Thursday."

"Why don't you just put the meeting off for a week cause this week is going to be stressful enough and I don't need you going into a meeting an emotional mess? This is my future we're dealin' with," I say with a smile.

She looks at me and smiles. "Yeah I guess you're right. I'll get Andrea to make some schedule changes. You can be so clear in situations like this. That's why you should be partner."

"Hey, I'm not getting my hopes up. You've got Clarke to get past."

"Oh Andy don't even think it. Yuk!" She makes a funny disgusted look. We both break into laughter.

"On a much more sombre note and saner one at that, I'll have Andrea take care of flowers for Tom. We'll talk later about the funeral arrangements." She stands and gives me another hug. "Oh Andy what would I do without you? I love you."

"I love you, too Laurel, I'm sure you'd have someone that would take care of you almost as well as I do, but not quite. Someone who isn't gay would probably fit the bill quite nicely I'm sure."

She giggles again. "Well Mr. McTavich, I do think it's time you get some work done around here."

"Okay, I'll talk to you later, Miss Pickford," I say as I leave her office. I can feel eyes watching me as I walk down the hall to my office. I'm sure that there's number of people in the office who suspect that there is something going on between us. I walk up to Trish's desk, "Are you free in about five minutes Trish?" I ask.

"Yes, Mr. McTavich, I'll bring in coffee if you'd like?"

"That'll be fine," I say as I walk into my office and close the door behind myself, hang up my overcoat and put my brief case on my desk. I sit down and open it. I don't know where to start. There's a knock on the door and Trish enters my office with a cup of coffee for me. "Did you make arrangements with Anna, Joe and Harvey that you'd be with me?"

"All done."

"Well you might as well grab a coffee..."

"Mr. McTavich...," she starts.

"Andy, please."

"Well?"

"Is there something wrong?" I ask

"It's, there's an awful lot of talk in the office about...," she pauses.

"About Laurel and me?"

"Well yes, that. And the pool seems to think that I'm using it to my advantage. That when you get your partnership in the firm you'll not go to the pool to get your..."

"Oh, I see, let's just stop there. For one there is nothing going on between Miss Pickford and myself, as you know the reason why. Secondly, it's only talk about partnership. It hasn't happened yet and with Clarke I have my doubts. Third if I did get offered a partnership I would of course go to the pool, even if for appearances sake, and yes, you would be offered the position of my secretary, but taking the job would still be totally up to you. So I say let them talk.

"Okay Mr.....Andy."

"I know Anna and Joe don't like it when you call me by my first name. I think it just makes things a little more relaxed in an already hectic world." I can see her tension ease a bit. "Well anyways, Laurel and I have just lost a very close mutual friend last night. That's why I've been in her office this morning."

"I know, I met Andrea at the water cooler earlier."

"Good, so you know that Andrea is taking care of sending flowers. Well I'd like you to do a couple of things for me this morning." She nods. "My friend Gerry will be helping with the funeral arrangements, so I want you to give him a call, his number is in your roll-a-dex and tell him that we've made lunch arrangements, just get the address of where he and Tom will be and we'll get Georgio's to cater out to them." She writes this down on her pad of paper.

"I'm sorry, Andy," she says.

"It's okay." I stop; I don't want to talk anymore about Gord's death. "Are you free for lunch?" I ask out of the blue.

Trish looks at me with a confused look on her face. "Andy, they are already talking about me taking advantage of my position."

"Well, if they are going to talk, Trish, we might as well give them something to talk about, right?" I say. "Anyways, this will be a working lunch here at the office. I'm just about finished the Davenport year-end and I'd really like to get it finished today, so I could use your help. So what do you say?"

She sits for a moment, and then says, "Shall I order Chinese or Thai?"

"Your choice, it's on me," I say. "Trish thanks and let them talk. They're just jealous 'cause you're good."

She smiles. "Thanks Andy, I'll clear my calendar with the others for this afternoon," she says as she leaves my office.

I sit back down, pull out the Davenport files, open them and start to work on finishing them.

Hours have gone by and Trish and I, amidst take out boxes, files and paper, are finally finished.

"I'll print off the draft statements and then you can go over them, make any adjustments you want and then I'll do the final copies. Shouldn't take more than an hour and we'll be done," she says.

"Great. Coffee?"

Trish looks at me, again confused as to our roles in the office. "Look I can pour coffee just as well as anybody else in the office."

"It's just going to take a bit of getting used to," she says, "having your boss getting coffee." She finishes with a smile.

"Black or blonde and sweet?" I ask.

"Black will be just fine, thank you."

I walk out with our two cups and head for the coffee machine. As I come around the corner into the coffee room, I almost walk into Laurel.

"Lots of talk on the floor today about you." she says.

"I know. I don't have time for these games."

She smiles at me, "I love the way you don't always follow office etiquette. How's Trish doing with it?"

"She'll be fine if she ignores it."

"Oh, Gerry called. Friday is the day. Both he and Tom thank you for lunch, said it was fabulous." Her eyes get teary.

She clears her throat and says, "I guess we'll go the funeral together, so I'll send my car around to get you."

"I could drive, I don't mind. I'll pick you up early and we'll do lunch first."

"Okay, that'll be better," she says. "Have you heard from Rick yet?"

"No, probably a real big problem and with his father and all." She looks at me with that I bet look. "He said it was serious," trying to reaffirm myself.

"Hey, I didn't say a thing, Andy."

"No, but I know what you are thinking." She doesn't say a thing.

"So how's the Davenport account coming along?" She changes the subject, knowing that she wouldn't get anywhere with me about Rick.

"Trish is just running off the draft statements and we'll go over them and will have final statements on your desk first thing in the morning."

"Great, so you won't be working late tonight?"

"No, shouldn't have to. Why?"

"No reason, I'll talk to you later." She says as she leaves the coffee room.

I get our coffees and walk back to my office. Trish is sitting at the computer and the printer is working away.

"Just about done," she says.

"Good. Any calls Trish?"

"No, I checked the voice mail while you were getting coffee and there's nothing there either. Are you expecting a call?"

"Just Rick."

"You haven't gotten any since this morning's call from Davenport," she says. "You don't mind watching this for a few minutes, I've got to go to..."

"Sure, go on, I'll be here to make sure this old thing doesn't jam."

She leaves the room. I wonder why Rick hasn't called. Up until Laurel has mentioned it, I wasn't even concerned that he hasn't called. It really must be serious trouble if he's still at his father's place. I'm sure that there is a lot of tension between the two of them and the site problem won't make it any easier. I sip my coffee as I stare out of my office window at the New York skyline. I look down and see the cars and people on the streets below. How impersonal and cold, almost ten million people. One would only know a handful of them, and the rest, well, no one really cares. The warm April sun warms my face as I gaze over the city. It's so big. If someone didn't want to be found they could do it down there on those streets. I wonder if Rick is really at his father's. Why am I questioning him like this? He hasn't given me any reason to. Just because he hasn't called me today to let me know how things are is no reason to not trust him. He's probably still with his father and they are busy. The printer stops. I look over and check to see if it's jammed. Trish comes back in and starts tearing off the sheets of paper and putting them in numerical order. I sit at the desk and start to go over the numbers again.

Five past five and Trish turns off the laser printer.

"Done. We're finished."

"Good work, Trish. You go on home. I'll tidy up and bring these down to Laurel's office."

Part way through the door, she turns and says, "Thanks again for lunch, Andy. Good night. I'll see you in the morning."

I pick up the phone and dial my home number. It rings five, six , seven and the answering machine kicks in. I hang up. I'll deliver these to Laurel and then try again. I walk down the hall and say good night to the last of the office staff still on the floor. Andrea is sitting outside Laurel's office with her coat on writing down one last memo for herself.

"Andy, she just went to the girls' room. She'll be right back. Go on inside. I'll let her know that you're here."

I sit in one of the two big leather chairs facing her mahogany desk. What a rush these last few days have been, I think to myself. If I didn't have this job I'd have probably gone crazy. Well three more days then the funeral will be over with and then everything will be back to normal. I look out the open door of the office. She's still not coming. I'll just give home a call again. I pick up the phone and dial, it rings, and again the answering machine picks up. I hang up.

"Still not home yet?" Laurel says from in the doorway.

"Ah no, he's not yet," I stammer, "here's the Davenport statements."

"Good and ahead of schedule, too." she says as she takes them from me and places them on her desk. She looks tired. "Wanna get a drink? I could sure use one."

"Sure, why not."

She grabs her coat and purse and we leave. We walk silently to the elevator. She slides her hand around my arm as the elevator doors close and we descend to the city streets below.

The big white ford pulls up to the back door of the restaurant. The writing on the doors is obscured with mud. The driver gets out and makes his way through the puddles in the gravel parking lot. He, too, is covered to his knees in dried mud. He pulls open the screen door to the kitchen and walks in.

"Tony? Is that you?" comes a woman's voice, heavy with an Italian accent.

"Yeah Mama," Tony replies.

"Don't you move till I take a look at you," she commands. "With all this rain I don't need you bringin' in mud through my kitchen."

"Okay, but could you hurry I gotta..."

"Tony don't you be talkin' to your mama like that, you hear me," the voice says sternly.

He stands there and takes inventory of himself. What mud he had on his pants has since dried and been brushed off. He figures he's cleaned himself off pretty good. He takes off his mackinaw jacket, and checks the back of it to make sure there isn't any dried mud he's missed. He hangs it on one of the coat hooks behind the kitchen door. He notices a patch of mud on his forearm, still tanned from the summer. He steps outside and brushes it off. As he walks back in he almost steps on a short, heavy, dark haired, dark complexioned woman.

"Oh mama," he says.

"Let me look at you." She ignores his greeting. "You still got some mud on your backside. Go outside and brush it off," she commands.

He steps out once again, stretches around to see if he can tell where the mud on his backside is. His broad shoulders stretch the white, sweat and mud stained t-shirt, pulling it tight across his flat stomach as he looks for the mud he has missed on his butt. He takes his hands and brushes off the mud caked to his Levis, that hug his butt. He walks back into the kitchen and waits for his mother's approval of his appearance.

"How's this mama?" he asks as he turns around on the spot so she can inspect him for mud.

"Much betta," she states. "Now come give me a kiss hello," she commands with a big smile. He walks over to her standing by her prep table and gives her a kiss, once on each cheek. She smiles and wipes her hands in her apron.

"So what's for supper?" he asks.

"Your favourite, spaghetti and meatballs," she says. "And Italian stew. But I don't know why I'm makin' you stew. Where have you been the last couple of nights? You haven't been home. You maka me worry so much. I don't know where my Tony is. No phone calls no nothing."

"Mama, I'm twenty eight years old. I'm old enough to take care of myself. Anyway with all this rain this spring some of the basements have flooded and I've been getting them cleaned out. Vacation season is just around the corner."

"Well, what 'bout my basement?" she says.

"Oh mama you haven't got a basement."

"You never know, with all this rain I coulda been washed away and you wouldn't have even known."

"You know you won't get washed away," he says to her. "Papa built you your house on the highest rock on the cape." She makes the sign of the cross on herself as he says 'papa'. "And yes, I know how you worry about me before you get into that speech." He smiles at her and gives her another kiss.

"Oh Tony, you know how to make your mama happy,"

she smiles at him. "Now if only you'd marry Elaine. You two have been engaged for six years now..."

"Mama, I told you before we're not ready yet. We're not in any hurry."

"I think it's you who's not ready yet. You'd betta watch it. She might not wait much longer Tony. She's gonna want to have children. She's not getting any younger."

"Mama," he says looking at her lovingly.

"I know Tony in this day and age people don't get married as young as they used to," she says. "But I'm not getting any younger either and I do want to enjoy my grandchildren."

"Maria and Joe have given you three lovely granddaughters and Paulo and Rita a grandson to carry on the diMarco name," he says to her as he lifts the lid to the pot of Italian stew simmering on the huge cook top.

"It's just because you look so much like Papa," she says, crossing herself again as she talks about her dead husband. "A child of yours and Elaine's. No, I'm not going to say anything more. You kids seem to think you know what's best. I'm just a mother, what do I know?" she states.

"Oh mama," he says to her, "I'll go and sit at the staff table." He turns and walks out into the dining room, ignoring her second attempt at making him feel guilty.

She watches him leave the kitchen, shakes her head, picks up a wooden spoon and continues her work at the stove. "Holy mother of God what's a mother to do?" she mutters to herself.

Tony walks into the diner part of the restaurant. The dining room is closed except on weekends and holidays during the off-season, but during tourist season Mama's Diner is the best and busiest Italian restaurant on Cape Cod. He sits at a table with a stack of menus. Maria, his sister, comes over and stands by the table. She works with their mother a few days a week, just to give herself some pantyhose money as she calls it.

"Hey Tony, how's it goin'?" she asks.

"Busy these last couple of days," he replies. "You?"

"Last couple of days it's been dead in here with all that bad weather, but it's picked up a bit today," she says as she sits down across the table from him. "You been busy with Elaine I take it. Mama says that you ain't been home for a few days, so we been guessin' that the two of you have been spendin' these rainy days and nights together."

"You and Mama both think alike. No, a couple of the houses we look after have flooded basements, so I've been busy cleaning them up. And since we haven't any extra help since Garth broke his leg two weeks ago, I've been going it alone," Tony says scornfully, but not too seriously. Maria, older by less than two years, and him are close. They never really get mad at each other and if they do, it doesn't last for very long. They've been that way all their lives. Paulo and him, since Papa died, have never seen eye to eye. Tony thinks it has to do with two things. First, Paulo thinks he has waited too long to get married to Elaine. Him and Elaine had been engaged for two years when Papa died and Paulo has, many times, said that they should get married and start a family, as it would help Mama with her depression. And secondly, there is twelve years between them. Paulo being older has always thought that Mama and Papa have treated Tony differently because he is the youngest in the family. When Papa died Paulo took over Papa's fishing boat. Mama thought that both her boys would work together, but Tony had decided to stay on with Cape Development and Maintenance. He's worked his way up to being one of two year round employees looking after a good number of vacation homes along the coast of Cape Cod Bay. He's helped maintain some of the nicest vacation homes of the wealthy from up and down the east coast for the last four years and has developed one hell of a green thumb, if he did say so himself. He's sure that his difficulties with Paulo will eventually iron themselves out as the two of them get older, but so far they haven't.

"I believe you, Tony," she says back.

"Yeah, sorry." He apologizes for being short with her. "Mama just hit me with all that stuff in the kitchen."

"We're just worried that she ain't gonna wait for you, that's all."

"Of course she's going to wait. She loves me," he says.

"Sure, she loves you, but, hey Tony, a girls' got a clock inside that says if she wants babies..," she says. "You never know, she just might get pregnant."

"No I think your wrong there, Elaine and I've talked about waiting."

"Tony, I hope you're right," she pauses, "Wanna beer?"

"Sure, please," he says as she gets up to get him a beer. He stares out of the window and thinks about the last time he and Elaine had sex. They take precautions. He always uses a condom, and anyways they don't have sex very often, maybe once every two and a half to three weeks. They both have very busy careers, and for the last month they haven't really even seen much of each other so it's been longer than usual. With all the rain this spring, the maintenance on the vacation homes has kept him out twelve to sixteen hours a day. Elaine has been helping the insurance company she works for open a new office in Sandwich, so there hasn't been much time for anything but maybe a lunch in passing. Elaine has her own place, which she shares with a girlfriend, Sara. He lives with his mother still. He knows that he should be out on his own but he decided to live at home when he and Elaine agreed not to live together until they were married. They had agreed that it would be a waste of money to get his own place, so until then he's living at home with his mother. Elaine has, only a couple of times, mentioned her biological clock ticking and babies but then in the same sentence she said that she wasn't ready to give up her career to settle down with children, so Tony's sure that there is no rush to get married.

Maria comes back and puts a beer on the table in front of him.

"Thanks." he says. "How are my favourite nieces?" he asks.

"Oh, Tony they're just perfect. Amy asks about you all the time," Maria says, her face lights up with a happy glow as she talks about her daughters. A bell rings signalling that someone has entered the diner. "We'll talk later," she says as she turns away to do her job.

"Okay, Tony, here's your supper." Mama says as she places a hot platter of spaghetti, meatballs and stew in front of him. "Watch it, the plate's hot." Steam rises and the aroma fill the area. It brings back memories of Tony's youth before

Mama had the restaurant and this smell could only be found in their home kitchen.

"This was Papa's favourite." she says, crossing herself. "It's getting busy." she states matter of factly, standing beside her youngest child while he eats. "You gonna be home tonight?" she asks. She sounds lonely.

Tony doesn't say anything for a few seconds "Yeah I was going to go to the Ayer's home, but that can wait until tomorrow. They haven't been out since Mrs. Ayer's was admitted into that nursing home a couple of years back." He watches her as he speaks. Her face lights up. "I'll just finish here, go home, shower, give Elaine a call and then when you get home we'll settle in for a game of canasta."

She kisses him on the cheek, squeezes his shoulder. "You're such a good boy Tony," she says as she retreats back into her kitchen.

The Diner starts to fill up. The two women working the diner move like a well-oiled machine. The other part time dinner staffs arrive and fit into the sequence of events that make this one of the best places to eat on the Cape. Tony watches, as he finishes his dinner, this fine tuned team work the dinner crowd. He scans the room and recognizes just about everyone, most recognize him. He nods to a few of them as he gets up from the table and walks back into the kitchen. Mama and Maria are busy working at getting the plates assembled. He walks up behind Maria and gives her a slap on the ass.

"Tony!" she says in a controlled yell. "Asshole!"

He gives her a kiss on the cheek "Bitch," he says back.

"Maria! Tony!" Mama scolds. "You two dont'a use that kinda language here! Tony you leave your sister alone, she's busy." She hears the two of them giggle. She smiles to herself.

"Sunday dinner?" Maria asks.

"No promises but I'll try," Tony says. "Bye, love you, give kisses to my nieces." He walks over to his mother and gives her a kiss on the cheek. "Magnifico! See you later Mama." He grabs his jacket from behind the kitchen door and walks out of the restaurant, into the puddle dotted gravel back parking lot to his truck. As he gets into the pickup truck, tosses his jacket on the passenger seat, he can smell himself. The mixed odour of sweat and mud confirms he needs a shower. He turns the key in the ignition and starts the big white truck, backs up and pulls out on to Main Street and heads off home.

As he pulls into the driveway, the outside security lights come on. The gardens are looking a bit of a mess with all the rain. The yard needs a little TLC. He's going to have to spend a good day or so getting things ready for spring Tony thinks to himself. Once he checks out the Ayers' place his time will be a little freer to do the gardens. He lets himself in, hangs up his jacket and checks the mail in the entrance hall. Nothing for him. As he wanders slowly up the stairs to his second story bedroom he starts shedding his clothes. First the socks, then the stained t-shirt, then the top button of his Levis, then the other four buttons. He starts to pull his Levis down, stops three steps from the top, sits and pulls them off, leaving him in just his white Calvin Klein's. He gets up, adjusts himself and continues to the top of the stairway and the short distance down the hall to his room. Tony enters his room and tosses his clothes into the laundry basket by the door. He checks his answering machine, no messages. He doesn't think too much of it. He picks up the phone and dials Elaine's number.

"Hello," comes the voice from the phone.

"Hi Sara, is Elaine there?" Tony asks.

"Tony. No she's still in Sandwich. She said to tell you that the driving was getting to her and she convinced her boss to put her up in a motel while they got the new office going. She said that she'd be home by Friday."

Tony was lost for words, but only for a moment. "Well, I guess that makes sense, better than all that driving. Did she say what time on Friday?"

"No, she didn't, but she sounded pretty tired. She said the computer stuff was really giving them a hard time."

"Don't know much about that stuff," he says. "Well, I'll talk to her on Friday then. Bye Sara," he says as he hangs up the phone. He gets a jogging suit out of one of his dresser drawers and tosses it on his bed, as he goes into his bathroom. He leans over the sink and looks at himself in the mirror. His face has a light dusting of mud. There are little rivulet sweat stains on his forehead. He moves over to the bathtub and starts to run the hot water. Tonight it'll be a bath he decides. The steam starts to rise as the tub fills. Tony slips out of his Calvin Klein's and tosses them on the floor by the bathroom door. He runs his open hand over his chest and down his washboard taut stomach. He thinks that he's in pretty good shape for twenty-eight. His hands roam over his body, tracing his tan line, over his thighs and stomach, feeling the hardness of his body. No wonder Elaine finds him physically attractive. If he was a woman, he'd find himself attractive too. It sounds rather conceited, but it's not as if he flaunts his body or his looks. He's just a regular guy, he thinks to himself. He turns off the hot water in the half filled tub and steps into the hot water. He slowly lowers his body into the tub as he gets used to the hot water. He moans as he finally rests his head back and closes his eyes. This feels good. A good long hot soak will do him good, he says to himself. He slowly drifts in and out of sleep as he lays still so that his immersed tired body can absorb the heat of the hot water. He soon hears his mother come in downstairs. His bath water has gotten cool. He must've fallen asleep. He drains a bit of the cold water, and tops it off with more hot water, takes the bar of soap from the soap dish and washes his tired body. After he dries himself off he puts on the sweat suit he's gotten out for himself earlier. He walks downstairs to the kitchen thinking that that's where he'd find his mother. But as he walks past the living room he can see her sitting in her favourite easy chair, asleep. Must've been a tough day at the restaurant.

"Mama," he says quietly, "Mama?"

She stirs and mumbles something unintelligible.

"Mama," he says a little louder and shakes her shoulder.

"Oh, Tony, I fell asleep waiting." she says sleepily.

"Why don't you go to bed, you're tired," he says as he rests his hand on her shoulder.

"What about canasta?" she questions dozily.

"Another night Mama. We'll play cards another night," he says, knowing that she'd try and stay up to play cards with him even is she can hardly keep her eyes open. "I'm a bit tired too, so I think maybe I'll just grab something to eat and head off to bed myself."

She smiles at him. "You're such a good boy, Tony. You remind me so much of Papa. He was such a good man." You could tell she still misses him. She'll probably never get involved with anyone because of that. She stands up slowly and stretches her legs. "Yes, I think I had better go to bed." She gives him a kiss.

"Night Mama," Tony says.

She starts off to her bedroom, which she's shared with Papa. "Will you be by for lunch tomorrow?" she asks.

"I hope so. I'm going out to the Ayer's place tomorrow and there's usually not much to be done around there. Nobody's been there for years." Tony replies.

"I've heard that before, especially when you go to the Ayer's place," she says cynically, then adds, "it is such a nice house and property. Such a waste."

"Yeah, it's my favourite," Tony states.

"Okay, goodnight Tony," she says as she continues to her room. "Oh, don't make a mess in my kitchen," she says as she closes the door to her bedroom.

Still by her chair, he thinks about his mother and what her life is; her restaurant, Maria, Paulo, their children and himself. Would she be able to cope without him living with her? He imagines that she'd probably do just fine. She keeps trying to get him married off. He chuckles to himself and shakes his head, his still damp hair falls in his face, he runs his hand though it and pulls it back out of his face. Six o'clock comes awfully early. He walks back upstairs to his room. It's Friday tomorrow and Elaine will be home in the evening. He'll want to get an early start so that he can get off work early or at least on time. He closes the door to his room and takes off his sweat suit, folds it neatly and puts them on the chair next to his closet. Turns down his bed sheets and slides his naked body between the cold sheets. For a moment he is awakened by their crisp coldness, but as they warm from the heat of his body, he relaxes and falls into a deep sleep.

Black. I hate wearing black. It makes my neck look too skinny. But what else do you wear to a funeral, but black. May 1st. and it's warm already. The weatherman said that it was going to be unseasonably hot today, so it'll be the linen suit not the wool one. Enough complaining, I've got to get going. I've got to pick up Laurel in an hour.

The phone rings. Watch, it'll be Rick. We've been playing telephone tag, well a sort of one-sided tag. I've missed all of his calls home. I rush out to the kitchen and pick up the phone before the answering machine gets it.

"Hello?"

"Hi? Andy?"

"Rick, How's it going at your father's?"

"Good, I guess. I should be home tonight."

"Good, I'm just getting ready to go to Gord's funeral. So I don't think I'll be good company, but it'll be nice to have you home."

"Well, I'll probably be late, I'm going to dinner with my Dad so I was, ah, just phoning to let you know that I'd be home some time tonight and not to wait up, 'kay?"

"Well, how late do you figure you'll be?"

"I don't know, but I'll probably leave here after ten or so."

"That late, huh?"

"Well I could cancel..."

"No, you go on, I'm sure that you and your father need this time. We'll have the rest of the weekend. So I'll see you Saturday morning."

"Sure. Andy?" Rick says, " I really don't know what to say about Gord."

"Well, don't say anything." I could sense that he really doesn't know what he should say. "Sometimes it's okay just not to say anything."

"You sure?"

"Yes, I'm sure. So I'll see you Saturday morning then."

"Okay, Saturday morning. Bye," Rick says as he hangs

up the phone.

I hang up the phone and stare at it. There's something not quite right with this whole situation. I pick up the phone and dial star 69. The computerized voice on the other side of the phone starts "The last number that." I hang up. What am I doing, I think to myself. If I make that call it'll only prove that I really don't trust him. But if I did check that it came from his father's, it would make me feel better, then I'd have no reason not to trust him.

I start to reach for the phone again, it rings as I pick it up and push the talk button.

"Shit. Oh sorry, Hello." I say into the handset.

"Well I should hope so, honey. What's all this cussing for anyway?" asks Gerry

"Oh, Gerry its you."

"Of course it is honey, so what about the cussing?"

Think fast. "I, ah, stubbed my toe turning around to pick up the phone that's all. I'm standing here half naked trying to get myself together and out the door. I've got to pick up Laurel in less than an hour."

"Half naked, you say." Gerry says inquisitively. "Hmmm. sounds interesting. So what's the naked part?"

"Gerry, I've got Calvin's on, what can I do for you?"

"White ones?"

"Of course. Gerry, what do you want."

"Oh honey, you're such a tease," Gerry says so matter of 'factly'. "Well I just wanted to let you know that you and Laurel have reserved seating in the second pew behind the family with me okay. I've left your names with the doorman at the funeral chapel so they'll know where to seat the two of you. Okay?"

"Sure that's fine, thanks for letting me know."

"Are they jockey style or boxer?"

"Gerry, I gotta get ready or I'll be late."

"You're such a poop honey, this could have been better than those 1-900 numbers..."

"Gerry!"

"Okay honey, I'll see you later then, bye."

"Bye." I hear the click of the phone as Gerry hangs up. Boy, I wonder what he's on today. This is not the same man from a few days ago. He's almost back to normal. Damn, I won't be able to check and see where Rick has called from. Must be meant to be this way. I guess I'm supposed to trust him on his word, but I still don't feel comfortable about it. Maybe it's just the funeral.

"How far away did you have to park?" Laurel asks.

"Two blocks, there wasn't a parking spot anywhere."

"Well come on," she says, "they're about to start." We climb the stairs to the funeral chapel.

There is a handsome young man in his early twenties stationed at the doors to the inner chapel. He has the looks of a mid western farm boy, strong jaw, blue eyes, straw blonde coloured hair about six feet tall all fit nicely into a black tuxedo.

As we approach he asks, "Family or friend."

I reply, "I'm Andy McTavich and this is Laurel Pickford."

He reaches into his jacket pocket, pulls out a small card, reads it, and then places it back into his pocket. "This way please." We follow him to the pew behind the family pew where Gerry is already seated.

"Sweet isn't he," Gerry says.

Laurel smiles and nods and I give Gerry a big grin. I think to myself I'll scold him later.

Laurel leans over to me and whispers, "Did you see who's here?"

"Yes, there's quite a few very well known celebrities sitting behind us."

Gerry leans over, "They were clients of Tom and Gord's. Isn't it grand."

"Gerry, this is a funeral not a...," I start to say.

"Oh honey, just you wait and see."

Father O'Brien walks in and the organist stops playing. Then all of a sudden the music starts. I look at Laurel, then at Gerry, the club mix version of We Are Family.

Gerry leans over again, smiles and says, "Only Gord."

We get up from the pew and leave after everyone else has left. Gerry has a big grin on his face. Laurel looks rather shocked.

"What just went on in there?" I ask bewildered. "Are

you sure that was a funeral?" I look at Laurel. She starts to giggle.

"My god," she says, "that puts some Broadway productions to shame, doesn't it."

"It was fabulous, just fucking fabulous!" Gerry exclaims. "Oooh! I can hardly wait for the reception."

I look at the two of them and we all start to laugh. Tom comes through the chapel doors and joins the three of us. "It was just the way Gord planned it. I think we got his instructions down to a tee, don't you think Gerry?"

"Yes," Gerry says in between laughs, "I think it was perfect."

"Well, I guess I'll see you three at the reception in a while?" Tom asks. "There's more show yet to come," he says as he walks down the stairs to the sidewalk.

We all start in at one time, "We'll be there, we wouldn't miss it for anything."

This time parking isn't a problem. I park the jeep in the back parking lot at Georgio's and walk around to the front doors where I had dropped off Laurel and Gerry. The three of us walk into the restaurant lobby, where we are again greeted by the same handsome young man, except this time he's in skintight jeans, a white tank, and a body to die for.

"Oh my, my, my," Gerry says. "I think I'll just linger out here for a while. Why don't you two kids go on in. I won't be long."

Laurel and I look at each other and start to laugh. "Gerry, you can come back after you've gone in and seen Tom and the rest of the family."

"Oh, there won't be any family here. They supposedly got on the first flight back to Chicago after the service. Tom and I had warned them about what was going to be going on at the chapel. They were quite reluctant to say the least but they stayed," Gerry says as he runs his hand down the chest of the doorman. "And when we explained what Gord had planned for the reception they said that they would be leaving immediately after the service. I'm surprised that they actually made it through that opening number."

Laurel goes to Gerry's side, slides her arm through his and says, "Gerry dear, you are going to walk me in there and we're going to mingle with the other people."

"Oh Laurel, you're takin' all the fun out of this," he complains.

"Yes, Gerry," I add, "I think you should go inside. You can always come back later."

The young man standing there with Gerry's hand planted firmly on his chest says, "On your way in, you can sign the guest book. It's just through the open door."

"Oh, I don't want to go," Gerry whines.

"Gerry!" Laurel and I say in unison.

"Okay, okay. I'll go, but I'll be back sweetie," he says to the young man.

We leave the entrance lobby and enter the main dinning room. The room looks the same but there is something different about it today. The music is playing rather loudly and it's not the same quiet classical fare normally played here. It's club dance music. Laurel signs the guest book, followed by myself then Gerry. There are about two hundred people milling around the room. Most are people from the funeral.

"Did you see who signed the book six up from us?" Laurel asks.

"I know, I didn't see them at the funeral did you?"

She shakes her head. "No, but they're here."

"Gerry, was all this planned by Gord before?" I ask.

"Oh, he had everything planned, even to what is on today's menu. Except that young man out in the lobby. I must've missed that when Tom and I were going over all the details." he says as he starts to walk back toward the lobby. Laurel reaches out and grabs his hand.

"Later, lover boy," she giggles. "You and I are going to get us a drink."

I watch the two of them disappear into the sea of people in the room. I can't believe the famous people here. Tom and Gord must have had a lot of connections. I slowly make my way to the bar following my two friends through the crowd of people.

"There you go, one Bud," the bartender says.

"How much?" I ask.

"It's by donation, honey," Gerry says as he sneaks up

beside me and slips the bartender a twenty. "All donations go to the AIDS Foundation. Georgio said that all the money generated by the liquor sales will be donated to the foundation. That's the way Gord had negotiated it with him. I'm going to say hello to a couple of old friends. You be good."

I search the room. Laurel is talking to a handsome man. He looks about thirty, six one, dark, very easy on the eyes. Oh, I hope he's straight, for her sake. I continue to look around the room. There in the doorway is Alberto. I casually make my way to him. Nodding and saying hello to the people I know on my way over to him. I assume he must be working today.

"Alberto, hi."

He looks at me with his dark eyes. "Andy, Hi. I didn't expect to see you here?"

"Well, Tom and Gord are friends of mine."

"Oh, I'm sorry."

"Hey, it's okay, did you know them?"

"I, ah really didn't know either of them. I'm here with a, ah, a friend of theirs," he stumbles through a sort of explanation of why he is attending.

"So, you're not working today?"

"Well, not here at the restaurant," he says as he looks away.

"Oh," not really knowing what else to say.

"It's not what it looks like," he says.

"Look you don't have to explain to me..."

"No, I know, I don't. It's just I'm working my way through med school and it's very expensive and well I'm not exactly from a wealthy family," he explains.

"Alberto, you don't have to explain, I understand. Sometimes you got to do things that you don't like, to get what you want." What was I saying? Of course there are other ways to get the things you want in life. You don't have to hustle. This really isn't the time or place to lecture someone on morals and virtues. He looks at me. He knows I'm lying. He knows that I don't approve of it. He looks into the crowd. I follow his gaze, it takes me to three elderly men, he raises his glass. The man in the middle raises his in return.

"Mr. Alsworthy," I comment. "I had a suspicion, but I

wasn't quite sure."

"You know him?" Alberto asks.

"I've met him a couple of times," I say. "The company I work for has done some work for him off and on the last couple of years. He seems like a very nice man."

There is silence. Alberto looks a little nervous.

"So, which lucky man is your partner?" Alberto asks.

"Well, actually he's not here. His family well, ah, it's really quite a long boring story, and actually he's out of town right now. So I've just come with Gerry and Laurel."

"Yes, I saw you come in with Gerry and that very beautiful red head," he says, as he nods to where Laurel is standing. She glances up and smiles towards us.

"Yes, she is quite beautiful, she's also my boss."

"Really?" he says.

She says something to the handsome man, and walks over to us. You can see the man watch her walk over to us. You can see that he likes what he sees.

"I could tell that I was being talked about. My ears were ringing," she says as she stops in front of us.

"We were just saying how beautiful you look," I say.

"Andy, you know you shouldn't talk about a girl like that behind her back." She smiles. "And so Andrew, who's your handsome friend here? I know I've seen you before but I just can't place you. I'm Laurel Pickford." She puts her hand out to shake his.

"This is my friend ah...Alberto...ah," I stutter. I don't know his last name. I can feel my face turning a bright shade of red.

He shakes her hand, "Alberto Cortez. The pleasure is mine," he says smoothly and breaks whatever tension that might have been building. "I work here as a waiter. I may have served you here before."

"So, then you're working today?" she asks.

"No, I'm...." He looks at me for help.

"Alberto here has been seeing Mr. Alsworthy, and has met Tom and Gord a few times." I hope that's what he was looking for in an explanation.

"Mr. Alsworthy, I suspected but I wasn't sure," she says. "Good catch though, very nice man." She seems indifferent to the fact that Mr. Alsworthy is gay. "I want to talk to Tom a little later. He seems to be handling things very well. Anyway, I think I'll just mingle a bit." She looks back at the handsome man she has left. "Have you seen Gerry?"

"I think he went back out into the lobby," I say.

"Wouldn't you know it," she laughs as she gives me a hug then turns and walks back towards the man she has left five minutes before.

"Thanks, Andy," Alberto says. "I didn't know what to say. I don't like telling people that I do this. They look at me like I'm a whore when they find out. They..."

"Alberto," I interrupt, "you don't have to explain." I put my hand on his shoulder to reassure him that it isn't necessary for him to explain. I can feel the hard shoulder muscles under the suit jacket. It's been a while since I've touched a man, seeing as though Rick has been away for the last week. I look at my hand, then into his eyes. He is looking at me very intensely and smiles. I quickly remove my hand from his shoulder. "I guess I had...ah better find Gerry," I stammer. "It's been nice talking to you, Alberto."

"Maybe we could do coffee sometime, Andy?" he asks. "You've still got my number?"

"Ah , sure that would be fine, I guess," I reply. "Well I'd better find him before he gets into some kind of trouble. Yeah, we'll do coffee sometime." I say trying not to commit to anything too concrete. As I walk away, I turn and see him watching me, nod, then go off in the direction of Mr. Alsworthy. Gerry where are you when I need you I think to myself as I search the room for him. There, right back at the lobby doors talking to the young man in the skin tight jeans, should've known I'd find him there.

"Hi, Gerry."

"Oh pooh, are you here to take me back inside?" he says.

"No, just taking a break from the crowd, before I talk to Tom, and then I'm going to head off. Rick's coming home tonight."

"Who?" he says. "Oh yes, honey, your other half. Forgot about him," he says with a big grin on his face. "Oh Andy honey, this is Troy. Troy, this is Andy. He's my best friend."

I shake his hand, "Hi Troy." He's young, maybe twenty, quite good looking; just the way Gerry likes them.

"I saw you with Alberto. I told you he was family," Gerry says. "So are you and he ...?"

"Gerry!"

"Okay honey, not another word." Gerry and Troy continue on with the conversation they were having before I had joined them. I turn and glance in the direction of Alberto and Mr. Alsworthy. Alberto has positioned himself so that he can see me. I turn and say, "I think I'll find Tom and give my condolences. Do you want to come with me Gerry?"

"No honey, you go on. I'll be fine right here." He smiles, "Oh, I won't need a ride home, I'll just get my driver to come around."

I make my way through the crowd to where Tom and Tom's family members that attended were seated.

"Hi Tom."

"Andy." Tom says as he gets up and gives me a hug. "Everything is okay."

"Good, I'm glad," I say. "I just wanted to let you know..."

He puts his hand over my mouth and says, "No 'sorrys', Gordon didn't want them, you know that. No Rick today?"

"No, he's out of town and won't be back until late tonight. He sends his condolences."

"Excuse me, Tom may I have a word?" A tall dark man in a white jacket interrupts.

"Will you excuse me, Andy?" Tom asks.

"Sure, I'm just on my way out and wanted to say goodbye."

"So early, but okay. We'll get together soon right?"

"Yeah, of course," I say as Tom and the other man leave the dining room through the kitchen door.

I decide to find Laurel and we'll be on our way. I head in the direction to where I had last seen her. I walk past Alberto and Mr. Alsworthy. They both nod. I finally end up back at the lobby door where Gerry is still talking to the young man in the tight jeans.

"Have you seen Laurel?" I ask them.

"She's already left," Gerry says. "She said to say that she'd see you in the office Monday."

"Was everything all right?" I ask.

"Oh everything is all right. She left with a gorgeous hunk of a man so I'm sure everything is all right."

"I don't believe it. All of this is just crazy today. This is supposed to be a funeral. Doesn't anyone get it?" I say in disbelief.

"Andy honey, I think it's you who doesn't get it. You know Gord wanted it to be just like this. He planned all this. He didn't want us to cry and feel sorry. He wanted us to carry on, that's why he threw this party. He wanted us to keep on living starting now. He didn't want life to stop because he died, because he knew that life doesn't stop. He wanted to get us going and live. Do you understand now why it's like this today?"

I stare at him. I know deep down that he is right but the thought that we had just lost a good friend, to me this whole event really shouldn't be happening, this party, we should be mourning. Oh, Christ, am I that anal! Who am I really feeling sorry for? Me?

"Gerry, can we talk for a minute?" I ask.

He looks at the young man he is with.

"Only for a few minutes, I promise."

"Well only a few, honey I don't want to let this one get away," Gerry says as he pats the young man on the butt. "Now you just stay right there and I'll be right back." The young man smiles and gives Gerry a wink as the two of us walk towards the entrance doors.

"I think Gord planned him for me. So what do you need to talk about?"

"Well, it's just all this. I guess I'm really very anal."

"Anal honey isn't quite the word," Gerry adds. "Look, if it'll make you feel any better, when Tom told me of the arrangements that Gord wanted and that all of this was in his will, I was a little taken aback also, but then I thought about it and I thought why not. Having us sit around crying and feeling sorry for ourselves wasn't Gord. This party is Gord. It's like he's here with us. He'd rather have us have fun and get on with life, don't you think? Anyway what would you want?" he asks.

"I guess you're right. I just wasn't prepared for this," I

say.

"Well honey, no one is quite prepared," Gerry says as he glances over towards the entrance to the dining room. "Well I've got myself a little, ah, business that I think that I'd like to attend to. So honey, if you don't mind I think I'll just make my way back over to them there doors being held open by that hunky young thing."

I smile, "You'll never change. Okay, I'm going to go home," I say as I pull the keys to my jeep from my pocket. "Oh, Gerry, thanks."

"Hey honey, no problem." He smiles and gives me a kiss on the cheek. "I'll talk to you real soon, okay."

The sun is shining as I walk through the large double doors out onto the street. I guess this is the way it's supposed to be I think to myself as I walk to the back parking lot to my jeep. I've got a free evening on my hands. I'll pick up some Chinese take out and then go for a walk if the weather holds.

Rick closes the door behind him as he leaves the small cubicle. He finishes wrapping the towel around his waist and makes his way to the showers. It's been a long time since he's been here. Being here is something like therapy. He feels he's getting in too deep with Trevor. Coming to a bathhouse will sort of set him back to reality. He hasn't frequented a bathhouse for the last year since he's been seeing Trevor. Rick learned early on in his relationship with Andy, that their sex life wasn't complete. He needed extra sexual activities that he couldn't have with Andy. It was more of a companionship relationship that he needed or wanted with Andy. His and Andy's sex life was not as active or very fulfilling. Nor did Rick find that it was that important for him to have a sexual relationship with Andy. They still have sex but it just doesn't satisfy him. It's more like going though the motions than anything else. Rick hopes that Andy gets something more out of it, or maybe Andy feels the same way he does about their relationship. With Trevor, it's different. He's definitely not as well educated as Andy but they connect.

Sex with Trevor has been the best he's had in years and it's still exciting. That's why he's here, at the bathhouse, to remember why he first started seeing Trevor, just for sex, just pure raw physical sex with no emotion. He's not supposed to want to be with Trevor outside of bed. That's Andy's domain. He's here to put everything back into perspective, at least that's what he thinks is supposed to happen. It's been two days and he's had sex with many men, but its not like sex with Trevor. He's always had extra-curricular sex while with Andy and never once had he ever felt guilty, but with Trevor he does. At the entrance to the shower room, he unwraps the towel from his waist and lays it on a bench. He enters the room; it's full of hot steam from the showers that are running. There are three men there, each standing under a showerhead spraying hot water over their bodies. Rick moves under a showerhead, eyes meet eyes as Rick scans the bodies of his three shower mates. He turns on the water and adjusts the temperature as the water hits his body. Rick forgets Andy and Trevor, right now it's just sex.

The sky lightens, as the sun gets closer to the horizon, Tony watches as his room slowly brightens and the darkness slips away. He reaches over and turns off his alarm clock, and slowly rolls out of bed. His tan line from last summer's tan is still very evident as it circles his waist and thighs. He'd much prefer not to have tan lines but he didn't get much time to sunbathe nude last summer. He spent a lot of time with Elaine last year instead of out at the Ayer's place where he could sunbathe nude. That isn't why he likes going to the Ayer's, it is the whole place itself. It is secluded, at the end of Rocky Beach Road sitting on five undisturbed acres with a crescent shaped beach of its own. The beach is not like the name the road suggested, but a fine white sand beach. With two large rocky outcroppings on either side of a small part of the beach gives the beach its privacy. Tony figures that his footprints are probably the only human footprints that have been on that beach in the last five years. Then there is the old house; a large Victorian style house built around 1910, perfectly situated to take advantage of both the sunrises over the Cape and the sunsets in Cape Cod Bay. The Ayer's who built the house must have spent at least a year just watching the movement of the sun so that they could build their house in that exact spot designed to take advantage of both the sunrise and sunset. Out of all the homes that Cape Development and Maintenance take care of during the off-season the Ayer's home is his favourite. It isn't the most grand or elegant it just is very well done. It feels like it could be home. He is sure that at one time it was. The other homes are sterile and functional, as an interior designer would describe it. They feel cold and unwelcoming. The Ayer's home is friendly. It makes him feel warm and relaxed. It's sad to think that no one ever uses it anymore. He steps out of the shower and dries off his body. Tony finishes buttoning his shirt as he enters the kitchen. The smell of coffee fills the air. His mother is already up. He can hear her in the back pantry. She comes out into the kitchen wearing her big pink fuzzy housecoat and an apron.

"Tony!" she says with a start. "Don'tcha go scarin' you mother so early in da morning."

"Morning Mama," he says.

"Your breakfast will be ready in a couple of minutes, you sit down and I bring you a coffee," she says.

"No I'll get...," he starts.

"Sit. I bring," she commands. Tony sits and she brings him a cup of coffee.

"Is everything okay, Mama?" he questions.

"Everything is fine," she says as she works over the stove preparing his breakfast. "Are you going to see Elaine tonight?" she asks.

"Yeah for a bit, I guess." He guesses that this is what all the fuss is about, Elaine and him. He had hoped that she wasn't going to start first thing this morning, about them getting married. "She's coming back from Sandwich today. I talked to Sara last night. She said that they were having troubles getting the computer system working so her boss put her up in a motel there to save her from driving. It's probably cheaper to put her up down there than have to pay her travel time and mileage." Tony said. "And we both know how cheap Mike Flannery is."

"Now Tony, he may be a little tight with his money but that's why he's got a lot of it," his mother says. "You never know, with as much money as he's got a woman can find him quite a good catch."

"Mama!" Tony exclaims. "You wouldn't consider seeing a man like him. I mean he's not bad looking, but Mama he's only eight years older than me."

"Tony, heavens no, not me. Since Papa died I never had a thought of wanting a man in my life again. But Elaine...?"

"Oh Mama, get those silly ideas out of your head. You just want to plant ideas in my head so that I get jealous and Elaine and I will set a date and get married. I can see what game you're playing. Anyways, he's much too old for Elaine and I don't even think she's his type." He smiles at his mother.

She looks at her son and he can tell, by the look that she can't understand why the two of them are waiting. "A mother's got to do what a mother's got to do when it comes to her baby." She smiles back at him. She brings his breakfast and puts it down in front of him. "You two come by the restaurant tonight and I cook you two something special, okay?"

"I'm sure that would be just fine," he answers her.

"You better hurry and eat before your breakfast gets cold," she says as she nods towards his plate. "I gotta go to the fish market today, so I gotta get ready. Just putta you dishes in da sink before you go. See you at lunch?"

"Sure Mama, I'll see you at lunch," he replies as she disappears down the hall leading to her room.

He rinses his dishes in the sink, gazing out the window as he dries them. The sun has risen and it looks like it is going to be a nice day. The trees in the backyard have started to leaf and the flowering cherries and plums are budding. There is a myriad of activity in the yard. The spring birds have started to arrive back from their long winter south, a few rabbits still in their winter colour can be seen in the dead underbrush, but mostly the plants have started to awaken from their long winter sleep. Soon the backyard would be green and bursting with colour. Next to summer, spring is one of Tony's favourite times. He stops his daydreaming, grabs his jacket and heads out to the big white mud covered Ford. He pulls out of the driveway and heads back into town. He stops at the office to leave a report on the flooded basement, picks up the key to the Ayer's place and is gone before anyone else arrives.

He pulls up to big wrought iron gates and stops. He gets out unlocks the heavy duty lock holding the chain around the gate, and then puts the old rusted key to the gate itself in the lock and unlocks it. He is surprised that it opens so easily. He pushes the gate open and hooks it so it won't close on him before he drives through. The driveway is bordered on both sides by Lombardy poplars and maple trees as it winds its way down to the house and beach. The sunlight filters through the branches as he drives down the driveway. He is excited about being there today. It has been nearly four months since he was here last and then it was only to check if everything was okay for the winter. He hopes he wouldn't find too many things that need attending to.

As he drives up to the house he notices that a couple of windows on the second floor have been broken. He speculates that the last storm might have caused a bit of damage. Deep down Tony hopes that he can spend a lot more time here. Tony gets out of the truck and walks around the house. As he returns to the truck he notices a large branch from one of the trees next to the house has broken off and lodged itself between the house and the large trunk. Some smaller pieces of the branch are strewn over the yard. That is probably what has broken the two windows. The broken windows are too high for anyone to break into. The large porch that faces the driveway also wraps around the house to face the beach. The porch that faces the beach is deeper than the part that faces the driveway. The main entrance is on the driveway side of the porch. Two massive solid cherry wood doors lead into a large foyer with a granite-tiled floor. Tony lets himself in and walks through the foyer. He checks the room with all the French doors. Everything looks like it has on his last visit, the doors are bolted, the furniture still covered in their heavy off white canvas sheets. He moves from room to room on the first floor of the house, the library, the dining room, the bedroom that probably served as a maids' or nanny's room and the large kitchen with a washroom off the back side of the house. Nothing seems out of place. He checks the pantry room, with its empty shelves and the door that leads to a small basement, used as a cold cellar. It is still locked. He returns to the entrance foyer and ascends the stairway that leads to the second story. He checks the two rooms with the broken windows. A bit of broken glass and some water damage on the hardwood flooring from the rain coming in through the broken panes is all he can find. There isn't much damage to the frames themselves. Tony figures it might take a bit doing to find some antique glass to replace the five broken glass panes, but for the time being he would just board them up. As for the water damage nothing that a little sweat, sandpaper and varnish wouldn't fix. Then he checks the other two back bedrooms and the upstairs washroom. This room he figures has been added long after the house was built, maybe in the fifties. It probably was another bedroom or nursery as it was larger than the average bathroom, with a free standing sink near the back window and a claw foot bathtub that looks like it was specially made to hold two. He then goes to the large bedroom that faces the ocean. It has large windows across the outside wall with two single French doors on either side of the bed leading out to a small, railed deck, large enough for two chairs and a small table. Tony stands by the French door and stares out across the bay. He crosses his arms on his chest and wonders why somebody isn't using such a magnificent house. He knows that if the house were his he would be there constantly. On the other hand if the owners used the place more than they did he couldn't be here as often. He is sure that one day this place will end up on the market and some wealthy Boston family will buy it so he'd better enjoy it while the Ayers' still owned it. He returns to the kitchen and opens the pantry and unlocks the door leading to the small basement. There should be some lumber down there, he could use to board up the broken windows. He walks down stairs. He can feel and smell the dampness; that could only mean that the basement has been flooded. Just as he steps off the bottom step he feels the cold rush of water inside his work boots. He's not expected this. He reaches for the string that's attached to the light and pulls it until the light clicks on. As he surveys the floor he notices that the water is contained at the bottom of the stairs and one corner. Rainwater has been leaking through a small window that has been broken. He needs to repair that also. Tony scans the basement, but can't see any lumber. He walks over to the dry side of the basement and checks the bank of cupboards that line the wall. Each cupboard has a separate lock on it. Against the far wall next to the cupboards is a small worktable, clean except for a thick layer of dust. He checks below it hoping to find something he can use to repair the windows. Nothing. He'd have to come back tomorrow with everything he needs to do the repairs. He can hear his feet squishing in his wet boots as he walks back to the main foyer and out the front door. He locks the doors and walks around to the front porch. He sits on the top stair of the wide stairway leading down to the front yard that opens up onto the white sand beach. He takes his wet shoes and socks off and lays them out to dry. He leans back against the railing and looks out across the bay. The view is spectacular. There is a slight breeze and in the distance there are a few sailboats. He thinks they probably belong to avid sailors that are probably out there every day of the year. The smell of the salt from the bay is evident on the breeze.

Barefoot he gets up and walks down to the beach. The sand is wet and cool from the spring storm, but it doesn't bother him as he walks along the shore. Soon enough the sand would be too hot to walk on barefoot. At night, from the rock outcropping on the south side of the beach you can detect the glow of lights of Provincetown. From the top of the north rock outcropping on a clear moonless night you can make out the faint glow of the lights from Boston across the bay. He walks towards the rock outcropping. This is his favourite spot. Here the rocks split and when he goes through the split there appears a small beach, about thirty feet long, protected by the rocks on three sides, just high enough to block anyone's view but not high enough to block the sun. It's the perfect spot. Tony sits on a large log smoothed by the rain and water from the bay over the years, and listens to the quiet rhythmic sound of the waves lapping onto the beach. The tide is coming in and soon this part of the beach would be surrounded by water. He thinks about the times he has spent here over the years. He remembers sleeping on the beach on a hot summer night, and of sunning his body in the little alcove beach between these rocks. He feels that he belongs here. Other homes on the bay don't make him feel like he does when he's here. It's got to be the house; no other place on the bay gives him this feeling. He gets up from the log and brushes the sand from his Levis. There is a wet patch from sitting on the damp log that stuck to his backside. His jeans would dry by the time he gets back to town. As he walks back to the house he hopes that nothing would change, at least for this summer.

After washing the big white Ford truck, Tony parks in front of his mother's restaurant. "Cape Development and Maintenance" in green lettering on the doors are visible after he washed the mud off. He walks in and takes a seat at the staff table. Maria brings him a coffee.

"Hi Tony. Lunch special today?" she asks.

"Hi Maria, sure the special," he replies as she turns and walks into the kitchen. That isn't like Maria, Tony thinks to himself. She's usually chattier. She comes back out and makes a quick round with the coffee pot to the other patrons in the diner. She puts the coffee pot back on the burner and then sits with Tony.

"Soooo...?" he says.

"So what?" she asks.

"So what's this mood all about?" he presses her.

"Oh nothing."

"Come on now Maria, you can tell your baby brother. What's up?" he asks again.

"Well...," she hesitates, then blurts out "I think I'm pregnant again."

"Oh?" is all Tony can say. There is a long minute of silence that hangs between them. "Is that okay?" he asks.

"Sure, I guess. But I wasn't planning on another child at least not yet."

"Have you told Mama or Joe?" he asks.

"No, I'm hoping that I'm not. I mean not yet. I know they both want a boy. It's just that I wasn't planning on having a baby yet. I was hoping to...," she stutters.

Tony looks at her and can see tears starting to well up in her eyes. One trickles from the corner of her eye. He takes his hand and wipes it away with his thumb.

"Everything will be all right," he assures her. "How late are you?"

"Just a couple of days, but I'm like clock work. You can set your watch by my period."

"Hey, you know you're getting older, and you are under a lot of pressure here at the restaurant. You know what they say about stress. It can change just about anything," he reassures her. "So give it a couple more days, then start to panic. Then come and see Uncle Tony and we'll get you one of those early pregnancy test things."

"Oh Tony, you're no help," she says as the bell rings signalling that there is an order up. She gets up and slaps him on the shoulder.

"Hey, what did I say wrong?"

She returns and puts his meal in front of him.

"Mama's not back from the market yet?" he asked trying to get her mind off of her dilemma.

"Anytime now," she replies. It's obvious that her mind is elsewhere. He decides to leave it alone and hopefully things would be the way she wanted them to be in a day or so for her sake. He hurries and eats his lunch because he wants to get to the lumberyard and pick up a couple sheets of plywood before they close for the day. He gets up from his table and walks into the kitchen to say good-bye to Maria.

He gives her a hug and whispers to her, "Everything will be fine."

"Thanks Tony," she says as she gives him a kiss on the cheek.

"Oh Tony you're still here," his mother says as she walks in the back door of the kitchen..

"Just leaving," he says.

"Before you go, could you get the box of groceries out of the wagon for me?" she asks him.

Tony walks out to her station wagon and gets the box from the back and brings it into the kitchen for her.

"How was your lunch," she asks as she puts on her apron.

"Good Mama. How's your morning going?" he asks.

"I'm behind," she says as she walks over to her desk and starts to cross things off a list. "Now don't you forget dinner."

"Okay Mama, we'll be here around seven?"

"Sounds good, I'll see you then." She sounds a little preoccupied as she hurries around her kitchen. He blames it on being Friday and a busier night for her. He goes back out to his truck and starts off to the lumber yard to pick up the lumber he would need to cover the broken windows at the Ayer's place, then back to the office to pick up a sump pump and his other tools before calling it quits for the day.

Tony gets home just after five p.m. As he reaches his room, he checks the answering machine, there are a couple of messages, probably from Elaine. He pushes the play button.

"Hi Tony." It's Elaine's voice. "Just wanted to let you know that it's four forty five and we haven't left Sandwich yet. We're having such a terrible time with these new computers and the phone lines; I'm lucky I got a line out. UPS dropped off some much needed parts a half hour ago and we're just about finished installing them, should be about an hour or so more. Just wanted to let you know that I'll call you in the morning. Night Tony, I'll see you tomorrow," the message finishes. Damn he thinks, he's just missed the call by about fifteen minutes.

The next message starts with, "Hey, Tony, Garth here. Calling to let you know that a bunch of the guys are gettin' together at my place for beers and maybe some cards. So if you ain't got anything to do tonight then come on over. So maybe we'll see you later." The second message finishes.

Tony starts to strip down for a shower, and thinks that it's quite obvious his evening is free now that Elaine is going to be late. He picks up the phone and dials up the restaurant.

"Hi Mama."

"Oh Tony its you, boy we're busy here tonight. So what time you two gonna be here tonight?" she asks. She sounds run off her feet.

"That's why I'm callin', Elaine's going to be late so I don't want you to make that special dinner that you were planning, okay?" he says. "Anyways if you're real busy then it might just be for the better that you don't have to do anything too extravagant tonight."

"Oh that's too bad Tony, maybe tomorrow?"

"That might be better, but I'll still be 'round for dinner later. I'll just eat at the counter."

"Sure Tony, I'll talk to you later." she hangs up the phone, not waiting for him to reply.

He hangs up the phone and continues stripping his body of his clothes. He tosses his dirty work clothes into the clothes hamper in his room and walks over to the bathroom sink, rubs his hand over his face and thinks to himself that there is no reason to shave tonight. He can hear the raspy noise of his callused hand rubbing over his whiskered jaw. He likes the sound and feel of it. He starts caressing his well formed chest with one hand while the other roams his abdomen, he traces the thin trail of black hair that runs from just above his belly button and disappears down below the elastic of his Calvin's. He strips his shorts off and gets into the hot shower. He lathers up his body in the hot water of the shower. He takes time to lather the soap in his crotch; he closes his eyes, enjoying the feel of his rough hands. He doesn't mind it when Elaine does it, but it just isn't the same. This feels good as he lathers his chest, down over his flat stomach, while his other hand lathers his hard round muscular buttocks. His fingers slide through the crack between the two cheeks. Tony gets out of the shower, gets out a pair of 501's and decides to go bare under them tonight, a white t-shirt to top everything off. He pulls the t-shirt over his head, it fits tightly over his torso, he tucks the shirt into his jeans and puts on a black leather belt. He likes the feel of not wearing underwear. He returns to the bathroom and wipes the moisture from his shower off the mirror. He runs his fingers through his cheekbone length thick, dark brown hair and pulls it back out of his near black coloured eyes. He brushes his teeth while he takes stock of his face. His beard is just noticeable and rough to the touch. It gives him a rugged look. He likes this look. He'd even like to grow a goatee and moustache but Elaine doesn't like them. She prefers a smooth shaved face. He brushes his hair back and gets the tangles out before it dries. He grabs his leather jacket, puts on a pair of work boots and leaves his mothers' house.

"Refill, Tony?" Maria asks.

"No thanks, Maria, I'm 'coffeed' out," he replies.

"Your pasta was okay?" she asks him. Her mind really isn't on her job tonight, and he can tell.

"Yes, for the fourth time in ten minutes, everything was perfect like it always is."

"Oh Tony, I'm sorry, my mind isn't quite where it should be tonight."

"Maria," he tells her. "Everything will be fine. So why don't you just do your thing and forget about it. You're probably so worried about not having it that it's prevented you from getting it."

"Yeah, your probably right," she says in agreement. "So Elaine is going to be late tonight?"

"Yes, they're waiting for computer parts," he says. "But we'll be at your place for Sunday dinner."

"Good, it'll be nice to see her. She's been out of town for over a week," Maria says. She reaches around and touches the small black box attached to her belt, as it softly buzzes. "Got to go, next order is up. You're off to Garth's now?" she asks.

"Yeah, for a couple of beer."

"Well you behave, you know how the cops have been with drinking and driving."

She leans over to take his plate away from in front of

him. She looks him square in the eyes and says "Thanks Tony."

"Like I said, everything will be fine, I know it," he reassures her. He knows that if she is or isn't pregnant everything will be just the way it was supposed to be. "I know Mama is really busy in the kitchen so just tell her that I'll talk to her later."

"Okay Tony," she says as she hurries off to the kitchen to get the next order.

He gets up and leaves the busy restaurant, he nods to a few people he knows that were eating in the dining room as he leaves. His family has lived in Rocky Beach since his mother and father were married in 1959, and have owned and operated the restaurant since the early eighties. His family is probably the last old-time family here in Rocky Beach, other than Mrs. Belmont. She owns a small bed and breakfast on the beach in town, just a couple of blocks from the restaurant. She's quite an eccentric woman, but nice. Most of the newer residents of Rocky Beach think she's just weird. He pulls the big white Ford onto Rocky Beach Road and drives in the opposite direction from where he went earlier during the day when he went to the Ayers' place. Garth lives a couple of miles south of town and away from the beach. He's bought the place a few years ago and has spent most of his time and probably money on fixing it up. So far he's done a real good job, but Tony's sure that the broken leg Garth suffers from will slow him down by at least six weeks or more. He pulls into a wide driveway and stops behind a red Chevy pickup, there's no other vehicles in the driveway. He figures he's early. As he reaches the front door and reaches to ring the doorbell, the door opens and Garth is standing there.

"Hey, Tony come on in," Garth greets him. "How's it goin'?"

"Good," Tony replies, "you?"

"Good as it can get with this thing on me," he says as he taps the hard plaster full leg cast. "Here, give me your jacket and I'll hang it up," he says as he starts to teeter and lose his balance. Tony grabs Garth's shoulders and steadies him.

"I'm not quite used to moving around with this thing on and these sticks yet, it's a real bitch," Garth says with a big smile. "Or maybe it's just the beers."

"Probably both if I know you," Tony says.

They both start to laugh, as Tony hangs his jacket over the banister of the stairs that lead up to the next floor.

"Come on into the living room and have a seat," Garth says as he leads Tony into the large living room. Tony watches Garth as he uses the set of crutches to move from the entrance to the living room. He's right it's either the crutches or the beer, he doesn't move very well yet. As Tony watches Garth move across the room to a large wingback chair he's had refinished last year, he realizes just how well Garth's body is put together. He's seen Garth without a shirt on during the summer and for a young guy of twenty-two he's quite well built, quite beefy for his age, but he's never really noticed his lower body. He's seen his calves before when Garth has worn shorts to work, but he's always worn those surfer shorts that cover just about your whole leg, but now because of the cast he's wearing short boxer type shorts. His thighs are very muscular and his butt is round and looks solid. Tony catches himself staring as Garth swivels on his good heel and turns himself so that he can seat himself in the big chair, and as he does he catches Tony looking at him.

"So what you lookin' at?" Garth asks.

"Boy, you sure need some practice with those crutches. I wasn't sure you were going to make it across the room," Tony says as Garth finally sits down. Hoping that his staring would only be taken as concern.

"Yeah they're tough," he says. "So what's your poison? And don't just stand there have a seat."

"I'll go into the kitchen and...," Tony says.

"No, Joey, my, ah, could you just help me lift my leg on the stool, Tony?" he says as he adjusts himself awkwardly in the large chair. "My cousin will get you what you want. Shit this is uncomfortable." Tony goes over to Garth, stands between his legs and lifts the plaster wrapped leg onto the stool.

"Wow, that's quite heavy," Tony comments as he rests

Garth's foot on the pillow on the stool.

"Tell me about it, so what do you want to drink?" Garth asks as Tony stands between Garth's spread legs, "and please have a seat."

"A Bud will be great," Tony says as he sits on the sofa across from Garth.

"Hey Joe, bring in another Bud will ya?" Garth yells towards the doorway that leads to the kitchen.

"I've only had this cast on for a week and it's already driving me crazy," Garth says. "It's fucking heavy and it itches. They shaved everything from my hips down, even my balls. It's murder in bed and taking a dump is another story. Hopefully I'm a fast healer." He takes a long drink from the beer he has on the table set beside his chair. Just as he puts down his beer a young man about the same age as Garth walks through the doorway leading from the kitchen. He's clean cut, well groomed, quite handsome, not too tall around five foot nine, and looks like he spends a lot of time at the gym, like one of the young guys that spend five days a week at the gym he goes to.

"Tony, this is Joe, my cousin Joey." he reiterates. Joey looks at Garth for a long moment and then at Tony. "Joe this is Tony, this is the guy I told you about, the guy I work with."

"Hi, good to meet you." Joey puts his hand out. Tony stands and shakes Joey's hand.

"Likewise, I'm sure." Tony replies, and then returns to his seat.

Joey seats himself in another large wingback chair next to Garth, a small table between them.

"So," Tony says, "Who else is coming tonight?"

"I don't think anyone else is coming," Garth says, "Bob was here earlier, but had to go, said his wife was on the rag and you know what she can be like when she's bleedin'."

The three men in the room start to laugh. Soon, after a few more beers each, the three relax into casual conversation, but it all seems to be centred around Tony mostly. Tony always felt that he was a very private person and normally wouldn't share any intimate information about himself or his love life. He feels that he is a bit old fashioned that way. Never kiss and tell he'd always say. So during the evening he mostly avoids any question that would lead the conversation in that direction.

"Oh hell," Garth says. "I gotta take a leak," he announces. "Could one of you give me a hand?" he asks, and looks at Joey and Tony. "I mean just to get out of the chair, the rest I think I can handle myself."

Both Joey and Tony get up and almost run into each other trying to help Garth out of his chair. They finally get him up on his feet and propped on his crutches and stand there and watch him hobble off to the bathroom. Still standing both the men look at each other, it's an awkward moment.

"I hope he makes it okay," Tony says, breaking the silence.

"He's doing okay, he'll get much better once he gets more practice on his crutches," Joey says as he looks towards the bathroom door. Again there is silence.

"How long are staying with him?" Tony asks.

"For a couple of weeks, I've taken some holidays so I can help him out then it's back to Boston, but I'll be back on weekends to help him out. In two weeks he should be able to manage just about anything," Joey says. "At least I hope he can."

Tony takes a sip of his beer. It's quiet in the living room again.

"So Joe," Tony says, "you guys are really not cousins are you?" Joey looks at Tony, not with a surprised look, but with one of just being caught.

Just then the bathroom door swings open and Garth almost falls through. "Damn these things are going to kill me. So where did we leave off?"

"I was just telling Joey that I have to go and fix windows at the Ayer's property tomorrow. A couple of them were broken during the storm last week. And since my help has broken his leg, I am running behind and have to work weekends." Tony and Garth start to laugh. Joey, still looking at Tony, slowly joins in. The three of them finish off their beers and Joey gets up and asks if anyone would like another.

"No, I think I'd better head off home, I've got to work in

the morning," Tony says.

"Here, help me up and I'll see you to the door," Garth says.

"No, you just relax, I'll see Tony out," Joey says.

Tony walks to the door with Joey just a couple of steps behind him. He takes his jacket from the banister and slides his arms in and does up the zipper.

Joey reaches for the door and opens it for Tony. "Well nice meetin' ya Tony."

"Yeah, nice meeting you too, Joey," Tony says. "I want to apologize for what I said earlier."

"Hey, no damage done," Joey says.

"No really, I shouldn't..."

"Forget it, Tony, really," Joey says.

"Well then good night," Tony says and puts his hand out and shakes Joey's hand.

Tony sticks his head back into the living room and says, "Hey Garth, take it easy eh? I'll stop by sometime next week. I'll call first before I come over."

"Anytime Tony, I don't think I'll be going anywhere too soon."

Tony leaves the house and gets into his truck and pulls out onto Rocky Beach Road and heads off towards town. Joey stands in the doorway and watches him pull away. Joey closes the door and walks back into the living room and sits down in the big chair next to Garth.

Garth looks at Joey, who is looking at him. "What?" Garth asks.

"He knows," Joey states.

"Knows what?"

"He knows, at least about me, but I'm sure he's now questioning about you."

"You didn't...," Garth starts.

"No I didn't, but when you were in the bathroom he asked me if we were really cousins, and thank God you came out of the bathroom before I had to answer. I didn't know what to say, but I think he knows and you know what? I don't think it really matters to him."

They sit there in their chairs in silence for a few moments, and then Garth reaches over to Joey and takes his hand in his and gives it a gentle squeeze. "You really think it doesn't matter to him?"

"Really, I don't think it does, as a matter of fact I'm sure he's really okay with it," Joey says as he gets up and walks behind Garth's chair and starts to massage his shoulders. "And I don't know why you have to hide. You've been openly gay as long as I've known you. It's only since you got this job two years ago that for some reason you felt the necessity to hide your sexuality. I understand about small towns and all, but if you don't wear your sexuality on your sleeve who's gonna know and who's gonna care."

"Yeah I know we've talked about all this before, but with Tony it's different. He's basically the one person in this town who's taken the time to be my friend. Sure there are other guys in town who I call friends but they're all married and got lives of their own, families. If they ever find out I'd be blackballed. And I don't want Tony to be one of them, because not only is he a friend but I've got to work with him also."

"You worry too much, Garth," Joey says as he squeezes Garth's shoulders. "Anyways, I think Tony's family, he just doesn't know it."

Garth looks at Joey with a big grin on his face and says, "You think everyone is gay!"

"You don't believe me, just you wait and see. He's much too good looking to be straight," Joey states as a matter of fact.

"What about his girlfriend, Elaine?" Garth asks. "You think she's just a cover to hide behind?"

"No, I think he actually cares for her genuinely, but that he has some very serious issues about his sexuality, which probably at this time in his life he's just not able to face, or doesn't even know that he has sexuality issues to face," Joey states. "And I think that eventually he'll just get tired of not being honest, especially with himself that he'll just let it happen and be himself."

"You mean he'll come out."

Joey looks at him and smiles, "If that's what it is then it'll happen."

"So you think he knows about us?" Garth asks.

"If he doesn't actually know, I'm pretty sure that sometime in the future he'll have some pointed questions." Joey leans over and kisses Garth on the forehead, and continues to massage his shoulders. "And you'll be the one that he asks."

"Thanks a lot," Garth says, and sighs, "I don't know if I'm ready to talk to him about it yet."

"Don't worry about it, you won't have any control over it," he says as he yawns and stretches his arms over his head. "I guess it's time to hit the sack. So let's get you up stairs," Joey says as he reaches for Garth's arms to help him out of his chair.

"Damn, I hate going up stairs with this cast and these walking sticks," Garth curses.

Joey slaps his ass. "Hey I kinda like helping you up the stairs."

"You only like it because you can put your hands all over my butt."

"Yeah, so what's so bad about that?" Joey questions. "And anyways you love it."

"So what's your point? You gonna help me or not?" Garth questions playfully. Both men start to climb the staircase, Joey behind Garth helping him balance his way up the stairs.

Tony drives cautiously through town. He's had a few beers too many and really shouldn't be driving. Boy, he thinks to himself, that was a weird evening. He hopes that he hasn't stepped over the line with Joey by asking him that question. For all he knows they really are cousins and Joey is there to help Garth for a couple of weeks now that he's home with a full leg cast. But they sure look nothing alike. He just feels that they have some sort of chemistry going on between them. Even if they were, you know... Tony stops himself. I can't even think the word to myself. "Gay," he says out loud to no one but himself. So what if they are gay? It wouldn't change things; actually it would be really okay having a gay friend. Not that it mattered anyway, he likes Garth. He's a good guy, he works hard and he's fun to be around, and he acts pretty straight. He pulls into the driveway of his mothers' house, turns off the truck ignition and just sits. Tony feels envious. It must be nice to be able to let yourself be free. Free from expectations from other people. Free just to be yourself without having to worry about what other people think. He runs his fingers through his hair and looks at himself in the rear view mirror. You make your bed and you lie in it, that's what Papa used to say. You live by the decisions you make. He gets out of the Ford and goes into the dark house, quietly climbing the stairs to his room. He strips and climbs naked into his bed. God what if they aren't gay he thinks to himself, I've just made the biggest fool out of myself. Maybe they didn't get the implication. If they did I'll just blame it on the beer. I'll play dumb like that's not what I meant, 'the you two don't look like you could be cousins`, it's the easy way out. Even if they were gay it wouldn't make any difference to him, he thinks as he lies in the darkness of his room. Tony wonders what they would be doing right now if they were gay. Would they be having wild sex? He smiles, probably not with that cast on Garth's leg. He feels the stir of blood pumping in his groin; he rolls over and quickly falls asleep.

Tony wakes up to sound of his mother's station wagon leaving the driveway. He's slept longer than he intended. He rolls out of his bed and makes his way into his bathroom, stands in front of the toilet and rubs his hardness a few times and then takes a leak, and watches his stiffness relax. He goes back out into his room and picks up the phone and dials Elaine's phone number.

"Hello," the voice on the other side says sleepily.

"Hey, hi Sara, is Elaine up yet?" Tony asks.

"No Tony, she's not, she got in real late; you want me to get her?" Sara asks.

"No, let her sleep, just tell her I called and that my mom is makin' dinner for us. I'll call her later, I've got to go out to the Ayer's place and fix some broken windows," he says. "So there's no rush. I should be finished around noon or so."

"Sure Tony, I'll tell her," Sara says as she hangs up the receiver. Sounds like she's still half asleep, knowing those two, they have spent half the night catching up.

Sara hangs up the phone and starts back to her room and nearly walks into Elaine coming out of the bathroom they share.

"Oh that was Tony," Sara says. "He's got to go and fix some broken windows somewhere, I wasn't paying much attention, but he said he'd give you a call later today, sometime after twelve," she continues.

Elaine doesn't answer her.

"Are you okay Lainey?" Sara asks. "You look a bit pale."

"Yeah, I'm fine, just an upset tummy," Elaine says. "Must have been something I ate that's not agreeing with me."

"Did you get sick?" Sara asks.

"No, just some dry heaves. I took some antacid, I should start feeling better soon," Elaine says. "With all this eating out this past week, I guess I must've had something that didn't agree with me."

"Are you trying to convince yourself of that?" Sara asks.

"No, what do you mean?" Elaine asks as she leans against the door.

"Are you just trying to tell yourself that it has to be something you ate rather than something else?" Sara says.

"What are you actually trying to say Sara?"

"Oh come on Elaine," Sara says, "this sickness could be, you know like morning sickness?"

"Oh please Sara, it isn't morning sickness. Anyways, I had my period two weeks ago and," Elaine pauses, "and I haven't had sex since before that, so it has to be something that I ate or a flu or something."

"You're sure? You know I'm a nurse and I deal with this all the time it just seems so typical of morning sickness," Sara says.

"Of course I'm sure," Elaine states so matter of factly and in a slightly angry tone.

"But you know how irregular your periods are, we've talked about this before."

"Yes, I know we've talked about this subject before when I thought that I might be pregnant but this is not one of those times, I'm sure of that," Elaine says, this time quite agitated.

Sara stops and looks at Elaine, she looks a little white and her tone of voice is somewhat anticipatory, like she is calculating Sara's next move. Like she's got something to hide.

"You would tell me if there was anything...," Sara starts

"You know I would, you're my best friend," Elaine says as she leans over and gives Sara a hug.

Sara rubs Elaine's back and says, "Remember that, anything, you can tell me anything and you know it won't go anywhere." She steps back and looks Elaine in the eyes, looking for something in her face to tell her what her best friend is up to. Sara gives Elaine another hug and goes into the washroom.

Elaine stands there at the doorway for a few moments and then goes off to her room and closes the door behind her. She lies on her bed and thinks. What if she was pregnant, how could she let this happen? And if she was pregnant what is she going to do. Well there is one way to find out if she was or wasn't pregnant and that would mean be tested. She'll show Sara that she's not pregnant, but she decides it's more for herself, to prove that she's not pregnant. She ties her long blonde hair into a ponytail and slips on some blue jeans and an old sweatshirt, grabs her jacket and heads out to the drug store. She decides that it's best not to buy the pregnancy test here in Rocky Beach, so she heads towards highway six; it'll take her to one of the small towns along the freeway. She has a few hours before Tony will be calling her back.

Tony returns to the bathroom and showers and shaves. As he gets out of the shower he hears the click of his answering machine. Damn he thinks to himself, he has the world's worst timing. He walks out into his room with a towel wrapped around his waist still dripping from his shower. He pushes the play button and continues to dry off his wet body as he listens to the message on his answering machine.

"Hi Tony." It's Maria. "Guess what?" the message continues, he knows what the rest of the message is; he can hear the excitement in her voice. "You were right, maybe I was just a little stressed but I got it today. Can you believe it someone being so happy to get her period? Anyway, dinner is still on for Sunday and oh yeah erase this message after you listen to it, I don't want Mom to know, okay? Love you, bye." The message ends and Tony pushes the erase button. He knew everything would work out the way it was supposed to. He finishes drying his body and gets himself dressed, he pulls on a pair of faded and rather ragged pair of Levis, a white t-shirt and an old sweater.

The sun is shining as he drives the big white Ford pickup down Rocky Beach Road towards the Ayer's place. He notices that spring has taken a strong hold on the trees and bushes along the roadside as the fresh young leaves start to sprout along their branches. There is a slight breeze from the west he can see the tall grasses leftover from last fall sway. Tony gets glimpses of Cape Cod Bay through the trees along the roadside, the view only blocked by tall fences or hedges of some Bostonian or New Yorker's vacation home. He concludes that none of these places along Rocky Beach Road is as nice a spot as the Ayer's property. He feels, only few houses could rival it. Not that it is very big or lavish. It just has a character that few houses along this stretch of the cape have. It has personality. He stops the big truck in front of the wrought iron gate, takes the keys and opens it wide and hooks them back so they won't swing shut. Tony wonders what it must have been like here a long time ago. He knows that it's been years since the gates were open. Maybe one day someone will open these gates again. He gets back in his truck and drives down the long tree lined driveway to the house. As he arrives he can see the five broken windowpanes on the top floor and the other window in the basement. Luckily there isn't more damage. He'd have to get Carol at the office to check around to see if they'd be able to find some period glass to replace them properly, so for the time being he puts up plastic and a plywood barrier over the whole windows to keep out the elements and whatever small animals that might consider the house a good place to nest. He brings the truck to a stop, grabs his tool box from the back of the pickup and walks to the beach side of the house and climbs the stairs to the veranda and unlocks the centre set of French doors leading into the living room. He checks out the floor, and notices that his foot prints from his visit a couple of days ago are now only slightly visible in the dust on the floor. As usual Carol would be making arrangements to have the homes cleaned before their owners start their annual trek. This one would be the last on her list. Tony walks back out to check out the branch leaning against the house. It's not that big so he should have that off in no time.

Tony hammers home the last nail into the plywood covering the upstairs window and climbs down the ladder. He steps back a few paces to admire his workmanship. He tosses his tools into his toolbox and puts it back into the truck and checks the time, ten o'clock. Plenty of time to get the pump working in the basement and the other piece of plywood ready to put up before he leaves for the day. He takes his ring of keys, the sump pump and hose and heads off for the basement. This time before he gets to the bottom stair he pulls the string to turn on the light. There is water at the bottom of the stairs. He's lucky there is an electrical outlet about half way down the basement wall but he'll end up getting his feet wet again. After getting the pump set up and running, he goes back outside to cut the plywood for the basement window. He knows that no one would ever see it but he's particular about what kind of job he's doing. After measuring and cutting the last piece plywood to the exact size Tony checks to see that the water is still coming through the hose from the sump pump. He has some time to kill, but he doesn't mind that. He sits on the front stairs leading to the large veranda, and stares out to the bay. There are more sailboats out on the bay today. He takes his shoes and socks off and lays them in the sun to dry. He knows that Mrs. Ayers would die soon and the family would put the house up for sale. It probably won't take too long before new owners change the whole place. He hopes that when that happens he can turn this house over to Garth. He closes his eyes and dozes off leaning against the large pillar. He wakes to the sound of the sump just pushing air through the hose. He checks his watch, twelve forty. He puts his damp socks and shoes back on and heads down to the basement to check the floor. He reaches the bottom of the basement stairs and finds that the sump has sucked up most of the water. He turns off the sump pump and starts his cleanup.

Tony takes a last walk around the house to make sure that everything is secure before he leaves. He locks the big iron gates at the end of the driveway, looks towards the spot where the house sits and sees that the sun is shining on that spot through the trees. He hopes that old Mrs. Ayers will live for a long time yet as he gets back in the truck and heads towards his mother's place.

Tony arrives at his mother's and goes upstairs to his room. As he enters he checks his answering machine. Nothing. He strips down and heads off to the shower. He can smell his own body odour, mixed with smell of mud and dust from his days' work. He turns on the water and washes them away.

Elaine drives up to the small white Cape Cod style house that she and Sara rent in Rocky Beach. It's not very big but it has a magnificent view of Cape Cod Bay from the back yard. She can see clothes being hung on the clothesline. Sara is doing laundry and hanging it outside to dry on this sunny April day. Elaine checks the sky and sees only a few fluffy white clouds. It probably won't rain she thinks to herself. She sees the clothes slowly move out on the line. Sara is out back right now. This will give her a few minutes to get into the house without Sara noticing. Elaine tosses her jacket on her bed as she passes her bedroom on her way to the bathroom, quickly locking the door behind herself. Well, let's get this over with she thinks to herself. She pees into the little cup provided in the early pregnancy test kit and puts in the little indicator stick. Now wait. She realizes that her queasy stomach has long since gone. She has nothing to do but wait. She thinks back to her conversation with Sara earlier this morning, telling her that she's had her period a couple of weeks ago. She thought she'd had it. She'd had the cramps, the headaches and the usual mood swings, just that this time there was no flow. She'd just thought she got off lucky this time. Her periods were not regular anyway. Sometimes she barely knows she is having it, other times it's like a flash flood. She looks over at the little cup. The indicator stick hasn't changed colour. She takes out a brush from the drawer and starts to brush her hair. As she brushes her hair she looks at herself in the full-length mirror attached to the back of the bathroom door. She caresses her tummy with her hands. She takes another look at the indicator stick sitting in the little cup. There is some colour starting to show on the stick. She picks up the box and reads the instruction sheet again to see what colour would tell her she's not pregnant. Elaine picks up the stick and looks at the colour that the stick is turning to. She feels the blood rush from her face. There's a light knock on the bathroom door.

"Elaine?" Sara asks. "Are you all right?"

There is a moment of silence. Elaine wonders if she can find her voice. What will she say? What will she do? She wasn't planning on having a baby now.

"Yeah, I'm okay." Elaine's voice cracks. "I'll be out in a minute." She decides that she needs to do another test. Maybe this one is wrong. She'd try it a little later. She cleans up and stashes the pregnancy test equipment in the vanity drawer where she keeps her personal bathroom stuff. She can hear Sara in the kitchen, so she heads off in that direction. She is making tea.

"Cup of tea?" Sara asks.

"Sure, that sounds good," Elaine answers back.

Sara looks at her. "Are you sure your all right? You look a little pale. Your tummy still bothering you?"

"No I'm fine, everything is just fine," Elaine says curtly. Sara looks at Elaine, surprised at the tone of voice. This is totally out of character. As they stand there looking at each other, Elaine realizes what she's just done. She can see the shocked look on Sara's face. She has never spoken to Sara or anyone for that matter in that tone of voice before. Elaine sits at the small round table in the kitchen and runs her hands through her freshly brushed blonde hair.

She looks at Sara and says in a quiet voice, "Of course there's something wrong." Sara sits down across from her and reaches for her hand.

"Well?" Sara says. "Are you going to tell me?"

"I don't know where to...," Elaine stammers. "I think you're right. I think I might be pregnant," she blurts out. "I started to think about what you said earlier..." The tears are starting to trickle down Elaine's cheeks. "It's not like I was planning this. The last thing I want is a baby." Sara wipes the tears from Elaine's cheeks with the sleeve of her sweatshirt.

"Have you done a pregnancy test?" Sara asks.

"Yes, I went this morning to get one of those home tests. I'm hoping that it's wrong. I'll do another later."

"I hate to tell you this, but those tests are pretty accurate. If it says you are, then chances are you probably are." Sara sits back in her chair realizing that isn't what Elaine needs or wants to hear at this moment, but she figures that there is no point in drumming up false hopes.

"What am I going to do?"

"It doesn't seem that complicated, Elaine. After you get medical confirmation from your doctor, you plan on having a baby." Sara pauses for a moment and then continues, "Then you tell Tony that he is going to be the proud father of a baby boy or girl in about nine months and life goes on."

"Oh my God!" Elaine exclaims, "Tony."

"Lainey, Tony's a smart and decent man, you don't think he is going to be a problem do you?"

Elaine falls silent. The kettle on the stove starts to whistle and Sara gets up to make tea for the two of them. The phone rings, once, twice. Sara picks it up on the third ring.

"Hello?"

"Hi," says the voice on the other side.

"Oh hi Tony," she says as she is looking to Elaine for direction. She stares at Sara wide eyed and shakes her head. She doesn't want to talk to him right now. "Elaine's out shopping. She's out shopping. She shouldn't be too long. I'll get her to call you when she gets in."

"That's okay, I'll just pop over and wait for her," Tony replies.

"That might not be such a good idea. She's not feeling well. She actually went to the drug store to get something to help her feel better. You have a dinner date right. And she did say she might want to have a nap this afternoon. I think it's a touch of the flu that's going around. We've seen a lot of it at the clinic this past week."

"Okay, okay Sara, you nurses are all alike. Tell her to call as soon as she gets in. If she's not feeling well enough for dinner then maybe a night in bed might be just what the doctor ordered. We can go to dinner anytime. And speaking of dinner Maria invited us out for Sunday roast, so if she's better by tomorrow we'll go there."

"Sure Tony, I'll do that."

"Oh, and remind me to tell her about Maria and her latest pregnancy scare."

Sara stares at Elaine sitting at the small table and says, "Pregnancy scare?" She can see Elaine's face turn white.

"Yeah, its pretty good," Tony says with a chuckle in his voice. "Tell Elaine I'll be waiting to hear from her, 'kay? Bye Sara."

Sara slowly replaces the receiver and walks back to the cupboard counter, gets the tea pot and pours two cups of tea.

"I'm sure he won't be a problem. It'll probably be a shock initially but with Tony, he's pretty level headed, it won't last long. He'll be fine," Sara says, hopefully as convincingly as she can possibly sound.

"Oh Sara...he'll want to know how this happened. He's always been so careful."

"You mean you're on the pill and he always uses a condom, right?" Sara says.

"No, I've never been on the pill, I use a diaphragm and he always uses a condom just in case."

"Well those two are good forms of protection, but they're not fool proof."

"Yes I know, but the only problem is that last time we were together we never had intercourse because he didn't have a condom with him. So he was never even inside me."

"So Lainey, what are you trying to tell me? That this is an immaculate concept?" Sara hesitates. "This is Tony's baby, isn't it Lainey."

Elaine remains silent.

"So when was the last time you two actually had intercourse?"

"You mean when he actually had an orgasm?"

"Of course that's what I mean. You can't make babies without eggs and sperm." Sara sighs.

"You know I've told you that he rarely has an orgasm when we have intercourse and I usually end up giving him a hand job."

"How long Elaine?" Sara asks her best friend firmly. "How can I help you if you don't tell me these things?"

"I think the last time he actually had an orgasm in me was about six months ago." The tears start to flow again down her cheeks. She wipes them off with her sleeve.

"And you've had your period since?" Sara questions in her nursing fashion.

"Yes, every month except I'm not so sure about the last," Elaine sobs.

"Oh Elaine, how could... with...oh my god...Lainey what have you done?" Sara reaches over and squeezes her best friend's hand. "What are we going to do?"

The two women sit there, one quietly sobbing, the other holding her hand.

"Do you know who…?" Sara finally breaks the silence.

"Yes, of course I know who," Elaine says in between sniffles. "It only happened once. I thought it was safe. It was just a moment. Oh god, what have I done?"

"So who was it Lainey?" Sara persists.

"Mike," she answers back through the tears.

"Mike Flannery? Ah Lainey, not your boss."

Elaine looks at Sara. "Maybe that test was wrong, maybe I didn't do it right?"

"Well let's do it again, or I'll take a sample into the clinic, or maybe you should see a doctor in Sandwich while you're there next week," Sara suggests. The two women get up from the small table and walk into the bathroom. Elaine gets the pregnancy test box out and Sara reads the directions. She hands Elaine the little cup and walks out of the bathroom. "I'll call Tony for you and tell him you feel awful and tonight isn't such a good idea."

"Thanks Sara, what would I do without you?"

She walks into the kitchen thinking to herself that she

can't really help much more. But she knows that Elaine needs some time to think about what she is going to do. There aren't many options. She knows that Elaine will have to face Tony eventually. They can probably keep this weekend's visit down to a bare minimum but she knows Elaine can't be sick all the time. A pregnancy is something one can't hide for very long, especially in a small town. Sara picks up the telephone and dials Tony's number.

Tony hangs up the phone. Elaine seems to be quite sick. It is probably a good thing that they spend this weekend apart. Hopefully Elaine will be better as she has to go to Sandwich again next week. I guess I've got a free weekend again with no plans Tony thinks to himself. He picks up the phone again and dials Garth's number.

"Hello?"

"Hi," Tony says. "Is Garth there, Joey?"

"Yeah. Is this Tony?" Joey asks.

"Yeah. I'm just callin' to see what he or you guys are up to?"

"I'll get Garth for you, just hang on a second," Joey says.

There's a pause as Joey puts the phone down to get Garth. He hears Joey in the background calling Garth. A couple of seconds later Tony hears someone pick up the phone.

"Hey Tony he'll be right here. He's not very quick on his crutches yet."

"No problem, tell him not to rush. I don't want him to hurt himself anymore. We're going to be busy soon and we'll need him at work." Tony can now hear the creaking sound of the crutches as Garth walks across the room.

"Hi Tony, what's up?" Garth responds.

"Not much, I, ah, just ended up with a free weekend and was kinda wonderin' what you were up to?"

"Well we ain't got much on our agenda, so if ya want to come over there'd be no problem." Garth suggests. "I'm really havin' a hard time gettin' around on these crutches. And I don't have much to wear that goes with this cast, so I'm keepin' my public appearances down to a minimum. Well, at least until I can get out of the house dressed half decently."

"Sure," Tony says, "I'll be over in a while." He hangs up. For some reason it excites him to be going over to Garth's. Maybe it is finding out about Garth or at least what he thinks he knows about him that excites him.

Garth slowly hangs up the telephone.

"So what's that all about?" Joey asks.

"I really don't know," Garth says. "I thought he mentioned that he had a date with Elaine for tonight. Wonder what happened there." Garth turns and stares at Joey. "You don't think he's coming over here because he figured out that I'm gay do you?"

"If he did figure it out and that's the reason he's coming over so what?" Joey says.

"So what!" Garth says excitedly. "So what! Maybe he has a problem with it and can't deal with it. Oh shit!"

"Hey calm down Garth. You don't even know why he's coming over. It could be something as simple as what he said, nothing much to do, ended up with a free weekend I think were his words, and just wants the company of a good friend," Joey says confidently. "So just be yourself and I'm sure even if he brings it up, and you just act normally and don't turn into a flaming queen, everything will be fine."

"Do you think so?" Garth asks.

"What do you think?" Joey asks him back. "Do you really think that he's gonna care, especially if he's as good a friend as you say he is?"

"Well you know this kinda thing has turned best friends into worst enemies," Garth replies.

"Yeah it has, but you gotta believe in human nature. Anyways, like I told you last night, I think Tony's family."

"No way, he's as straight as they come," Garth says so matter of factly.

"Well, if he's straight then my 'gaydar' is way out of whack. And you know I haven't been wrong before," Joey says with a big smile. "So just one step at a time and don't panic even if he does say something. Remember you got me here."

"Yeah I know," Garth says, "but I hope he doesn't bring it up."

The two young men move into the kitchen, Garth sits

at the kitchen table while Joey makes a pot of coffee.

Joey says, "Worst case scenario is that if he can't handle it, it's his problem."

"But I have to work with him," Garth reminds him.

"Right, you just work with him and nothing else," Joey says. "I thought we were past the days when we had to hide in closets to survive in the world."

"Of course we have, it's just that this is such a small town and things get around quickly. I'd be blackballed I'm sure."

"You're just speculating now. You don't know this for sure," Joey replies. He continues to get the cream and sugar for coffee. "Or you could quit your job and come back to Boston and live with me instead of me leaving Boston and coming here."

There is silence. Joey knows that this isn't an option but to get the situation back into reality with Garth he thought that he'd throw it out as an option. Joey can feel Garth staring at him. He turns and stares back at him.

"Well, it is an option," he says to Garth. "Do you think Tony may want a beer instead?"

"No, you know that it's not an option. The reason I'm here is so that we can get away from the big city, the rat race and all that fuckin' gay activist bullshit, and start a life where we don't have to worry about who we are or who we sleep with and just be normal."

"So then, what's the problem?" Joey asks as he looks over at Garth.

"I guess the problem is that I want Tony to like me, us, just for who we are and not have it depend on our sexuality," Garth replies.

"I don't think you're giving Tony enough credit here. If he's the person you've talked about it isn't going to make any difference. And actually it may not be a bad idea to tell him. You know, the you trust him with your life kinda thing, sharing your secret with him, may be what you need to do."

"I don't know, I..," Garth starts.

There is a knock on the door. Joey starts to walk out of the kitchen to answer the front door. "I think it's a good idea, then there's no pretending," he says as he leaves the room. "If he wants a beer, we have beer."

Garth knows that Joey is right. In Boston he'd have no problem doing it, just telling it like it is. Like it or leave it. But here in Rocky Beach, small town USA, he's not so sure. He's not even sure about how the man he considers to be his best friend would take it. And if Joey is right and Tony can't handle it, it's Tony's problem not his. He hears Joey greet Tony at the door.

Tony and Joey return to the kitchen where Garth is still sitting at the small wooden table in the centre of the room. His plaster-covered leg sticks straight out towards the doorway. He's wearing a long sleeved t-shirt and ragged cut off denim shorts. He starts to get up from the table to greet Tony.

"Hey don't get up just 'cause of me. Sit and stay off your good leg." Tony smiles. Garth resettles himself in his chair. The coffee maker starts to gurgle from the counter signalling that it is ready.

"Coffee anyone?" Joey asks. There seems to be an air of tension. "Why don't we go and have coffee on the back veranda? It's turned into quite a nice day," Joey suggests, as he proceeds to get mugs out for their coffee.

"Sure, sounds like a good idea. The weather for this time of year has been great," he says as he starts to get up. "We'll meet you outside."

Tony reaches over and puts his hand under Garth's armpit to help him get his balance. He can feel Garth's hard bicep and shoulder muscles work as he gets up and manoeuvres the crutches.

"Thanks," Garth says as he looks at Tony.

"Hey no problem," Tony says as he breaks Garth's stare. "Joey? Need a hand with anything there?"

"No, I'll be fine. Why don't you two go outside? I'll just be a few minutes with the coffee. I'm sure that cripple there's gonna need more help than I do."

Garth feels the tension build. This isn't what he wants with Tony. He doesn't want Tony to feel uncomfortable when he's around him.

"Sure, take your time, it'll take me a few minutes to get there and settle," Garth says snippily. Garth hobbles out onto the sun drenched back veranda, with Tony following a few steps behind him.

Tony watches Garth from behind and like last night finds himself admiring Garth's body. The ragged shorts are cut off very short and Tony can see the muscles of Garth's butt work as he moves in front of him. He can also tell that Garth is wearing a jock strap, as the straps are showing in the creases where Garth's round butt cheeks meet his thighs. He's probably wearing them because of the cast. That makes sense. Tony finds his interest in Garth's body quite fascinating. He can feel his juices start to flow and stiffness appear in his crotch. He's always been able to tell whether a body, either male or female is nice or not, but why are things like the shape of a man's butt or how well formed a guy's arm is, such a fascinating thing? Why Garth? Is it because Garth's a friend and he's never noticed before that Garth is physically well put together or is it something inside himself telling him that he's been neglecting his own body, that maybe it's time for him to get back into his workout routine. Garth sits down in a wicker patio chair with his plaster-covered leg sticking straight out. Tony sits down directly across the table from him.

"So what's up Tony, I thought you had plans with Elaine?" He is still a bit apprehensive as to why Tony is there today.

"Yeah, we had dinner planned, but Elaine has the flu so it's a no go for tonight, and since I had some free time and well, I just thought that..., well, we had such a good time last night that I'd just come over and just hang with you guys," Tony says. It sounds like he has to work at an explanation, but Garth can tell that Tony is sincere, that he really is there just to hang out for no particular reason. Garth takes a long hard look at his friend. He's a good soul. There can't possibly be a bad bone in his friend's body.

"Coffee will be right out," Joey yells out through the kitchen window. Tony looks in the direction of where the voice comes from.

Garth is still looking at his friend's face. He's very good looking. He has strong straight lines in his face. His jaw is square and his lips are full, but not too big, very kissable

Garth thinks. His eyes are dark; you can barely tell the pupil from the iris they're so dark. His cheekbone length dark brown hair still has faint red streaks from last summer's sun. His dark complexion finishes off a near perfect look. Garth knows that Tony's good looks go hand in hand with Tony's very nice body. He's seen almost all of it, and it has been the subject of many late night fantasies. He knows that Tony has a very strict workout regime that keeps him in near perfect shape. Just looking at him and thinking about him, makes Garth feel the material of his shorts tighten as his cock starts to harden. He decides that Joey is right. It is time to tell his best friend about himself and Joey.

"Ah, Tony I'm glad you came over today. There's something that..."

"Okay coffee's ready," Joey says as he comes out onto the veranda, not realizing that he has walked in on Garth's moment of truth. Tony gets up from the table to catch the screen door from swinging back and hitting Joey with his tray of coffees.

"So what have I been missing?" Joey asks.

"Not much, we just got me settled," Garth responds.

"Yeah," Tony says, "so Garth, you were saying that there's something that...?"

Joey looks at Garth and quickly figures out that he walked in on Garth telling Tony about being gay.

"Ah yeah, that I'm, ah," Garth stutters, "ah, I'm really grateful for you taking over some of my houses at work." That's all Garth can think of saying. He should have been able to say it in front of Joey, especially since they are partners.

"Hey no problem, you know that it's no big deal," Tony replies. "You'd do it for me."

"Yeah, you know I would," Garth says.

Joey can sense the tension mount; he knows that isn't what Garth was going to tell Tony. He looks at Tony and then at Garth. He says, "You know what? I think I'll go and put on another pot of coffee." He turns and walks back into the house, giving Garth the opportunity to really talk to Tony without interruption. Joey smiles outwardly as he starts to make another pot of coffee. He feels very proud of Garth.

This is a big step for him, especially where Tony is concerned.

Tony and Garth sit silently across from each other. Tony runs his hands through his hair pulling it back. He puts his hands behind his head and stretches. Garth can see Tony's biceps contract and his chest stretch the white t-shirt he is wearing. Tony leans back on the back two legs of his chair, so that his face is in the sun. He closes his eyes as he lifts his face to the sun. Garth looks at his friend and lets his eyes wander down the front of his friend's body and then back to his face.

"Tony," Garth begins. "There's something else I want to tell you." Tony remains in the same position, his face in the sunshine. Garth figures that with Tony's eyes closed it would be like talking on the telephone, like he's not really sitting in front of him. He starts to scratch nervously just underneath the cast where it meet his crotch. He can hear Joey in the house. Garth knows he won't come back out onto the veranda for a while. Garth thinks to himself, it has to be now or never. "I'm gay." Silence. Tony doesn't move from out of the sun, his expression doesn't change, he doesn't open his eyes, he doesn't say a thing.

Finally after a few seconds Tony brings his chair back down. His eyes are open and he looks at Garth. He can see small beads of sweat on Garth's forehead. He thinks that it must've been tough to say this. His eyes search Garth's then he says, "So." He pauses, "I kinda figured that out." His tone of voice doesn't change; he doesn't seem upset. He pauses again.

Garth can see that he's searching for the right words. He fears that Tony isn't okay with this and that he's made a mistake, but it's too late now. "I wanted to tell you before but I wasn't sure how you'd take it," Garth interjects. "I know that I've had plenty of opportunity but I just didn't want to ruin what we had, our friendship and our working relationship. Both are important to me, and I didn't want..."

"Garth," Tony says as he looks at his friend. He can tell that it took a lot of guts, just by the look in Garth's eyes. He knows that it doesn't bother him in the least. "I'm okay with it," Tony adds. "Really, I'm okay with it. I value our relationship and that's really the reason I've come over today. I know that it must be tough living a life where you can't be honest, especially with yourself. I didn't want you to be afraid to be yourself around me. I've come over to tell you that it is okay," he finishes. Tony feels envious. He wishes that life were simpler. He thinks that Garth is lucky to be able to live his life without restrictions. Without having to have the approval of family or church. Are these things really so important that millions of people live lies their whole lives? He knows deep down that it is people's fear of things that are different or unfamiliar that keeps people like himself from truly being happy. It's not that he is unhappy with his life. He keeps telling himself this. He knows he loves Elaine; he cares deeply for his family, even for his brother, Paulo. But for him there's something else that's just not right in his life. It's not like he's got a secret life or anything like that, just something that makes him feel like his life is not whole, and he hasn't quite figured out what's missing.

Tony breaks the silence again. "So are you and Joey...?" he starts to ask.

"Yeah, Joey and I are partners. We've been together for over two years."

"Hey Joe!" Garth yells into the house. "Why don't you get us some hot coffee and join us out here." Garth turns and takes a long look at Tony. He doesn't look like this has affected him, at least right now. He'll really know just how much Tony is okay with him being gay in the next couple of weeks. "Tony. Thanks."

"For what?" Tony asks his friend back.

"For being okay with this, I guess," Garth says.

"Hey Garth, like I said, I'm okay with you being gay." Tony smiles, "And anyways, you're not the first gay person I've ever known." Tony thinks to himself that Garth really is the first gay person he's known personally. The only other person that Tony really knew was gay was Harry Belmont. He was an older man maybe in his forties. He lived with his mother Fiona and another man Jim, who was about the same age as Harry. Harry died six years ago. Every one in town sort of knew about Harry and Jim but no one ever said anything. Jim and Mrs. Belmont still live in the house the three of them converted into a Bed and Breakfast. They've done a great job restoring the old Cape Cod style house. Harry was the only person that Tony could say he really knew was gay, but he wasn't going to admit it.

Joey comes through the back door onto the veranda, and takes a long look at both of the seated men's faces, trying to read them. He decides that it is fine, otherwise Tony would have been long gone by now. He steps up to the table and fills the coffee mugs with fresh coffee and then takes the seat next to Garth facing Tony.

Elaine comes out of the bathroom and hands Sara the cup with her urine in it. Sara takes it from her and puts it in the centre of the tiny kitchen table and places the indicator stick into it. Both women stare at the cup in the centre of the table. Elaine starts to cry as the stick turns colour. Sara picks up the box and says, "Well, these test are sometimes wrong Elaine." She tries to comfort her friend, knowing full well that these tests are nearly ninety nine percent accurate. "So I think that when you get to Sandwich tomorrow you should find yourself a good doctor and have a test done so that you can be sure." Sara says, "And being there will give you some time to think about what you are going to do if the test is positive." Elaine has a lot to think about, and she hopes that she comes up with the right answers.

"Sara," Elaine says, "I've got quite a problem haven't I?"

"Yeah you do, but you've got options Elaine."

"Do I really?" she says between sobs.

"Sure you do. This is not the end of the world. People have babies all the time by accident and the world doesn't end. They just look at what options they have, make their decision and get on with life."

"Are you suggesting that I have an abortion?" Elaine asks.

"Heavens no!" Sara exclaims. "I would never suggest

such a thing, you know I'm pro life no matter who is having a baby. There are just a few other things you can do."

"Such as?" Elaine asks.

"Well, for starters you gotta make sure you're pregnant," Sara says, knowing full well that what Elaine will find out will just confirm their suspicions. "Then, when you find that out, and it turns out you aren't then you have nothing to worry about. But if you are, well then you got to tell someone, like Mike."

"Tell Mike! Tell Mike that I'm carrying his child but I'm going to marry Tony. I don't think so!" Elaine snaps.

"Oh come on Elaine that would be the honest thing to do. He'll find out eventually. And of course you'll have to tell Tony..."

"Tell Tony that I'm carrying some other man's baby. Well that'll be the end of Tony and me," Elaine says.

"Look Lainey I'm just trying to help, I didn't get you into this mess," Sara snaps back. "You do have another option. You can put the baby up for adoption. There are thousands of couples in this country that can't have children and would love to have a baby."

"Oh Sara, I don't know if I could...." Elaine's voice cracks and she starts to cry, her sobs choke out anything else she is trying to say. Sara comes around the table, hands her a tissue, and puts her arms around her best friend and holds her while she cries.

"So, I'll get you an appointment through the clinic with a good doctor in Sandwich next week and we'll get things going," Sara says, all the while Elaine nods in agreement, tears roll down her cheeks.

The phone rings.

"Hello?" Gerry sings.

"Hi Gerry."

"Oh Andy honey, how have you been? We haven't seen much of you lately? What have you been up to?" Ending the barrage of questions from Gerry I answer, "I've been around, haven't done much."

"You okay honey?" He asks. "You sound a bit under the weather?"

"I'm fine," I reply. "Are you busy today?"

"Well, I've got a dinner date tonight with Troy."

"Boy the two of you have really hit it off haven't you?"

"Is that such a bad thing Andy?" Gerry questions. "You know it's been a few years since I've had anybody in my life."

"Oh Gerry don't get me wrong, I think it's great that you have someone in your life again." I hope that I have myself. "And believe me I won't lecture you the way you lecture me."

"Need to talk, hey Andy?"

"Well I wouldn't mind, maybe lunch with my best friend. We haven't done anything since the funeral."

"It's Saturday, where's you know who? " Gerry asks.

"Rick's at work again, he's been working a lot lately."

"Well okay, let's meet at Georgio's in an hour, is that okay?" Gerry queries.

"Sure meet you there," I respond as I hang up the phone.

It's been four weeks since Gord's funeral and all the problems with Rick and his dad and his company are still there. I'm sure things are happening, just that they're not happening with me. I seem to be at a standstill. Gerry has a new love interest. Laurel has a new man in her life. Both of my best friends are extremely happy and moving forward. I feel like my life has stalled. Everyone looks like they are alive and growing and I feel stale. It's almost the end of May and summer is just around the corner. New life is everywhere. Maybe I just need some contact with my friends. I have been spending a lot of time alone since Rick has been putting in so much overtime at work. I can't fault him for that. The weather has been great so far this year and business for his father's company has been very good. His relationship with his father seems to have gotten a lot better also. He's been spending just about every Sunday for the last month at his parent's place. Rick figures, that he'll be able to have me with him and his family by this time next year. I know that it's important for him to make amends with his family and I have been encouraging it. So much so that when he gets a day off and suggests that he'd like to see his dad, I almost push him out the door. I grab the keys to my jeep and start towards the door.

The door to the apartment opens and a small dark plump woman appears.

"Oh hallo Mr. Andy," Rosie says.

"Hello Rosie, how are you today?" I ask as I take my leather jacket from the hall closet.

"I am fine Mr. Andy. Is Mr. Rick home, today is cleaning day, you know?" she says.

"No I'm the only one here and I'm just on my way out for lunch with my friend Gerry. Rick is at work so he won't be home till late," I say.

"Okay," she states as she lays the large bouquet of fresh flowers on the kitchen counter and starts to get herself ready for her afternoon of cleaning in the apartment.

I close the door behind me and walk towards the elevator at the end of the hall. I can hear the phone ringing from my apartment. I hesitate for a moment trying to decide whether I should go back in and answer it. I decide to let the answering machine do its job, and continue down the hall. I hear the door to my apartment open and hear a voice call my name from the other end of the hallway.

"Mr. Andy, Mr. Andy," Rosie says. "Please Mr. Andy come back quick."

I walk quickly back to the open door of my apartment.

"What is it Rosie?" I ask.

She looks at the phone and then the answering machine. “It was your mama. She says it’s important you call right now,” she says as she motions to the telephone. “She say it’s your grandma.” She points to the answering machine.

I push the message button.

“Hi Andrew, it’s Mom,” the voice says. I don’t know why she always says that. I always recognize her voice. After the short pause the message continues, “I’m here at Gram’s nursing home and well Andrew please just call me here as soon as you get in.”

I dial the number to the home.

“Greenville Sound Nursing Home, Jill speaking how may I help you?”

“Hi, Jill, this is Andy McTavich. My mother just called and said to call her back. Is she there? That’s Catherine McTavich.”

“She was just here a second ago. One moment Mr. McTavich and I’ll page her to a house phone.”

There is a click and some piped music starts to play over the phone. It seems like ages before someone picks up the phone again.

“Hi Andy is that you?” his mother’s voice comes through the receiver.

“Yes mom, what’s up? What are you doing in Wilmington?” I ask. “You’re not due back from LA till July fourth.” She lets me ramble on. “Is everything okay with Grams?”

“Well Andy, that’s why I called. Grams passed away last night.” She pauses, “They phoned me first thing this morning and I flew right out. I thought that I would be able to call you from the airport but my connections kept me running and I forgot my cell in LA so as soon as I got to the home I called you and the rest of the family.”

“You okay?” I ask.

“Yes hon, I’m fine, not much anyone could have done, she just slipped away while watching TV in her room late last night.” There is silence for a moment. Then she says, “Will you be able to come down in the next day or so? Grams had everything taken care of, in case of this happening. It’s just that I’m sure that I could use you to help me with your two aunts." She pauses for a second, "They were both hysterical when I called them."

"Sure Mom, I just have to make a few calls and I'll get back to you to let you know what time I can be there. Where are you staying?"

"I haven't got that far...," she starts to say.

"Well don't worry about that. I'll arrange for something for us at the Hilton. So you just go there. I'll do that right away, and I'll leave a message at the desk for you about when I will be getting in. You sure you're okay?"

"Oh Andy you're a good boy. No wonder Grams liked you best. I'd better go. I'm going to see the resident doctor in a few minutes. Bye Andy." She hangs up the phone.

"Bye Mom," I say as I hang up the phone.

I stand by the phone not moving.

"It's no good, right Mr. Andy? I just know it," Rosie says as she makes the sign of the cross.

"No, my grandmother died last night."

"I'm so sorry Mr. Andy," Rosie says.

"Thank you Rosie. There wasn't much anyone could do. Mom says she just slipped away." I fall silent, for a moment,. I've got to make some arrangements. I hang my leather jacket back in the hall closet. "Rosie, I've got to make some calls, so I won't be leaving just yet."

"That's okay Mr. Andy, I understand, I'll come back on Monday," she says as she finishes putting the flowers in a vase on the dining room table. "You just do what you have to do, and when you see your mama you tell her I'm sorry for you both okay?"

"Thanks Rosie, I will."

"Okay Mr. Andy, I will let myself out. Bye. You take care."

I stand there leaning against the wall. Damn, this sure hasn't been a very good start to this year. First Gord dies, and now Grams. Things can't get any worse. I pick up the phone and push speed dial number two. I'll tell Rick what's going on and then make the other arrangements to get myself to Wilmington. The number automatically dials and starts to ring. Once, twice, three times, then a woman's voice comes on the phone.

"Long Island Construction. Jill speaking. How may I help you?"

"Hi Jill, Andy McTavich here. Is Rick around."

"Oh hi Andy, he's not on site today."

"He's not there, are you sure?"

"Yes, I've just done a personnel count and he's not on site. Is there something I can do for you?"

I fall silent. He's supposed to be there. "Did he go out for lunch?"

"No, he hasn't been here today. Why should he have?"

"He said he was going in to work today. Would he be out with his dad?" I ask.

"No, Mr. and Mrs. Campbell have been at their condo in the Virgin Islands for the last two weeks and we're not expecting them back for another three weeks."

I fall silent again.

Jill asks "So Andy, can I help you with anything?"

"I'm sorry, I just thought that Rick is there. It's just that my Grandmother died last night and I have to leave for Wilmington today, and I'll probably won't be back until the weekend."

"Oh I'm so sorry Andy. You know he may have had some errands and may be on his way to the site yet. So why don't I just make sure he calls as soon as he shows up, okay Andy?" Jill suggests.

"Sure that would be great, thanks Jill," I say hesitantly and hang up the phone.

There's something not right with this. Rick's not where he's supposed to be and his parents have been in the Virgin Islands for the last two weeks. So where has Rick been for the last two Sundays if his parents have been away in the Virgin Islands? Where in the hell has he been, better yet where is he now? I get that sick feeling in the pit of my stomach that tells me that I've been walking around blindly when it comes to Rick, that all my friends have been right all the while. My hands are shaking. Wait I tell myself this isn't right he's probably got things to do, so he hasn't shown up at the construction site yet. And as far as the last couple of Sundays I'm sure that there is a perfectly good reason. Then why do I feel sick about this situation?

My hands are still shaking as I dial Gerry's phone number. I hope he hasn't left yet. One ring, two rings, three rings.

"Hello?" Gerry answers.

"Hi Gerry, good I caught you before you left, I'm going to have to cancel."

"Sure, he came home did he?" Gerry says sarcastically.

"No, actually I just got a call from my mom. My grandmother just passed away in Wilmington."

"Andy I'm sorry. Are you okay?"

"Yeah I'm fine I guess. I just got off the phone with her. I've got to go to Wilmington, so I've got to make some arrangements here."

"If you need anything Honey you just call, okay?" Gerry offers.

"Yeah thanks Gerry, you could do me a favour while I'm out of town."

"Sure Andy just name it."

"Could you keep an eye out for things at the apartment?"

"Sure Andy, is Rick going with you?" he asks.

"No," I reply

"I don't understand. Why do you need me to look after things at the apartment if Rick is going to be home?" he questions.

"Not the apartment per say, just an eye around you know the apartment."

"Andy you want me to watch what your Rick is up to, don't you?" I can sense the excitement in Gerry's voice. "You mean spy on..."

"All I want you to do is just call or drop in sort of unexpected once or twice next week," I say. "I was going to talk to you about all this at lunch but it'll have to wait."

"Do you think he's up to something or better yet someone?" Gerry exclaims.

"Actually I don't know. Maybe this wasn't such a good idea."

"No Andy, don't be silly I'm sure you have your reasons and we'll talk about them when you get back, but I'll just pop by once or twice okay. Nothing too suspicious, okay?"

Gerry suggests. "Why don't you go on and get yourself off to Wilmington, I'm sure you'll have enough to do there."

"Yeah thanks Gerry." I hang up.

I pick up the phone receiver and push speed dial number one. The phone rings once and a man answers.

"Hi is Laurel there?"

"One moment, can I tell her whose calling?" the man's voice queries.

"It's Andy," I say. I can hear the man tell Laurel that it's me on the phone as he walks across the space that separates her from the phone.

"Hi Andy. What's up?" Laurel asks.

"I, ah, I'm sorry if I interrupted anything."

"No we're just sitting on the patio. So?"

"Yeah, I'm going to need some time off this week. Actually probably the whole week."

"Is there something wrong, Andy?" she questions.

"Well, Grams died last night and I have to go to Wilmington."

"Andy, I'm so sorry. Are you okay? How's your mother doing? Of course you take all the time you need. Oh shit Andy I'm sorry."

"Hey Laurel, there wasn't much anyone could do."

"You sure you're okay? I wish I was there with you now so that I could give you a hug."

"Yeah me too. But hey, I've got to get myself off to Wilmington, hopefully today or tomorrow morning at the very latest."

"Like I said Andy, you take whatever time you need, and don't worry about anything at the office, okay? I'll make sure that someone covers your accounts this week. Just keep me informed, 'kay?"

"Yes, thanks Laurel. I've got to go. I've got to start making my travel arrangements." I want to tell her about what I'm feeling about Rick, but I figure that can wait till I get back. It would probably all be worked out by then and there would be nothing to talk about. It's probably nothing but a simple misunderstanding.

I walk to the den, get my day timer and look up my favourite travel agent. I pick up the phone in the den and dial his number.

New York to Baltimore to Raleigh to Wilmington is the best I can get on such short notice. I'd be in Wilmington by ten thirty tonight, not bad considering the up and down flights, the two-hour layover in Baltimore and one and a half hour layover in Raleigh. I leave a message for mom at the hotel to pick me up at the airport. Now, I just have to pack a few things, call a cab, leave Rick a note and I'm off. I walk back into my bedroom and start to put the clothes on the bed I would need to take with me while I'm away this week. I dial the phone again and call the cab company to make my arrangements. They would be here in forty minutes. It doesn't give me much time. I continue to pack. I go to the closet and pull out the black suit I just wore to Gordon's funeral. Wow, I think to myself, it's been over three weeks since his funeral. Time sure moves fast. I would have to give Tom a call when I get back. I put it on the bed with all the other clothes; and then I go into the bathroom and start to gather up my bathroom stuff, toothbrush, toothpaste, razor, deodorant, and brush. Where's my brush? I walk back out into the bedroom and look around the room, trying to remember where I last used it this morning. I retrace my steps. Right, I must have left it in Rick's room. I was putting away some of his laundry earlier this morning while I was getting myself ready for the day. I walk into the room where Rick keeps his stuff. His bed is still made. He's either sleeping in my bed or at his parents lately. There it is, on his dresser. I walk over and pick it up. There on the dresser top is a picture of him and me when we were on holiday in Key West three years ago. We look so happy. I notice that Rick has a pile of unopened mail at the back of his dresser. He's always so bad at handling his mail. I pick up the pile and start to flip through, just to make sure there is nothing urgent. When I write his note I'll remind him to go through it. Credit card bills, it's a wonder he doesn't have financial problems. Here's one stamped personal and confidential. It's from a free clinic from across town. I stare at it and I get this awful sick feeling. I put the pile of mail back on his dresser. Why would Rick have mail coming from a free clinic, I wonder to myself. I tell myself that it's probably old from when we had our last HIV testing a few years ago. I know he used a free clinic then. I examine the envelope; the stamp cancellation date is only two weeks old. I sit down on his bed holding the envelope and consider opening it. He is my partner. It wouldn't be so wrong to open his mail. I've never done it before, open his mail that is, and he's never opened any addressed to me. I continue to stare at the envelope. I wouldn't want him to open my mail so why should this envelope from the clinic be different. It is a matter of trust. Anyway, I'm sure it's nothing. I slide the envelope back into the pile of envelopes and put them back on his dresser. I pick up my brush and walk out of his room back into my bedroom and grab my suitcase and start to put the things into my suitcase. I check the clock. The cabby will be here in about ten minutes. I finish packing and take everything to the front door of the apartment then go into the den to write Rick a note:

Rick

Grams died last night. Had to go to Wilmington. Mom's there. I'll be at the Wilmington Hilton if you need to get a hold of me. Will be there for at least a week. I'll call in a day or so when I know more about what the arrangements are. Handle that pile of mail you've got on your dresser. I'm sure you've got bills in there that need to be paid.

Love Andy.

I walk back out into the kitchen and put the note by the phone. I pick up my bags, walk out of the apartment and head towards the elevator.

As I reach the main floor of the apartment building, that same sick feeling I had when I was looking at the envelope from the clinic comes back. I should have opened it. The doors of the elevator open and I can see a yellow cab just pulling up to the curb. It's too late to go back up and get it. I walk out towards the front door of the apartment building and think that I shouldn't have mentioned the pile of envelopes in my note to him. Maybe he won't deal with the pile of mail until after I get back. He's usually quite slow when it comes to that kind of stuff. I walk through the big door out onto the sidewalk. An older man, maybe in his fifties gets out of the yellow cab.

"McTavich?" he asks.

I nod. "Yes."

"Where to?" he asks.

"La Guardia," I say.

The cabby opens the trunk of the cab and takes my luggage from me and puts it into the trunk. I get into the back seat as he returns to the drivers' seat of the car.

"Where you off to kid?" he asks

"Wilmington."

"Business or pleasure?" the cabby asks.

"Neither," I reply.

"Hey kid, just tryin' to be pleasant. We've got a bit of time till I get you to the airport."

"I'm sorry, family funeral," I say. I hope he doesn't feel like talking all the way to the airport.

"Hey sorry kid, didn't mean to be rude," he says as he pulls away from the curb in front of my apartment building.

"What time's your flight and which terminal."

"Three forty-five, American," I answer back.

"We should be there about an hour and a quarter before your flight if traffic is normal for a Saturday."

Silence. The cab driver doesn't say a word to me the whole way to the airport. He checks in periodically with his dispatch, but other than that no conversation is exchanged between us. He watches the traffic go by and I watch the city go by as we travel towards the airport. He pulls up to the curb in front of the domestic departures gate and gets out of the car to open the trunk and retrieve my luggage. He sets it on the curb.

"Got you as close as I could get ya kid. You've got about a block to walk back to the terminal," he says. "That's thirty bucks for the ride."

I hand him two twenties. "Keep the change," I tell him. I pick up my bags and start walking into the terminal. I head straight for the ticket counter to pick up my ticket.

"Boarding will commence in thirty minutes, Mr. McTavich," the young blonde girl at the ticket counter says. "The check in counter is just about a hundred yards down from here." She points towards the check in counter. "It doesn't look too busy so if you go down there now you'll be able to move through the line quite quickly." She smiles.

"Thanks," I say, as I take my ticket and move off towards the check in counter.

The airport is crowded. My thoughts drift away from the envelope back at the apartment as I watch people saying good-bye, couples embracing as if this was the last time they'd see each other. I wish that I had someone here to see me off. I reach the check in counter and present another pretty young woman with my ticket.

"You've got quite an up and down ride in store for you Mr. McTavich," she says as she looks at my ticket. "Would you like to take your bags as carry on or would you like to check them in?"

"I'll do carry on, thanks," I reply.

"Boarding will commence in thirty minutes at gate number Fifty-six," she says. "Have a nice trip Mr. McTavich."

As I walk towards Gate Fifty-six, I can see more people saying good-bye or hello, embracing and kissing. I feel envious. It's been a long time since I've been hugged or kissed. I know that Rick isn't a very affectionate person at the best of times, but this seems to be one of those times when I need him to be and he's not here. I continue on to Gate Fifty-six knowing that something is missing from my life, and at this time I really don't know what to do about it. First things first. I'll deal with Gram's death and then I'll deal with my life. I may be just feeling this low because of Gram's death. I hand my boarding pass to the attendant and move down the hall to the entrance of the plane. I find my seat and settle in for the first leg of my trip to Wilmington.

The fasten seatbelt light comes on and the pilots' voice can be heard, "This is Captain Kelly, on behalf of the crew of Flight 211 to Wilmington. We hope you have enjoyed your flight. We will be landing in approximately five minutes at New Hanover International. Local time is ten twenty; the temperature at New Hanover International is currently a warm sixty-eight degrees. Again, thank you for flying American." The intercom cuts out as we start our descent into New Hanover. I look out of the window next to me for the first time and notice that it's a clear night and the stars are brilliant. As the plane banks towards the landing strip I get a panoramic view of the city and all its' lights. I hope that my mother is here as I really don't want to be stuck in the airport for long. I'm feeling quite tired. It's been a long day. I look around the plane. It's really the first time all day that I've taken any notice of my surroundings since I left La Guardia earlier this afternoon. The plane is about three quarters full. The other passengers have all returned their seats to the upright position and are preparing themselves for the landing. A couple of kids in seats a few rows behind me start to giggle as the plane's wheels first touch down. I feel a smile on my face. It seems good to have nothing much to worry about except having fun in life. That's the way it was when I was a kid. Spending summers at the beach with Mom, my aunts and my cousins Emily and Trisha, Grams and Grandpa while he was still alive. Grams, Grandpa and I used to fly kites down on the beach. Grandpa was the best kite flyer in the world; well that's how I remember him. He used to say that when you fly your kite real high, close to the clouds, that you were flying with the angels. I think that this was one of the happiest times of my life, on the beach with my Grams sitting on her blanket, Grandpa and me just a few feet away holding on tightly to the string of the kite flying high in the sky. Grandpa would say, "Can you feel the angels holding up the kite boy?" and of course I'd say that I did. At six years old I really thought that the angels did have hold of those kites we flew. Today I really don't think there are any, angels that is. I've grown to be a little sceptical. I don't know what in my life has made me think that way. The plane has come to a stop and I can hear the doors opening and the other passengers starting to move out of the plane. I stand up and take my bags from the overhead compartment, and make my way out of the front door of the plane.

As I go through the door the stewardess says, "Hope you enjoy your stay in Wilmington." Little does she know as I nod to her. I walk down the long corridor and into the arrivals' gallery of the terminal building. People are standing around the stainless steel luggage carousel waiting for their luggage to come out of the chute. I scan the large room and there by one of the exit doors is my mother. She is dressed in a long flowing skirt, a light sweater, a lacy shawl over her shoulders and white boots, a sort of early eighties Stevie Nicks look, a bit dated but it looks good on her. Her curly blonde hair is tied back in a loose ponytail. Her complexion is still tanned from the sun in California. From this distance she looks rather relaxed. As I get closer to her she starts to walk towards me. I notice that she has aged a bit since the last time I saw her, a few wrinkles, laugh lines I'm sure she'll call them, but she still looks good. In moments she puts her arms around me and gives me a long, firm hug. I put my arms around her and squeeze her back. She pushes back, takes a long look at my face, searching my eyes. She gives me a kiss.

"Hello son," she says.

"Hi mom," I say, "it's so good to see you."

"And you too. Are you alone?" she asks as she looks behind me to see if anyone else was traveling with me.

"Yeah, Rick is away at his parents," I lie. I really don't have a clue, at that moment as to where he is. "I couldn't get a hold of him, so I just left him a note."

"Well I guess that's okay," she says. Mom has never said much about my relationships. And she has never commented about the people I've been involved with. She's always said as long as I was happy what more could she ask for. I believe her. I know that's how she lives her life. As long as a person is happy with the situation that they have for themselves then why should anyone else interfere. She slides her arm through mine as we make our way out onto the street.

"You look great Mom," I tell her.

"Thanks, I've been going to the gym and it's starting to pay off." She smiles and says, "Can't expect to catch a man with fat now a days you know."

"You're getting your monies worth, you look really good."

"Thanks. I have a cab here. We're only about fifteen minutes from the hotel."

"So how are you doing?" I ask her.

"Oh I'm fine. Even though Gram's death came sort of as a surprise, we've been sort of prepared for it. Her doctor said two years ago that it could be anytime. So after a year we all thought that she'd probably outlive us all," she says with a smile. "Your aunts, by the way, are a mess."

"You said that they were when you called them." I smile back. "I think that you were kinda figuring that they would be."

"Of course I was, those two are the most predictable people I know." She stops talking as we reach the taxi. The driver puts my luggage into the trunk and we both get into the back seat of the cab.

"The Hilton, please," she says as the driver gets back into the car. "They started blubbering the moment I told them and I don't think the two of them have stopped since." We both start to laugh. "They are quite a site!" she finishes.

The two of us stop laughing. Again she looks at me and searches my face and eyes.

"Are you okay?"

"Oh I'm fine, just that it hasn't been a very good spring. First my good friend Gordon dies, no promotion yet, and now Grams," I say. "It's just been a rough start this year." I don't want to get into anything else right now. I don't want to talk about things at home, how all my friends don't like Rick, or tell her about the letter from the free clinic for Rick.

She continues to look at me. She reaches over and grabs my hand. It is warm and for the first time in a long time I feel like someone who genuinely cares is touching me. She brings her other hand over and rubs the top of the hand she's holding. I can feel the warmth of her hands run up my arm and through my body. I think she knows how this makes me feel. "Em and Trish will be here tomorrow. Your aunts are a couple of floors below us at the hotel. I don't think I could bear being on the same floor as those two blubbering fools," she continues. "Grams had all of the arrangements for her funeral made in advance. She was such an organized woman, your grandmother. And I really don't think that she'd have left any of those arrangements up to us. She was particularly fussy about these things. The funeral will be held on Monday at ten in the morning. The reading of her last will and testament is on Thursday at four in the afternoon at Peabody's office."

"Grams still retained that old codger?" I ask.

"She always said that he knew more about what she had and that because he was a good friend he would make sure that everything in her will would be carried out just as she wished. She wouldn't trust any other lawyer to do this. He's coming out of retirement for this."

The taxi now drives into the hotel parking lot and then into the front portico of the Hilton. A doorman comes to the rear passenger side door and opens it. As I start to get out of the car, I notice that the doorman is young, maybe in his mid twenties. He has deep blue eyes and blonde hair. He looks at me and holds my stare. He smiles and nods at me. He reaches in and helps my mother out of the back seat, while the taxi driver unloads my luggage from the trunk of the car. A bellhop runs out and picks up my luggage as soon as the taxi driver puts the cases down on the sidewalk. I take out my wallet and pay the taxi driver. We walk into the lobby and my mother walks over to the registration desk. She leans over and talks to the young man behind the counter. A moment later he reaches over and hands her another cardkey to our suite. Mom walks over to the bellhop and hands him the key, and a ten spot.

"We'll be in the lounge, please return the key to the front desk," she says as the young bellhop turns with my luggage and walks down the corridor to the elevators. She walks over to me and gives me another hug and says, "Let's go and have a drink, okay? I'm sure your aunts will be there. Probably trying to figure out how much Grams left in her will."

"Mom, they're not like that," I say.

"You haven't seen them. Those two have been worried about Grams money ever since she's moved into this home in Wilmington ten years ago. They've always said that it was too expensive and that Grams really wouldn't need the kind of care." She stops and looks around the lounge to see if she can see her two older sisters. "Ah yes, there they are. So I guess we're obligated to join them."

Mom has always had a problem with her two older siblings. She finds them superficial, their lives revolving around the almighty dollar. Husbands were for climbing the social ladder and better alimony cheques, which ever could provide them with a better standard of living. Their motto was first you marry for love, second for children and then for money, and the quicker you get the first two out of your system the quicker you could get on with the job of going for the money. It seemed to have become a competition between the two over the years. Mom never bought into their game. They ridiculed her for not having done so after my father died. They kept telling her that she was young and had already experienced love and had a child, and it was time for her to start looking out for herself and make sure that she was set in life. Set financially that is. But Dad has left Mom pretty well off with insurance money. She's always said that she wasn't going out there specifically to find a man, and a man with money at that. If anything was going to happen, it would more than likely happen naturally. We make our way over to their table. They seem quiet; at least it looks like it from this distance. Mom's oldest sister, Ellen, gets up as we approach the table. She looks a lot like my mother; through most of their childhood and teenaged years people often said they looked so much alike they could almost pass as twin sisters. She comes forward and gives me a big hug and a sloppy kiss.

"Andrew how are you my boy?" She asks.

"As well as can be expected I guess Aunt Ellen," I reply.

Aunt Audrey, my mothers next eldest sister pushes her chair out from the table and opens her arms wide and says, "Hi Andrew, come and give me a hug." Aunt Audrey looks the most like their father. Her features are not as fine as mom's or Aunt Ellen's. She is big boned and chunkier. But all three women have the same eyes, Gram's eyes. They all have the same twinkle as Gram's.

I move around the table and give her a big hug. It's good that the three sisters still get along, other than their disagreement on how one should live ones' lives and of course their excessive drinking which my mother doesn't like. My two aunts return to their seats and my mother and I sit at the two empty chairs at their table. A waiter comes over and takes our drink order.

"I'll have a glass of white wine," my mother says.

"I'll have a Bud," I order.

"Oh you two should have something with more kick to it than just a glass of wine and a beer," my Aunt Audrey says.

My mom shoots her older sister a look that could kill. "I'm sure we both know what we would like to drink," she says sternly.

"Oh Katy, I'm sure Audrey just means that under the circumstances...," Aunt Ellen starts to say.

"Under any circumstances people should be able to order whatever drink they would like," my mother says sternly to her two sisters.

There is a short period of silence between the four of us. Then Aunt Ellen says, "Andrew did your mother tell you that Em and Trish will be here some time tomorrow?"

"Yes, she told me on the way in from the airport. Are they bringing the crew with them?"

"No the kids have school and with such short notice they decided that it would be best to keep them at home," Aunt Ellen says as she picks up her glass and takes a drink.

"A funeral is really no place for young kids anyway," Aunt Audrey says. "The children hardly knew Grams." Again there is silence around the table. All three of the sisters have had a good relationship with their mother, I'm sure that deep down, for all of them, and this loss is hard to cope with. But they all seem to be holding their own. Even though my mom's two older sisters are so money oriented, I'm sure that they would miss their mother just as much as my mother was going to.

"Did your mother also tell you that Grams had all of her arrangements made already?" Aunt Ellen asks.

"Yes, Mom filled me in on everything on the way over from the airport," I say. "Mom told me that she even made arrangements for the reading of her will on Thursday at old Peabody's office."

"Can you believe it, old Peabody is coming out of retirement to do this one last thing for Grams," Aunt Ellen says. "I'm sure that after Grandpa died Peabody was trying to court Grams," she chuckles.

"Oh please," Aunt Audrey says. "I'm sure that Grams

would never have had anything to do with him."

"Could you imagine being raised by Grams and old Peabody," Mom suggests.

The three of them break out into raucous laughter. Finally our drinks arrive. I take a long pull on my beer; The coldness of the liquid feels refreshing as it trickles down my throat. As I relax in my chair I realize that it's been a very long day. My thoughts wander off to the events of earlier in the day. My problem of getting a hold of Rick. Where has he been anyway? He should have been at work like he said he was. And what has he been up to these past few weekends when he's said that he's been at his father's? I realize that trust is the basis of all relationships but this situation just doesn't sit right. And then there is the envelope from the free clinic.

"Andy, Andy," my mom interjects. "Andy is everything all right?" She shakes my shoulder.

She brings me back to reality from my daydream. " Oh yeah, I guess I'm just tired from traveling today. I think I'm going to head off up to the room, if you ladies don't mind?"

"Oh sure Andy, you go on ahead. We have all day tomorrow. The funeral isn't until Monday morning so we'll have plenty of time to visit," Aunt Ellen says.

I get up from the table and leave my half full bottle of beer behind. I give each one a kiss on the cheek and say goodnight. I make my way to the lobby and to the front check-in desk to get a key for the room. After getting direction from the night clerk to where the elevators are I make my way to them. As I'm standing in the corner of the elevator I wonder if it was the right thing to do, to ask Gerry to check up on things at the apartment while I'm away. I think that I want him to find out that he's been wrong about Rick, that he's isn't fooling around on me and all this talk about him has been uncalled for. No this just means that I don't trust Rick. I'll call Gerry when I get upstairs and tell him that it's not necessary for him to check on the apartment. I have to trust; otherwise I don't have much in the way of a relationship. For all I know Rick might be thinking the same things right now about me being away in Wilmington, but if we trust each other then we don't have to worry about these things. The elevator stops, the doors open and I walk towards the suite and unlock the door. It's eleven thirty. Gerry will still be up, and so should Rick. I pick up the phone and dial my number. The phone rings, once, twice and on the third ring someone picks up the phone.

"Hello?" I say.

"Hi, Andy."

"Hi Rick. You got my message?" I ask.

"Yeah, I got it when I got home from work at six," Rick says. "Everything okay?"

"Yeah everything is fine, well I guess it is," I say. "It's good to hear your voice, Rick."

There is silence for a moment then he says, "Are you sure you're okay?"

"Yeah I'm fine, just a bit tired," I say. "Didn't Jill tell you I called to tell you that I was going to Wilmington?"

"Ah yeah, she mentioned that you called but she was in such a hurry to get out of the office she didn't say what it was about."

"Geez, I told her it was important and she said that she'd get you the message as soon as you got to the site," I say. I'm finding it hard to understand why Jill wouldn't mention something like this Rick, it's really not like her.

"Hey, I'm sure she probably meant to tell me, but like I said she was is such a hurry to get out of the office today it probably just slipped her mind. There's probably a little sticky note on her desk." There is silence again for a moment. "So how's your mom doin'?" he quickly changes the subject.

He never asks about my mom. My mother never says anything that would indicate she really doesn't like him. It is her body language towards him. She has difficulty including him with me, but she tries, which is more than I can say about some of my other friends who don't really like him either. 'As long as you're happy, what more could a mom ask' is what she always says.

"She's doing okay. It's my aunts that are basket cases right now. But that should change by the time they have the will read, then they'll be just peachy," I say. "Grams had all her funeral arrangements made already. She'd never leave anything like her own funeral arrangements up to her daughters especially to my aunts."

"So when's the funeral then?" Rick asks.

"It's on Monday," I say.

"So you'll be back on what, say Tuesday night or Wednesday?" Rick asks.

"No, the reading of Gram's will is on Thursday, but I'm planning to stay until either Saturday or Sunday and visit with the family. My cousins Emily and Trish are coming in from Dallas tomorrow and will be staying the week." I find myself getting irritated with the fact that I've given most of this information to Jill this morning. Why didn't she give him the message? She's usually not that incompetent. The only other reason that Jill would not have given Rick the message would be if Rick never showed up at the site. "You know I gave all this information to Jill this morning. I'm going to have to have a talk with the girl when I get home." I'm sure I sound irritated.

"Andy, I told you she was in such a hurry to get out of the office, that it probably just slipped her mind. She may have had a crisis of her own, you know women," Rick says, "and if it really bothers you that much I'll say something to her on Monday."

"Yeah maybe I'm just being a bit too hard. I guess I'm just tired from traveling today," I conceded. "Well on that note I guess I'd better let you go as I'm bushed."

"Well good night Andy, I guess I'll see you sometime on Saturday or Sunday. You don't have to call. I'm sure you'll be busy with family things."

"Talking about family, how's things going with your dad?" I ask.

"Coming along just fine, we've got plans to go golfing tomorrow," he says. "And you know how much I hate to golf."

"Yeah, I know. Anyways, night Rick."

"Night Andy," he replies and hangs up the phone.

He is lying to me. He's up to something. Maybe everyone else is right about Rick. Maybe he is seeing someone else. I hesitantly hang up the hotel phone. I don't think I'll phone Gerry tonight. Shit, here I am falling for it all over again. Trust, I say to myself, I have to trust him. Maybe Jill didn't give him the message because she was really having a crisis of her own and really was in a hurry to get out of the office. She could have mistaken me for someone else. The Campbell's have partners in business. It could have been them she was thinking about being in the Virgin Islands. I'm sure that it was probably something like that. Rick isn't like that anyway, and our relationship is sound, and there is really no need for me to question Rick's commitment to our relationship. And the letter from the free clinic...

I hear the door to the suite close. I turn to see my mother coming into the small living room.

"Andy, I thought you had gone to bed," She says as she walks across the room towards me. She puts her arms around me and gives me a hug. She pushes herself back and looks at my face intensely. "Is everything all right?"

"Yeah, I'm just tired from traveling today. All that up and down and waiting in airports, you know how that is," I say.

"Sure I do, just went through it two days ago. But there's worry in your face I can see it. Is everything all right at home?" she asks.

I know she's concerned, I guess any mother would be concerned about her child. "No everything is good as far as home is concerned," I say to her, hoping she can't sense that I'm not being honest with her. "Work's been a hassle lately, no promotion yet. One, which I think I deserve, but other than that everything is just fine."

"Okay, I can't help you much on the promotion bit if that's the only thing that's not going well right now in your life. You can always use your mother as a sounding board if you want," she says and smiles at me.

I feel myself breaking into a big grin, "That's why I love you so much."

"I know, so why don't you get yourself ready for bed before I get into the bathroom. That way you don't have to wait for an hour to get in there."

I make my way to my bedroom in the suite to grab my bathroom stuff. I turn and take a good look at my mother. "Thanks mom. I'll see you in the morning." I watch her turn towards me. She looks so much like her mother did in her younger years. "I love you."

"I love you too, Andy," she says back to me. "We'll have breakfast on the patio. We'll do room service, say 'tenish'?"

"I wouldn't miss it for anything," I say as I walk into the bathroom.

Rick hangs up the phone and starts back to his room. He feels a big grin spread across his face. This is perfect; actually it's more than perfect. Trevor has been nagging me to bring him to our apartment. Andy's grandmother's death couldn't have happened at a more opportune time. This will get the apartment thing out of Trevor's system, and after this week of being here for a night or two they can get on with things just the way they have been for the last year. He makes his way to the bedroom. As he enters the room he takes off his clothes, leaving his underwear on. He walks into the bathroom and turns on the shower. The steam starts to fill the room and clouds the mirrors. Rick steps into the steaming shower and washes away the sweat left on his body. As he soaps up his body he thinks that this week with Andy away he'll have more time to think about how he was going to deal with Trevor. He knows that if he lets things go on further the way they are, the more difficult it will be to keep it secret. But for the time being, well at least for the next week, he'll just have some fun. It'll be good not having to always be looking over his shoulder.

Elaine takes the turnoff onto Interstate Six, driving on the freeway will keep her mind off of her problem. Her nausea has just about gone, the package of saltine crackers on the seat next to her are half gone. Sara has said they would help with the nausea. Sara has set up an appointment with a doctor friend she has in Sandwich for eleven o'clock that morning. Elaine knows that the doctor wouldn't be able to tell her anything that she doesn't already know and fear. She knows that early pregnancy tests are usually ninety nine percent accurate. Of course she'll have to take another test, just to confirm that she is. Somehow over the last twelve hours she has come to the realization that she is pregnant, and has also come to the conclusion that no matter what, she is not going to give up this child, not to adoption nor to abortion. Her problem is what to do about Tony and Mike. She knows she loves Tony and he's the man she's always wanted to spend the rest of her life with and of course have children with. But then Mike excites her. He makes her feel like a young girl again and the sex is extraordinary. She thinks about what she's told Sara, that it had only happened once. She knows she's lied to her best friend and she hopes that she's been convincing enough for Sara to believe her. She hasn't been looking for it, sex that is, but her sex life with Tony lacks real excitement. Handsome, well put together as Tony is, there just doesn't seem to be a real sexual connection. Not just for her, but for Tony also. She is sure that Tony needs or wants something else, well at least sexually. She knows for a fact that Tony loves her. It has nothing to do with his equipment either, for God had been generous there. Mike on the other hand has not been so lucky, but he hasn't been shortchanged either. Mike has a sexual magnetism that Tony lacks. Does she love Mike? She isn't sure, but what she feels is definitely different than what she feels for Tony. Elaine knows that this pregnancy will be very difficult to hide so she has to make up her mind about what she was going to do about the men in her life. She'll have a few days to think. She won't see Tony until the coming weekend and Mike won't be in Sandwich till Thursday morning. She'll have the results of the test by then. She looks down at the speedometer and notices that she is traveling ten miles an hour over the speed limit. She takes her foot off the accelerator to slow her car down to the speed limit. The hour and a half that it takes her to drive to Sandwich seems like forever. She has phoned Mike last night and has told him that she has an appointment and will be in the Sandwich office by noon. This week they would be putting the finishing touches on everything, making sure that the computer system works and is properly linked to the home office in Rocky Beach and of course hiring some staff. She and Mike have two full days of interviews lined up for Thursday and Friday. Those two days were going to be hell. She smiles, something, she thinks to herself, she hasn't done a lot of lately. She notices the sign for the Sandwich turnoff go by. It will only be a few minutes and she'll be turning off the freeway.

Elaine pulls up to the clinic and parks in the parking stall closest to the front door. She gets out of her car and brushes the cracker crumbs from her business suit. As she walks to the front door of the clinic she sees her reflection in the glass windows. She can't imagine what it would be like to be fat, pregnant fat that is. She lowers her right hand to her tummy and thinks there is a little baby in there. The door to the clinic opens and an elderly man walks out. He startles her.

"Sorry miss, didn't mean to frighten' ya," he says.

"Oh that's okay," Elaine replies "Guess I just wasn't paying much attention to what I'm doing."

He holds the door open as Elaine passes through. She walks up to the counter and checks in with the nurse at reception.

"Hi, I'm Elaine Carter, I have an appointment with Dr. Miller at eleven o'clock."

"Yes Ms. Carter. You're a new patient for Dr. Miller?" the receptionist asks.

"Yes, this is my first visit with Dr. Miller," Elaine replies.

"I'll need you to fill out these forms. Do you have medical insurance?" the nurse asks. Elaine nods. "I'll also need your medical insurance card when you finish filling out those forms. So just have a seat over there. The forms only take a few minutes to fill out and we'll have you in to see the doctor in about ten minutes." She points to a small desk in the corner of the reception room. There are only a few people in the office, she hopes that the receptionist is right and it won't take too long to get in to see the doctor. She sits at the desk and fills out the standard forms that doctors' offices make you fill out. She returns the forms to the receptionist and also gives her medical insurance card.

"Please have a seat Ms. Carter," the receptionist says.

No sooner than Elaine sits down a nurse comes in through an opening at the back of the office and says, "Ms. Carter."

Elaine says, "Yes?" as if she hasn't been expecting anyone to call her name.

"Doctor Miller will see you now."

That's been quick, she thinks, not even enough time to pick out a magazine let alone read one. The nurse leads her down the hallway to the last examining room on the left hand side of the hall, opens the door and ushers her in.

"Please have a seat. The Doctor will be with you shortly." Then she closes the door.

The office is sparsely furnished and very sterile looking, a small cupboard with a sink, an examining table, a desk and three chairs. Elaine sits in the chair next to the desk. She scans the room again. There are a couple of charts on the wall, an eye chart and one of a pregnant woman. She stares at the woman on the poster; again her hand reaches down and rests on her abdomen. The door opens and a woman in her early fifties in a white coat comes in. She has a stethoscope around her neck with the loose end neatly tucked into to her white coat pocket. Her hair is shoulder length and greying. She's not wearing any makeup and her complexion is pale. She's not very tall and looks a little over weight.

The woman picks up Elaine's chart and sits in the chair behind the desk.

"Elaine Carter, I'm Doctor Miller." She pauses for a

moment as she looks at the chart. "So what can I do for you this morning? Your chart here doesn't give me much information other than you're from Rocky Beach," she finishes.

Elaine thinks for a moment. "I think I'm pregnant."

"You think you're pregnant. So why do you need to come all the way to Sandwich to see a doctor about a pregnancy? You do have your own physician in Rocky Beach don't you?"

"Well, yes I do, but I'm working here right now and I thought and....," she starts to fumble with her words, "and my friend Sara Johnson suggested that I should see a doctor as soon as possible and I wouldn't be able to see my doctor for a few weeks."

"Oh Sara sent you. She went to nursing school with my daughter. My daughter is my receptionist. The two of them squeezed you in this morning."

There is silence again as the doctor starts to write something in Elaine's file.

"Sara says that you have done an EPT already, is that correct?"

"Yes," Elaine says.

"Well? What were the results?"

"It confirmed that I was pregnant," Elaine replies. "And I've been nauseous every morning lately, and I don't think I've had my period."

"Okay," the doctor says. "First we'll do an official pregnancy test, but I'll be honest with you Elaine, you are more than likely pregnant. Those tests are pretty accurate, and not having your period is something of a give away, but to be on the safe side we'll wait for the results of the test." The doctor gets up from her chair and goes to the cupboard to get a small container and hands it to Elaine. "If you can you fill this and leave it with us, we should have the results back by Wednesday afternoon or Thursday morning at the latest. Have you got a number here in town where we can reach you?" the doctor asks.

Elaine gives her the motel phone number and her room number.

"Elaine," the doctor says, "Sara also mentioned that you were not quite sure what you were going to do if you were pregnant. I just want to let you know that you do have some options."

"Actually, Doctor Miller," Elaine cuts in, "I have decided that I'm going to keep the baby."

Doctor Miller sits back in her chair. "Well that's good there's nothing like a pregnancy without having to worry about a fickle mother trying to figure out whether or not she's going to keep the baby." Again the doctor scribbles in her file. She takes a good hard look at Elaine. "Are you married?" she asks. "Not that a woman needs to be married these days to have a baby."

"No," Elaine says.

"You do know who the father is?"

"Are these questions necessary?"

"The questions are, but the answers, they're up to you, Elaine," the doctor responds.

Elaine hesitates, the doctor is right. The questions are necessary but the answers are up to her. "Yes, of course I know who the father is." Again she hesitates. Elaine decides Doctor Miller is just like Sara said she was, hardened, direct and to the point. She obviously doesn't put up with any bullshit.

"Well are you going to tell me?" the doctor questions.

This is it, the time she's been dreading. She thought that she'd have a few days to really think hard about this answer. She feels pressured, but she also knows she needs to give the doctor an answer. "It's Tony, my fiancé."

"His full name please," the doctor says.

"DiMarco, Tony diMarco," Elaine says.

Dr. Miller again stops and takes a long look at Elaine. "I don't understand. If your fiancé is the baby's father why would you consider giving it up or aborting?"

Elaine starts to fidget and continues to stare at the floor, "We never really talked about having children, well at least not yet. We both have careers that are just getting off the ground and I'm not quite sure that having a baby right now would be fair to either Tony, myself or the baby for that matter." Elaine starts to sniffle. "But after thinking about it, adoption or abortion are not options."

The doctor hands Elaine a tissue. "So keeping the baby

is best for all?"

"Other couples do it, have a family and careers, they make it work so why couldn't we."

"Good answer," the doctor says. "You haven't told him yet have you?"

"No, I wanted to be absolutely sure that I am."

"Okay, I can understand that. No point in getting two people worried or stressed especially if children are not part of the plan yet." The doctor continued to write in Elaine's file. "So why don't you take your jacket off and we'll do a quick examination and then have you fill the bottle."

Elaine removes her jacket and sits down on the examination table.

"Oh thank God that's over with," Ellen says to her sister Audrey as they quietly file out of the funeral chapel.

"It wasn't so bad. I suppose it was just like Grams would have wanted it," Audrey says.

"Of course it was," my mother says sternly to her two sisters. "She's planned the whole thing, remember?"

Trish, Em and I walk behind the three sisters, all dressed in black, out into the small courtyard in front of the funeral chapel.

"So Andy, which one is going to be the first one to say, I could use a drink about now?" Em questions. Emily is Aunt Audrey's daughter from her second marriage. She, myself and Trish are the only children that the three sisters had. Both the girls look so much like their mothers and that is a good thing, because their fathers were, let's just say not pretty. "I bet it's my mother," she continues.

"No," Trish says, "It'll be mine. I'm sure she's had a drink even before breakfast this morning."

I start by saying, "I don't think it'll be my mom, so why don't I just say that no matter who says it first the other will only be seconds behind in saying that's a good idea, then my mother will follow and berate the two of them," I add, "and to make things interesting who ever gets it right gets dinner bought." The three of us nod in agreement.

The three of us look at each other and start to laugh. My mother looks at the three of us affectionately. When we were younger the three of us were so close. When we summered on the Cape with Grams and Grandpa you couldn't separate us. It was two months every year, until Grandpa died that we summered with them on the Cape. I think she longs for those days again, that's when the sisters were closer.

"What's so funny you three?" Aunt Ellen asks. "Boy it sure gets hot early in the day down south," she says mimicking a southern drawl. "I sure could use a drink with all this heat. It's not too early is it?"

"Oh what a good idea, I'm a little parched from this heat too," Aunt Audrey says.

"It's way too early for a drink, unless you mean a coffee," my mother adds.

Again the three of us start to laugh, uncontrollably this time. Em is almost in tears and Trish is doing a little dance and saying that we're going to make her pee her pants. The three sisters look at us in surprise. As the three of us start to gain our composure, a short, robust man with wispy white hair in a black suit approaches my mother and her two sisters. A plump little woman, no taller than the man, wearing black, follows him: Peabody, Grams' lawyer, and his wife, Martha.

"My condolences girls." He's always called my mother and her sisters girls. "I just wanted to let you know that I'll sorely miss your mother," he says with a southern accent. "As you know, my wife Martha and I have spent a lot of time with your mother over the last few decades since your father passed away."

"Why thank you, Mr. Peabody," Aunt Ellen replies accepting the condolences on behalf of the family. "Hello Martha, you keepin' okay?" she asks the plump little woman.

"Yes, thank you," Martha stammers in between sobs.

The three of us look at each other and we almost start to laugh again, but this time we are all able to keep it under control. The five older people stroll towards the street. The three of us follow walking towards the limos that'll take us back to the hotel.

"So where are the two of you going to take me for dinner tonight?" I ask.

"Your choice," Trish says.

"Pick seafood, Andy" Em pleads. "We don't get much real fresh seafood in Dallas."

We can barely hear what the older group is saying, but Peabody's voice carries even when he's trying to be quiet. Guess it's from all those years of yelling in court.

"I know this really isn't the time or place, but we've got a meeting on Thursday afternoon to settle up your mother's estate, but what I'd like to do instead of having it at the office downtown is to have all of you out to our place in the country. It's not too far from town. We'll have dinner. Martha and I insist so you can't back out."

"Melvin just hates to go into the city if he can help it," Martha says. That's the first thing I think that I can recall her saying other than the thank you between sobs. "It gets so hot in the city at that time of day," she finishes.

Melvin opens the door to the first black limo parked at the curb in front of the funeral chapel and my mother and her sisters get in. Just as he closes the door he reminds them, "Don't forget to bring the young ones, your mother didn't leave them out of the will, so they should be there for this. I'll send a car around to pick you up say at two o'clock. We'll have lemonade on the veranda." He closes the door to the limo and steps back from the curb. Em, Trish and I are already getting into the second limo. Martha and Melvin wave to us as our limo pulls out from the curb.

Gerry taps his foot as he waits for the elevator door to open. Come on; come on he thinks to himself. I must talk to Andy about this building. It must have the slowest elevator in New York City. Finally the door opens and Gerry moves quickly out into the corridor and heads down the hall to Andy and Rick's apartment. He glances at his wristwatch. Oh hell, he thinks it's already eight thirty Thursday morning, it'll be too late to catch Rick at anything. Gerry is quite sure that Rick would eventually get caught. Hopefully it wouldn't hurt Andy too much. Andy's much too good for Rick. Everyone knows it, but Andy. He finally reaches the apartment door and he starts fumbling with the keys.

"Which one is it?" he mumbles softly. "Ah, there you are, I knew I'd find the right one." He inserts the key into the lock and quietly unlocks the door and pushes it open.

"Hello," he yells as he waltzes inside the apartment. "Hello Rick are you here?" he calls again. He hears nothing. "I know you and I don't see eye to eye Rick but Andy called before he went off to Wilmington and asked if I'd stop over and water the plants while he was gone. He said that you'd probably forget to do them even if you had a note tattooed to the inside of your eyelids." Still nothing. He looks around, notices dirty dishes in the sink, unopened mail on the kitchen counter. Hell, he's not here, but it looks like he's been here. Gerry counts the dirty plates in the kitchen sink, one, two, three, four, short one plate except Andy did say that Rick was going to his parents for Sunday so that's the right number of plates for one person since Saturday. Doesn't look like he's had company, well at least for dinner. Gerry goes to the kitchen sink and gets out the watering can from underneath and fills it full of water, "Well I'm here now I might as well do what I promised to do," he says out loud to himself. At least if he comes home while I'm doing this it'll be self-explanatory. Gerry wanders through the apartment and waters the jungle of plants Andy has accumulated over the years. He goes into the bedroom that Andy and Rick share and waters the few plants Andy has set by the window. Gerry thinks that if Andy ever lost his job as an accountant he would have no problem getting one at an arboretum or nursery, he has such a green thumb. The room looks like a tornado has gone through it. Gerry checks the bathroom, no plants to water in there and only one toothbrush. He walks into the spare bedroom, the one that Rick has for his personal belongings. Two plants to water there, one on the windowsill and another on the dresser. This room is neat and tidy; no one has slept here for a long time. He waters the plant on the windowsill and then waters the plant on the dresser. As he looks around he notices the pile of unopened mail, except for the one envelope on the top of the pile. Gerry looks to see whom it is addressed to. Gerry picks it up and then puts it back down. Well, he thinks, it is open, what if it just happens to fall off the dresser while I'm watering this plant here and the contents of the envelope falls out and I'm able to read some of it as I put it back into the envelope. That wouldn't be like snooping would it? Gerry feels that it is very easy to convince himself that sometimes there is a need to be nosy and this may be one of those times. He picks up the envelope and pulls out the one sheet of paper, unfolds it and starts to read it:

Dear Mr. Rick Campbell

The results of your tests are in. Please call the number below and set up an appointment to discuss your results.

Short and sweet, Gerry thinks. He checks the top of the letter. It is dated the beginning of May. Andy hasn't said anything is wrong, and he also knows that Andy handles all the mail, so it is probably nothing. He refolds the letter and replaces it inside the envelope and slides it into the pile of unopened ones. Weird he thinks to himself. He's thought that the two of them had finished their HIV tests over two years ago. It's probably for something else. Rick's probably too cheap to go to a regular clinic where you pay for the services. He picks up the watering can, returns to the kitchen and empties the remaining water in the can into the kitchen sink. Maybe Andy is right. This is the most opportune time for Rick to be bringing his tricks home. For one split second

Gerry thinks that he might be wrong about Rick, but quickly changes his mind. No, he's sure that Rick is screwing around on Andy and that one day he would get caught. He walks out of the apartment and locks the door, casually walking to the elevator. The elevator is already on its way up. Gerry has concluded that this is New York's' slowest elevator and it would take a good ten minutes before it gets to this floor. Surprisingly the elevator stops right in front of him. As the doors open Gerry notices a handsome young man with beautiful blue eyes. Along with him are two women. The three of them all look to be about the same age and all are carrying grocery bags. They all get out on that floor. As the young man passes Gerry their eyes lock and they hold a stare. Gerry bits his lip. What a hunk he thinks, I wish I were one of these women.

He turns and pushes the button for the lobby. As the doors close he watches the perfect globes of the young man's butt move in his tight jeans as he walks down the corridor with the two women. Finally the door closes and the elevator starts its journey to the lobby. Well, the trip hasn't been a complete loss. The plants got watered and the eye candy was worth the trip, even if he didn't find anything.

Trevor turns and looks back at the elevator as the doors close. He recognizes that man from somewhere. He knows he's seen him around somewhere, but he can't place where. Trevor stops at Rick and Andy's apartment and pulls out a key from his Levi pocket and unlocks the door. The two women continue on down the hall, tuning once to say goodbye to Trevor. He enters the apartment and locks the door behind him. It's his night to cook. He's getting tired of take out. Tonight he's planning a good old-fashioned steak and potatoes dinner. But first he'd clean up the kitchen and then retrieve his laundry from the laundry room in the basement. It has been nice spending the last two nights together like a real couple. If Rick is right, the therapist Andy is now seeing has done wonders and it won't be too long before Rick will be able to leave his friend and move in with him. Rick says the therapist is trying to convince Andy to sell this apartment and move somewhere else in the city where there won't be as many memories. Trevor agrees it's probably a big part of the problem. Apparently just about everything in this apartment was Andy's lovers' before he died and Andy just inherited everything. Andy was a lucky guy. His lover had great taste. Trevor quickly puts the groceries away and starts to clean up the kitchen. Trevor likes the feeling he has with this pseudo living together he's had with Rick these last couple of days. He feels good about Rick and thinks that the two of them make the perfect couple.

Tony walks into the office of Cape Development and Maintenance and hangs his ball cap on the hook behind the door. Marcy, the secretary, is seated at her desk pouring over the vast mountain of paperwork that takes place at this time every year. Maintenance orders for work that needs to be finished up before the vacation season starts. There is a big push on to get all the odd jobs done.

"Marcy?" Tony asks. "Have we had any word on that glass I ordered for the Ayers' place?"

Marcy looks up from her desk and smiles, "Actually Tony I received a letter here from the window place just this morning. Let me find it." She starts to rifle through a pile of opened envelopes on the desk. "Ah yes, they say they have to special order it from Boston and it'll take about a week to get it here."

"That's the soonest, eh?" he questions her.

"Looks like it," Marcy replies. "Oh and talking about the Ayers' place, we also received a letter from a lawyer in Wilmington today. Looks as though the old lady has died and there are changes in the title in the works. I've got it around here somewhere. Here it is," she says as she picks up the envelope and pulls out the sheet of paper from inside. She hands it to Tony to read.

It is written on special bond with Melvin Peabody, Barrister and Solicitor in bold letters across the top of the page. It starts with 'to who it may concern', please be advised that Mrs. Alice Ayers of....Tony skims the letter hoping it would say what will be happening to the property. He's hoped that they wouldn't lose it, but the letter doesn't give much more information than notifying Cape Development and Maintenance of Mrs. Ayers' death and through her will the title and deed to the property will be passed on to a family member that at the time of the letter writing he was unable to divulge due to the fact that the family hasn't had the chance to have a formal reading of Mrs. Ayer's will. And that Cape Development and Maintenance will be informed of the changes in the form of a written document from Peabody's office.

Tony looks at Marcy, "Gee I hope we don't lose this one, it's the easiest property to look after, never a money problem or anything."

"I've known that this was going to happen eventually. She was pretty old, and no one ever came to the house anymore," Tony says. "Well, I guess there's no real hurry then for the glass." He stops and looks around the office. He is trying not to seem upset about the situation. "So what's next on the agenda?" he asks Marcy.

"The Thompson's and the Callaway's just need to have the pruning done on a couple of trees and they're all set for the summer and then a couple of bigger jobs at the Steinman's. You're going to need some help there. How's Garth? When is he coming back to work?" she questions him. "I hate doing all this casual labour, it's a lot more work than having a regular payroll." she complains.

"He's much better, he just got his cast off and he's walking around with a cane," Tony says. "He's also going to some physiotherapy clinic in South Yarmouth. His doctor figures he'll be back in a few weeks." He pauses, "So I guess I'll have to go and find some help again for the Steinman's job. First, I'll handle the pruning jobs. I'll worry about the Steinman's tomorrow." He takes his ball cap from the hook behind the door and slips it on his head as he leaves the office.

Marcy watches Tony as he walks out to the white Ford truck parked in front of the Cape Development and Maintenance office. She figures that the letter from the lawyer in Wilmington about the Ayers' place bothers Tony more than he lets on. She shakes her head. Must be a guy thing she thinks to herself.

Tony gets into his truck and pulls out of the parking lot in front of the office and heads off down Rocky Beach Road towards the Thompson place. He figures he'd leave the Callaway's till last today. He knew that this was going to eventually happen, that old Mrs. Ayers' would die and now as he thinks about it, it'll only be a matter of time before the place goes up for sale. He doesn't like it but there isn't much that he can do about it. He wishes he hadn't gotten so attached to the place.

Elaine opens the door to her motel room and walks inside. She goes to the nightstand and checks the telephone to see if the message light is blinking. It is. She picks up the phone and dials "O" for the motel office. It rings a couple of times before it is answered.

"Front desk how can I help you?" is the answer from the girl at the front desk.

"Hi, this is Elaine Carter in room two twelve, my message light is blinking."

"Yes, Ms. Carter, Dr. Miller's office has called and would like you to give them a call anytime. Do you have their phone number?" the girl's voice asks.

"Yes, I have it thank you," Elaine says as she hangs up the phone. It is almost noon Thursday and they are finally getting back to me with the results of my test. She feels a little annoyed about that. She and Mike have started interviewing for positions in the new office and she thinks it's best to skip out to her motel room to make this call rather than make it from the office with Mike there. She picks up the phone again and dials the number for Dr. Miller's office. She waits while the phone rings. She hopes she hasn't caught them during lunch.

"Hello, Dr. Miller's office, please hold," is what Elaine hears when the phone is picked up. She patiently waits for a couple of minutes before the voice from the other side of the phone comes back on. "Sorry to keep you waiting. How may I help you?"

"Hi, this is Elaine Carter, I have a message to call your office back."

"Oh hi Ms. Carter, yes the doctor would like to talk to you for a moment, can you hold a moment and I'll put you through to her office." Again Elaine waits.

"Hi, Elaine? Doctor Miller here."

"Hi doctor, well?" Elaine asks.

"Well, you were right, you are pregnant. So I guess congratulations are in order?" the doctor says.

Elaine hesitates on her end of the phone. She's known before that she was pregnant and this just makes it formal. "Ah yes," she stammers "Thank you," she finishes.

"So when you get back to Rocky Beach you make sure that you get in to see your regular physician and I'll courier your file up, okay? Again, congratulations," Doctor Miller adds.

"Yes, thanks Doctor Miller. I'll do that next week," Elaine says as she hangs up the phone. Now she has to tell Tony and somehow keep this a secret from Mike for the time being. She sits on the side of her bed. A tear rolls down her cheek as she thinks to herself, what have I done. She wipes it away with the sleeve of her blouse. I can't change things now, so I'd better get on with it. There's only one person on this planet who knows the truth and that's Sara. Elaine feels she can trust Sara with her secret, but she figures she'd better fill Sara in about the decisions she's made. She picks up the phone and dials the number for Sara's work.

Sara answers. "Afternoon, Rocky Beach Clinic."

"Hi Sara, it's Elaine."

"Hi. Have you got the results back?"

"Yes, I just got off the phone with Doctor Miller."

There is a long pause. "Well?" asks Sara

"I'm pregnant." Another long pause.

"I don't know what to say Lainey."

"How about meeting in me in an hour at that truck stop at the junction of one thirty four and I-six?" Elaine asks.

Sara hesitates for a moment. "Could do, it's very quiet

here today. I should be able to leave early."

Elaine hates to put Sara on the spot like this, but she needs to talk to her to let her know everything. Everything, meaning that she's told Doctor Miller that Tony is the father of her child. Tony's name will be the official name as the father of the baby not Mike Flannery's. She needs to tell the only other person who knows the truth, what she's done, and how she will be going to play this out; and that needed to be done before anyone finds out she's pregnant.

"Thanks, I'll see you in an hour," Elaine says. Now I'll just skip out on Mike this afternoon. That shouldn't be too hard she figures. He'd do anything for her. She gets up from the bed and walks into the bathroom and checks her makeup in the mirror. She puts on fresh lipstick and heads back to the office.

It is almost one o'clock when Elaine drives into the large gravel parking lot of the truck stop. She sees Sara's car parked at the far end. She hopes she hasn't been here too long. She parks her car and enters the crowded diner. There is a lot of noise. She looks across the diner, but she can't see Sara. She starts to walk down the small aisle towards the far wall checking the booths as she walks. Elaine finally comes up to the booth where Sara is sitting with a couple of menus laying on the table and a cup of coffee, which looks like it has just been poured. The booths are pretty private with long high backed seats. No one can see into the booth and with the noise in the diner at this busy time of day one shouldn't be over heard.

"Hi," Elaine says. "I'm so glad you could make it Sara," as she seats herself across the table from Sara.

"Hi Lainey, I don't know what to say."

"How about congratulations," Elaine says.

Sara looks at her with a puzzled look.

"I've had some time to think and I've made my decision about what I've got to do."

Sara's puzzled look disappears from her face, "I'm glad you've thought about things. So I take it you're going to keep the baby?"

"Yes, I am," Elaine says. She stares hard at Sara. She

hopes she can trust her friend. "I sure could use a cup of coffee."

The two women wave down a waitress and order a cup of coffee for Elaine, and both place an order from the menu for something to eat.

"Well," Sara says, "I'm waiting to hear."

"First," Elaine starts, "I thought about the baby. I knew I couldn't give it up. I don't think that I could bear the thought of someone else raising my child. And of course you know abortion is completely out of the question. So, there is really no other option but to keep the baby."

"The next thing I've had to decide was what to do about Tony and Mike." Elaine stops and again stares at Sara intensely. "I really wasn't sure how or what I was going to do about that until I was at the clinic."

The waitress comes over and places two burgers and fries in front of the two women and says that she'd be right back to top up their coffees.

"So what happened at the clinic?" Sara insists.

"Well, you know that they have to ask you all sorts of questions about, well you know, you work at a clinic, about pregnancies. When your last period was, if you took an early pregnancy test, if you're feeling sick in the mornings," Elaine continues. She knows she is just beating around the bush trying to set herself up, "And things like if you're married and..."

Sara interrupts her "And who the father is?"

"Yes, that too," Elaine says.

"Well, what did you say to that one?" Sara asks.

"Well, I thought about it for quite some time, and I had some things that I had to weigh before I could answer that question," Elaine rambles.

"That's not a hard question to answer, Lainey," Sara says.

"Well, actually it's quite difficult. You see I had to look at what was not only best for the baby but what was best for me."

"Lainey, please tell me you told the doctor the truth," Sara says.

There is silence. Elaine and Sara's eyes are locked.

Elaine is not so sure that this has been a wise idea. She hadn't figured that Sara was such a prim and proper person. She's thought that their friendship would be able to surpass this situation.

"Lainey, I can't believe you didn't." Sara pauses, "Lainey, the reason you've asked me to meet you here was so that you could tell me that you told the doctor that Tony is the father of the baby you are carrying, which as we both know is not the truth." Again Sara pauses. "And to ask me not to say anything to anyone, to keep your secret. To lie to my friend Tony, to play this charade with you. Lainey how can you ask me to lie?"

"Sara, I've had to think about what is best for both the baby and myself. The baby will never know who it's real father is other than the man it grows up knowing as it's father. For myself, as selfish as this may seem I know I love Tony. I'm not really sure what I have with Mike," Elaine says.

"A baby is what you have with Mike, Lainey," Sara says. She looks Elaine square in the face. Both women know that Sara is right. "And as far as Tony is concerned you love him enough to have had sex with another man while being engaged to him."

"That's not fair, Sara." Elaine retorts. The diner is still noisy. Elaine is sure that no one is paying attention to them.

"Not fair to who Lainey?" Sara points out.

"Look Sara, I've made a mistake, and I want to do what is best for everyone. Don't you think that if Tony ever found out I had a one-night stand with another man that would hurt him? I didn't mean to, but it happened and now I'm paying for it. I love Tony and I don't want to hurt him. Do you?" Elaine asks. She knows she isn't being fair to Sara, but this is obviously the only way she can have Sara keep her secret. "What do you think I should do? Do you want me to ruin Tony's, Mike's and this baby's life? And what about me? Shouldn't I have some consideration in this situation?"

"I'm sorry Lainey, but you should have thought about that before you slept with Mike," Sara snaps.

Both women stare at each other.

"That was uncalled for Sara."

"Lainey, I'm sorry but it's the way it is, and truly I am

sorry that you're in this mess," Sara says. "I wish for your sake that you weren't pregnant, but the reality of the situation is you are."

"Thanks a lot Sara for reminding me."

"Look, you're missing my point." Sara stops and thinks for a moment. The truth for Elaine at this moment doesn't mean a thing so preaching about honesty isn't going to help things get any better. "Let's just say I know you're going to do what you're going to do and there isn't much that I can do or say about it. You've already got the ball rolling. So as your friend I promise you I won't say anything, and also as a friend be warned that I won't ever be put in this type of situation again."

"What do you mean this type of situation again?" Elaine asks.

"Just that, I won't lie for you again. Don't ever ask me for anything a friend would ask for ever," Sara says. She is still staring at Elaine sitting across the table from her. She can feel her face flush. She hates what has just transpired between the two of them. She is angry not only with Elaine but with herself for actually agreeing to lie for her, Tony is her friend also. Sara places a ten-dollar bill on the table for her untouched meal and gets out of the booth and turns to walk down the aisle to the door of the diner, leaving Elaine sitting alone at the table. Without looking back she gets into her car and starts her drive back to Rocky Beach.

Elaine puts another ten-dollar bill on the table and leaves the diner She gets into her car and pulls back onto Interstate Six. She doesn't like the way things are left between her and Sara, but she thinks that Sara would eventually come around and see that her decision is for the best. As for getting her to promise not to say anything about the real father of her baby, Elaine got what she wanted. Now the only thing she has to do is to devise a way to tell Tony.

Back in the diner Joey can't believe the conversation he's just overheard from two women in the booth behind him. Man he thinks, these small towns are just like the big cities, just a regular soap opera.

"I've rented a car, Mom. Em, Trish and I will follow you there," I say to my mother.

"I'm sure that there will be enough room for all of us in the limo Andy."

"No, this will be better. If the three of us want to leave then we can," I reply. "Not meaning that we don't enjoy your company but you know old Peabody. It might be just a bit boring for the three of us young people." Em and Trish start to giggle. "There's really not much reason other than listening to the reading of the will for us to be there."

"I get your point," my mother replies. "Well, then I guess we should get going. The limo is waiting outside the lobby entrance."

"So we'll be right behind you," I say.

My mother and her two sisters get into the limo and it pulls out from the curb and turns right onto Market Street and heads out of the city. Em, Trish and I in our rented Cavalier pull out onto Market Street behind them and follow them through the city. Wilmington is a beautiful small city and it's no wonder Grams' liked it here. The climate is very nice due to its proximity to the ocean. I guess it's a good place to be a retiree. After traveling for about fifteen minutes the limo takes a left onto Gordon Road, and we follow. The road is lined with large plantation style houses with large yards. We follow the limo for about another mile or so and it pulls into a driveway and stops. The big iron gates slowly open, the limo continues on through and we follow behind it, hoping the driver of the limo has explained that we are with them.

"My Melvin Peabody has done well over the years now hasn't he," Trish says.

"By the looks of this place he's done very well," Em confirms.

We pull up behind the limo parked on the circular driveway in front of a large whitewashed two story plantation house. It looks to be in impeccable shape.

"Wow!" I exclaim. "He's done extremely well."

We all get out and gather with our mothers on the front veranda. The whitewashed pillars shine like new. It looks like the house has just been freshly whitewashed, and the front gardens look like they were professionally tended.

The double front doors open and Melvin steps out onto the front veranda.

"Welcome everyone," he smiles. He's wearing a light linen suit with a light yellow cotton shirt topped with a straw fedora. "I see we all made it in one piece."

He ushers us into the grand foyer of his home. I can hear the slight hum of the fans pushing the air around in the house. Melvin leads the way to the back veranda of the house. The dark coloured tiles of the floor emit coolness as we walk through the centre of the well-decorated southern style home.

"Mr. Peabody," I start to ask.

"Oh please Andrew, call me Melvin," he interrupts.

"Okay, Melvin, I just wanted to comment on the wonderful collection of antiques you have," I finish.

"Why thank you, it's mostly my wife, Martha's doin'. She's the one with the eye for the antique. I'm just the guy with the wallet," he laughs.

My mother adds as we enter the back veranda through large opened French doors, "Well she's very good at keeping with period collectibles. Your wife must be very knowledgeable."

"Well, when I was younger I worked in New York City at an antique store. That's where I learned all about antiques. No formal training in college, just practice on the selling floor," Martha says as we walk onto the back veranda. "Please every one sit if you'd like."

There are a few patio tables on the veranda with numerous rattan chairs strategically placed. There are flower baskets and containers, all uniform in shape and size, all equally spaced or hung on the veranda filled with a barrage of colour and scents. It is a beautiful and relaxing space.

"So, before we get started on the formal paper work, why don't we have lemonade," Melvin suggests. "Martha makes the best lemonade in the South. She makes it from our own lemons." He looks at her lovingly. You can tell by looking at these two people that they indeed are in love with each other. "You know if it hadn't been for your mother I'd never have met Martha? Yes, if she hadn't turned me down I would have never married this wonderful woman." Martha gives him a little kiss on the cheek as she hands him his glass of lemonade.

"And your mother," Martha steps in, "thanked me every time we visited her for taking this pesky lawyer out of her hair." Everyone on the veranda starts to laugh. As the conversation goes on I realize that Melvin, Martha and Grams had been very close. The three of them had forged strong friendships that had started in Melvin's thwarted attempt at courting Grams after Grandpa's death. After listening to the two of them reminisce about Grams, it occurs to me that these two people have truly lost a very dear friend in Grams. It also makes me feel very good that Grams had two such wonderful and close friends. As the lemonade slowly vanishes from everyone's glass Melvin clears his throat and announces, "Well we must get on with the business of the day so if I could have y'all follow me into the parlour we'll get on with the reading," he says in his most southerly accent.

Martha moves ahead and opens the large oak door to the parlour and then as the last of our party enters the room closes the door quietly, leaving my Mother, Aunt Ellen, Aunt Audrey, Em, Trish, myself and Melvin in the large room. Melvin walks over to an antique partners' desk over by the floor to ceiling bookcase and picks up an envelope. He turns and says, "If everyone would please take a seat, we'll get this started." He waits for a moment and scans the six of us in the room. He opens the sealed envelope and starts to read:

"I, Alice Catherine Ayers, of sound mind and body, do swear that this is my last will and testament, done so in my own hand, witnessed by my council Melvin J. Peabody on this day the second of January in the year nineteen hundred and ninety nine. That on my death I bequeath all my worldly goods to be divided between my three daughters, Ellen Francis, Audrey Patricia, Catherine Anne, and their children Emily Marie, Andrew Matthew and Patricia Alice as follows.

To my daughters Ellen Francis, Audrey Patricia and Catherine Anne I bequeath the monies in all my accounts and investments with an estimated value as of this day the second of January in the year nineteen hundred and ninety nine of six hundred and twenty two thousand five hundred and thirty seven dollars and fourteen cents, less fifteen thousand dollars to be divided equally between my three daughters. The fifteen thousand dollars to be paid as fee for services rendered to Melvin J. Peabody for the reading and execution of this my last will and testament. To my granddaughters, Emily Marie and Patricia Alice I bequeath the property and house in Palm Springs, California; market valued as of this day the second day of January in the year nineteen hundred and ninety nine at four hundred and forty thousand dollars. And to my grandson Andrew Matthew I bequeath the property and house in Rocky Beach, Massachusetts; market valued as of this day the second day of January in the year nineteen hundred and ninety nine at one hundred and ninety five thousand dollars.

Melvin continues with the rest of the legal jargon of the will, but I don't really hear anything else he says. I don't think I believe what I've just heard. I wasn't expecting anything of the sort. And anyway, I thought that Grams had sold all of her real-estate years ago.

I lean over and I whisper to my mother seated next to me, "There must be some mistake, I thought Grams..."

"Ssshhhh," she says to me quietly. "I'll explain later after Melvin is finished."

Melvin continues reading out the rest of the details of Grams' will. I think we all knew that Grams had money but I guess we didn't know, or at least I didn't, how much Grams actually had, except for maybe mom.

"I trust this is what you all were expecting, " Melvin says as he scans the room. The six of us sit there quietly. I'm sure that none of us really knows what to say at this moment.

"Actually," I say, "I honestly didn't expect this." Trish and Em both nod in agreement. "I thought Grams had sold all of the properties she and Grandpa owned years ago."

"Well Grams told me about three years ago that she

hadn't sold these two in particular as they were their favourites and she thought it would be nice if she could keep these two in the family," my mother says. "I suggested to her at that time that she leave them to the three of you."

"Hmmmph," Aunt Audrey says just loud enough for everyone in the room to hear.

"She also said that certain people in this room, who will remain nameless," as she gives her older two sisters' a hard glance, "would probably just sell them off for the sake of the almighty dollar, and she didn't want that." My mother continues, "That's when I made my suggestion and she loved the idea. She said that the three of you would get years of use from these two places."

Melvin steps to the centre of the room and says, " I've checked with the state laws and I can foresee no problems in the change of titles. As a matter of fact, I've taken the liberty of informing the management companies that are currently looking after the properties of the changes on your behalf. And if you'd like I'd like to do the final transfer of titles for you three kids, which would be covered in the fee paid by your Grandmother's will?"

We all agree.

So far Aunt Ellen hasn't said a thing. My mother looks at her eldest sister as she sits in a large armchair. She stands up and walks over to the table and picks up the will left on the desk. She looks it over quickly. She turns to my mother and then to Aunt Audrey.

Trish, Em and I exchange looks. I can just imagine what is going to happen, she'd announce that she would contest the will as she figures that the three of them should have gotten it all.

"Is there a problem, Ellen?" Melvin asks.

"Actually," Ellen starts to say, "I think that everything is order." She looks at my mother and smiles. "I think that Grams did the right thing in listening to your suggestion about the properties Catherine. Don't you think so Audrey?" Her tone has changed to the eldest sister tone. "Well Audrey, I have to agree with Grams and Catherine, the kids will benefit more from these properties than we would." Still Audrey just sits there getting redder in the face.

"Ellen do you remember what we agreed to the other night in the hotel?" Audrey asks. "That if the will didn't say an even three way split that we would contest it."

Before my mother can say anything, Aunt Ellen continues, "That was before we knew about the properties. They weren't in the equation before." At that my mother relaxes and lets her oldest sister continue. "And anyway it is an even three way split, so the properties are irrelevant." She pauses for a moment and looks like she is reaching deep for the right words. "I don't want to seem harsh but we just lost someone we all loved very much and these are her last wishes, so if you feel that you've been short changed by our mother then do what you have to do otherwise just hold your peace." This last bit is meant specifically for Audrey, who sits, red faced, on the overstuffed lounge.

Audrey looks around the room and then at her two sisters and says, "You know, I didn't mean anything by that," she stammers, "and if you all think that it's fair then of course I do also." She covers herself quickly.

Aunt Ellen walks over to her younger sister and puts out her arms. Audrey rises from her seat and gives Ellen a hug. Ellen then looks at my mother and waves her over and the three sisters embrace.

Ellen says, "I sure hope that we do more of this in the future," as she looks at her two younger sisters. "Mom would want this for us."

I watch the three women hold on to each other. I can hear Em ask Trish for a tissue. I too can feel the warmth of tears well up in my eyes as the three sisters hug.

Finally, after a long moment of silence the three women release their hold on each other.

Melvin, who's still standing in the centre of the room, suggests in his strong southern drawl "Why don't we have another glass of lemonade on the veranda?" He walks over to the large doors and opens them to let us out of the parlour. "I'll have all the papers finalized in about a week, then I'll have them couriered to you shortly thereafter, and after that I'll get back to retirement," he says with a chuckle, as we all move through the large doors out onto the back veranda.

"See you later." Elaine says as Sara leaves their house. Sara doesn't reply. Elaine knows that Sara is still angry with her about what she's told the doctor. Elaine thinks that deep down Sara understands that this is the only thing she can do. If she were in her shoes she'd probably have done the same thing. She tells herself that she can't worry about it because today's the day she's going to tell Tony. She hopes for everyone's sake it goes as she's planned it. He's due any minute.

A few minutes later there is a knock at the door and Tony walks into the front hall. He is wearing Levis and a white t-shirt, his arms, neck and face are already turning brown from the sun. Elaine walks up to him and gives him a long kiss.

"So what's going on with this?" She pulls at the sleeve of his t-shirt "A farmer's tan?"

"No," he says, "you just say that so you can get my shirt off."

"Is that a bad thing?" she asks as she un-tucks his t-shirt.

"So what's all this excitement?" he asks her. "What couldn't you tell me over the phone. I thought we didn't have secrets?"

"Oh come on in and sit on the couch and I'll tell you. And it's really not a secret," she says. This is all part of the scheme, the excitement. If she is excited about having this baby it would rub off on Tony. Elaine figures she knows him that well.

"Well?" he asks.

"Right, do you want a beer?" she asks. "I've got cold Buds in the fridge. I'll get you one." She bounce up and heads for the kitchen to get him a beer.

Tony hears her in the kitchen, opening the refrigerator door and clanking the glass bottles in the fridge as she retrieves a beer for him.

"So what's this all about Lainey?" he shouts to her.

"It's just I have a surprise for you," she yells back to him from the kitchen.

"A surprise?" he questions. "You're gonna tell me that you don't have to go back to Sandwich anymore right? And that you'll be bringing me lunch everyday at work from now on? Right?"

"No nothing like that," she says as she returns to the living room couch and sits down beside him. She hands him his beer and he takes a sip.

"Okay so what is this surprise?" he demands.

"So what do you think about children?" she asks.

"I love kids, why?" he replies.

"How about one of your own?" she asks.

"One day, we'll have one," he says hesitantly to her as he puts his beer down on the table beside the couch. He's not sure whether he actually believes what he's just said.

"Well Tony my dear, it's one of those days now," she says to him. He sits beside her with that deer in the head light look. "Don't you get it Tony? We're going to have a baby." She smiles at him. "Isn't it exciting. That's the news I didn't want to tell you over the phone."

"How? When?" he stammers.

"I'm sure you know how. When exactly, I can't quite pinpoint. You know how spotty my periods are, so I guess one of those times we've had an accident," she says excitedly.

"Are you sure?" he asks.

Elaine feels that she hasn't quite pulled this off yet. "Of course I'm sure. I've gone to the doctor already and it's been confirmed. I know we weren't planning or even trying to have a baby."

The colour drains from Tony's face. "Holy shit!" he says.

"Aren't you excited? Tony, we're going to have a baby!" she looks at him, searching for a clue in his eyes to show that she's pulled this off. "This doesn't mean that anything has to change. It just means that we've had an accident and we're going to have a baby. Isn't it wonderful!"

"It's just that we've never really talked about children and now we're having one," he states. "You are sure?"

"Of course I'm sure. I wasn't going to say anything

until I had the tests done and the results were in," she says. "Oh Tony I'm so excited! We're having a baby."

Tony sits on the couch and doesn't move a muscle as Elaine cuddles up beside him. He doesn't know what to think. All of a sudden he feels as if his whole life has been turned upside down. He's not quite sure why he feels this way but he does.

She looks up at him and says, "You are excited about this baby aren't you?"

Before he can say anything she says, "Tony! You want to have this baby with me don't you?" she sits up and faces him.

"Elaine it's just that we've never discussed children."

"Well then I'll just have it by myself," she states. "I don't need you," she says angrily as she slaps him on the shoulder. "I thought you would be as excited as I am about this child of ours." She continues to use us and we to help convince him that this is their baby she is carrying. "Just the look on your face tells me that you aren't!"

"It's not that. It's just I wasn't..., we weren't even planning on children yet," Tony says. "We haven't even decided when to get married."

"We don't have to get married to have children, mind you it would be nice," she says.

"Wow, this is really not what I expected today." Tony gets up from the couch and starts to pace the living room floor. "Does anyone else know?"

"Just Sara, you know us girls, I needed to talk to someone when I first realized that something was wrong with my period and with Sara being a nurse and all, one thing led to another, you know," Elaine says. "I wanted to be one hundred percent sure before I told you. I didn't want to get you all excited about having a child of your own and then find out it was something else."

"Oh, I understand that Elaine," Tony says as he paces back and forth, "I just don't understand the how and when. We've always been so very careful." He pauses, "And I just can't remember when, we've ever had an accident."

"All I can tell you Tony dear is that we must've because I'm pregnant," Elaine says as matter of factly as she can. “If it makes any difference Tony this is not the way I wanted things to go for us, but this is the way they are.”

There is a long silence. Tony walks to the living room window and pulls the curtains open watching the slow local traffic drive by. Elaine is still sitting on the couch. She figures that this is a good sign, knowing Tony. She'll just let him think. He'll put things in order and then we can start making plans. She decides to let him take the first step. He's an honourable man, and he'll do the right thing.

Elaine gets up from the spot on the couch and walks up behind him and puts her arms around him. “I know this is a bit of a shock, but we've got to deal with it eventually. I know that you probably need some time to think about what we should do.” Elaine knows that by telling him this he'd end up going and talking to his mother, and staunch Catholic that she is, would tell Tony that they have to get married. “So why don't you take some time to think, she says to him as she holds him. She still has her arms around his waist; her hands hold his flat stomach tightly.

Tony turns around in her arms and looks at her face, “Yeah, I guess I need a little time to think about this. It's quite a shock.” The colour has returned to his face, “I just wasn't expecting...” Elaine puts her fingers across his mouth to stop him from saying it all again.

“I know, we've said all that before, but we've got to move forward with this,” Elaine says. She releases her hold on him, walks back to the couch and sits cross-legged on it. Tony tucks in his white t-shirt again and sits beside her. “Tony, I'm gonna have this baby with or without you, I want you to know that,” she says bluntly. “I don't believe in other options like abortion or adoption. I couldn't go through with either one,” Elaine states. “Do you understand that?” she asks.

“Look Elaine, I've got to think,” Tony says. “And of course I understand about abortion or adoption not being options.”

“Good,” she says. “I know I've unloaded a lot on you tonight. Just remember I'm not the only one responsible for how I got this way and I understand that you need some time to think. God knows when I found out, I did.”

"Of course I know you're not the only one responsible," he says.

Tony gets up from the couch and walks towards the front door.

"Don't take too long, Tony," Elaine says. "Tony," she pauses, "I love you."

He turns and looks at her, "I love you too Elaine." There is just too much happening. He knows that saying these words his heart isn't in them. He hopes that she can't sense it. She walks up to him and gives him a gentle kiss on the mouth.

"I know you do," she says.

He opens the front door of the house and walks down the steps to the driveway.

She closes the door behind him and leans with her back against the door. She smiles to herself. The hard part is over. The rest would be easy. Elaine knows that Tony is a very trusting person and would never question her fidelity. That's just the way he is. But she also knows that he is a stickler for details and would want all the information she could possibly provide about when she actually conceived. She's sure that she can skirt her way around that. She would just use the fact that her periods are so inconsistent that she doesn't know the exact time, and doctors in all their wisdom and training also have a hard time pinpointing these things. She's sure that she'll get all the back up support from his mother and sister, Maria, in these matters. She can feel herself smile; her hands reach down and rubs her abdomen. "Even though he's not your real daddy, he'll love you just as if you were his own, not that he'll ever know that he's not your father." She says softly. Elaine walks into the kitchen and looks at the calendar hanging on the wall by the refrigerator. Independence Day is in five weeks. She figures that she would be Mrs. Tony diMarco by then. She knows what she needs to do with Tony. Everything else would fall into place.

The quickest and easiest way to get home is to catch the red eye into La Guardia Airport. He would be home by seven, seven thirty, once he gets through the baggage claim and gets a taxi. He could have called Rick or Gerry to meet him at the airport but they would have had to leave at three in the morning. It is quite busy for five a.m. Saturday, people coming and going. Everyone has someplace to go. He picks up his suitcase and walks down the long air-conditioned hall of the arrivals terminal. He stops at a coffee vendor and gets a large cup of coffee to go; then he continues to make his way out of the arrivals building. As he walks outside the warm June air hits him. We just like to complain about the weather like a bunch of Jewish mothers. Outside the terminal there is a row of yellow cabs. It wouldn't be hard getting one. More people are filing out of the building. The cabbies are busy trying to attract customers into their yellow cars. He looks over the selection of cabs and realizes that the old cabby who drove him here last weekend is standing at the front fender of his cab reading the morning paper. Andy makes his way over to him.

"I need a ride to Manhattan please."

He looks up and smiles. He doesn't say anything, just walks past me, opens the trunk of his car and I put my suitcases in. He looks at me again, this time with a curious look on his face.

"Hey didn't I give you a ride before?" he questions me.

"Yeah, last weekend you brought me here," I reply.

"I knew I saw you before. I never forget a face," he says. "Where to?"

I give him my address. He comments that he remembers exactly. I know that he really can't recall, but I go along with him.

"So where'd you get in from, kid?" he asks.

This time I don't mind the talk. Actually it's kind of nice talking to someone who doesn't require anything from you except maybe some talk. "Wilmington. I had a family funeral to go to."

"Oh yeah I remember, last weekend sometime I picked you up." He stops and thinks for a moment. "Saturday, if I remember correctly."

"Right." I could be wrong. Maybe this old guy really does remember. It actually makes me feel good.

"Well, get in kid," he says. "Let's get ya home."

"Hey do you mind if I sit in the front with you?" I ask the old cabby.

"It's against company policy," he states, as he looks me over. "But you look like a good kid. Sure, why not. It wouldn't be the first time I've been in trouble with dispatch."

I get into the front seat of the cab. I notice that attached to the lower inside door panel is a small handgun I guess this job is as rough as they say it is in the papers."Thanks," I say as he starts the cab and pulls away from the curb.

As we pull up in front of my building, I get out and so does the cabby. He opens the trunk of the cab and gets my bags out and sets them on the curb. I hand him a couple of twenties even before he tells me the fare. Then I slip him another fiver.

"Hey thanks kid," he replies as he walks back around to the drivers side of the car. "If you ever need another cabby, ask for Bert when you call in."

"Thanks Bert, I'll do that," I say as I watch him get into the drivers seat of the car and pull away from the curb leaving me standing at the front entrance to my building. Seven forty-five and I'm home. Rick should be still asleep. I'll just go up and make coffee. I'll surprise him.

Trevor rolls over and lays next to Rick, both of them staring at the ceiling. Rick looks over at him and smiles.

"Gotta like that," Rick says. "No more condoms."

"Mmmm, yeah," Trevor says in agreement.

"I'm gonna have a quick shower to clean up this mess," Rick says as he smears the cum he spewed on his chest and abdomen. "So why don't you go to the kitchen and make us coffee, and I'll meet you back here in a few minutes," he suggests.

Trevor gets out of bed and slips his boxer shorts on.

Rick walks towards the bathroom. He stops, turns to Trevor and says, "Hey Trev, I ah, I love you, you know that don't you?"

Trevor looks at Rick standing there looking back at him. "You know that's the first time since we've been seeing each other that you've said that to me," Trevor says. "I love you too Rick, now go and get cleaned up. I'll make us some coffee." He walks out of the bedroom and down the hallway to the kitchen. Just as he enters the kitchen he hears the lock on the door being turned. He thinks it is probably Andrew, Rick's roommate. Rick did mention that he was away and would be returning sometime this weekend. Rick figured he'd be here on Sunday, so he's a day early. Oh well, he lives here, and there's no reason why he shouldn't be in his own home even with Trevor there. Trevor continues to make coffee as the front door of the apartment opens. Trevor thinks that it is probably time that he meets some of Rick's friends seeing as though they are a couple, and what a better one than to start with his roommate.

As I walk into the entryway, I can hear water running in the kitchen. I close the door behind me and drop the suitcases on the floor by the door. I would get them later. I move down the hall towards the kitchen.

"Hi, I'm...." I stop saying as I walk into the kitchen and almost walk into this stranger in my kitchen, dressed in just a pair of skintight boxer shorts.

"Hi," says the barely dressed young man. "You must be Andrew. I've heard so much about you. And now we finally meet."

"Who? What?" I'm startled. I really don't know what to say. "Do I know you?" I know I've seen this young man before but I just can't place him at the moment. I think the shock of him being in my kitchen with barely anything on has made me lost for words. He has such gorgeous eyes, I should remember those eyes, but I can't at this moment remember where I've seen him before, but I know I have. "How'd you...?" I continue as I look towards the front door.

"Oh I'm sorry, I'm Trevor," he puts his hand out to shake mine. "I'm a friend of Rick's."

"Rick?" I question.

"Oh yeah, he's just in the shower. He'll be out in a few minutes," Trevor continues to make coffee. "He is a bit of a mess this morning," he smiles.

"A bit of a mess?" I'm confused. "What kind of mess?"

Trevor looks at me for a moment. "You know, mess." He continues to stare at me. "Oh I get it. He hasn't told you, probably because of the therapy you're going through, probably thought it best not to say anything."

"Told me? Therapy, I'm going through?" I'm beginning to sound angry.

"Oh, I'm sorry. I guess I shouldn't have said anything about that. He did say you were sensitive about admitting you needed, you know professional help."

All of a sudden everything clicks and it has become crystal clear to me that what all of my friends have been warning me about Rick has been true all along. I think to myself that I've got a couple of options here. I can go off the deep end right here and now or I can play along with this and actually see where it goes. As I stare at this very good looking young man, standing in front of me with nothing more on than a pair of boxer shorts, I realize that he has absolutely no idea that Rick and I are partners. Well, at least I thought we were partners. So in that split second I decide to play along. Let this situation play itself out.

"Oh right the therapy, Rick is right I don't like talking about it," I say "What else has Rick told you?" I ask him.

The coffee machine on the counter starts to gurgle as it finishes making the pot. The aroma of the fresh brew fills the kitchen.

"Not a lot really, just that since your lover died a couple of years ago that you've basically relied upon him for emotional support while you've been goin' through therapy," he says as he motions to the coffee he's just made. "That's pretty much it. Would you like me to pour you a cup?" he asks.

I nod yes. My lover died. I think to myself, my lover will die shortly. I can feel myself turning red.

Trevor notices the colour change in my face. "I hope I didn't embarrass you. I'm sorry if I did," Trevor says sincerely as he hands me a mug of fresh hot coffee. "Actually I've been wanting to meet you for quite some time. I told Rick that you couldn't be in as bad a condition as he makes you out to be."

"Quite some time? How long might that have been?" I ask. I'm not so sure I want to hear the answer to this question. As I stand there with Trevor, my worst fears have come true; Rick has been screwing around on me for quite some time now.

"Well let's see we've been seeing each other for about a year..."

I sputter on my hot coffee as he says a year.

"You okay?" he asks.

"Yeah!" I reply. "Hot coffee," I finish saying as I put my coffee down on the counter and grab a towel from the counter to wipe up the coffee I have sputtered. "A year, eh? So you've been wanting to meet me for some time then?"

"Yeah, I told him that I could help him help you through, you know, your hard time."

I stand and stare at Trevor; I look him square in the eyes. He actually thinks that this is all true. Boy has Rick pulled one over not only on me but on this young man standing in front of me. Trevor catches me giving him the once over, and takes note that he's wearing barely anything.

"I think that I'll go and put some more clothes on. I'll tell Rick that you're here."

Trevor starts to walk back to the bedroom.

I watch him walk. He's the innocent in all this. He has absolutely no clue as to what Rick and I have, or had. That's it though. I'm done with Rick. I've given him my trust and he's betrayed it. I don't think I can forgive him for this. If he's done this to me he'll probably do it to Trevor, I feel sorry for him already, unless...

"Trevor," I call him before he reaches the bedroom door. "Don't tell him I'm here. Let's surprise him. So once you get yourself semi decent let's have him come out here for coffee, okay."

He looks at me and says "Sure why not." He disappears into the bedroom only to return a moment later after pulling on a pair of my sweat pants and a white t-shirt. I can feel my face turn red again. "Are you sure you're okay? Your face just turned the reddest red I've ever seen."

"Yeah I'm fine," I say trying with all my might to control my anger. "It's been a long night of travel from Wilmington. Not much sleep, you know how it is in airports and airplanes."

"Not too comfortable," he says as though he is quite aware of what it is like. He sits down on the large overstuffed couch facing the bedroom. I sit across from him in the matching overstuffed chair. This time there is silence between us as we wait for Rick. I want to tell him what's going on here, but I figure that when Rick makes his entrance into the living room and finds both of us sitting here things will start to come together or fall apart.

"Rick tells me that you inherited this apartment from your lover when he died," Trevor says.

Behind me from the bedroom I hear, "What did I tell you? Who are you talking too?"

"Hey, Rick come on out here. You'll never guess who's here."

As Rick walks up the hallway and enters the living room with nothing more than a towel wrapped around his waist, I say, "Yeah Rick come and see who's here."

"Oh fuck!" is all he says as the colour drains from his face. "What are you...Shit!" he turns and goes back down the hall to the bedroom.

Trevor looks at me and then gets up. "What was that all about?" he asks as he moves towards the bedroom where

Rick has gone.

"I don't really know. Why don't you go and find out," I suggest, even though I know exactly what has just transpired in the living room. Rick has been caught. Trevor looks at me then heads off down the hall to the bedroom.

As Trevor enters the bedroom he finds Rick pacing back and forth saying out loud to himself "Shit, shit, shit, shit."

"Shit what?" Trevor says. "Rick what the fuck is goin' on here. How can you treat Andrew like that?"

"You've got to get the hell outta here," Rick says. He isn't paying attention to Trevor.

"What is goin' on here? Why do I have to leave?" Trevor questions him. "Andrew seems like a nice guy. He's not like you said he was."

Rick starts to pick up his clothes and puts them on as quickly as he can. "Please Trevor, you've got to go. You never know what he'll be like now that he's caught you here with me."

"I really don't understand, what do you mean caught?" The two men stand there looking at each other. Finally the light goes on. "How fucking stupid I am. Andrew is your lover. That's why all this time you've been avoiding having me meet him. I can't believe that for the last year I've fallen for the story that he's in therapy and that you're needed to help him through it. Fuck, I thought that was so honourable that you'd do such a thing for a friend. I thought that you were different from all the rest, that you had some morals, fuck was I wrong."

"Look Trevor you just got to get outta here now. I'll explain everything later, okay?" he hands Trevor his jeans. Trevor stands there for a moment and holds onto his jeans. Then he slips the jogging pants off, puts his jeans on and slowly tucks in his t-shirt.

"Would you hurry the fuck up, I don't want to..." Rick is cut off short as the clenched fist of Trevor's right hand round houses him and knocks him back into the door. Rick slides down to the floor, as a small trickle of blood runs down his jaw and drips onto his lap. His eyes are shut.

Trevor yells in pain as he connects his clenched fist

with Rick's jaw. "FUCK!" He grabs his hand with his other hand and holds it tight. "Shit, I think I broke my hand."

I jumped up with a start from the chair where I'm sitting listening to Trevor and Rick in the bedroom. The bedroom door opens slowly and Trevor comes out holding his fist. There are tears on his cheeks. He looks at his fist and then at me, "I think I broke my hand."

We hear a moan coming from behind the door, and it slowly closes. Neither of us looks at the door as it closes.

Trevor starts walking down the hall towards me with his head hanging down. "For what it's worth, I'm sorry." There are fresh tears rolling down his cheeks. Trevor is hurt not only physically but emotionally. "I really honestly didn't know that you two were lovers."

"Trevor, I have to apologize to you too," I say.

"What do you have to apologize for?" he asks.

Really, I don't have to apologize for anything, but I say, " I want to apologize because as soon as we started talking earlier I figured it out. Rick screwed us both around, but I thought that you should find out just like I had found out that he was screwin' with you."

"So, do you want him? He's up for grabs," I state.

Trevor shakes his head and asks, "You okay?"

"Actually, I'm fine," I say to him. "As morbid as it may sound to you, I honestly believe you really didn't know about us, but screwin' up his relationship with you couldn't be more satisfying right now. So you see, I do owe you an apology."

"Maybe I should be thanking you," he says.

"Right now while you're angry with him, maybe. Tomorrow you may feel different about things." I pause and look at the closed bedroom door. "I'll probably feel different about things tomorrow, too." We start to walk towards the apartment door.

Trevor stops and without looking at me he says, "I've got some things here, should I get them?"

"I'll give you my work number, give me a call in a day or so and we'll make some arrangements." I go to my desk and get him one of my business cards. He slips it into his pocket without looking at it. I open the door and he walks out neither of us saying good-bye. We just look at each other and he turns and walks towards the elevator still holding his hand. I close the apartment door behind him. I stand there with my forehead against the shut door. I can feel the tears fill my closed eyes. I decide that I need some time to think. I walk back down the hallway, through the living room and down the short hallway to the closed bedroom door. I sit on the floor on the other side of the closed door. I can hear Rick moan from the punch he received from Trevor.

"He's gone," I say to Rick on the other side of the door. "He wasn't the first was he?" I ask. I don't get an answer, which is answer enough for me. I'm just guessing. I really don't know and right now I don't care. "I need some time to think about what I am going to do..." I feel the tears slowly run down my cheeks. I wipe them away. "So, I'm going to see if I can spend a few days with Gerry."

"Andy, I'm...," Rick starts to say.

"Rick, don't say anything, just listen, 'cuz right now I don't want to hear anything you have to say." I don't want him to see me cry. I don't want him to see what he lost today. "So this is what I want you to do, I'm going to go into the den and you're going to get yourself together and leave the apartment. Do you understand? Rick?"

"But Andy, if you just let me explain," he pleads.

"No Rick, I don't want to talk to you right now."

"Andy, please."

"No." I stand firm on my decision, "We'll talk, I promise, just not today." I think this might help him get out of the apartment until I can gather up some of my stuff and go to Gerry's. I get up from the floor, walk into the den and lock the door behind me. I look out of the window. Everything I see is blurred through the tears. I wipe them away and look down at the street. I can see Rick's truck parked by the curb. There is a knock on the den door.

"Andy?"

"Rick, I can see your truck from the window. As soon as I see you get in I'll come out." I honestly don't want to see him. The locked door seems to create this impassable barrier between us.

"Aw Andy, please," Rick pleads again.

This time I don't reply. Moments pass into minutes.

He could kick the door open, but I know he wouldn't. After ten minutes I hear the apartment door close. I stand and watch the street below. In a few minutes he would be there. I continue to watch his truck. Soon Rick enters the street, he looks up towards the apartment windows. He is rubbing his jaw where Trevor has hit him. I know he can see me standing in the window like I said. He unlocks his truck and gets in. It takes a few more minutes before the truck pulls away from the curb. As I watch the truck move down the street I can feel myself let go. The tears stream down my cheeks.

It takes me an hour to leave the den, but when I finally do, I begin to feel slightly human again. Even though Rick has betrayed my trust and love for him, I feel kind of relieved. Deep down I think I've known this was coming. As I look back, our life together was rather boring, comfortable, but boring. It had become an existence, not really living. We had become companions that had sex every once in a while. Was it love making, I'm not really sure, I thought it was. As for Rick, I'm not even going to guess what he was getting out of our relationship. I pick up the phone and dial Gerry's phone number. It rings twice before he answers.

"Hello," I say.

"Andy, Honey you're home," Gerry says. "How was your trip?"

"Oh the trip was fine," I say.

"And your beautiful mother, how is she?" he asks.

"She's fine."

"Everything else is okay, Honey?" he asks. I'm sure he can tell that something else is up. Before I can reply he says, "Look Andy Hon, I really don't feel like pulling teeth to get information out of you, so let's skip the preamble and get to the meat of the situation." He pauses then says, "Sooo?"

"Well, I guess I really don't know where to begin," I say. "I just want to know if I can come and stay at your place for a few days?"

"Stay at my place a few days? Andy I don't understand?" he questions.

"Just say yes, okay Gerry," I say to him.

"You know you can stay here for as long as you like Andy but why?" he asks again. "It has something to do with Rick right?"

There is a silence between us for a moment, and then I say, "You were right about him." Silence again.

Gerry says, "Oh Honey, I don't know what to say. I guess sorry would be a good place to start. Are you okay?"

"I guess I am."

"I'll send my driver around to get you. You just get your stuff together and he'll be there in about half an hour," he says.

"Thanks Gerry," I say to my friend.

"No problem," he replies. "Hey Hon, everything will be okay."

"Thanks for the reassurance, but I'm not too sure."

"It may take some time but it always gets better," Gerry says. "These things change for a reason you know. It's obvious that this wasn't the way God wanted things to go for you in this life."

"You really think that?" I ask.

"Of course I do, all things happen for a reason," he says. "And I believe that this has happened to you now for a reason. We may not know for what reason, because the reasons are sometimes not obvious to us but they are there." He pauses then says, "So you get some things together and I'll have you picked up. We'll talk more when you get here if you want."

"Thanks Gerry." I hang up. I look around my apartment, as neat and tidy as it looks it has an unclean feeling about it. I make my way to the front hall where I left my suitcases. I lock the door as I leave my apartment.

As Tony drives down the tree lined driveway of the Ayer's place, he figures that this might be one of the last times he would be able to come to his favourite house in Rocky Beach. Life has changed in the last couple of days. First old Mrs. Ayers dies and the house is changing hands, probably to someone who'll sell the place, and second Elaine announces that they are having a baby. That's the biggest change; the one he hasn't expected. He's told his mother and sister Maria and after a few moments of questions like how and when and are you sure, they both kicked into wedding mode. Maria said that she'd figured that it would eventually happen; that Elaine would get pregnant before they've actually set a wedding date. She was ecstatic. Mama on the other hand was a little more reserved. When they were alone, Mama had asked him if he was happy with his situation. He told her that he had some difficulty in trying to figure out when this accident had occurred but of course he was happy, even though it didn't show. He didn't see he had much choice. His mother said that they should have a small quiet wedding, something low profile so the two of them could get on with life and have their baby. She never got angry, like he expected his hot-blooded Italian mother would, but then she didn't get too excited over the situation either. She was just a bit too calm and this bothered Tony.

He pulls up to the old Victorian house at the end of the driveway. He looks at the well preserved home and thinks that it would be sad to see it sold to some wealthy Bostonian family who would either tear it down or have it gutted and remodelled. Hopefully when that happens Cape Development and Maintenance wouldn't be in charge of the house. He didn't think that he could bear the sight of this beautiful house being destroyed. He gets out of the truck, walks up onto the front veranda facing Cape Cod Bay and sits on the top stair. As Tony stares out over the water he thinks that two things as simple as a death and a new life can have such life changing effect on so many people. He feels a strong connection with this place; he knows that its existence would change just like his would in the next few weeks. It is as though they both have no choice, as though their paths have been chosen for them, and he isn't so sure that it is the right path, at least he isn't very sure about his. Tony gets up from the stair and walks along the veranda's length, looking at the old glass windows, the weathered wood that had stood up against the elements.

"Look old girl," he says out loud to the house, "hopefully you'll find a new owner that'll appreciate you. Your quality and strength, your character," he says as he runs his hand over the hardwood doors that open onto the veranda. "They don't build places like you anymore." It is as though he is talking to a close and dear friend. "But I guess we have to travel roads we don't necessarily think we should," Tony says this last bit for himself. Deep down in himself he knows that he wasn't meant to marry or have children. His life was destined for a different road than the one he is traveling now. He stops at the open stairway that leads down to the beach. He thinks about what his father would be saying right now, "You've made your bed, now you have to lie in it." His father was probably right, he was most of the time, but he doesn't like it. He walks down the stairs and heads for the beach. Maria, Elaine and Sara are at his mother's making plans for the wedding on the fourth of July. They've asked him for his input, but he's told them he'd probably just get in their way in making the arrangements. He's asked Garth to be his best man, and of course Sara will be maid of honour for Elaine. Garth had been a bit shocked when he told him, but he came around and seemed quite happy for them. Sara on the other hand didn't say much. She seemed quite aloof about the whole situation. Elaine says it's a girl thing. She's just a bit jealous. He reaches the beach. The tide is out. He can walk at least a hundred yards out into the bay before he gets his feet wet. He takes his runners off and places them on the beach by the big rock outcrop and starts to walk out onto the exposed sand left by the receding tide. At thirty yards into the bay he walks into the salt water of the bay. Tony picks up a rock and skips it across the water. He continues walking along the waterline towards the north end of the property, the small receding waves lapping at his feet. He turns and looks at the house set back on a small rise above the beach. The sun glistens off the windows, the second floor balcony off the master bedroom seems, from where he stands, the perfect spot to watch the sailboats out on Cape Cod Bay. He makes his way to the secluded beach between the rocks and sits down beside the large log set at the back of the beach. He pulls his t-shirt off and lets the sun warm his upper body as he places his head on the log and closes his eyes. He is going to miss this place.

I've been a week at Gerry's and I still don't feel like going home. I've had Rosie clean up the apartment since Rick has taken all his personal stuff out. Gerry had met Trevor two nights ago at my apartment so that he, too could pick up his few items. I haven't spoken to Rick since Monday afternoon when I had decided that it really was over. He argued with me about the lack of time that I gave myself to think about my decision, but I told him that the longer I gave myself the more I would find myself hating him. He said that I wasn't being fair to him. I couldn't believe he would suggest that I wasn't being fair. I replied I wasn't the one sleeping around and for all I knew Trevor wasn't the only one he had been 'dicking' around with in the last six years of our relationship. I gave him until Thursday to get his stuff out of the apartment as I had asked Rosie to go in and clean on Friday afternoon. It wasn't an easy thing to do cold turkey, quit a six-year relationship; especially one that I had felt was the "one." It's the trust quotient. I couldn't trust Rick anymore so I don't feel that we can ever have the kind of relationship that I need. Since then I've been at Gerry's, and he has been very good about the whole situation. Last Saturday when I got here he said that he'd say it only once, 'I told you so'. And ever since then he's been great, very supportive and comforting to be around. But I don't want to wear out my welcome. I know he doesn't mind me being here. But I think, even though I don't want to, it's time for me to go home.

"Gerry?" He is sitting across the table from me reading the morning paper and having his coffee.

"Yes Hon?" he says to me.

"I think it's time for me to go home."

"You're probably right," he says as he puts down his paper. "It's been a week and you should be getting your life back to normal." He takes a sip of his coffee. "But you can't go today. Tomorrow would be better." He takes another sip of his coffee.

"Why can't I go today?" I question him.

"Well Hon it's Saturday and I've gone and invited a few of our mutual friends over for dinner and cocktails this evening. So tomorrow is a much better day for you to go home."

"So who's all coming?" I ask.

"Laurel and Joshua, don't you just love that name?" he muses.

"Yes and who else have you invited? I hope you're not trying to fix me up with anyone of your new young friends," I say.

"Oh Andy Hon, I wouldn't even think of it, with you just a week out of a lousy relationship," Gerry says. "Anyways, they're all couples that I've invited." He stops abruptly realizing what he's just said. "Oh Honey I'm..."

"Gerry, it's all right, I'm sure that you didn't mean anything by it," I say.

"Oh shit, they are all couples," he says. "I'll just cancel the whole thing."

"No you won't, not with this short notice. It'll be fine. I think it would be better if all the guests tonight are couples, it will be easier to get back into the social scene sort of one step at a time." I suggest.

"Are you sure Hon?" he asks. He seems so sincere

and concerned with how I feel about being the only single person in attendance at tonight's dinner party.

"Of course I'm sure. Just look at my history while being part of a couple. I've always gone single or with you as my escort."

There is a short silence then Gerry says, "You're probably right. I can't think of a time when you two ever went out as a couple other than to a club."

"So who else is coming?"

"Well there's Laurel and Josh, Tom and a new friend of his, I think his name is Alan if I remember correctly. Lillian and her lover Brenda, Cynthia and her husband Mark, Roger and his gorgeous wife Melissa. Bret, you remember Bret? He's that muscle bound hunky straight guy with that wanna be actress girlfriend of his. Oh her name always disappears from my mind when I think of him. If anything, he's great eye candy for a party. Ronny and Bill, and let's see Sandy and Jim. Oh and of course Troy will be here too." He pauses for a moment and takes another sip of his coffee. "Lillian and Brenda are bringing a lesbian couple along with them that are new to the city. And I think that's about it for the guest list." He takes another sip of his coffee and says jokingly, "Would you like to inspect the dinner menu for final approval?"

"No," I smile at him "I'm sure it will be just perfect like your dinner party menus always are."

"So, that's settles it then. You'll be spending another night here with me," Gerry states.

"How could I turn down an evening like this? It'll be like having my very own coming out party."

"Well, it's sort of a coming out party," he says. "A coming out of a lousy relationship party." He looks at me for some sign as to whether I've taken offence to what he's just said.

"That's a perfect reason to have a party," I reassure him. I can see him relax.

Gerry picks up his newspaper and continues to read while he drinks the remainder of his coffee. I get up and go to the buffet and pour myself another cup of the hot coffee from the silver coffee service Juanita has set up earlier.

"Would you like a refill Gerry?" I ask him.

"Why sure Honey, I'd love a warm up," Gerry answers without putting his paper down. "Andy Honey?" he queries.

"Oh that sounds like you've got a serious question to ask," I reply as I put the steaming cup of coffee I've just poured down in front of him. He rustles the pages of the newspaper and sets it down on the table in front of him.

"You're not worried about that test Laurel and I made you get earlier this week are you?" Gerry asks.

"Do you think I should be?" I ask him back.

"Well, you know about that letter from the free clinic that you know who got, and I was just wondering if you were worried about your results." He looks at me and I can see from the look in his eyes that he is genuinely concerned.

"I really don't think about it, and I don't think I have anything to worry about." I sit down in the chair beside him. "The results will be in by the end of this week and we'll know for sure. But if there is one thing that I'm quite sure of is that what little sex Rick and I've had was always safe. Rick always used a condom, said it made him last longer." I pause for a moment to reflect on our sex life. It really wasn't much of a life. Well at least it didn't happen very often with me. "Anyways Rick's a bottom. I can't remember how many years ago that I did the receiving and I know that back then we practiced safe sex. Come to think of it, it never really happened as Rick couldn't keep it hard, so we gave up." I smile and chuckle. "That was so long ago, almost at the beginning of our relationship. We thought that it was just because we were so nervous about getting together." I sit back in my chair next to Gerry. He studies my face. He can see that my eyes are tearing up and that I'm doing my best to be strong.

"Andy, I'm really sorry that he did this to you, I mean screwed around on you that is. It's obvious that you really did love him." He reaches out and holds my hand.

"Yeah I did," I say. "But love isn't the only thing that a relationship needs to succeed." I pause for a moment then continue, "Trust and honesty are just as important."

"I'm sure that you'll find it out there somewhere. There will be a man that holds all those values."

"I don't know Gerry, if there is such a man out there. I

really don't think that I can give myself as fully again as I did with Rick."

"Never say never Hon."

"I don't know if I can trust another man with my heart again. It hurts too much when things go wrong."

"Don't be too sure of that. I'm a firm believer that there is a perfect someone for everyone alive. It just has to happen at the right time and place." He squeezes my hand and continues, "Rick was supposed to be in your life for just this period and now it's time to move on because life has something else in store for you."

"Fate. I believed in it once but I now don't think that all things happen for a reason."

Gerry looks at me with a hard stare. "All things in life really do happen for a reason. We are put here to learn life's lessons and all the ups and downs, the pitfalls and the triumphs all take place to help us learn the lessons we need to learn in this life."

"Oh Gerry, you sound way too philosophical for this time of day." I smile at him.

"Christ, I do don't I?" he smile a Cheshire cat size grin. "Oh, I've got to stop this. I must be getting old." We both start to laugh.

"So what do we have to do to get ready for tonight's party?" I ask.

"Juanita is looking after all the arrangements. All we have to do is look pretty for tonight and by the looks of that perfect cloudless sky it's going to be a hot one, so wear as little as possible. Something sexy would be appropriate."

"Why would I want to wear something sexy when all the invitees are part of a couple?" I ask.

"It'll make you feel good about yourself if everyone thinks you're sexy..." Gerry stops mid sentence. "There I go again bein' philosophical, thank God I caught myself before I got in too deep."

I shake my head in disbelief and smile at my best and closest friend. "I think then, I'll have to go to my place to pick up something to wear for tonight's soiree."

Gerry looks up from his newspaper and coffee. "Are you sure you want to? Do you want some company when you go?" he asks.

"No, I think I can go by myself. I'm a big boy, I'm sure I can cross the street without having someone hold my hand."

"It's not that. It's been quite obvious that since last weekend you've been avoiding your apartment," Gerry cautiously responds. "I can understand that. And as far as holding your hand I'm absolutely positive that you'd probably much prefer a tall dark and handsome man as opposed to me, I know I would." Gerry hesitates again, "I don't think that came out right did it?" After a short pause he says, "What I meant Hon is that if I were you I'd prefer someone other than me holding your hand."

"Well, that sounds better, especially if you are trying to cheer me up." I smile at him. I know he's being so careful with everything he says to me, trying not to say something offensive. I guess that's why I consider Gerry my very best friend. "And who says I wouldn't want you to be holding my hand?"

"Oh don't say things like that Honey, I just might have to drop my young buck and latch onto you," he says. "But really, I don't think I'm your type."

"Actually Gerry I don't think I'm your type. I'm a few years too old." We both break into laughter.

"Well then, when you go back to your apartment, remember it's just the place the events happened in not the event, okay?" He rustles his newspaper together in a half assed sort of order. "And don't forget to make sure you dress sexy for tonight. It's gonna be a hot night, temperature wise."

"Oh, I'm sure it'll be a warm evening, especially if you have anything to do with the agenda, and I'm not referring to the temperature."

"What on earth are you suggesting Honey?" he asks, not really expecting me to answer. He gets up from the table and starts to walk towards his bedroom. "Well I must get myself ready for the day, my young Greek god Troy will be here in an hour. So you go about your stuff and just remember cocktails at six. Hmmm, love that word cocktails." He enunciates it slowly as he disappears into his bedroom.

I smile and shake my head as I watch him leave the room. He's so special I think to myself. I get up from the table and pick up the breakfast dishes Gerry and I have left at the table and make my way into the kitchen. As I load them into the dishwasher that strange 'déjà vu' feeling comes over me. I know it's just the act of cleaning up the dishes I normally would do on weekends for Rick and I as we've had our Sunday breakfasts. I pause and think, it seems like such a long time ago, maybe almost a year ago. I guess that's when Rick met Trevor. Everything seems to be explainable now that I've had that bit of information. It explains the beginning of the distance. I tried to justify it to myself that we were just becoming comfortable with each other and our routines. I guess it also explains why our sex life almost died a year ago. God, was I ever stupid. I saw all of this happening but I never wanted to believe that it could be happening to me. All along my friends had been telling me that this was going on right in front of me, but I chose not to believe them. There must be something in my genes that makes me learn the hard way. As I finish putting in the last of the dishes into the dishwasher I hear the front door open and close. A few moments later I hear the distinct footsteps of Juanita coming down the hall towards the kitchen.

"Good morning, Juanita."

"Oh good morning Meester Andy. Is Meester Gerry out of bed yet?" she asks in her Puerto Rican accent.

"Yes, he's just getting himself ready for the day," I reply. "We've already had breakfast and I was just cleaning up."

"Oh no, no, no!" she exclaims. "Out of my kitchen! Only Juanita clean in kitchen." She starts to shoo me out of the kitchen back into the living room. "Juanita do dishes, you no worry," she says as she ushers me out. "You go enjoy sunshine. Juanita has to do lots for party. Delivery boy be here soon." I grin at her and give her a big sloppy kiss on the cheek, turn and walk towards my room.

As I walk down the hall Gerry comes out of his bedroom and says, "I thought I heard the door. Is Juanita here yet? She has a lot to do for tonight."

"Oh she's here. She just kicked me out of the kitchen. All I was doing was putting the dishes in the dishwasher..."

"She'll have them out of there so fast you won't know

what happened. She's like a tornado when it comes to cleaning and she hates the dishwasher, says 'machine no clean good'," Gerry mimics her. "I just don't know what I'd do without her, but I'd never let her know that."

"Why not, if she's that good? Why not let her know that you appreciate her?" I suggest.

"Heavens no Honey, that's the way our relationship is. I act as if I don't appreciate her and she acts as if she hates working for me. I actually did start telling her that I appreciated her just shortly after Paul died, but she told me that she didn't want to work for me anymore if I was going to be nice to her and treat her like everyone else. How'd she put it? Like old furniture, she wanted to be treated like old furniture."

"Old furniture?" I question my friend.

"Yeah, you know old furniture is more comfortable, you don't mind putting your feet up on it. You don't cover it in plastic and not let anyone sit on it." Gerry says and smiles. "It works. We're both happy." He turns and walks down the hall towards the kitchen.

I can hear the two of them chattering about the dinner party. Their voices disappear as I close the door to my room. The room feels like a hotel room, it's not like home. I want to go back to my apartment, but I have this overwhelming fear that I won't feel comfortable there. I know that I have to go back, because I can't stay at Gerry's forever. I'm sure Troy wouldn't be too happy with that kind of arrangement. I take off the kimono that Gerry has given me to wear in the mornings. He says that if I was to walk around here half naked he'd have a major problem all the time. I take stock of my body in the floor length mirror that hangs behind the bedroom door. I have neglected myself. I stare at myself in the mirror, almost thirty and single again. I don't think I'd ever able to trust another man. I also know that from now on I'd always hold something back. I wouldn't let myself get hurt like this again. I pack up the clothes that I brought with me a week earlier and close my travel bag. I'd ask Gerry if his driver could give me a ride to the gym.

There are only a few guys at the gym this morning, so my workout is quick. As I walk out of the building I can feel the heat from the pavement and concrete of the buildings. I have a five block walk back to my apartment in the heat. This was going to be the hard part. As I walk along the streets towards my apartment, more people start to crowd the sidewalks. I try to keep my mind off the events that drove me from the apartment, but as I get closer, the thought of Rick and Trevor and god only knows who else he has shared my bed with races through my mind. I suddenly realize that I'm standing outside the front doors of my apartment building. I put the key into the door lock and push it open. At the far end of the lobby are the elevators. I push the number seven button and wait for the doors to close. Once they do I get this ominous feeling, one of fear and hate. I'd never felt this way about a place before. Maybe Gerry is right, it's not the place but the event that took place. I lean my head back against the wall of the elevator as it starts its climb. I begin to worry that I won't be able to differentiate between the place and the event. I can feel the sweat start to bead on my forehead. It is very warm inside the elevator. I try to change my thoughts to the events of the coming evening. The elevator comes to a stop and the doors open. I look down the corridor towards my apartment. I feel stuck, like I can't move. If I walk down that hall and open the door of the apartment it would happen all over again, Rick and Trevor. The doors start to close, I reach out and stop them from closing. I hear the elevator start its descent back to the lobby or another floor. I can't turn back. I fumble with my keys and finally put the door key into the keyhole and turn. I slowly turn the doorknob and push the door open. I stand in the entranceway of my apartment and look in. Rosie has been here. The strong fragrance of fresh cut lilies comes to greet me. I walk in and look around; I have left the door open. I continue to walk through my apartment, checking that Rick's belongings are gone. It looks as though he'd packed all his belongings. I walk towards the bedroom, which Rick and I had shared, open the door and look inside. I can smell the peppery smell of freesia's, Rosie's touch again. I turn and go to the room where Rick kept most of his personal belongings. As I turn the doorknob to open the door I find myself holding my breath as if I was expecting something to jump out at me. The room had been cleared of his stuff. There are fresh sheets on both beds. All the rooms look as if Rick had never been here. I walk back down the hall towards the front door and shut it. I turn the deadbolt and lock myself in my apartment. I slowly walk through all the rooms again to make sure to not get that feeling I'd feared. I pick up my bag, walk into my bedroom and toss it on the bed.

It is then I notice that I smell of sweat and perspiration from my workout and the walk to my apartment. I make my way into the bathroom where I strip my clothes off my body. I take a close look at my face in the mirror above the washbasin. I need a shave. I rub my hand over my jaw. I take out my razor, and look at myself in the mirror. Why not I say to myself. I could use a change. I'll grow a moustache and goatee. I shave my jaw and face where I didn't want hair to grow; I splash water on my face to remove the leftover shaving cream. There is a dark outline of beard where I didn't shave. I stand back and look at my whole body in the mirror. Not bad for twenty-nine. It hits me again, almost thirty and single. This isn't the way I had been planning my life, but it was better than being in a relationship where you can't trust your partner. I step into the shower and wash the smell off my body. After showering and drying off, I put on a pair of shorts and t-shirt and start to take a closer look around the apartment. Rick had left nothing to even remind me that we had just spent the last six years together. Not a photo, no lost sock or t-shirt of his lying around forgotten. I open the window in the living room to air out the apartment. I walk into the kitchen to pour myself a glass of water and notice the pile of unopened mail sitting on the countertop next to the phone. I start to sort through it. Most of it is junk mail, except for a couple of bills of mine, a brown manila envelope from Peabody, and a letter from the free clinic for Rick. It's the same one I'd seen before I went to Grams' funeral. What do I do with this? I don't want to open it. I rub it between my fingers. It feels like only one sheet of paper. Even if he's been for HIV testing, I have been tested also since finding out that he's been screwing around. It's really none of my business why he's obviously avoiding these letters from the clinic. I know that on Thursday I'd be hounding my doctor for my test results. I didn't think I could move forward in my personal life without knowing the results. I take a black marker pen from the drawer beneath the phone and write: Return to Sender, Moved no Forwarding Address. I feel a twinge of guilt. I know I should be telling him it's here, but I know he already knows about the letter, he received one in May and he'd opened it. Maybe I'd give him a call at work from my office later in the week, so I decide to hold onto the letter until I talk to him. My feeling of guilt subsides, after thinking this out. I place the envelope back on the counter by the phone and walk back into the den. I place the two bills in the centre of the blotter on my desk, and reach for the letter opener and cautiously cut the manila envelope open. It is quite thick. I slide the papers out. There is a cover letter with Peabody's letterhead. I quickly read the letter. He needs my signature on all of the transfer papers, so that by July the fourth everything would be complete. He also states that he'd informed the management company, Cape Development and Management Company, of the transfer in ownership. He also attached a copy of a letter he'd sent to a local bank in Rocky Beach about the change in ownership, seems as though there is also a small bank account that's attached to the house for the sole use of maintaining the house. The maintenance company has signing authority. If I see fit to make any changes then I should inform them both. No real need to do that. I live in New York City and the house is way up north on Cape Cod. It would be much better for them to have control over the maintenance bills, rather than having to call me every time they need to have a cheque written. I'd just have to have them send me a statement or something detailing what was being paid for. I take out the phone book, flip through the pages and stop at the name, Richard Spence, Lawyer. I call him to see if he'd witness my signature so that I can get the papers off that afternoon. I saved him a lot of money on his taxes the last couple of years so maybe he can do me a favour. It wouldn't take but a half hour at the most. I pick up the phone, dial his number and listen to it ring.

As I leave the UPS office after lunch with Richard and his girlfriend, I walk down the sidewalk towards my jeep. I feel for the first time in a week, that things are starting to get better. Almost thirty and single, it's not so bad. Things could be worse. Life isn't going to stop just because I've had a few personal setbacks this year. If I'm going to move forward, I've got to take that first step. The first couple of days after I'd caught Rick and Trevor together I blamed myself. What did I do to make Rick look for something outside of our relationship? When I finally figured out that it wasn't me that made Rick look for something outside of our relationship, but Rick's own needs that couldn't be fulfilled within our relationship, I turned an important corner. Gerry also helped a lot. He kept reminding me that I was the one who had been faithful in the relationship. Back in my jeep, I pull out into the street and start my drive to Gerry's condo.

As I walk into Gerry's condo I can hear voices coming from the kitchen. It's Gerry and Juanita. They're arguing about something to do with the evening's event.

"Now look Meester Gerry, you want tonight to be good, then do as Juanita say."

"Juanita, this has to be perfect," Gerry says.

"Then let Juanita do," she snaps back. "You go from Juanita's kitchen."

I walk past the entrance of the kitchen trying to avoid being seen, but I don't have much luck.

"Hi Andy Honey."

"Hallo Meester Andy," Juanita greets me.

"Hi, I ah, don't want to interrupt," I reply.

"Do you mind giving your opinion on something?" Gerry asks.

"Gee Gerry do you really think...," I start to say trying to avoid being dragged into the argument.

"Of course we don't mind another opinion." Both Gerry and Juanita stand in the centre of the stainless steel kitchen and wait to see if I'd be their third opinion. Just then Troy comes into the kitchen from the dining room.

"Hi Andy," Troy says giving me a hug. "I could hear what was going on from the other room and thought you might need some help."

"Thanks Troy, I think I'm going to need it."

Troy walks over to Gerry and puts his arms around

him. "Why don't we leave our guest out of this little argument?" he suggests. "You two didn't listen to me, so why do you think you'll listen to Andy?"

"Of course you're right, Troy," he stops and looks at the counter. "Okay Juanita, you do what you have to do. I really should know better than to try and change things we have already planned."

"Thank you Meester Troy," she returns to the cutting board and continues to work on whatever spurred the argument. "Such a nice boy," she mutters just loud enough for Gerry to hear. Gerry smiles behind her back. The two of them thrive on the friction.

The three of us leave Juanita to finish her preparations for the evening's dinner party.

"So how was the apartment?" Gerry asks.

"Not as bad as I thought it was going to be," I reply. "Thought that I was going to have a big problem but when I got there it never materialized. I guess I thought that there would be this flood of memories and emotions that would make being there difficult but it never happened."

"Well that's good," Gerry says. "Everything is almost done for the evening."

Troy and Gerry sit on the sofa close to each other. Troy reaches out and holds Gerry's hand. I can see Gerry tense up.

"I hope you don't think that your public display of affection is going to bother me?"

"Well...," Gerry starts.

"Well it's not. I think it's wonderful that the two of you are together. After this last week I've done a lot of thinking and I realize that life, both mine and those around me are not going to stop just because I've had a bad month."

"See I told you Gerry," Troy says. "You don't give Andy enough credit."

I give Gerry a strange stare.

"It's not like that Andy. And you don't have to look at me like that," Gerry says. "I wasn't completely sure how you'd take things if you saw people showing affection towards each other."

"Looking at my past with Rick, it was never openly

affectionate. You know I've always wanted more but I never got it, so believe me it's not something I'm going to miss."

"Yeah, I guess you're right."

"Hell, we hardly ever did anything together outside of my apartment."

"True," Gerry agrees.

"Shit, that must have been awful," Troy says.

"You get used to it. But now things are different. I get to start all over, fresh."

"Well, it's about time I hear those kinds of words coming from your mouth," Gerry says. "I thought you were going to wallow in self pity forever. What made you change?"

"You know Gerry, I really don't know. After I got to the apartment, and I didn't have all those feelings that I feared I was going to have, I just decided that if I don't get on with things life will pass me by. I really don't want that to happen. So what if I don't ever have that someone special to share the rest of my life with, I still can have a good full life. I have you two, Laurel and Tom and all my friends. What more could I ask for?"

"Well that's quite a change in attitude from a few days ago," Gerry notes.

"I figure that the mourning period for my bad relationship is over and it is time to get on with things."

"Good for you," Troy says. "But I don't think I'd count on being alone for the rest of your life."

"Well let's just say that I'm in no rush to meet anyone. I know that there's this trust issue that I'm going to have to get over."

"Hey don't lump the rest of the single available guys in the same category as Rick," Troy adds..

"I know I can't do that, but I do know that I'll be awfully damn cautious from now on."

"Understandably Honey, but don't close all the doors, you never know what or who you'll miss."

"Right now that's a chance I'm willing to take," I reply. "I don't think there is someone special for me out there. I already thought I had him."

"Well give yourself some time Hon," Gerry says. "Damn it's hot. Thank God for air-conditioning."

Troy gets up and walks over to the windows that overlook Central Park. "So is it sit down or buffet, Gerry?"

"If Juanita gets her way it'll be buffet. Speaking of which, we should arrange a few tables and chairs on the terrace. You know a few intimate groupings."

"Good idea," I say. "Just let me put my bag in my room and I'll give you a hand."

As I return from my room, I can see Gerry and Troy out on the terrace. They are holding each other. Seeing the two of them holding each other doesn't bother me. It actually makes me feel good. Gerry had been alone for so long since Paul had died that it was good seeing him with someone again. Troy seems to be a good person. He's employed and genuinely seems to like Gerry a lot. Not some street hustler looking for a free ride. He's ambitious also, taking some evening courses to finish his BA. He says he wants to be a teacher. He comes across much more mature than what he looks. I'm happy for Gerry. I walk through the sliding door in my room out onto the terrace.

"Of course you had to have the sunset side of the building didn't you?" I say to the two of them.

"Positioning is everything, whether it be seating in a room or where you live," Gerry announces. "And it will be a great sunset tonight."

We start to shuffle the tables and chairs that Gerry had rented for the evening, setting some of the tables with four chairs, some with two. Troy follows us and sets up the market style umbrellas in each of the tables. Gerry stands in the doorway of the dining room and surveys the terrace.

"Perfect, every table will still have a view of the sunset," Gerry proclaims. He glances at his wristwatch. "Oh hell, the other guests will start to arrive in just over an hour and I'm not ready. If you don't mind I'm off to get ready." He turns and skips off to his room.

I pull out one of the chairs from a table near the terrace railings and look out over Central Park. Troy in the mean time had slipped back into the condo. A few moments later he returns with a couple of Buds. He hand one to me and takes a long drink from his.

"It's very hot today."

"Yeah, it sure is." I take a drink from my cold beer. "Thanks, that hits the spot."

Troy pulls out the chair across the table from me and puts his feet up on the terrace railing.

"Gerry and you look very happy."

"We do don't we," Troy says. "Andy I know that you and Gerry are close friends so I want you to know that I really care a lot for Gerry. I know that you care for him, too."

"So what are you trying to tell me?"

"I just want you to know that I am very serious about Gerry, and I don't want you to worry," he continues. "He's asked me a number of times to move in but I've told him not yet. I want him to be sure that I'm not just someone filling in for lost memories of Paul."

"I understand, Troy, I think people should be cautious. At least I think that now."

I pause and take another drink of the cold beer. "But I think Gerry knows what he wants. He's not one to let memories get in the way. He's much too mature for that."

"That's what he says too," Troy says. "I've just got to be real sure, and I guess that seeing you over the last week and what you've gone through has made it harder to take that last step."

"Do you love him?" I ask.

"More than anything." His reply is quick. It leaves no doubt in my mind that he does.

"So step into the unknown."

"You think so?" he asks.

"You'll never know if you don't." Where in the hell is Gerry? Just as I think of him he appears through the doorway of the dining room.

"You two look like you're having a deep conversation. Can I join you?" he asks as he walks onto the terrace.

"Actually," I start to say, "I'd like to have a quick shower and change before your guests arrive, so if the two of you'll excuse me?" I get up from my chair, guzzle down the last of my beer and head towards my room.

As I leave the terrace I hear Gerry ask Troy, "Is he okay?"

"He's fine," Troy says as he gives Gerry a kiss. "He's

just doing what a good friend does."

Gerry looks at him with a puzzled look on his face. "I don't...?"

"We'll talk later, okay. We've got just a few things left to do before the others arrive. Flowers on the table and that infamous last check of Juanita's perfect job that you'll want to do."

"It's just part of the game..."

"Oh you two kill me," Troy says with a smile as he takes Gerry's hand. The two of them walk back inside to finish the last of the arrangements.

By the time I have showered and changed into my clothes for the evening, jeans and a white skin tight muscle shirt, some of the guests have arrived. When I walk into the living room there are already eight of the eighteen guest here. Laurel comes into the living room from the dining room looking as beautiful as ever. She is wearing a cotton sundress in a washed out jade green and is bare foot. Joshua, her new man friend is sitting in one of the comfortable armchairs in the living room. Tom and Alan are out on the terrace with Troy and Gerry, Roger and his wife Melissa are seated on the sofa. Gerry has done his 'hostessing' well. Everyone is armed with cocktails and is seated comfortably. I say my hellos to my friends seated in the living room. When I get to Joshua, whom I've never met formally in person, he stands up.

"So you're Joshua. It's good to finally meet you," I say as I reach out to shake his hand.

He takes my hand and shakes it firmly. "It's good to finally meet you, too. Laurel has told me a lot about you."

"All good stuff I hope?" I say as she walks up to the two of us.

"Good, you've finally met," she says as she wraps her arms through ours and starts to lead us to the bar Gerry has set up. "Why don't you two handsome men let a girl buy you a drink?"

"I'd be most flattered to have a pretty young lady like you buy me a drink," Josh says. He has learned quickly about Laurel. She doesn't mix words and she's not shy.

"I'll have a Bud."

"Oh, I was sure you would," she says as she looks at me with her striking green eyes.

"Witty, are we?" I say back slyly.

She gives me a kiss on my cheek. "It's so good to have you back. I've missed you. I have so much to tell you about what's going on."

The doorbell rings and Gerry makes his way towards the front doors. As he walks by me he says, "Nice shirt, and the jeans fit really well. Good choice. Not only is the weather hot but so are you."

"Gerry!"

"Oh Honey! You are! Now get yourself a drink, I've got guests at the door."

Soon all the invited guests are here and dinner is underway. Juanita has out done herself. She is a magician in the kitchen. She has made it an international affair with dishes from around the world and each done to perfection. After everyone has finished eating, Troy, Laurel and myself quietly clear away all of the dishes to the kitchen where Juanita and a friend of hers are busy cleaning. Troy leaves us as Juanita shoos us from the kitchen stating that he doesn't want to get in her way.

Laurel and I walk into the hall towards the living room where she turns to me and asks, "You okay? I know you've gone through a lot of shit this last week."

"Yeah I'm fine, I'm gonna be okay."

She searches my face with her green eyes, "Okay, I believe you."

"Well, that's a good thing," I smile. "So what's new? No let me guess." I grab her by her shoulders and hold her at arms length studying her hair and face, I spin her around and she starts to giggle.

"Well!" she says.

"Well, lets see, hair, eyes, face, legs and all other visible body parts, oh just wait, open up." I command.

"Open up? Open up what?" she queries.

"Your mouth lets see if there's been any new dental work."

"No new dental work, take my word for it," she says.

"So then, hair, eyes, face, legs and all other visible

body parts and teeth are unchanged, so it must be your love life."

"Yes! yes! yes! Can you tell?" she asks excitedly.

"Of course I can tell, you glow." I respond. "And by the way so does he when you're around him."

"You think so?" she asks.

"I'm very sure," I confirm. "Just look at him." Josh is standing alone by the French doors. "He looks lost without you, but the moment you go into that room you just watch him glow, and you do too."

"He does look kind of lonely doesn't he?" she sticks out her lower lip in a pout.

"Why don't you go to him, and watch him change. He loves you, you can tell." I give her a little nudge. "I can hear wedding bells," I say teasingly.

"Oh you're such an asshole," she slaps my shoulder. "It's so good to have you back home where I can keep an eye on you."

"I think you'd better keep your eye on Josh. He's quite an attractive man."

"See, I told you you're an ass." This time she says it with such a grin on her face. "So I guess that's what I was looking for, your approval."

"You don't need my approval, you know that I'd never stand in your way when it comes to love."

"Yeah I know it's just that, believe it or not you are a very important part of my life and yes your approval is important to me. You're my best girlfriend." She pauses mid thought. "Even though your approval or disapproval would never make me change my mind about a man it's still important for me to hear it."

I look at her and smile, "Girlfriend? You're such a nut case."

She wraps her arms around me and squeezes, then whisperes in my ear, "I think I'll have you as my maid of honour," she giggles.

I whisper back to her, "Only if the best man is handsome and gay."

She stands back, "Like I said it's good to have you back."

At that moment I understand it's not just a 'physical glad' to have me back but more an emotional, intellectual glad to have me back.

"Hey" I say to her as I point her towards the dining room. "I think he needs you. And don't forget to watch him as you get closer." I slap her backside, "Get going." She turns, smiles then disappears into the dining room. She looks like a young girl as she walks off around the corner of the room. I walk back into the kitchen and head to the refrigerator. Juanita gives me that what are you doing in my kitchen look.

"I'm just getting a beer Juanita," I say to her. I quickly grab a Bud from the refrigerator and leave the kitchen. As I enter the hall the door bell rings. I stick my head around the corner of the hall to catch Gerry on his way to answer the door. "I'll get it," I say to him as he is about half way through the dining room. He turns and retreats to the terrace. That is odd. Gerry normally doesn't let anyone else get his door bell, especially during a party.

"Alberto?" I say.

"Hi Andy, sorry I'm late but I was in the middle of..."

"You know you don't need to explain..."

"Of course, but I don't want you to get the wrong idea, like I said I was in the middle of typing a paper for my Anatomy class and completely forgot about the dinner party tonight," he says.

"I'm sorry Alberto, I didn't mean to imply anything."

"That's okay, no harm done. Like I said, sorry I'm late." He is still standing outside in the corridor.

"Oh shit forgive me, come on in." I swing the door wide so he can enter. "You've missed dinner but I'm sure Juanita can put something together. Gerry and everyone else are out on the terrace. There is a bar set up in the dining room so why don't you go out and say hello to everyone and I'll go and talk to Juanita about some dinner for you."

"Thanks Andy," he says.

Moments later Gerry comes into the kitchen to find Juanita and myself preparing a dinner plate for Alberto.

"Oh I see, Alberto finally made it. He's such a nice man." He checks what we are doing. "Oh I was just coming in to see about getting a dinner plate done up for him, but you two seem to have everything under control." He turns to leave the kitchen.

"Oh Gerry, you failed to mention Alberto was on the guest list earlier this morning," I say to him firmly.

"No, I think I mentioned him, and if I did miss him it was just a small oversight." He goes to the refrigerator and takes out a couple of satay skewers and puts them in the microwave to warm them. "Troy and I were out for dinner earlier this week at Georgio's and Alberto was our waiter. He was telling us about how busy he has been with term papers and exams. We thought it might be a nice gesture on our part to invite him to our party. But if we forgot to tell you that he was coming it was really just an oversight."

"Are you sure you're not trying to fix me up with him Gerry? You did say that one week was long enough to be in mourning."

"Heavens no Honey, you're definitely not ready to be fixed up. I would never consider trying to fix you up only one week after a failed relationship." He smiles at me, "But then, if anything should happen on its own, well you never know." He winks at me and leaves the kitchen.

I can't believe he did this. I can hear the laughter from the other rooms. I finish helping Juanita with Alberto's plate and go to the refrigerator to get myself another beer. I crack the cap and take a long sip from the bottle. Just as I put the bottle on the counter top Laurel comes into the kitchen. She gives me a shy look.

"You knew too?" I say to her.

"Well, I knew that Alberto was coming, but we were not trying to fix you up honestly. Actually we talked about trying to invite some single people but none of us knew anybody that wasn't on the prowl. We thought that Alberto was a safe bet. We didn't tell him about you and Rick so he thinks you're still part of a couple and that he's the only single person here."

"So he's here under false pretences also?"

"No, he knew you were here and as far as he's concerned he's just been invited to a party. That's exactly what is going on. I swear to you the only reason he's been invited is that he's the only single person we could think of. Troy knows a lot of single guys but he says they're all sex pigs so we didn't figure that they would be appropriate. We wanted someone here that you might like to talk to not just all of us couples."

"You're sure about that?" I ask.

"I'm not going to lie to you Andy. We just thought that with all of these couples in the same room it might depress you." She smiles at me, with her green eyes wide and sparkling. "Forgive us, if we've touched a nerve. We never intended anything, honestly." How could I not forgive her when she looked at me like she did?

"Of course I forgive you, I just wish you'd remember to make me aware of these things."

"I promise that if we ever do anything like this again you'll be fully informed."

She gives me a kiss on the cheek and leaves the room. Juanita hands me the hot plate she put together for Alberto and sends me out of the kitchen. I slowly look around the room and find that Alberto is out on the terrace, seated at one of the tables with Bret. Nice choice of company. I can see he has a cocktail, so as I walk towards him I pick up a napkin and cutlery from the buffet table. As I walk across the terrace towards the table Bret excuses himself and leaves Alberto alone. I walk up, place his plate in front of him and set out his napkin and cutlery.

"This is quite a switch," he says.

"What do you mean?"

"You serving me dinner?" Alberto points out, "usually it's me placing plates in front of people."

"Yeah, I guess it must seem strange to have someone you normally wait on serve you."

"Feels great," he says.

"Juanita has out done herself as usual," I reply. "Too bad you weren't here earlier. There were a few extraordinary dishes that didn't last long." I turn to walk away and let him eat his dinner.

"Andy would you like to join me?" Alberto asks. "It would be nice to have some company while I eat."

"Sure, I guess. Would you like another drink?" I ask.

"White wine would be great, thanks."

I walk to the bar, grab a couple of wine glasses and start to fill them.

"Just take the whole bottle with you," the voice says from behind me.

"Gerry, you almost scared the shit out of me," I say. "It's not like it looks you know. I'm just keeping him company while he eats. No one should have to eat alone especially at a dinner party."

"Of course not Honey. I wasn't implying anything, but go ahead take the whole bottle." He smiles at me.

"Wipe that smirk off your face, Gerry, it's not what you think."

"I didn't say a thing, Hon and I promise I won't." He still has that silly grin on his face. "I have other guests to attend to so if you'll excuse me I must see to them." He winks at me as he returns to the other guests.

I return to the table and place the two glasses and the bottle of white wine on the table and sit down across from Alberto.

"It's very good. Would you like some? There's a lot?" He pushes his plate closer to the centre of the table.

"No, thank you. I think I ate too much already and there's dessert yet."

"Gerry has quite a place. Terrific view of Central Park and the sunsets from this terrace must be spectacular," Alberto says.

"Yeah, they are," I agree with him as I look over the terrace railing towards the park. I havn't paid much attention to the sunsets over the last week, but I'm sure that Alberto is right. The sunsets probably are spectacular. I look towards the sun and realize that it would be setting soon as it is very low on the horizon now.

"So, haven't seen you around much," Alberto says, not that he and I run with the same crowd.

"I've been out of town, my grandmother died. I was away at her funeral."

"I'm sorry," he says. "Are you a close family?" Alberto doesn't seem to have a problem asking personal questions, especially to someone he hardly knows. It just seems to come to him naturally.

"Yes, we are. I guess we're as close as most families are."

"Not all families are close, mine isn't," he offers. "Well not close to me, at least since I told them I was gay. I haven't spoken to my parents for eight years," he says in between mouthfuls. "I have one sister that keeps in contact with me, but if my parents ever found out that we talk she'd be disowned too."

"That's sad that there are still people out there that can be like that, especially parents." I sympathize with him.

"Hey, no big deal. You learn to live with it. Got to, you know, go on living your own life," he says nonchalantly. He finishes his glass of wine. I pour him another.

"Thanks."

"So you've been busy with exams and papers, eh?"

"Yup, just finished writing my last paper for this term. This will be the last summer that I'll work at Georgio's. This fall I'm hoping to go to UCLA."

"UCLA, wow. California, that's quite far from home."

"Yeah, but if you think about it I really don't have anything to keep me here. Family would probably be the only thing, but I really don't have much of one so I might as well go to one of the best medical schools in the country."

"I can understand that," I say to him. I feel sorry for Alberto for not having a very supportive family. "Going to California that is. The family thing, I don't know if I understand that, probably 'cause I'm an only child."

He reaches for the bottle of wine, pours himself another glass and tops mine off. He smiles at me.

Laurel has made her way back onto the terrace, comes up to us and places her arm around my shoulder. "Hi," she says. "So what are you two gorgeous men talking about?"

"Alberto was just telling me about going to medical school in California this fall," I offer.

"California. There must be some good medical schools on this side of the country you could attend instead of going to California," she says like a true New Yorker.

"Sure, there's the University of Boston, Harvard Medical School to name a couple, but I thought the sunny skies of California would be a nice change."

"Well, I can understand California for a vacation but to actually live there, I'm not so sure," she states.

"Laurel!" I exclaim, "you talk of California like it's still a distant outpost." She brakes into a big grin. "Oh shit girl, you're just yanking my chain."

Giggling she says, "Of course I am. It's absolutely beautiful there. What school are you planning to attend, Alberto?"

"UCLA, doesn't look like it'll be much of a problem getting in. My grades are good enough."

"So you'll only be around for the rest of the summer, eh?"

"Probably only July. I'm planning to drive across the country and get myself set up there before school starts."

"Sounds exciting," she says. "Maybe before you leave, Andy will invite us all to that lovely sounding property he inherited on Cape Cod, hey Andy?" She giggles again, I can always tell when she's a little tipsy. "That's if you haven't decided to put it on the market?"

"No, I haven't decided what to do with it yet," I say. "But if I do decide to keep it, that would be a great idea."

There is silence. I'm not going to bring up Rick and all the shit that's happened last week.

Laurel squeezes my shoulder and says, "Everything will be fine. I need to get another cocktail, so if you gentlemen will excuse me." She leaves us sitting at our table. Alberto has finished eating and pushes his plate to one side. His wine glass is almost empty again. He pours himself another glass.

"I guess you haven't heard," I say to him.

"Heard what?" he replies.

"About Rick and me. We're not together anymore. I caught him and..."

"You don't have to say anything Andy. I'd have never guessed though," Alberto says. "If I heard correctly you and Rick never did much anyway."

"Yeah, you're right. We never did." I agree with him.

The sun is almost gone, and the sky has turned a brilliant red. A mix of cloud and smog from the city cast a warm glow over the terrace.

"So tell me about this place on Cape Cod."

I stare out over the park and think about my Grandparents' summer home and the wonderful childhood memories I have of the place. "Well let's see." I hesitated, "It's been so long since I've been there. I think the last time I was there I was ten." I pause for a moment. "That was the year my Grandfather died. Actually we all had thought Grams had sold it years ago. It wasn't until we had the reading of her will that we found out she still kept a couple of her properties."

"So where about on the Cape is it?" Alberto asks.

"It's in the small resort town of Rocky Beach."

"Can't say I know where that is," he says. "I'm not that good at geography. Human anatomy, well that's a different story," he smiles.

"It's not that far from the Cape Cod National Seashore Park." I ignore his attempt at a possible pass. "At the end of a dead end road. I can't remember too much about the house except that when I was younger, Mom and I and my aunts and cousins spent most of our summers there up until Grandpa died. After that we never went back." I stop again and stare out over the park for a long moment. Alberto doesn't ask anything more. "What I do remember about the place is that when I was there it seemed the most fun place on this planet," I continue, "and flying kites. My Grandpa was the best kite flyer I have ever known. He used to take Grams and all us grandkids down to the beach and bring one or two of his kites and we'd have a picnic and fly kites. He and I used to walk out on the beach when the tide was out and see how high we could get one of his kites. Sometimes we would get it so high he'd tell me a story about when it gets that high it meant that it was flying with the angels." I smile as I remember the story. "He used to have me hold the string sometimes when it was out that far so that he'd say, "can you feel the angels pulling on the kite, boy?" That's what he used to called me." I pour the last of the wine into our glasses. "Other than that I can't really remember much about the house. It always seemed so big, but I'm sure that was just a ten year olds' perception."

All the while I'm telling Alberto what I remember about the house, we are oblivious to the last of the sunset. The colours have faded from reds to purples to black, and if the glow from the city hadn't been so intense I'm sure there would have been stars in the clear night sky. As we continue talking, the guests start to leave the party, and soon only Gerry, Troy, Laurel and Josh along with Alberto and myself are left.

"It sounds like you had quite a fun childhood," Alberto says. "It must be great to have memories like that. I grew up on the other side of the tracks. We never had summer vacations to speak of. I'm envious."

"Oh don't get me wrong, I didn't grow up with money. My grandparents had the money. I grew up very middle class. I don't think my mom really wanted money. The only financial help I got from my Grams was with some of my schooling. I was like you, I worked to put myself through school," I say.

"But you had parents who supported you," Alberto says.

Just then Laurel and Josh come out onto the terrace.

"Well you two have talked away the whole evening," Laurel says.

"I guess we did. I didn't realize that it was getting so late."

"Thank god it's Sunday tomorrow. Do you have to work tomorrow Alberto?" she asks.

"Yes I do, but not until four," he answers.

"That's good. We just stepped out to say good night to you two," she adds. She bends and gives me a kiss on the cheek. "I'll talk to you tomorrow Andy. Nice seeing you again Alberto."

Alberto and I say good night at the same time as they leave the terrace arms around each other. I look through the French doors to see Gerry and Troy walk Laurel and Josh to the front door of the condo. I can imagine what the four of my friends are saying at the front door about Alberto and me. They are probably all proud that they were able to find someone that I could spend the evening with, without having to worry about me getting depressed about not being a part of a couple. I guess it worked. I have to admit that it had been quite an enjoyable evening talking with Alberto. I pick up Alberto's plate and walk into the condo. I can hear him get up and follow me in. Gerry and Troy are talking in the kitchen. I can barely make out what they are saying, but by the sound of it, it's about how the evening being a success.

As I enter the kitchen, plate in hand with Alberto right behind me I hear Gerry say, "It was a wonderful party. Everyone seemed to have a good time, and of course Juanita had out done herself with the buffet like she always does."

"Yes it was good," Troy responds.

I put the plate into the dishwasher and say, "Looked like everyone enjoyed themselves tonight."

Gerry looks at me strangely. "What are you growin' on that pretty face of yours Andy Hon?"

Before I can say anything Alberto says, "I like goatees. I think Andy has a great face for a goatee."

"Thanks, Alberto," I say.

"Oh I like them too," Gerry replies, "I just hope with all that blonde hair you have on your head that it doesn't come in red. But of course that'll depend on what the colour of the rest of your body hair is, know what I mean?" He smiles at me and gives my body the once over from head to toe, with his stare lingering a little longer on my crotch.

"Gerry! You're such a pig sometimes," Troy says.

"I agree with you there, Troy."

Alberto takes a step back and edges his shoulder down to Gerry's, while giving me the once over from head to toe and says, "Well, I think Gerry has an interesting point, one I think the government should spend some research money on."

Troy starts to leave the kitchen, "Come on Gerry, I think that's our cue to leave."

"I don't think we have to leave the room just because the conversation has turned to pubic hair," Gerry says in protest.

"Gerry! Come on!" Troy growls and winks at his partner.

"Oh! Oh, I get it." Gerry follows Troy from the kitchen. A moment later we can hear the door to their bedroom close.

"Those two make a great pair," Alberto says.

"They do don't they?" I agree with him.

"So how about one last drink before we call it an evening?" Alberto suggests.

"Only if you're not driving," I say.

"No, I taxied. Med. school hasn't left me much extra cash for a car, and I can get around the city easier without one. I guess I'm going to have to get one before I leave for California."

We both laugh. I reach into the refrigerator and get out another bottle of white wine, which I hand to Alberto. "The bottle opener is on the buffet table in the dining room. I'll get a couple of clean glasses and meet you in the living room, okay?"

Alberto turns and leaves the kitchen. I quickly glance at his disappearing body. I don't know is it just the wine or am I actually attracted to this man. Physically Alberto is nearly perfect. His mulatto colouring is set off wonderfully by the white t-shirt he is wearing. It's tight enough to accentuate his pecs and show his flat stomach. It doesn't look like there's an ounce of fat around his waist. His light brown biceps stretch the sleeves of the shirt just enough to make a snug fit but not enough to cut into his skin. His blue jeans are of the baggy type but they show enough of the shape of his buns to let the viewer know that they are round and firm. The crotch area is hard to tell as his jeans are baggy in the front. But if Alberto was anything like they say these Latino's are, the package is more than likely sizable. I can understand why men like having him around. He is definitely good eye candy, and very intelligent, too. But can he cook? It's got to be the wine I think to myself as I enter the living room. As I go from kitchen to the living room I turn off lights leaving only the lamp at the far end of the sofa. I find him sitting on the large overstuffed sofa facing the windows that overlook the terrace. He is still holding the bottle of wine. I notice that he's just finished wrapping it in a napkin the way that waiters do at restaurants. He gets an ice bucket from the buffet and sets it on the floor next to him. I sit down in the middle of the sofa, just far enough away that we don't make physical contact, but close enough so that if either of us wanted to touch, it wouldn't look obvious and awkward. I hold out the two glasses and he fills them. I sink back into the sofa and take a drink of the wine.

"Gerry has good taste in wine," he comments.

"He's a trained chef, but I don't think he's ever cooked commercially. He met Paul just after cooking school."

"Paul was Gerry's ex?" he asks.

"Sort of I guess. Paul died of sudden heart failure, about five or six years ago. So I don't know if you'd call that an ex," I say. "This is the first time since Paul's death that Gerry has been romantically involved." I pause and then ask him, "So what about you?"

"Me what? Involved romantically?" he asks.

"Yeah, romantically. Do you have someone in your life right now?" I ask him. I feel my face getting hot. Why am I asking him this? It must be the wine, because normally I would never be so forward with someone I barely know.

"No, can't be," he says matter of factly. "With the type of work I do it doesn't seem possible. I can't seem to find a man who is comfortable with their partner being an escort." He takes a drink of his wine. "The longest relationship I've ever had was three weeks, until he found out that I dated men for a living." He takes another drink of his wine. "Don't get me wrong I'd love to be in a relationship with someone. You get tired of the one night stands with people you'd like to have something special with, but you know, as soon as they find out how I earn my living they're gone."

"So what about the men you do date? Haven't you ever gone out with someone that you'd like to get to know and have a relationship with?" I ask him.

"A few times I've come across a guy who I thought would be great to get to know, but they usually have only one thing on their mind. Don't get me wrong sex does play a big part in the escort business, but that depends on the escort themselves."

"I don't understand. What depends on the escort? Sex? Most people who hire an escort are usually looking for sex, aren't they?"

"No, some clients just want company believe it or not. To spend an evening at an event or a movie with someone they consider to be good looking on their arm."

"No sex?" I question him.

"No sex, but then sometimes they want it, and usually they offer big bucks to get it." He pauses as he finishes off his wine and places his empty glass on the coffee table. "Don't forget you don't have to have sex. I think it's easier for a male escort to say no to sex than it is for a female escort for fear of getting beat up. I know I don't have a problem, especially when a guy wants to have unprotected sex. It's simply not on the menu."

Talking about sex and having it with multiple partners brings Rick back to mind; brings back my resolve to never again get that close to another man.

"Now that we've discussed my life, what's going on in yours?" he asks.

"What's to tell? I live a very unexciting life." I give him a short answer hoping he wants details.

"Oh, I'm sure it is," he says with a smile on his face. He reaches over and places his hand on my jaw and gently strokes my face. I let him; it feels good. It's the first time that a man has actually reached out and touched me first. "You're a very good looking man Andy, so you don't actually think I'd believe you when you say you lead an unexciting life do you?" His hand has left my face and is now resting on my thigh.

"I actually do have an unexciting life. I've been so immersed in my relationship with Rick over the last six years that I've forgotten to enjoy life along the way," I say. "If it didn't have anything to do with being a couple I just wasn't interested. You can get Gerry to attest to that."

"Oh come on, you must have had a life outside your relationship with Rick?" I shake my head in disagreement.

"Other than work, the gym and a few good friends, nothing. I didn't think you needed one, a life that is, once you have a relationship you consider to be forever."

"So what happened? With you and Rick, if you don't mind me asking?"

I sit and reflect about Rick for a moment. I can feel the wine. It is making my mind fuzzy. I notice that Alberto moves closer on the sofa. His shoulder is now against mine, his hand still remains on my thigh. I've touched his arm while we were talking. "In a nutshell, I walked in on him and his boyfriend. Simple as that."

"Harsh," Alberto says as he adjusts himself on the sofa so that he is sitting squarely in front of me. He reaches over and strokes my face again with his hand. "I like the feel of your beard," he says. He pulls my face towards his, his lips meet mine. I let a soft moan escape my lips. He presses his lips harder against mine. I gently push him back into his corner of the sofa. I kiss him again. We adjust our bodies to be comfortable. I rest my head on his chest. I can feel the hard muscles of his pectorals under his t-shirt against my cheek. Our arms are wrapped around our bodies. I have his right bicep cupped in my left hand; my right hand is holding his shoulder. I move my body up so that my face is tucked under his jaw. I move my hand and rub it over his chest. I can feel the contours of his pectoral muscles under his t-shirt. His nipples are hard as I lightly caress his chest. His left hand strokes my back, and stops at the waistband of my jeans. I can feel his hand slowly and lightly slide over my butt. Alberto's legs are now on either side of my hips as we lay on the sofa. I can feel the hardness in his crotch on my abdomen as he pulls me closer to him with his hand on my butt. My own hardness is straining the material in my jeans as we press our crotches together. I want to have him but something deep inside me isn't ready.

Without raising my head, but still holding him tight I say, "Alberto, I don't think I can."

"Andy, don't say anything," he says quietly, his free hand stroking my hair. "This is good. It's nice to have someone in my arms that isn't paying for it, someone I like," I hear him say. He is right. It does feel good just having someone hold you. I can feel his breathing get slower as he drifts off to sleep. The last thing I remember is the slow rhythm of the rise and fall of Alberto's chest as he sleeps, holding me in his arms.

"Well look what the wind blew in. How are you feeling Garth?" Marcy says as Garth and Tony enter the front office of Cape Development and Maintenance. She is opening the Monday morning mail. He smiles at her. She's teased him ever since he fell and broke his leg. "There's fresh coffee," she states as she continues to flip through the unopened envelopes. "Oh Tony that glass you ordered from that Boston glass shop came in for the Ayer's place late on Friday. It's in a UPS box in the back office." Tony disappears into the back office and returns with the box. He opens it carefully, removes one pane of glass and looks at it.

"Hopefully they got the measurements right," he says as he takes the ruler from Marcy's desk and starts to measure the piece of glass. "Looks like they got it right," he states.

"Oh, talking about the Ayer's place, here's another letter from that lawyer in Wilmington," Marcy says as she examines a thick legal sized manila envelope. She carefully slips the letter opener into the corner of the envelope and slits it across the top opening the envelope without damaging it's contents. She removes and unfolds the papers and starts to scan them. This catches Tony's attention.

"Well?" he says, trying not to sound as though he expects bad news. "Does it say what is happening to the property?" he asks. Garth steps up and hands Tony a cup of coffee. He places the other on the desk for Marcy, and then sits on the corner of Marcy's desk sipping his coffee.

"Thanks Garth," she says without looking up. "Well, it says here that as of the fourth of July this year the title will convert to Mrs. Ayers' grandson from New York City," she continues to read the letter. "Other than the change in ownership on title nothing else changes for now." She continues to flip the pages back and forth. "Humph, that's less than two weeks, just like your wedding Tony boy," she says to the two men at her desk. "So, talking about July the fourth, how are the arrangements for the social event of the year in

Rocky Beach going?"

Tony hesitates for a moment. Everything will be different pretty much at the same time. He's been hoping the change for the Ayers' place would take a little longer than two weeks. "All the arrangements are pretty much done. Elaine, Mom and Maria have taken care of almost everything already." He seems distant while he is talking about the arrangements for his wedding.

"Boy, you don't sound too excited about your wedding," she remarks.

He brushes it off. "It's two weeks away. You know I don't get too excited about things until the day before."

"If it were me, I'd be bouncing off the ceiling, not like you, more excited about a piece of old glass, must be a guy thing," Marcy says.

"It's not me to get excited about things like flower arrangements and invitations," he says. "That's girl's stuff."

"I thought you liked flowers?" Garth grins.

"Of course I like flowers," Tony says, "but in the ground. And hey, you're supposed to be on my side."

"Marcy, I'm having a rehearsal party on the third, you're still gonna be there to help aren't you?" Garth asks her.

"Oh of course I wouldn't miss it," she says grinning at them. "I wouldn't miss the last time I'm going to see our Tony as a single man," she says. "So am I going to meet your Joey at this rehearsal party?"

"Yeah, he'll be coming in from Boston that evening. He'll be late but he'll be here."

"Good, I can hardly wait," she says.

Tony doesn't say anything. He's been quietly sipping on his coffee, not really paying any attention to the banter going on between Garth and Marcy. He's realized that in less than two weeks almost every aspect of his life would change. He'd be married and would be having a baby. His favourite place in Rocky Beach was changing ownership and would probably go up for sale. "I have to go to the hardware store and get caulking for these panes," he says as he places his mug on the desk, picks up his ball cap and heads out of the front door. Both Garth and Marcy look at him curiously.

"Hey wait for me!" Garth says, as he puts his mug on

the desk and runs out of the office following Tony.

"It's gotta be a guy thing," Marcy says shaking her head, watching the two men leave the office.

The hardware store is just a block away, and Tony has chosen to walk there. His steps are long as he heads towards the store. He hears the door of the office close behind him for a second time and sees Garth coming after him.

"Hey Tony, wait up," Garth says. "I can't go that fast yet." Tony can see that he's right. There's an unmistakable sound of a limp in Garth's walk. He slows to let his friend catch up with him. "What's the hurry?" Garth asks as he reaches Tony's side. "The hardware store will be open all day and we have nothing pressing on our agenda today." He looks at Tony with concern. "Is everything okay?" he asks.

"Yeah, everything is fine," he says. "I just get tired of all the wedding talk." He is being honest about that. He really doesn't care for it. He hasn't felt excited or talked much about his up and coming wedding since it's been announced. "And the Ayer's place changing ownership sucks, too. I guess I just hate to see such a great place dumped on the real-estate market." He sighs, "If I could afford it I would buy it but it'll be out of my price range."

"It's just a piece of property with a house...," Garth starts to say.

"No, it's not just a piece of property with a house. There's something special about the place. I don't know what it does to me but it does something. No other place we take care of does it." He searches Garth's face for a sign that he understands what he is getting at. He doesn't know what words to use to tell Garth how or why the place makes him feel like that. "It's like me saying that your place is just a piece of property with a house on it."

Garth is silent for a moment. "I can understand that, but you really don't have a personal connection with it other than having maintained it for the last eight or nine years."

"That's just it though, I do have this connection with the place, it's just that...," he pauses and then continues to say, "I don't know what it is. The place just makes me feel good, you know." They continue to walk towards the hardware store at a much slower pace more suited to Garth. "I get this feeling that I belong there, none of the other places we maintain gives me that feeling. There's just something special about the Ayer's place."

Garth listens to his friend but doesn't say anything. He can understand Tony's connection with the Ayer's place. He has it with his own property. It's the interest he's not showing about his wedding and his unborn baby that have Garth really concerned. If it were him he'd be excited and probably a lot more involved. It just seems that Tony doesn't really care. Maybe when it gets a little closer he'll show more emotions, like he's showing now about the Ayer's place. The two men enter the hardware store and purchase the caulking they need to fix the windows. They say little as they return to the office parking lot where the big white ford pickup is parked.

Tony tosses the keys to Garth. "I'll get the box of panes and meet you in the truck," he says as he enters the office. In a few minutes he's back. The box is heavy, Garth can tell. The muscles of Tony's arms are pumped as he carries the box to the pickup. Garth reaches over and opens the drivers' side door and Tony slides the box to the centre of the bench seat between them. He starts the pickup, pulls out onto Rocky Beach Road and heads north to the Ayer's place. Both men barely say anything to each other as they drive to the property. Garth watches Tony as he drives the truck down the road. God is he good looking, he thinks to himself. He has a body to die for. Garth tries to look while avoid staring, but he is having a difficult time. He can feel himself starting to get hard. It's a good thing the UPS box is between them. It helps hide the straining material of his pants. He takes a quick check of his crotch and sees a small wet spot on his pants. He adjusted his arm to cover his crotch and the wet spot; he can feel the stickiness on his forearm.

"You know what I like most about the Ayer's place?" Tony finally says to Garth as he continues to stare out the front windshield. "It's such a different style of house for the Cape and it's the most private of all the places we take care of."

The white truck continues down the road. "I guess it's sort of serene, you know peaceful. At least that's how I feel when I'm here." He is silent again and the two continue without saying anything. Five minutes later they arrive at the gates to the property.

"I'll unlock the gates," Garth volunteers, and reaches out his hand to Tony for the keys. Tony takes the ring of keys from the dashboard, flips through them and selects the key that opens the lock on the gate. Garth gets out of the truck, unlocks the gates and opens them wide. Tony watches his friend as he moves in front of the truck. He looks at Garth's body movement. He has a slight limp from his broken leg; his white t-shirt is tight across his chest and shoulders. Tony can see the definition of his friends' upper torso. The looseness of his t-shirt around his waist tells Tony that Garth's waist is slim. He watches the movement of his butt under his baggy green work pants. He stands just out of reach as Tony drives the truck through the gates. As Tony passes the spot where Garth is standing he checks out Garth's crotch. It isn't difficult to notice the bulge and the small wet spot on his pants. Now, as he slowly drives past Garth he can see his crotch much closer. Tony quickly adjusts the growing hardness of his own crotch before Garth gets back into the truck. As Garth closes the door of the truck Tony says, "Too bad the old lady had to die."

"Yeah, it's quite a place," Garth says as Tony drives the truck down the tree lined driveway.

After replacing the broken windowpanes with the new glass from Boston, Tony and Garth sit in the sun on the front stairs of the veranda facing Cape Cod Bay. Tony takes his shirt off and stretches out on one of the lower stairs. Garth leans against the pillar on the top stair of the veranda. He can see Tony's body stretched out on the stair below him. His chest and his flat stomach, well defined abdominal muscles, a slim waist with the small trail of hair leading from his belly button disappearing under his jeans' waist. His narrow hips and thick well-muscled thighs stretch the denim of his jeans. The bulge between his legs looks large. Tony blocks the sun from shining in his eyes with his fore arm. His bicep is large and round; Garth decides that Tony spends a lot of time working on them. The hair under his arm looks damp from either the work or just from the heat of the sun.

Tony's dark nipples almost blend in with his suntanned skin. Shit, he thinks to himself, Tony is probably totally unaware of how much torment he's putting him through laying on the stair like that. Again Garth can feel his cock get hard. He should have worn underwear today, he thinks to himself. At least it would have helped keeping his cock restrained a bit, where as his baggy work pants just let it do its own thing.

"You know when old man Ayer's built this house he planned it really well. It takes full advantage of the sunset over the bay," Tony announces. "The way they removed the trees down to the beach lets the warm southwest winds blow up to the house. And if you noticed as we drove in the old man didn't remove the large oaks and pine trees along the eastern side, instead he just topped the larger ones. That's so they'd still get some morning sun, but it blocks the winter winds from the Atlantic. He planned out the placement of the house to get the most out of Mother Nature."

Garth looks around to check out what Tony is telling him. He strains back to try and see the trees behind the house without getting up and giving away his crotch problem. "You know you're right. I've never noticed these things before."

"Yeah, the old guy was really ahead of his time. Most people who built houses at that time just placed them on the property to get the best possible view of the bay. He didn't. He took all these other things into consideration before he started to build."

Tony lifts himself onto one elbow and faces the beach. This gives Garth a perfect view of Tony's back and butt. Tony's back is broad, well muscled, and darkly tanned. His hairless back narrows to his waist. Garth can see the lower back muscles disappear below the belt line and the roundness of the hard cheeks of his butt under his snug fitting jeans. He's sure Tony could crack walnuts with his butt cheeks. Garth pulls off his t-shirt and places it on his lap to hide the hardness of his crotch and the growing wet spot.

"That sun is sure hot," Garth says, averting his attention away from Tony's body.

Tony rolls back onto his back. "Yeah, it sure is. I like to go down to the beach and suntan there. There's a great secluded part of the beach in between those two large outcropping rocks." Tony points towards the north end of the beach. "If you really want to you can go naked on that part of the beach. You can't see it from the house at all." He pauses for a moment as though he's remembering all the times he has been on that secluded part of the beach with nothing on. "I've done it many a time," he says.

"You really like this place, don't you?" Garth asks. "You have gotten quite attached to it."

"Just look at it. It's the perfect place. End of the road, secluded beach where no one ever goes. A house that's almost immaculate, and hasn't had a human stay in it for years."

"Sounds rather lonely and a bit sad," Garth says.

Tony doesn't respond to Garth's analogy, maybe because it's those things that really make him like this place as much as he does. It could be the reason why he likes coming here because no one else does, a sort of sanctuary for himself. He stands up, faces Garth and stretches. Garth notices the definition of Tony's abs' muscles as he reaches for the sky.

"I'm gonna go down to the beach and take a nap. Do you want to come with me?" Tony asks.

Garth thinks he's gotten a reprieve with the talk of the house and property, now he really doesn't need to go down to the beach and strip naked with this hunk of man. If he thinks he has a problem now, naked on the beach with Tony would be a bigger problem. "Where?" Garth stammers.

"Down on the beach, between the rocks." Tony points to the north end of the beach property where some large boulders obscure the beach.

"I think I'll just stay here for a while, I'm quite comfortable," Garth says.

"Suit yourself," Tony says as he throws his t-shirt over his shoulder, turns and walks down the path towards the beach.

Garth watches his friend as he walks towards the beach. He notices that Tony doesn't have that same spring in his step. Garth wonders if it's the fact that the Ayer's property has changed hands or because of his forthcoming wedding or the baby. Garth knows he really should talk to Tony about it. He continues to watch Tony walk until he finally disappears behind the rocks. Tony is right, you can't see that part of the beach from the house. He removes his t-shirt from his lap so that the warmth of the sun can dry the wet spot on his work pants. Garth closes his eyes, leans his head back and takes a deep breath of the sea air. He continues to let the sun warm him.

Garth opens his eyes. He's lost track of time. He figures he'd been sleeping for about forty five minutes. He looks around the veranda and then looks off towards the beach. There's no sign of Tony. Garth decides that he'd better go down and get Tony. He checks his crotch and sees that the sun has almost dried the wet spot. He gets up and descends the stairs from the veranda and walks along the same path that Tony took to the beach. The marram grass sways in the slight breeze he creates as he walks towards the beach. He's not sure what to expect from Tony when he reaches him. He'll either have left something on or he'll be buck naked laying on the beach in all his glory. Garth thinks that Joey has been back in Boston for too long. Garth finally reaches the beach and finds the path leading to the secluded beach behind the rocks. As Garth reaches the hidden beach he sees Tony leaning up against a large log. To Garth's relief he's still wearing some clothes.

"Hey Tony," Garth calls out, not wanting to catch Tony by surprise.

Tony raises his arm to show Garth where he is. Garth comes up from behind the log, climbs over the log and sits next to Tony. He's wearing his jockey shorts, his long muscular legs are stretched out in front of him. The tide is in far enough that Tony has his feet in the water. Tony's strong arms are hanging loosely by his side, his face is turned up to the sky and his eyes are closed. Garth pulls off his work boots and socks, pulls up his work pants to his knees and puts his feet in the water.

"Water's warm for this time of year," Tony says.

"Is everything okay Tony?" Garth asks. "You don't really seem to be yourself lately."

"Yeah, I guess everything is fine," Tony says, still leaning on the log with his eyes closed. "Yeah, everything is fine."

"You sound a little sarcastic," Garth says. "Hey Tony if I'm outta line you can tell me but does your attitude have anything to do with your wedding and baby?"

Tony doesn't move from his position on the log. He says nothing for a long moment. "I guess it does. I was just sort of hoping that things would have happened a different way, you know what I mean?"

"Sure, I suppose I do," Garth replies. "You mean first the wedding and then the baby."

"I guess that's a simple way of putting it," Tony says. "It just wasn't the way I was planning how my life would go. There's so many things that I'm...," he stops.

"You mean about Elaine and you?" Garth says. "Are you saying that you're not sure about you and Elaine?"

"No, I'm quite sure about Elaine, it's just, oh never mind. It really doesn't matter," he says as he stands up and puts on his jeans. He sits down on the top of the log and wipes the sand off his feet before he puts his socks and work boots back on. "My dad used to say you make your bed you gotta lie in it. So I guess, I've made my bed."

Garth gets up and sits down beside Tony to put his socks and work boots back on. "I guess the shock of everything hasn't worn off yet?"

"Yeah, I guess you could say that," Tony replies.

The two men walk off the beach and up towards the truck parked next to the house. "So are all the plans made for the rehearsal party? Is Joey going to make it back in time for the party or just for the wedding?" Tony asks. It's really the first time Tony has mentioned his wedding without having someone else bring it up first.

"Yes, everything is arranged. It'll be fabulous, just like every other party put on by a fag." They both laugh. "But it's true. Tell me of one party ever arranged by a straight person that was fabulous. Come on you can't. I'm sure the white house uses us homo's to arrange all their events." Again they laugh. Both men get back into the truck and start their way back to town.

I sit, trying to concentrate on the work on my desk. I haven't written anything on the papers in front of me for over an hour. It's three forty in the afternoon and I haven't received any calls all afternoon either. Every time I hear the phone ring I wait in anticipation for the moment when Trish buzzes and says it's for me. Suddenly I hear a voice over the phone.

"Andy? Was that your call from the doctor?" Laurel's voice comes over the phone speaker.

"No, I was talking to Rick," I say back.

"Oh," she says curiously.

"I called him about the letter from the free clinic. You know, to find out where he wanted me to send it," I say.

"And?" she asks.

"He said he's already handled the clinic and for me just to toss the letter." There is a pause before either of us say anything.

"Well! Are you going to give your doctor a call?" she asks. "I don't know how you can sit there just waiting. I'd have called hours ago."

"Yeah, I know you would have. I'm just a bit nervous. I'm not quite sure I want to know."

"We've gone over this before. You know you have to know for your peace of mind."

"Yeah, yeah, I know you're right."

"Okay so I'll hang up and you call. I'll be watching my phone to see your light go on," she says as she hangs up.

I look at the telephone on my desk. Part of me wishes it would ring and another part wishes this whole situation would just disappear. I reach over, pick up the receiver and dial my doctor's phone number.

"Mayfair Clinic one moment please," the voice says. Music starts to play as I am put on hold. Waiting for the voice to return seems like an eternity.

"Hello, Mayfair Clinic, Janet speaking. How can I help you?"

"Hi Janet, this is Andrew McTavich, Doctor Conroy was to call me today with some test results, I was just wondering if he'd received them yet?"

"Doctor Conroy's a bit backed up today, just let me give him a buzz in his office. Will you hold please?" she asks as she automatically puts me back on hold not waiting for me to answer. Again time seems to drag on as the music plays.

"Mr. McTavich?" Janet says.

"Yes?"

"Doctor Conroy is just finishing up with a patient. He says that he'll call you in ten minutes. Are you at work this afternoon?" Janet asks.

"Yes, I'm at the office," I reply.

"Then he'll call you there." She hangs up.

It only takes seconds before Laurel's voice comes over the phone speaker again.

"Well?" she asks.

"Well what?"

"Oh come on Andy you know damn well what, your results?"

"He's gonna call back in ten minutes as soon as he's finished with a patient."

Only seconds later Laurel is in my office. She closes the door.

"He said he'd call you back. Is that good?" she asks.

"I don't know, I hope so," I say. "Actually, I only talked to the receptionist not my doctor."

"I hope so too," she says. "Can I wait here with you? You don't mind."

"I haven't got a thing done all day waiting to hear." Laurel sits on one of the leather chairs across from my desk.

"Yeah me too, I've been a basket case all day." I say as I tap the pencil on the desk. I look at my boss as she sits across from me. She looks very good, even when she's stressed. Me, well I probably look like I haven't slept since the weekend, which I haven't.

"You look like hell," she says to me. "But I like the goatee, it suits you."

"I know I feel like it too." I look into her eyes, ignoring

the compliment about my growth of facial hair. "I thought these few weeks of waiting would go by quickly but they've just dragged. I don't think I've slept since Gerry's party."

She smiles and says, "Yes I've heard about how you slept at Gerry's party. Seems as though you and Alberto looked like a picture from a Steve Walker calendar."

"Who told you that?" I ask. "Anyways nothing went on between us."

"Well, will there be?" she asks

"Will there be what?" I ask her back.

"You know, goings on between you two."

"No, I don't think so. I mean Alberto's a nice enough guy but you know I don't think I'm really his type and anyway it's a bit too soon for me."

She gives me a long look of concern. "Well, it may be a bit too soon right now but I'm not going to let you wallow in it."

She is cut off by Trish's voice, "Andy, there's a call for you on line one."

"Thanks Trish," I say. Laurel sits up in her chair and looks at me. As I pick up the phone she crosses her fingers for good luck.

"Hello," I say into the receiver.

"Hello, Andrew?" comes the deep raspy voice.

"Yes, Hi Doctor Conroy."

"Sorry, I didn't call you earlier today, but we've been swamped here at the clinic. I have your results here." I can hear the flipping of paper from the other side of the phone. "Ah yes, here they are. Normally I wouldn't give these results over the phone." It sounds ominous. "But you've been a patient of the clinic since I started here. Well, let's see." There is another pause as the doctor reads the results of the test. "Everything seems okay no signs of STD's, Hepatitis negative and your HIV test came back negative."

"You're sure?" I ask.

"Well, unless they've made some horrendous errors at the lab I'm pretty sure they are correct. Of course you know you'll need to come back and do a follow up HIV test in six months."

"Of course. Thanks Doctor Conroy," I say as I hang up

the phone.

Laurel has since moved to the edge of her chair and is waiting patiently as I hang up the phone. I get up from my chair and walk behind her to the window, she turns and follows me around the room.

"Well, tell me?"

"Negative," I say to her.

"Oh thank Christ," she says as she gets up from her chair and comes up behind me to throw her arms around me. "Don't you ever go and do this to me again, do you hear me Andrew McTavich?"

"What do you mean? You and Gerry made me go for testing?"

"That's right and like I said don't you ever make me have to go through this again. Do you understand?" she is smiling, tears in her eyes.

"No crying," I say to her. "You'll screw up your makeup."

"It's not my makeup you're worried about," she says grinning at me.

"I don't wear makeup," I say to her.

She picks up my phone and starts to dial. "Who you calling?" I ask her.

"Gerry and Josh. They're waiting to hear." She pauses for a moment then says, "Gerry? Hi, he's negative. Yes, at seven thirty. Okay we'll see you there. Bye."

"What are you two up to?"

"Dinner that's all, a little celebration dinner," she says as she dials another number on my phone. "Josh, Hi, Laurel here, everything is fine. Meet us at seven thirty. Bye." Her phone calls are quick and to the point and obviously pre planned. "I wonder if I should cancel the meeting with Berkwitz and Clarke tomorrow. No, I think we'll just have it after lunch, what do you think Andy?" she asks.

"Do you actually think that by having me in that meeting with Clarke it's going to make any difference?" I ask her.

"You never know until you try," she says.

"Clarke is such a homophobe that he'll never agree to having me as a senior partner, no matter how much business I drag into this firm every year," I say.

"Just maybe if we talk dollars and cents he'll see that

it's important we make you a partner. He understands money really well."

"I think he'd understand better if I wore a skirt and had boobs," I say to her. "Look, I really don't think he's going to go for it Laurel."

"We'll see," she says confidently. "I wish I had some dirt on him."

"I don't want a partnership if you have to blackmail him into it."

"It's not blackmail. We call it office politics," she smiles. "Unfortunately I don't have anything to pin on him."

"Good, I'd rather make partner through my ability to be good at what I do rather than have a deep dark secret about another partner."

"Oh you're no fun!" she giggles. "Let's leave and get a drink across the street at Bailey's."

"Sure, I haven't been able to get anything done all day, so why start now. And it seems I have a dinner date tonight." We both leave my office. Trish is just cleaning up her desk.

Laurel picks up her phone and dials a couple of numbers. "Andrea?" She pauses, "Before you leave could you call Berkwitz and Clarke and change tomorrow mornings' meeting to a lunch meeting?" She pauses again then says, "Yes, that's a great idea. You go ahead and make those arrangements okay, thanks." She hangs up. "I'll just get my purse and we're gone," she says as she walks down the hall towards her office.

"You don't seem to be as tense as you were earlier, Mr. McTavich?" Trish says.

"Yeah, everything is just fine now," I say to her. "Thanks for your concern Trish. And how many times do I have to tell you to call me Andy?"

She picks up her purse and starts towards the elevator. "Good night Andy," she says smiling at me. I watch her as she walks down the hall and disappears around the corner to the elevators, just as Laurel appears at the other end of the hall walking towards me.

As she nears me she says, "So first we go to Bailey's for a couple of drinks. Then you're going to accompany me to dinner at Georgio's."

I put out my arm in a gentlemanly fashion and say, "Shall we then?"

She slides her hand through my arm and giggles. "You know if you decide that now you're not gay...," she starts to say.

"Hey, I thought you already had a man."

"Oh not for me, you snooze you lose bucko, but I do have a few very available friends," she offeres.

"Well, if I can't have you, then there's really no point in being straight." She giggles again as I say that while we walk down the hall towards the elevators.

It's almost twelve thirty and time for the lunch meeting with Berkwitz and Clarke. Any moment now Trish will be buzzing me in my office to remind me. I feel a little apprehensive this morning, not to say a little hung over from last night's celebration dinner at Georgio's. Laurel also has a bit of a headache this morning. Both of us decide at the water machine, that when we do these celebration dinners we're going to have to cut down on the wine. Last night she'd said that she was hoping we'd have to do this all over again tonight if everything went as planned today.

"Mr. McTavich, I mean Andy it's time for your lunch meeting." Trish's voice comes across the speaker on my phone.

"Yes, thank you Trish" I reply. I check myself, tie is straight, jacket hanging on the coat rack is not wrinkled.

Trish looks up from the work on her desk and quietly says as I pass her desk, "Good luck Andy, I hope you get it."

"Thanks Trish," I say as I walk towards the men's room just down the hall from the board room where the meeting will be. As I enter the board room Andrea and Laurel are just going over the small buffet table set up at one end of the room.

"Andy, we're just checking what the caterer has done for lunch. Looks absolutely delicious," Laurel says.

"Afternoon Mr. McTavich," Andrea responds.

"Hi Andrea," I say as I check out the buffet table with

the two women. "Looks fabulous."

"You look a bit flushed Andy," Laurel says.

"Just a bit nervous and a bit hung over. You don't look so..."

"Don't go there Andy," Laurel warns as the door opens and Clarke enters the room.

He walks up to the table and says, "Looks and smells great. Thai. What a great idea Laurel. We haven't had a lunch meeting for quite some time."

"Clarke, you can thank Andrea. Lunch was her idea."

He gives her a nod and puts the folder on the table in the boardroom. He returns to the buffet table, picks up a plate and starts dishing out his lunch. "Berkwitz was just on his way from his office when I left. He had to make a quick call to his wife."

So far he hasn't even acknowledged that I am in the room. I can tell already that this isn't going to go the way that Laurel thought. Andrea picks up a plate and also starts to dish out her lunch. Laurel and I follow their lead and make a short line behind the two of them. I figure that I should say something so at least I won't look like I'm nervous about why we are having this lunch meeting.

"So Clarke," I say. "Speaking of wives, how's Margaret since her operation?" I ask, hopefully coming across as concerned.

"Maggie is doing fine, the plastic knee joint is just what she needed, McTavich." He looks at me with a sort of shocked look upon his face. I guess he wasn't expecting a gay man to actually be concerned about a woman. He returns to the seat at the table where he's placed his folder earlier. The door to the boardroom opens and a bald headed man in a black suit enters the room. He is just finishing up loose ends before he retires next Friday. He's a very nice elderly man. He works hard and pretty much keeps to himself. He never has anything bad to say about anyone. His motto is everybody who has income could be a client. Life here at Pickford, Berkwitz and Clarke is strictly business for him. He conducts himself in that fashion and expects everyone else at the firm to conduct themselves accordingly.

"Good afternoon everyone. Sorry I'm late. I just had to

make a quick call home. Some last minute details for our trip to Europe next week," he says as he walks up to the buffet table. "Looks and smells very good. Let me guess. Andrea this must be your doing today. Good job."

"Thank you Mr. Berkwitz," she replies.

"I knew I should have kept you as my personal secretary. Probably would never have missed my anniversary last year," he says to her with a smile. "I'll just get myself a plate of this wonderful smelling food and we'll get this meeting started." He fills himself a plate and sits down at the table. Laurel is a the head of the table with Andrea on her right, with all her secretary paraphernalia. Clarke is seated across the table from Andrea and Berkwitz is seated next to Clarke. I'm seated next to Andrea across the table from the two male senior partners. There is an empty seat next to Clarke. I figure that it would be best if I didn't sit right next to him. It might make him too uncomfortable. As we eat our lunch we talk about what Berkwitz and his wife's plans for their retirement. We are all envious as he tells us about the house they bought in Palm Beach. After about thirty minutes of light banter about Berkowitz's retirement plans, a young Asian woman enters the room and starts to clean up the plates and cutlery from in front of us and pushes the wheeled buffet table out of the boardroom.

Laurel stands up and says, "There's coffee and tea on the back cabinet so if any of you would like to get yourself a cup do so now so we can get started with business this afternoon." She walks down the length of the table and gets herself a cup of coffee, for Andrea a cup of tea and returns to her seat. The three of us men follow suit, with myself pulling up the rear. I've been included in an increasing number of these meetings in the last two years, but this is the first time that I feel nervous. It could be that the main agenda for this particular meeting is to replace Berkwitz with me as senior partner when he retires next week.

Laurel starts the meeting with a short overview of the firms performance over the last six months. "Business has been very good for the first half of the year. We have increased our client base by twenty percent since January, that's the largest increase we've ever experienced at Pickford,

Berkwitz and Clarke." As Laurel is speaking Andrea is taking notes. She has started the tape recorder to catch anything she misses. "That projects us to three quarters of a million dollars in increased revenue for the year even if we go flat for the rest of the year." She pauses as she flips through the paper placed neatly in front of her. "We have picked up quite a few large firms from the financial district and an enormous number of small businesses."

"Look Laurel," Clarke rudely interrupts her. "Why don't we just get on with what you really are planning for this meeting this afternoon?"

"Clarke you know that all this information is important."

Again he interrupts her, "Of course it is," he says patronizingly. "But this is Friday afternoon. I'm sure that we'd all like to get out of the office at a reasonable time today. Let's just skip all the number crunching. We're accountants we do that all day, so let's just cut to the quick and get on with it."

Laurel is silent for a moment. I can tell that she still has a headache from the night before and Clarke's interruptions are irritating her. "Sure why not Clarke," she says. Andrea continues to write down what is being said at the table. "Well then, as you all know Mr. Berkwitz' retiring next Friday leaves a vacant seat at the senior partner level, and according to the firm's incorporation mandate this position must be filled prior to his retirement. In the past month or so I have brought Andrew McTavich's name forward to fill this position as the only capable..."

"We can shorten this meeting rather quickly," Clarke says, cutting Laurel off. "You know that as senior partners we all have to be in complete agreement about who fills that position and that each of us are allowed by mandate to bring forward any name we feel could and should deserve that position. And as Mr. Berkwitz has opted not to bring forward any candidates he also forfeits his vote as per mandate."

"Thank you Clarke for clearing that up for us." I can sense that Laurel is getting fed up with Clarke by the tone of her voice and the fact that her face has gotten red. By now I can tell where this meeting is going. I'm hoping that Laurel sees it also and cuts it short. "I would like to point out for the record that a major part of the twenty percent increase, as a matter of fact that sixty percent of that increase was done solely by Andrew. And if any member of this firm deserves to be asked to be a senior partner then it's him."

"His numbers are impressive. Let's face it none of us ever came close to increasing the firms business in those proportions." Berkwitz adds. "There also hasn't been any other member of this firm senior or junior who has worked as hard this last couple of years."

"I'm not saying his performance is lacking. We all know that numbers don't lie." Clarke says.

"Well then what's the problem? It's obvious that Andrew is the most likely candidate to fill the up and coming position," Laurel says.

There is silence around the small table. I'm not sure whether this is either a good or a bad sign, but the silence feels worse than death.

"I suggest that we just decide right here and now so that we can get on with our weekend within the next half hour," Laurel suggests.

"It's not that easy," Clarke says.

"What's not easy? We just agreed that Andrew is the most competent person we have to fill Mr. Berkwitz's shoes," Laurel says pointedly.

"She's right Clarke, from a business perspective he's the right man for the job," Berkwitz adds.

"That's where you're wrong," Clarke stares at me. "He's no man, he's just a fucking faggot, a lousy fucking faggot. And if you think that I'll ever allow a fucking faggot to have an equal seat with me in this firm you're all out of your minds," Clarke says. While he stares at me, I can see the hatred in his eyes.

"You mean because he's gay means he can't be...," Laurel starts to rebuke him.

"Yes, because he's gay. He should never be allowed to hold any position of authority or power. He's an abomination to creation."

Laurel and Berkwitz are saying something to him, the voices in the room are getting very loud. Laurel is challenging him, Berkwitz is trying to get him to shut up before he gets himself into trouble. Andrea has stopped writing in her steno pad and is watching the ugly scene unfold in front of her. I watch Clarke spew his hatred for my sexuality and me on the table before the other senior partners and myself and Andrea. His face is red and puffy. I am still seated in my chair; I can feel that I'm gripping the arms of my chair tightly. I'm afraid that if I let go of them I would do something to harm Clarke. That is probably what he wants, then he'd get his way if I hit him. He'd be able to fire me. The next thing I know is I push my chair back and I'm standing at the table. The room is silent. Everyone looks at me.

"Andy are you okay?" Andrea asks.

My fists are clenched. I can feel my temperature rise. I know that my face is probably a deep red. I really should have hit him, but to what end? "Am I okay?" I say back to her. I make eye contact with Laurel. "What the hell do you think? Of course, I'm not okay. I can't believe this." I pause. I scan the others in the room. Andrea is still looking shocked. Laurel is now standing staring at me. Berkwitz is shaking his head, hopefully in disgust. Clarke has pushed his chair back from the table probably in anticipation that I'm going to attack him. I look back at Laurel and lock eyes with her. "I don't need this bullshit," is all I say. Everyone is still staring at me. I stop the tape recorder take the tape and walk out of the room. I can hear Clarke start to say that my kind will rot in hell. Then Laurel tells him to shut up. As I walk down the hall back to my office my mind is whirling. I know he is a homophobe but I hadn't realized that his feelings were so deep that it could be expressed as plain hatred towards me. The man barely knew me the person. There is a silence in the corridor. I'm sure that everyone in the office has heard and is aware of what has just transpired in the board room. No one looks at me as I pass by their desks. I finally make it back to my office and walk right past Trish. It takes her only a moment to get out from behind her desk and to follow me in. She closes the door behind her.

"Andy I'm sorry. The whole floor knows. We couldn't help but hearing it. Their voices, I could hear them all the way back here. I just wanted you to know that they're making a mistake."

"Trish I don't want to sound rude but I need a few moments," I say to her.

"Yes, I understand," she says as she moves towards my office door.

Before she opens the door I say, "Trish. Thanks."

She smiles at me. "Would you like a coffee?"

"No, but thanks anyway." She leaves my office and closes the door quietly behind her. I walk over to the window and stare down towards the street below. I go over in my mind what has just transpired in the board room. I can't believe that in this day and age people can still be so prejudiced. This is the first time in my entire life that I've experienced such overt hatred towards myself due to my sexuality. I've known about Clarke's attitude towards homosexuals but I've always thought he was a businessman first. Boy, have I been wrong about him. I've never expected him to be so vehement about having to work with a gay man. As I stare out of the window to the streets beyond I think to myself that the last couple of months of my life haven't been very favourable. Death, break up, the HIV scare and now this hatred directed towards me personally. I don't know why this is all happening. It's like this is my year when all bad things come together. I can hear the door to my office open and close behind me. I know it has to be Laurel, I knew it would only be a short time before she would come to find me.

"Andy, I'm so sorry. I never intended that to happen," she says sincerely.

"I know it's not your fault," I say. "I never really suspected he was as bad as that."

"He surprised me too," she says. "Are you okay?"

I hesitate for a moment deciding whether or not to be completely honest with Laurel about how I was feeling right now. "Actually Laurel, I'm right fucking mad."

"I don't blame you," she says. "But not so mad as to do something crazy? Right?"

"You mean crazy like quit?"

"Well, I was hoping we wouldn't use that word but I guess you're right."

"I wouldn't do that when I'm angry. You should know

me better than that. It's not the way I do things," I say.

"I know I'd have done it on the spot in the board room if I'd been treated that way," she pauses for a moment, walks up beside me and stares out of the window with me. "So what are you going to do?" she asks.

"I don't know," I say to her. "I need some time. God I've used that line too much lately; first with Rick and now with work. Christ I need to get away."

"Hey what a great idea. Why don't you take some time off? You know, go for a holiday," she says. "Take some time to really reflect."

"Sure, great idea. Just lost my boyfriend, family and friends are dropping dead like flies, one of my bosses hates me so much because I'm gay and I'm going on a holiday. Sure right."

"Look Andy, as your friend a vacation may be just what the doctor ordered. You are right. Your life these last few months has not been exactly peaches and cream so maybe some time away from work and the city would be in order. And as your boss, I don't want to see you leave this firm because of this situation. I consider you to be too valuable."

"I realize that these are not the right circumstances to leave. But how could I or anyone for that matter continue working at a job where you know that your personal life will determine your future?"

"That's why I think time off would be a good thing right now. It'll give you some time to put things back into perspective and not make a decision based on anger."

"I'll give you that," I say to her. "It does make sense but what happens when I come back?"

"I guess that's my job," she says. Both of us are still staring out of the window of my office.

"So you'll take some time then, two, three weeks a month? Your call."

"I can't afford a month and where would I go?"

"Don't worry about the money, you're still on payroll," she says. "Why not go to Cape Cod? You've inherited a place there. Why not go there?"

"Never thought of it. I guess I could, but I have some things that I have to finish up here before I go."

"No, I'll just have Trish bring me up to speed and I'll finish up for you." She puts her arm around my waist and leans her head on my shoulder as we both continue to stare out across the city. "So why don't you just get yourself on your way." I feel her pull me closer with her arm.

I put my arm around her shoulder. We stand there for a few minutes then I say to her. "You know I think I'll do that. I'll go home and pack and then head north."

"Oh please!" she says. "No you won't. You'll go home, wash clothes, make arrangements with Gerry to look after your plants."

"Okay, okay, I get your point. I'll be on the road first thing tomorrow."

"That's more like it," she says as she turns to face me. She is smiling now. "But you have to make me a promise."

"And what's that?"

"That you won't make any hasty decisions about work," she says looking at me square in the eyes. Her green eyes are sparkling. "Promise?"

"Of course I promise."

She smiles at me and gives me a kiss on the cheek. "Good," she says as she hugs me tight. She starts to walk back to my office door. "I'll deal with Clarke," she says as she reaches for the door.

"Laurel, thanks," I say to her.

She stops at the door, turns and faces me. "That's what friends are for Andy."

"One more thing, Laurel."

"What's that?" she asks.

I toss her the tape of the meeting. "Here's your dirt."

She looks at the tape and smiles as she slips it into her jacket pocket. "I'll arrange things with Trish. You just get out of here. Let me know how I can get a hold of you okay?" she says as she opens the door and leaves my office.

After Laurel has left I return to the window and stare out again. She's right, I think to myself. I shouldn't make any hasty decisions, especially in anger, and the more I think about it Cape Cod for a month might be just what I need. I go to my desk and start to look for my day timer. A soft knock on the door and it opens. Trish comes in.

“I hope I’m not interrupting anything but you’ve left this in the boardroom.” She hands me my day timer.

“No, you’re not Trish. I was just looking for that. Thanks.” I start to flip through the pages.

“I hope everything is okay?”

“As good as it’s going to get today.” I look at her. She has a worried look on her face. “No, I haven’t done anything rash, like quit.”

“Oh good.”

“But I am taking some time off. A holiday. I’m going to my place on Cape Cod.” It feel funny saying ‘my place’ as I flip through the telephone number section of my day timer. “Laurel will finish with you, on the accounts we’ve been working on.” I stop at the page with ‘C’ on top and run my finger down the page until I get to Cape Development and Maintenance. I start to dial their phone number. I hope I can get a hold of someone there. It is already after four p.m. on a Friday. They’d probably already gone for the weekend. The phone rings three times and the answering machine picks up.

“Hello, you’ve reached Cape Development and Maintenance. We’re sorry we can’t come to the phone as the office is now closed. Our regular office hours are Monday to Friday eight a.m. to four p.m. daily. To leave a message press one after the beep. Thank you. Beep.”

I press the one on the telephone keypad “Hi this is Andrew McTavich, I’m the new owner of the Ayer’s property in Rocky Beach and I just wanted to let you know that I’ll be in Rocky Beach and am planning to stay at the house next week. I’ll be in touch with you on Monday. Thanks. Bye.” I hang up the receiver.

Trish is still in my office. “Will you be gone long?” she asks.

“Only a few weeks maybe a month,” I say to her. “Don’t look so worried, Trish, as of right now I’m not planning to quit.”

“I just wanted to be sure. You’re one of the best to work for in this firm.”

“Thanks Trish, I think Laurel should give you a raise.” I smile at her as I pick up my day timer and head for the door. "Give Laurel all the information she's going to need to finish up those accounts okay?"

"Of course Andy." She still sounds unsure. "Have a good time." I hear her say as I leave my office and make my way to the elevators. The office staff has long since cleared out, almost all of the desks are empty with the exception of one or two stragglers, and of course Trish. Laurel's office door is closed as I pass by it. I decide that I would give her a call next week instead of stopping in before I leave today. I stop at the elevator doors and push the down button. In a few moments the doors open and I join the half dozen other people already on their way to starting their weekend.

I pull the zipper closed on the suitcases that I've packed. Gerry has convinced me that I might need something a little on the formal side just in case I happen to meet someone. I told him he's too big a romantic, but I pack a light linen suit anyway. I've gone over everything that I think I'll need for a month. If I've forgotten anything, I'll just buy it. It's almost ten a.m. Saturday. I'd hoped that I'd already be on the freeway out of the city, by this time. I figure it would take me four to five hours to get to Rocky Beach. I'm doing things I've never done before, just packing up and taking off. I don't even have a reservation at any place to stay when I get there. This is not like me. Usually I have everything planned down to the smallest detail. But not this time, I'm just winging it. I go into my bathroom and pack up my bathroom stuff into an overnight bag. I look at myself in the mirror and check out my goatee. It has grown in thick and dark. I think it looks good on me. I open the drawer next to the wash basin, take out the suntan lotion, a first aid kit and place them in the bag. There at the back of the drawer is an unopened box of condoms. I pick them up and check the expiry date. Still good for a few months. I toss them back into the drawer and close it. I start to close the zipper on the overnight bag and stop. I reopened the drawer and pull out the box of condoms and put them in the bag.

"What the hell, you never know. I'll be so close to Provincetown, I might just get lucky," I say to myself in the mirror. I slide the drawer closed and leave the bathroom. I pick up the two suitcases and head for the front door of the apartment. After I set them at the door I quickly walk through my apartment to make sure I haven't forgotten anything. It seems weird going on vacation alone, but I'd always gone on vacation alone even when Rick and I were together. In the six years we've been together we only went on vacation once as a couple. I get to the den and notice that I've missed my ghetto blaster and CD's. No point in going to the beach without my music. I pick them up and make my way back to the front door placing them on the floor with my suitcases. On the kitchen counter is a brown envelope. It contains a letter of introduction for me to Cape Development and Maintenance from Melvin Peabody. I'd need that to get the keys to the property. I pick up my bags, walk out into the corridor and head off to the elevator.

I step out into the parking garage under my building. I can feel the coolness of the concrete garage where my jeep is parked. I unlock the driver's door and put my bags behind the seat. I take down the soft top and tuck it neatly into its carrying spot, as the weather forecast is calling for temperatures in the nineties. I've dressed for the drive north to Cape Cod in cut off shorts, white tank, runners, a sweatshirt, ball cap and sunglasses. I reach the metal gates that block the exit to the street. There I tell myself that once I go through that gate I can't turn back, I've made this my point of no return. I push the button to activate the gate. As it starts to rise, sunlight pours into the exit way. It's like there is this whole new world out there this morning, though it's the same street that I go out onto every day. I drive out onto the street and make my way to the freeway.

The sun is already on my back as I take the exit off Highway Number Six to Rocky Beach. The last mileage sign said that it's now just five miles to Rocky Beach. Traffic is heavy, even though this is end of June. The holiday season seems already in full swing. This will be the first Fourth of July holiday weekend I've spent alone in six years. I come up to an intersection and stop. I read the road sign. It reads Rocky Beach Road; under it another sign with an arrow pointing to the right reads Rocky Beach Town Centre, two miles.

I turn right and continue driving down Rocky Beach Road. As I drive into the town of Rocky Beach I try to remember what it was like when I was a kid. The streets are all tree lined with maple and oak. There are overflowing flower baskets on every lamp standard throughout the centre of town. There is a boardwalk along the white sandy beach that skirts the town. There are people walking and sitting at various spots along the boardwalk. Beach umbrellas and people dot the beach. I pull off into a parking spot along the boardwalk and look out across Cape Cod Bay. There are at least a hundred sailboats out on the water. Their colourful sails look spectacular as they tack their way to wherever their destination is. As I sit and watch the sailboats in the bay, I feel a calmness come over me. It is the same feeling I had when I was younger. I decide that this was the best move I'd made all year. I get out of my jeep and walk over to the boardwalk to take a closer look at the beach. It stretches for miles in each direction. I watch the people and children playing or just sitting in the surf, their bodies brown from the sun. I take a quick look at the exposed skin of my own body, I feel so white compared to them. After about fifteen minutes of people watching I get back into my jeep and decide that I should find a place to stay for the next couple of days. I pull out onto Rocky Beach Road and continue to drive. I pull into a gas station and asked the attendant where I can find a place to stay. He tells me that I probably wouldn't get a hotel or motel room until Monday but I could possibly find a spot at one of the bed and breakfasts on Bed and Breakfast Row. He points me north and says that they are all together about a mile down the road. I drive off in the direction he had pointed out, and after a few more blocks of shops and businesses the streets turn residential. Most of the houses are of a cape cod style with the odd saltbox mixed in. The yards are neatly manicured and overflowing with the colour of summer flowers. Soon the signs of the various bed and breakfast establishments of Rocky Beach appear on gates and fences. Their names depict either the geography or the history of the Eastern States. I drive by the Lighthouse Bed and Breakfast, Cape Cod B and B and of course Rocky Beach Bed and Breakfast. All of the places are bedecked with flags, Old

Glory and the Massachusetts state flag were the most prominent. I stop in front of one, which not only flew the red, white and blue but a familiar flag which I didn't think I'd see here in Rocky Beach, a rainbow flag. The carved wooden sign on the fence reads Pilgrim House B and B. I may be assuming too much to expect a gay bed and breakfast here in Rocky Beach but anything is possible. I get out of my jeep and enter the manicured front yard and walk up the stairs to the front door of the Cape Cod style house. There is a sign on the door that reads Welcome to Pilgrim House B and B. If you have a reservation come on in, if you don't come on in anyway and we'll see if we can make room. I walk in the front door. There is a desk set up in the hallway with a bell on it. Above the desk is another sign, which reads, 'This guest house caters to both gay and straight people.' I ring the bell and wait. The walls of the hallway are covered in photos, probably of the owners and guests from over the years. The inside of the house is as neat and tidy as the front yard. I have a good feeling about the place. I can hear someone moving in the house. A couple of doors close as someone approaches the hall where I'm standing. A moment later an elderly lady wearing a large floppy straw hat comes through the white door at the end of the hall way. She moves like she is quite fit for her age. She appears at first glance to be in her late sixties or early seventies. She isn't very tall, maybe just five feet and a little on the chubby side. She is wearing a pink flowered cotton frock that reaches below her knees, and sandals on her feet. She has a smile that looks like it never leaves her face. As she moves down the hallway I can hear the bangles jingle around her wrists. When she reaches me she looks at my face.

"Hello young man," she says. "We're in the back gardening. I take it you're looking for a room."

"If you have a vacancy."

"Of course we have a vacancy. We find room for everyone who comes by," she says still smiling. "Single or double?"

"Single."

"All I have left is a room with a double bed. Is that okay? It's five dollars more a night?"

"That'll be fine," I reply.

"Okay, if you'd just fill out the guest book, I'll get your key and show you your room," she says as she hands me a pen and points to the guest book on the desk.

I fill out the guest book with the information it asks for. After I finish I hand her back her pen and she looks at the book. "Hello Andrew McTavich, I'm Fiona Belmont and welcome to Pilgrim House." She opens a drawer in the desk and takes a key out and says, "Follow me and I'll take you to your room Andy. You don't mind me calling you Andy do you?"

"No, I don't mind." She makes me feel comfortable right away. I follow her down the hall and through the white door at the end of it.

"I gave you the front room on the south end of the house, it has the best view of the bay," she says as we reach the top of the stairs. "So how long are you in Rocky Beach for Andy?"

I had been expecting her to ask that question when I filled out her guest book but before I can answer she says, "This will be your room here." She puts the key in and turns it unlocking the door. Walking into the room I follow her lead. She crosses the room and opens the window. "This room has a wonderful view." She takes a long moment and gazes out the window. She turns and hands me the key to the room. "You'll have to share the washroom with the other guests on this half of the top floor. It's just down the hall second door on you right. I'm sure you have some luggage, so why don't you get it and get yourself settled in. We've got iced tea on the back porch. Once you're settled in, come and join us," she says as she leaves the room. I can hear her footsteps on the stairs as she goes back down.

I look around the room. It is simply furnished; hardwood floors with a round rag rug in the centre of the room, a honey coloured oak highboy commode, and a closet. The double sized feather bed with a thick eiderdown quilt, with a beautiful multicoloured hand sewn duvet cover looks inviting. Next to that a small nightstand with an alarm clock and a lamp. There is an armchair and a small writing table close to the lace curtained window. I take a look through the window. It frames the part of Cape Cod Bay that is filled with sailboats. It is like a living picture. I place my hands on the window sill and take a deep breath. The smell of the salt water is strong as there is a slight warm breeze coming in from across the bay that rustles the leaves of the trees that line the street. I walk out of the room and head back down to the street to get my luggage. As soon as I get myself settled I go back to the main floor of the house and follow the sounds of people to the backyard of Pilgrim House. I walk through the squeaky wooden screen door that leads out onto the back porch of the house. Fiona is seated in a large rattan chair over looking a very English style garden, sipping on a large glass of iced tea and talking. I don't see anyone else in the backyard but her.

"Please join me Andy. Would you like a glass of iced tea? I made it earlier today, and it's a good batch if I do say so myself."

"Thank you, I'd be happy to." I search the backyard to see if I can see anyone else. Suddenly from about twelve feet out in the garden amongst the tall colourful plants and flowers a man stands up. This must be whom Fiona was talking to.

All of a sudden he says, "I told you these Shasta daisies were going to be trouble. They're taking over the whole garden, bloody weeds they are." He has a bit of an English accent but it's not very strong. "Oh hi," he says when he notices me standing on the porch behind Fiona.

"Andy let me introduce you. This is Tim. He's my son's partner," she says matter of factly.

"Hi," is all I can say, I guess I'm sort of taken aback. Tim is tall with a slim build, his skin is darkly tanned and weathered looking. He must have been close to fifty. He is wearing a plaid shirt, with the sleeves rolled up and bib coveralls. I can't see what he has on his feet but by the way he is dressed I'm sure he is wearing gumboots. He is standing in the middle of a huge patch of daisies with a pitch fork.

"Would you like another glass of iced tea Tim?" Fiona asks him.

"No thanks, mum," he says and walks off towards the back of the yard, where a large shed stands, covered in various flowering vines. I watch him go through the wooden door to the shed while Fiona pours me a glass of iced tea.

"Please sit down and join me for a bit Andy," she says.

I sit down in another large rattan chair across from her. Between us the small wooden table holds the tall jug of iced tea and an assortment of glasses. I take a sip from the glass she hands me. "Thank you. It's very good."

"Iced tea is always good to have on a hot day, don't you think?"

I nod in agreement, as I take another sip.

"Tim is very shy. Ever since my son, Henry, died he's turned into a bit of a recluse, hiding out in that old garden shed when guests come out and sit on the back porch." She sighs. "I've told him he has to get on with things but he says he's happy here with me, so I just let him stay around. Maybe one day he'll get over it, Henry's death that is." She looks towards the back of the yard at the vine covered garden shed. She still has that smile and sparkle in her eyes. After a moment she turns to me and says "So Andy, what's your story?"

"Story?" I question.

"Yes, you know, what brings you to Rocky Beach and for how long, you know your story," she says. "Everyone's life is just that, a story. They all have a beginning, climax, hopefully plenty of those," she smirks "and endings just like books."

I sip on my iced tea and as I place my glass on the table between us I say, "My story? I really don't think my story is very interesting."

"That's what every one thinks about their lives, but every life is full of stories that are all interesting. Everyone's story is just as individual as the individual telling it, or rather living it." Her eyes twinkle. "And just like stories, life does have those boring parts. They seem to be fillers until we get to the next exciting part. So go on, tell me your story."

"Well let's see, how 'bout it starts with why I'm here in Rocky Beach." Fiona nods and smiles. She sits back in her cushioned chair as I start to recall the events of the last few days of my life. As I tell my story the events unfold backwards to my friend Gord's death of Aids. We sit and talk for hours on the back porch. During my story telling Tim comes by a few times and listens in. He'd either sit just out of my visual range or in the shadows in the back yard. At one point he brings out another jug of iced tea and a bowl of gazpacho and a plate of sandwiches. He lites candles along the porch as it gets dark. The candle flames dance in the slight breeze. As we talk about the events of my life of the past four months she asks questions, but all of her questions are not about the events themselves but more about how I felt or was feeling about them.

"I guess I've reached the place where I figure I'm travelling the road of life alone. At least that's the way I want it for the moment. I really don't think I can trust another man, especially right now." I tell her.

She sits there in silence for a moment then says, "I take it that you're a man who believes that trust, along with love, are the foundations of a solid relationship."

"Aren't they?" I reply.

"Why of course they are," she says. "But by the sounds of things you're ready to write everyone off because you think you're not going to be able to trust anyone again. Don't forget that people are not perfect. They have flaws and believe it or not they make mistakes. It takes a lot of love to forgive and carry on."

"Do you think that's really true?" I ask her.

"Of course I do," Fiona says sincerely. "Of course I do, I think that's what makes our lives and the relationships we have during our lives so interesting. So don't go off living your life in a way that wouldn't permit someone to enter it and give you and that someone happiness, even if it is for a brief time. We all deserve to be happy."

I observe the elderly woman sitting across from me on the porch and think to myself, could she be right, am I so rigid about the way I think about relationships because of the way my one and only serious relationship ended? "I'm sure you're right about people deserving to be happy, but I'm not so sure that I haven't already used up my quota of happiness."

"That's where you young people are wrong." She smiles, "You all think that because you've had one or two relationships that go sour that you're destined to live your lives alone. That happiness will always avoid you." We both sit in silence for a few moments then Fiona says, "Some advice, Andy, not that you have to take it or even believe it, but don't close the door on people just yet, keep yourself open to love and you'll find that you can trust again."

"You really think so?" I ask her.

She just smiles at me, "Of course I think so. Your story is interesting and I can tell by just sitting here talking to you these past few hours that you have a lot to give and of course a lot of love in you. I'm sure that you'll find someone to share that with one day. Who knows maybe that's why you're here in Rocky Beach."

"Now you're talking predetermined destiny. I really don't believe that everything is already set out before us and we just travel life's road and take whatever it hands us as we go along. I think we make things happen in our lives."

"I don't agree with that completely. I think that our roads are planned but the choices we make along that road are our own. Sometimes we make the right choices and other times we miss them, and our road changes direction, but as we travel it those same choices are offered time and time again until we make the right one. Let's say we are going down the road of life and we say that happiness for example is not on our dance card every time we are in a relationship, that doesn't mean it's avoiding us, but that we've just taken a slight detour off the road and eventually the path will cross the right road again and if we're traveling our path with our eyes and soul wide open we'll see the right way to go."

As we sit and talk on the porch I realize that I'm telling a complete stranger all the details of my life, but I don't feel uncomfortable doing it. There is something special about Fiona Belmont. I know what Fiona is saying holds some truth, I'm just not sure that it relates to me. At one point during my story telling I say to her, "You must be an analyst."

She replies by saying, "Analyst.? I've been called that before but I don't claim to be anything like that. Most people just call me either crazy or eccentric. Maybe I'm a bit of both and maybe a little bit of a backwoods analyst, if there is such a thing. But I make no claims to anything other than just being a good set of ears for listening."

Soon darkness covers the whole backyard except for the candles on the back porch. The back garden shed has almost vanished from view. I can barely see its outline in the darkness. The breeze has nearly died away and the candle flames barely flicker. The scents from the night flowers are growing stronger. Fireflies dance under the trees and in the vines that line the back of the property. I can hear the sounds of the other guests as they enter the house. Some laughter and the sounds of footsteps ascending the stairs drift across our silence.

"It must be getting late," I say.

"Oh yes, it's just after eleven," Fiona says as she looks at the watch locket she has around her neck. "So you'll be here at Pilgrim house till Tuesday, I presume?"

"Yes, Tuesday at the earliest. Monday I'll go into town and see the people at Cape Development and Maintenance and arrange to have the house opened up and cleaned. My stay with you will depend on how quickly that we get that done. Is that okay?" I ask her.

"That would be just fine," she says with that same smile on her face. She looks at her locket watch again. "Oh I must go to bed now, six o'clock comes really early." She gets up and gathers the pitcher of iced tea and glasses onto the tray Tim left behind. After she finishes tidying up the porch she makes her way into the house. "Make sure you're down for breakfast between eight and eleven. Tim does a fabulous breakfast. He'd learnt all his cooking skills from my son Henry, before he died. Be so kind as to blow out the candles before you retire," she says as she leaves me sitting alone on the back porch. There is a calming silence over the back yard. Slowly the backyard recedes into total darkness as the diffused light from the upstairs windows are turned off. Now the only illumination in the back yard comes from the candles and the fireflies in the trees. The darkness is very peaceful, away from everything hectic on the other side of the house. I get up, blow out the candles and enter the house through the back screen door and quietly make my way up to my room. When I get into my room I notice that the lamp on the nightstand has been turned on, the bed has been turned down, a fresh set of towels has been set out on the foot of the bed. I go to the window and look out across the road to the bay. It is very quiet and dark, not like the city. The only sound is the sound of the waves crashing gently on the beach. There is no traffic noise, no sirens, just the sound of the waves. Quite peaceful. I return to my bed and undress. I decide to leave the window open for the night as I slip between the sheets under the eiderdown quilt. The sheets are cool next to my naked body. I turn off the lamp and let the waves lull me to sleep.

Monday morning comes quickly. I'm the only person staying at Pilgrim House Sunday night, as all of the other guests have left. I finish dressing after my shower and make my way down stairs to the dining room to find Fiona sitting in her spot at the head of the dining table sipping a cup of tea.

"Good morning Andy. How was your night?" she asks as I enter the sunlit room.

"I've never slept so soundly in years."

"Good. Please sit, Tim has made eggs benedict for us this morning. They should be ready shortly," she says as she pats the chair next to her. "You're off to Cape Development this morning?"

"Yes, I should get started getting the house ready for me to stay in. Not that staying here wouldn't be just as fine," I say.

"Why thank you," she says as the door to the kitchen swings open and Tim comes out with two plates for us. "Looks and smells wonderful Tim," she says.

"Thank you Tim," I say to him. He avoids my gaze as he retreats back into the kitchen without saying a word.

"Rocky Beach is a very pretty place," I say as I start to eat my breakfast. "I spent most of yesterday exploring the town. There's some really neat shops and eating places."

"Oh yes we do have our fair share of them don't we," she says. "Oh, I took the liberty of going through my old photos and I found a few of your Grandparents from a long time ago." She hands me a couple of old black and white photographs. They are of Grams and Grandpa at a fair.

"Those were from the nineteen fifty nine town fair, I believe. I think that was when your Grandfather took up flying kites. We had a kite flying competition at the fair that year."

"You knew my grandparents?" I ask her.

"I only knew of them, I worked part time at the Rocky Beach Bulletin for a couple of summers and did some photography work. Part of my job was to get pictures of the local celebrities. I think that year your Grandfather actually won the competition, so he was a very popular man in town. I have photos of lots of people from nineteen fifty nine and sixty, I kept the photos that weren't used in the paper."

"I find that really interesting." I smile at her. "I think one day I'd like to hear your story." She smiled at me, says nothing but continues to eat her breakfast. We both finish our breakfast in silence. Hopefully I haven't offended her by asking to hear her story.

"What I do know of your Grandparents is that he was the best kite flyer on the Cape and that he had quite a collection of kites. It was said that he had kites from as far away as Japan and that he even made his own. We always knew that the Ayer's were here when there were kites in the sky. I used to sit on the beach with my husband and we'd watch them fly high in the sky on summer afternoons. They looked wonderful, way up there dipping and diving and then climbing high again."

I could remember them doing that. My Grandfather was very good at making them do just that. Grams would sit on her blanket and give my Grandfather directions as to what she'd want the kites to do. He'd always say 'give me something more difficult Alice' and she'd try hard to give him some kind of configuration to do in the sky. Every time he'd pull it off without having to try a second time Grams would laugh and then clap as he completed the task set before him. My cousins and I used to watch in awe as he performed these tricks with his kites. We all thought that he could do magic, but he said it was the angels that helped him, and way back then we believed him.

"My grandfather was very good at flying his kites. He used to tell us grandkids that it wasn't really him but the angels that helped him make the kites do those tricks in the sky. I guess he didn't want to admit that he had a real talent for flying kites."

"Oh do I sense a little disbelief?" she says.

"You mean in the angel part of the story. I think it was just a good story to tell us grandkids."

"Could have been just a story, but he may have actually believed that his talent came from above. It wouldn't be such a bad thing to believe in now would it?"

"Angels?" I questioned. "I know that I may sound a little sceptical but I guess I do have a hard time believing in them. Do you believe in them?"

"It doesn't matter whether I believe in them or not, but whether you do," she says, not really giving me an answer to my question. She glances out through the dining room window across Cape Cod Bay. "Now all they ever have are sailboat races on the bay. No one flies kites anymore." She sounds a bit sad. "But the sailboats are pretty out on the bay."

I check my watch. "I guess I should be going. I don't want to leave this too late. I'm hoping I can get an extra set of keys to the place and take a drive out there this afternoon. Are we still on for dinner tonight? My treat. All you have to do is pick the spot."

"Of course we're still on for tonight. I never pass up being seen in town with a handsome man." The twinkle returns to her eyes and voice as I excuse myself from the dining table.

I drive the short distance along the beach into Rocky Beach town centre. Yesterday I had found the office of Cape Development and Maintenance so it is easy getting there this morning. I pull into a parking spot almost in front of the office, get out of my jeep and enter the building. There is a young woman sitting behind a desk. As I enter the room she looks up and greets me.

"Good morning, how can I help you?" she asks.

"Hi, I'm Andrew McTavich. I called on Friday and left a message about the Ayers' place."

"Ah Mr. McTavich, I'm Marcy Proust. Yes, got your message this morning. We have all the papers from your lawyer Mr. Peabody, I believe. I just wish you had given us a little more notice about your arrival. We could have had your place ready for you when you get here, instead of you having to stay at a motel."

"That's quite all right. It was really a spur of the moment kind of decision to come here, so if the place isn't ready that's fine. I'm staying at a quaint bed and breakfast here in town," I say. "And I'm sure it'll probably take the better part of the week to get the house into some decent shape, since no one has been there for years."

"Actually Mr. McTavich..."

"Please Ms Proust call me Andy."

"Sure Andy, only if you call me Marcy."

"Agreed," I say. "You were saying?"

"Actually the house is in extraordinary condition. It just needs a good cleaning and the furniture uncovered and checked and a few things like the plumbing and electrical systems checked. You should be in before the holiday weekend starts."

"That quickly."

"Yes, your grandmother...Oh I'm sorry."

"That's okay there's no need for an apology."

"As I was saying your Grandmother made sure that the property was well taken care of. Cape Development and Maintenance is one of the best property management companies here on the Cape." She gives me the sell. "So if you'd like you could go and inspect the property to see if there is anything special you'd like us to handle for you?"

"What I came for this morning was to find out whether you could arrange for cleaning and whatever needs to be done. But I guess I should take a look at the property first."

"Well, I have taken the initiative this morning to arrange for cleaning and the inspections. Cleaning will take place tomorrow and inspections tomorrow afternoon. Is that okay?" she asks "Our man Tony diMarco will be in charge of anything that needs to be replaced or repaired. He's very good."

"It seems as though you've got things under control," I say. "Are there papers that I have to sign or anything?" I ask.

"Well, I hope you don't think this sounds a bit suspicious, but I'll need to see some identification before I give you the extra set of keys. Your lawyer gave us some so that we could match, but you know how things are now a days. One can never be too careful."

I pull out my wallet and ask her what she needs, a drivers license, social security card? She says she needs them both which she checks with some papers she has in a file on her desk. Then I hand her the brown envelope that contains the letter of introduction.

"Oh good, I was beginning to wonder whether you had that," she says. "Mr. Peabody's instructions were very clear, that I was not to give the keys to the property to anyone who didn't produce this letter," she says as she opens the letter and quickly reads it and again checks with another sheet of paper from the file. Then she places the letter of introduction in the file, reaches into her desk, pulls out a single key, moves towards a cabinet against the wall and unlocks it. She retrieves a ring of keys and hands them to me. Three of the keys are labelled, front gate, front door and basement door.

"There's quite a few keys on that ring and I'm not sure exactly what they are all for except the marked ones," she says. "If you'd like I could have someone meet you there this afternoon? I'm not quite sure where Tony is at the moment, but I'm sure that at some point he'll be by and I could send him there to meet you."

"No thanks, I'd like to just go out by myself and nose around."

"That'll be fine. You said that you're staying at a bed and breakfast here in town. Do you mind me asking which one in case we need to get a hold of you?"

"I'm at Pilgrim House."

"Nice spot, I'll get their number from the phone book if I need to," she says as she writes down Pilgrim House on a small sticky pad and attaches it to the file on her desk. "Will you be staying long, Andy? When you're ready to leave we'll handle the lockup for you."

"I'm not quite sure how long but at least two or three weeks, maybe a month." She is very good at the sell. I guess the property management business must be quite competitive here on the Cape. "I'll keep you informed Marcy, and thanks for all your help. I'm sure you'll be hearing from me soon," I say as I leave the office. I'm just about to cross the street to where my jeep is parked when I hear the office door open behind me and Marcy's voice call my name.

"Andy," she calls "Do you have directions to the house?"

"No, I was going to rely on childhood memory to get me there."

"I've drawn a rough map for you." She waves a piece of paper. I return to the doorway and she hands it to me.

"Thanks."

"I wouldn't be doing my job very well if I let a client just drive around Rocky Beach trying to find their home, now would I?" she smiles.

"Thanks again Marcy, I guess I owe you."

"How about coffee sometime?" she says. I'm taken by surprise, I guess I don't look as gay as I thought I did, or maybe she's just not that aware.

I'm lost for words. I really don't know quite what to say. It's been decades since I've been asked out by a woman. So I say, "Sure, we should do that." Trying not to commit to anything too concrete. "You know where to find me," is all I can say as I make my way across the street to my jeep. I'm sure that I'll be able to find a way of not actually going through with a date with her. I pull away from the curb and pull a u-turn on the street heading back north towards the property. Marcy is still standing in the doorway of the office. She waves. As I drive north I quickly read the directions on the paper Marcy gave me. North on Rocky Beach Road past all the B and B's keep going until you come to the end of the road. There you are. Call me, with a phone number. I think she wanted me to have her number instead of the directions, which are so simple she could have just pointed. I continue to drive down Rocky Beach Road and past the numerous bed and breakfasts that line the road along the beach. Soon they give way to larger private properties. It takes only about ten minutes before the road stops at wrought iron gates attached to large stone pillars on each side. There, on a weathered brass plaque on the left pillar, Ayer, fifty nine ninety five Rocky Beach Road in large letters and numbers. I get out of the jeep and take the key marked front gate, place it in the lock and turn. It turns easily. I push the gates open and secure them so that they don't swing back onto the jeep when I drive through. I look down the long driveway and get shivers down my back. It's been almost twenty years since I've been here. I hoped it is like I remember it. I get back into the jeep and drive down the tree lined driveway. Around a last corner and I'm up to the house. It is just as I remember, except it doesn't look as big as I thought it to be. I guess that's the child's perspective of things remembered from the past. The exterior looks just as though I have stepped back in time. It has obviously been well taken care of. The trees and bushes around the property have grown thick. These were places where my cousins and I played, but by the looks of how thick and over grown the bush has become over the last two decades a child could never play in them now. They look as though they have been controlled in some fashion so as to not over take the lawns around the house which seem to be in great condition. By the looks of things around the house, Cape Development and Maintenance have obviously been true to their word about being one of the best property management companies around. They obviously care about what they do. I wander around the house seeing all the places where as a young boy I used to play hide'n seek with Trish and Em. Places we pretended were our castles and where dragons and pirates were slain. I find the spot where one summer we started to build a tree house, now all that remains are a few boards nailed into tree trunks, all overgrown with vines and bush. When I finally reach the front of the house facing the ocean, the memories came flooding back. I remember the rock outcroppings. We weren't allowed past those rocks alone until we were ten years old; Grams said that was because she could not see us when we went behind the rocks. Grandpa always said that an ogre lived there that ate children but only children that were younger than ten years of age, because children under the age of ten were still young and tender. We all believed him. I don't think that any of us ever went behind those rocks until we were old enough not to be eaten. I slowly walk towards the beach along a worn path bordered with long marram grass gently swaying in the breeze. When I get to the place where the grass gives way to the sandy beach I turn and look back at the house. It looks grand, framed in blue by a cloudless sky, just as I remember it. It feels like I've come home. I return to face Cape Cod Bay. It is Monday afternoon and the bay is full of coloured sails. I check the sky. Mrs. Belmont was right, no kites. I continue my walk on the beach, past the rock outcroppings into the secluded spot where my childhood ogre lived. Again I turn back to look at the house. This time it has disappeared all except the top of the roof. A person would have to stand on the rail of the top floor balcony to see anything in this spot between the rocks. I turn, and make my way back to the house. I see only one set of footprints in the sand. All of a sudden I feel terribly alone. I wonder if I will ever share my life with another person again. As I climb the slight hill back to the house I can see the large veranda that crosses the front of the house. We used to spend hours playing on it, have ourselves wrapped in towels, having hot cocoa after a swim in the bay. I can remember the time Em had fallen down the veranda stairs and we had to take her to the clinic to get stitches. She was so angry that she couldn't go swimming for a week until she had her stitches removed. I can feel a smile grow on my face as all of these memories come swimming back into my mind. I have to agree that the time I've spent here, as a kid has been good. It was a good idea to come here for a vacation. I jingle the keys as I search for the one labelled front door. After opening the door and stepping inside more memories come back. Inside, the rooms look a lot smaller than I remember, but the details are all the same. Hardwood floors, wooden banister leading upstairs to the bedrooms and bathroom, the wide open space that is the living room, lined with French doors that lead out onto the veranda. Through a French door at the other end of the living room is the dining room with the kitchen behind it. Grandpa's study, with its set of French doors that goes out onto the veranda is on my right before the stairs. As I walk across the floor into the living room I notice the amount of dust that I'm disturbing as I move. No one has been in here for years. I feel rather sad that we've never used this place after Grandpa died. I guess it held too many memories for Grams. After I tour the bottom floor of the house I make my way upstairs to the bedrooms. If I remember correctly there were five at one time, but Grandpa had the one at the very top of the stairs converted into an indoor bathroom. After checking out the smaller bedrooms, I proceed to the large bedroom that was my Grandparents room at the front of the house facing the bay. That is the room with the balcony. As a child I think I was allowed in it only once when Grandpa had taken ill. When Grams had taken Grandpa to the hospital in Boston the next day, we all went with her. That had been our last visit to the house. I open the door to their room and walk in. A small swirl of dust floats into the room from the movement of the door. The furniture is all still there, all covered in heavy canvas securely wrapped. I move to the balcony door, unlock the latch and step out onto it. The view of the bay is spectacular. I stand and watch the sailboats float by in the bay. This would be a great place for a telescope. As I stand and stare out across the bay I hear the sound of a vehicle coming down the driveway. From this part of the house it is impossible to see who's coming. I return to the main floor of the house, remembering now that I have left the gate at the road open. It could be anyone. As I reach the front door and quickly insert the key to lock it I notice that the vehicle is a big white truck. I walk around the veranda towards where the truck would park next to my jeep. The writing on the door of the pickup, Cape Development and Maintenance in red lettering is reassuring. I feel a sense of relief come over me. A man gets out of the truck. He is thirtyish, very good-looking, dark complexion, quite muscular, by the look of the way his work clothes fit. Marcy probably has sent someone to check the place to meet me.

"Hey!" I yell from the veranda. "Hi!"

The man looks up at the veranda and waves at me. He goes up the stairs by the side door to the house and walks towards me. Now that he's closer I can see that he's of Italian descent and extremely good looking. He must be Tony diMarco; the guy that Marcy said would be out.

"Hi," I say as he approaches me, "I'm Andy McTavich, you must be Tony. Marcy said that she might send you out."

I reach out my hand to shake his.

"Hi," he says, somewhat on the cool side. "Yeah, Marcy said that you'd probably be here, so I thought I'd come out and show you around."

"That's okay, it's just as I remember it. I used to summer here when I was a kid," I say. "It's pretty much the same as it was twenty years ago. Looks smaller than what I remember but I'm sure that's just the way things look to a kid."

"So you've been through the house already?" Tony asks.

"Yes, and I've walked around the grounds and everything looks as though it's in prime condition."

"The old house has faired well. We only had one mishap over the last few years, a few broken panes of glass during a late spring storm. But we sourced some antique glass panes out of Boston so that all the windows would still look the same," Tony says as he sits down on the veranda railing. "So are you planning to sell the place?" Tony blurts out.

"Sell the place? I really hadn't thought about it, but I guess it's a possibility."

"Should fetch you pretty good coin, given the condition of the place and the area. It's not your typical Cape Cod house," Tony says coolly. "And the beach is great."

"Sure, I guess." I sure hope this guy Tony doesn't treat all Cape Development and Maintenance's clients this way. Mind you he's real nice eye candy, I think to myself. "Right now I'm just here for a few weeks for a vacation." I figure that he doesn't need much more information than that. Selling the place hasn't really crossed my mind, especially since the house has come with a small maintenance fund to keep it running and maintained for a few years yet.

"Marcy has arranged for a cleaning crew to come in tomorrow morning and after they're done I'll do an inspection on the electrical, plumbing and go over the furniture. If there are any repairs to be made I'll contact you and we can make whatever repairs you'd like to have done. Marcy says you're staying at Pilgrim House, is that right?" Tony asks.

Boy, Tony is strictly business. "Yes you can reach me there."

"Good Mr. McTavich, we should have you in the house by Thursday, at the latest." He makes his way back to his pickup truck. "Don't forget to lock up the gates at the road, you never know now a days." He stops and turns "If we don't get all the repairs that need to be done by the weekend, I'll have another maintenance man finish up. I'm on holidays starting this weekend."

"Hey no problem," I say, and I mean it, with your 'too business attitude' towards me I think I'd rather have someone else a little more pleasant, but hopefully as easy on the eyes as he is. I watch him walk towards his truck. He has broad shoulders that stretch his shirt to the limits. I'm sure if he flexed his back the shirt would come apart at the seams. His shirtsleeves are rolled up past his elbows. The muscles of his forearms are well defined, probably a good sign that the rest of his body is in the same well defined shape. His green work pants fit snugly in all the right places. His butt cheeks move up and down with each step he takes towards his truck. He finally reaches his truck and gets in. As he drives away I give him a quick wave that he returns and then drives away and disappears down the tree-lined driveway.

Tony reaches the gates at the end of the driveway. Shit, he thinks to himself, am I ever a jerk. I hope he doesn't think I'm that way all the time. As he drives down Rocky Beach Road towards town, he knows he owes Andy an apology for his attitude that afternoon. He knows he was a little tenser than he should be, but that's because of his wedding this weekend. Andy McTavich shouldn't have borne the brunt of the tension he's feeling right now. While he is driving into town he thinks about the man who has inherited his favourite place on the Cape. He seems rather young to be taking over the family vacation home, but then stranger things have happened. He seems pleasant enough, for someone coming from a wealthy family. Funny, he noticed Andy had a goatee. For a blonde man it either grew in very dark or he dyed his hair blonde. Anyway, it looks good on him. Other than that Tony has paid little attention to Andy physically. Normally he takes good physical stock of his clients. He figures if they spend the time and money on making sure that they are in good physical shape they usually have no problem about spending the money to take care of their vacation home. He realizes that he's missed an opportunity to make sure that if Andy didn't sell the property that Cape Development and Maintenance, and of course himself, could continue to have the Ayer's property on their list of homes to manage. As he drives into town he wonders to himself if he should go back out to the place and apologize. He pulls into one of the parking stalls behind Cape Development and Maintenance's office.

"No, he'll be around for a couple of weeks, I'll just make sure that I apologize before my vacation." Tony says out loud to himself.

"Who you talking to?" comes Garth's voice, who is just leaving the office by the back door.

"Ah, no one, just thinking out loud," Tony replies. "Got time for lunch?"

"Sure," Garth says. Tony gets out of the truck and both men walk down the street to his mother's restaurant.

I get back into my jeep after I've locked the gates to the property and start the short drive back to town. I have spent a large part of the afternoon taking a good look at the condition of the house and the property. There shouldn't be much in the way of repairs to be made. I spent some time looking under the heavy canvas' that covered the furniture. Only a couple of the cushions on the living room sofa need to be recovered, so if the inspection on the electrical and plumbing are fine then I should be in by Thursday morning. I feel quite excited about the prospect of getting into my childhood vacation home. What I do need at the house is some patio furniture. I hope that there is a place in Rocky Beach where I can find some. I'll make that a project for myself tomorrow while the house is being cleaned. I want to be at the house while the inspections are being done. I drive to Pilgrim House, open the front gate of the B and B and notice that Tim is working on the front flowerbeds. He looks up at me, nods a greeting but says nothing and returns to his chore. I enter the front door and head directly to the back porch where I find Fiona sitting in her big rattan armchair. She is wearing a fabulously coloured cotton sundress and a big floppy white straw hat, with a scarf matching her dress wrapped around it. She is sipping on a tall glass of iced tea and reads a magazine. She has that smile that never seems to leave her face.

"Fiona? Would you mind if I make a long distance call to New York City?"

"No, that'll be okay. We just take an imprint of your credit card to pay for it when the charges come in."

"Thanks."

"Then, if you have time come sit and have an iced tea with me."

"Sure," I say as I walk back into the house and through the solid white door back into the front hall. On the small desk in the hall is the telephone. I pick up the receiver and dial the office phone number.

"Pickford, Berkwitz and Clarke, Andrea speaking, how may I help you?"

"Hi Andrea."

"Hi Andy, how's your vacation?" she asks.

"Great so far, Cape Cod is absolutely beautiful."

"I'm envious. Would you like to speak to Laurel? She's got a client, but she said if you called I was to interrupt her. So just hold for a second." I hear the click of the hold button and the piped music starts to play. In seconds Laurel answers the phone.

"Hi Andy," she sounds excited. "I was hoping I'd hear from you today. How's everything?"

"Just great. I just wanted to let you know how to get a hold of me if you need to." I give her the phone number of the Pilgrim House and of Cape Development and Maintenance. "The house is in great shape. It's just like I remember it from when I was a kid."

"So then maybe we'll all come out there sometime this summer for a weekend getaway or something?" she suggests.

"Sounds like a plan," I say.

"Andy, about Clarke the other day," she starts to say.

"Laurel, why don't we talk about that when I get back, okay? When I got here it felt like I left all of that garbage back in the city. For the next few weeks I don't really want to have to deal with it."

"Really, Andy?" she questions.

"Really."

"This doesn't sound like the Andy I know. Normally you'd stew over something like this for at least a week."

She's right. Normally I would stew over something like that for a while. "Yeah you're right. Must be all the fresh sea air," I reply. "I've got to go. Say hi to Josh and Gerry for me. Love you and I'll talk to you sometime next week. Okay?"

"Okay Andy, love you too and I miss you," she says as I hang up the phone. No matter how the situation with Clarke works out it really won't make that much of a difference. I return to the back porch and join Fiona for an iced tea.

"You're looking rather summery," I say to her as I sit down across from her.

"Why thank you. It's an old outfit I thought would be just right for today," she says with that marvellous smile and twinkle in her eyes. "And you're also looking fine today yourself. Is there something going on that we should know about? Another part of your story perhaps?"

"Actually, I guess there is. I've been out to the property and it looks great." I sound like an excited child after a first visit to the fair. "Being there brought back so many good memories."

"That's good," she says as she fills her glass and another for me.

"I've been giving some of the things we talked about the other night some thought. I've come to a conclusion about a few things about myself. I hope you don't mind me sharing this with you?"

"Of course not. I think that it's wonderful when people share things about themselves with others. I think it's like receiving a special gift from someone when they share something intimate about themselves."

"Good. Anyway, I've learnt that I am quite anal about things in my life. I take things way too seriously. And now that I've figured this out about myself I have to find an appropriate way to deal with it."

"Well, that's just great. But one step at a time. You'll find out for yourself what you have to do to deal with these things. I'm happy for you."

"So have you decided where I'm taking you for dinner?" I ask her. "Tim is more than welcome to join us?" I suggest.

"Oh, he'll never come with us, but I'll ask. He always refuses to go," she says as though she has said that a thousand times before. "We're going to Mama's Diner. I have already made the reservations. Eight o'clock, and after dinner we'll take a short stroll on the boardwalk along the beach."

"That sounds wonderful," I say to her as I sit back in my chair and sip on the iced tea she has poured. We sit and talk the afternoon away. I ramble on about the events of my day and the things I need to buy for the house so that I can move in. Dishes, bedding, some patio furniture and of course some food. Fiona says that I'm more than welcome to use their pickup truck to move the furniture to the house. She figures my jeep might be a bit small for the task. Fiona gives me information as to where I might find the best buys for the stuff I need. She suggests I do a day trip to the Yarmouth area. She's sure that I find just what I need there. As we talk, Tim makes several appearances but never says a word or stops long enough to be included in the conversation. I understand from what Fiona tells me and by his actions that Tim has been completely devastated by Harry Belmont's death. Fiona asks him at one point if he'd like to join us for dinner in town; he reacts just as Fiona has predicted. He politely says no, that he has many chores to do around the house. She accepts his refusal and just smiles at him. Soon it is time for the two of us to get ourselves ready for dinner. I leave Fiona on the back porch while she makes arrangements with Tim for the evening. About half an hour later I meet Fiona on the front porch of Pilgrim House Bed and Breakfast, and escort her down and into my jeep.

"I've never ridden in one of these before," she states

as she climbs into the passenger seat of the jeep.

"Well, it's great, especially with the top off like this," I say to her. "So hold onto your hat, we don't want it blowing off." She smiles and ties her hat in place with the silk scarf that matches her dress.

I pull into the front parking lot of Mama's Diner and stop the jeep. I barely get my door open and Fiona is already on the sidewalk waiting for me.

"Must be good food," I say.

"Oh yes, Mama makes the best pasta in Massachusetts." I put my arm out to escort her up the stairs into the diner. She gracefully nods her head as she leads the way in. A dark haired Italian woman greets us as we enter.

"Mrs. Belmont, how are you this evening?" the woman asks.

"Just fabulous Maria," Fiona says, her eyes twinkling.

"Your table is ready," Maria says as she leads us into the dining room.

"How is your mother, Maria?" Fiona asks.

"She's going to drive us crazy," she giggles. "With my brother's wedding this weekend that is."

"Yes, I heard about the wedding," Fiona says. "Oh forgive me Maria, this is Andrew McTavich. He's a new member of our community."

"Hi Andrew, welcome to Rocky Beach," Maria says.

"Thanks, I used to summer here as a kid. My grandparents owned a summer home here."

"Well then, welcome back. Are you planning to be a permanent resident?" she asks as she pours us some water.

"Actually, I live in New York City, I just inherited the summer house from my grandmother, so I really haven't given it much thought to what I am going to do with the place yet."

"He's here on vacation right now," Fiona adds.

"Well, I hope you enjoy your stay Andrew," she says as she hands me the wine list. I open it and start to read. "May I suggest the Barolo," Maria says.

I look at Fiona and wait for her reaction. She doesn't say anything. "Can we have a few moments?"

"Sure, I'll be back," she says as she leaves the two of us alone at our table.

"So, I take it that you'd prefer something else?" I say to Fiona.

"Of course the Barolo would be perfect, but save the Barolo for an occasion when you will share it with someone special."

"But Fiona you are special," I say to her.

"Why thank you Andy, but my favourite here is the Ruffino Chianti."

"Well then, the Chianti it is," I say. "What would you suggest we dine on this evening?"

"Mama makes the best spaghetti and meatballs in meat sauce in the world."

Maria returns to our table, I order the wine and our dinners. She takes our order and returns in a few moments with our wine, pours each of us a glass then sets the bottle on the table and slips away again to serve her other customers.

A few moments later I can hear Maria talking loudly at the front door of the diner. "Tony!" she says, "I thought you were going out with the guys tonight?"

"That was last week, Maria." I recognized Tony diMarco's voice from Cape Development and Maintenance. "How's Mama?"

"She's driving me crazy," Maria says. "I can hardly wait until everything is finished with this wedding of yours." There is a short silence then Maria says "You two here for dinner?"

"Yes, are there any empty tables in the dining room tonight?" Tony asks his sister.

"Yeah, just go on in and sit down. All this evenings reservations are in already. You guys want a beer? I'll bring them right over."

The two men walk into the dining room. I notice that Tony takes a quick scan of the dining room, looking for an empty table. His gaze stops momentarily at our table then moves on quickly to a table at the back of the dining room. The younger of the two men, follows Tony to the table. He too scans the room, except when his gaze meets mine, he holds it as he crosses the room. He smiles at me as the two men finally reach the table at the rear of the dining room. Maria makes her way over to their table and places a couple of Bud's down in front of them.

"That's Tony diMarco. He's Maria's brother, the one getting married this weekend. And the other young man is, if my memory serves me right, Garth, he works with Tony."

"Yes, I know, I mean I met him, Tony that is, at the house this afternoon, but I didn't know he was getting married." I glance over my shoulder at their table. Tony has taken the chair facing the front of the dining room. Garth is sitting across from him with his back to us. I decide at that moment that I've got the wrong seat at this table. Tony looks up and catches me looking at them. I quickly turn back to Fiona.

"Married eh? Too bad." I say.

"I was quite shocked to hear it too," she says. "I always thought...well, I guess I was wrong." She takes a sip of her wine and doesn't finish what she was going to say. "He and Elaine have been going out for almost ten years now. Word out there is that she got herself pregnant to hurry up things. You know how women are about their biological clocks and all?" she says. I give her that puzzled deer in the headlight look. "Well maybe you don't."

"Of course I know about that. I'm not just a pretty face you know," I say as I take a drink of my wine. "All the good ones are straight," I sigh. I now understand why he was a bit cool with me earlier today.

"I also understand that Garth is family. He has a partner, word has it."

"Thanks." I raised my glass to her. She smiles back at me and raises hers. Maria comes over with our plates and places them in front of us and then tops up each of our glasses of wine and leaves us to our dinner.

"Did you see that guy sitting with Mrs. Belmont?" Tony asks Garth

"Oh did I ever," he replies taking a quick glance over his shoulder towards Mrs. Belmont and the handsome man sitting with her.

"Hey, don't let your hormones get the best of you."

"Just because I've got a partner doesn't mean I can't look. I'm not dead. He's gorgeous," Garth says.

"I know you're not dead, that wasn't what I was getting at," Tony says.

"Well, he is very good looking and from what I can tell he's probably very well put together."

"Okay I agree he's good looking..."

"How would you know what a good looking man is? I thought you liked girls?" Garth interrupts him.

"Just because I like girls doesn't mean I can't tell a good looking guy from an ugly one," Tony says as he looks over towards Mrs. Belmont and Andy. "But that's not what I'm trying to tell you. He's the guy that inherited the Ayer's place."

"Oh, so that's him," Garth says as he takes another long pull from his beer. "Why didn't you say something?"

"Well, I guess I should have." Tony says.

"But?" Garth asks.

"Well I don't think I actually treated him quite the way I should have when I first met him this morning at the house."

"Really?"

"Yeah really!" Tony says. "I don't feel great about it, but I guess I was thinking that he...well that doesn't really matter. I just treated him rather coolly. I owe him an apology."

"Well?"

"Well what?"

"Go over and apologize."

"Not yet. They've just got their dinner, I'll go over and apologize when they're finished," Tony says. Maria comes through the dining room doors from the kitchen and places two large plates of spaghetti and meatballs in front of them and disappears back into the kitchen. Both men start to eat their meals. Tony keeps checking on the table where Mrs. Belmont and Andy are sitting. Garth watches his friend watch the other table. He can tell by Tony's eye movement that he's only watching Andy.

After about fifteen minutes Tony gets up from the table. "I'll be right back Garth."

"Sure," Garth smiles at him as his friend walks to where Mrs. Belmont and Andy are seated.

"Why Tony, how are you?" Fiona asks as Tony arrives at their table.

"Fine, thank you Mrs. Belmont."

Before he can say anything she said, "You know Andy McTavich don't you?"

"Yes, we met earlier today. That's why I came over. I hope I'm not interrupting?" Tony asks.

Again before he can say anything, "No of course not." She has a big smile on her face.

"Oh good, I just came over to apologize for how I acted earlier this morning." He looks at me and holds my stare. His eyes are dark, so dark that the black pupils almost blend into the colour of his eyes. I can feel my body temperature start to rise. I continue to stare into his eyes.

"Andy?" Fiona says.

"Oh! Sure, no problem. I understand that you're getting married this weekend. I'm sure you are just under a lot of stress with all that. Apology accepted." I feel very flustered. He reaches out his hand to shake mine. I take hold of it and he squeezes my hand. His hand is hard and strong. I can feel the calluses of hands that have worked hard.

"Good," Tony says. "Oh I'll be out at the house at three tomorrow afternoon to do the inspections, so if you'd like to meet me there I'd be happy to go through it with you."

"I'd like that."

"Good, I'll see you then," Tony says. I watch him as he turns and walks back to his table. He seems like a much nicer person than he appeared earlier today. As I watch him move I can see by the close fitting clothes he is wearing this evening that the assumptions I've made about his body were right. Tony is built like a Greek god, well a Roman god. He has the body and face Michelangelo would have used as a model, and one, I'm sure, that if Calvin Klein saw him, his face or body would be on every billboard in every major city across the country.

"Andy, you okay?" Fiona's voice brakes through my thoughts.

"Yes of course," I stammer as I return my gaze to her.

"Yes, he is very good looking, don't you think?" she asks.

"Oh yeah!" I say, trying not to sound too overwhelmed by him. "He definitely could make the cover of a lot of magazines with that face and body." We continue to drink our coffee and eat our dessert in silence. My mind keeps wandering back to Tony. Too bad he's straight, I think.

Tony sits down in his chair facing Garth and takes another look back at the table where Andy and Mrs. Belmont are seated. He looks just as Andy turns his head back to Mrs. Belmont. Was Andy looking at him as he walked back to his table? He probably thinks I'm rude for interrupting his dinner.

"Well?" Garth asks.

"Well what?" Tony replies.

"I hate that, answer a question with a question. Joey does that a lot to me," Garth says. "So tell me."

"So tell you what?" Tony asks.

"Hell, there you go again. Tell me, what's he like?" Garth says.

"I don't know. He seems like a nice enough person," Tony says as he picks up his beer. "He's got a very handsome face..."

Before Tony can say anything else Garth says, "You know if I'd didn't know otherwise I'd be almost convinced that you could be gay."

Tony just looks at Garth and smiles. He winks at his friend as he takes a sip of his beer.

"You're such a tease, especially since I told you about myself." Tony sits back in his chair as they wait for their dessert to come, still grinning. "See what I mean!" Garth says. "Next you'll be posing, driving me crazy."

It's almost three. I drive up to the gates of the property. They have been swung wide. Obviously someone is here, probably the cleaners and Tony. I don't know whether I'm excited about getting the house ready or about seeing Tony again. Well, at least I can say I've seen the best looking man that I've ever laid eyes on. Mind you, his buddy Garth is also easy to look at. As I approach the house I see a white van with Rocky Beach Maid Service written on the side in bold letters, parked next to the Cape Development and Maintenance truck. I park Mrs. Belmont's older pickup, loaded with the rattan furniture I've bought earlier this morning, as close to the front veranda as I can get it. I can see buckets and mops and baskets of cleaning products on the front veranda. It looks as though the cleaners are finished. I unload the furniture onto the front veranda. I can hear Tony's voice through the open front door, talking to someone in the kitchen. I can't quite make out what he's saying but the sound of his voice excites me. There is something so regular about it. He doesn't sound like some real butch straight man, just regular, if anyone can sound regular. I bring up the last piece of furniture on to the veranda and place it with the others. Tony and a couple of elderly women come out onto the veranda.

"Hi. I heard you talking so I just went on unloading my furniture. I didn't want to interrupt."

"Hi Mr. McTavich," Tony says. "This is Mrs. Finney and her sister in-law Mrs. Albert. They are the cleaning people we use." They both nod to me. "This is Mr. McTavich the new owner of the house."

Mrs. Finney says, "Hello Mr. McTavich. We knew your grandparents from a long time ago. It's good to see someone use this beautiful place again." Mrs. Albert just nods in agreement.

"Mr. McTavich, I've got just a few things to go over with these lovely ladies before they leave, then we can get on with the inspection," Tony says.

"Sure, take your time," I say "I think I'll just play with the arrangement of this furniture."

Tony and the two women walk down the stairs towards the white van, carrying their mops and buckets and their baskets full of cleaning paraphernalia. He is gone for about ten minutes before he comes back up the stairs. I've arranged the rattan furniture to take in the whole view of the bay.

"Looks good," he comments.

"Thanks," I say. "Oh, by the way, please call me Andy"

"Okay Andy, why don't we get this inspection done? It shouldn't take too long," Tony says with a smile. I think that this is the first time see him smile. His whole face lights up when he does. His white teeth gleam against his darkly tanned complexion and full red lips. I follow him into the house and we start inspecting everything he feels needs to be checked. I'm having a hard time concentrating on what he is saying. I just agree with everything. I'm not so sure that he doesn't notice. I know another gay man would have but I'm not so sure if a straight man would. We go over pipes and drains, what he's going to have fixed or adjusted. I spend most of the time just nodding in agreement. I wonder as we walk through the house whether Tony knows just how damn good-looking he is and how lucky his future wife is. Now if he were gay, this would be the type of man I'd want to have in my life. Tony glows as we walk through the house. He seems to have an affinity with the place. He looks comfortable here.

He checks his watch and says, "It's almost four o'clock. Are you in a rush?"

"No, I really don't have any plans for tonight," I catch myself saying. It's like I thought he might be asking me out on a date. I'm on vacation so no.

"So I guess it's okay to finish the inspection. All we have left is the basement and the old garage at the back of the house," Tony says.

He seems to be all work. "Hey no problem," I say. The more time I get to spend looking at him, well let's just say he'll probably be the subject of a lot of late night fantasies. We continue down into the basement. Here he shows me where the tree limb had broken the basement window during a storm in April. He explains that there was very little damage other than a few panes of glass. There's not much else to check in the basement. All the plumbing and electrical systems are in good order. There are cupboards along the far wall, the locks hanging on them.

"If you don't mind me asking, these cupboards, do they contain anything that I should take a look at?" he asks.

"Actually they contain or used to contain my grandfather's kites. He loved to fly kites," I say with a smile, as the memories of long past times come flooding back. "I'm pretty sure that they are empty. I'll have to check them out while I'm here."

"That's fine I was just wondering if there is anything structural that I need to look at," he says as he looks closely around the perimeter of the cupboards. "Doesn't look like there are any pipes or wires going behind." He steps back and as he does his arm bushes mine. I can feel the sun bleached hair of his arm brush against mine. I get goose bumps; Tony doesn't flinch, or even acknowledge that we touched. "Well, I guess we should go out and check out that old garage. The brambles have just about taken it over." I lead the way up out of the basement. I can hear Tony's footsteps coming up the stairs behind me.

As we reach the old garage I say, "I think this building has pretty much had it. It looks as though most of the wood has rotted. You are right the brambles sure have taken over."

"Do you think that you'll want to salvage anything here?" he asks.

I try to keep Tony to my side. That way I wouldn't have to watch his body move as we walk and inspect the property. It is getting very hard to keep my eyes from wandering and undressing him visually. The only problem with keeping him to my side is, that we brush each other quite frequently, which makes it even harder to concentrate on what I should be doing with him.

"If you don't mind I think I'd like to have the power cut off to the garage. I don't think you'd want it to be a fire hazard," Tony suggests.

"Yes, that's a good idea, I would have never thought of that," I say. Right now the only thing I can think of is how can a man so good-looking be so straight. We start on our way back to the house where the trucks are parked. Again he checks his watch. I take a look at mine. It is five o'clock. The last two hours have just flown by.

"I should be off," he says.

"You must be pretty busy right about now," I say. "I mean with your wedding happening this weekend."

"Yeah, I guess," he says "I've got a lot of things to catch up on before this weekend." I notice that his demeanour seems to change when I mention his wedding. I can't put my finger on it but there is a change. His eyes seem to cloud over, like a sadness coming over him momentarily, but it disappears just as quickly. He is probably under a lot of stress.

He quickly drops the subject of his personal life and said, "So you can move in anytime Andy." That is the first time he uses my name. All this time that we were walking and inspecting the property he's never used my name. I almost melt on the spot. I can't remember the last time I reacted that way when a man said my name. Wait until I tell

Gerry. He continues, "I'll drop off those cushions Thursday afternoon, and I'll do those couple of odd jobs we talked about inside then I'll disconnect the power to the garage."

He definitely is all work, or so it seems. I watch him get into his truck, drive up the driveway and disappear behind the trees.

Tony drives over the bump where the driveway meets the road. He looks in the rear view mirror at the large wrought iron gates. He doesn't stop to close them. As he drives back into Rocky Beach he thinks about the last two or so hours he has spent with Andy. Garth is right about him. He really is a good-looking man. He starts to take a physical inventory of Andy. He looks very fit. Both of them are about the same size in height. Andy is just as broad across the shoulders as he is and has a great set of arms. Andy has been wearing walking shorts. The muscles in his legs are well defined and strong looking. He has nice calves. It is obvious that he spends time at the gym. Tony feels comfortable with the fact that Andy takes care of himself. He thinks Andy would take good care of his favourite place in Rocky Beach. After deciding that, his mind wanders back to Andy's body. He finds himself noticing guys' bodies a lot more lately. Garth's, his partner's, Joey's and now Andy's. He knows that all his life he has noticed guys' bodies, but lately he has more than just noticed them; especially with Andy. He can feel a real stir within himself. It excites him. Even Garth and Joey, who he thinks are pretty well put together and well defined, never get him excited like this. Is it just a combination of things, the property, and his feeling that Andy would take good care of the property, and maybe just a little, that Andy really is quite a handsome man? He drives the truck into his mother's driveway. As he stops and gets out, he wonders about Andy's age.

"Hello," the voice says on the phone.

"Gerry. It's me Andy."

"Honey!" Gerry says. "We've been worried about you. It's Friday and you've just called now. So what's going on?"

"Well, I'm just calling to let you know that I'm actually moving into the house today and that if you want to get a hold of me you can leave messages here at Pilgrim House. Fiona has been kind enough to let me have message privileges."

"Well, isn't she a sweetheart," he says cattily

"Gerry, I'm not getting a phone, well at least not yet, so it's very nice that she's going to let me have messages left here."

"Well, I guess that's okay then. So Andy honey, tell me what's going on. We miss you, you know?"

"I know, I miss all of you also, but I've been very busy getting things ready at the house. I've been out shopping up a storm."

"Well of course you have honey. You've always been a good shopping fag, but this sounds serious. You're not planning to stay there are you?" he asks.

"No, but believe me it has crossed my mind. Life here just seems to be so much simpler. And the eye candy is just fabulous." I add.

"Just get those awful thoughts out of your head do you hear me? You belong here in New York City with the rest of us. Eye candy, what eye candy? You've been to Provincetown haven't you?" he asks. "You know you're only there for a month."

"No, I haven't been to Provincetown yet. There's plenty of hunky guys right here in Rocky Beach. Ones that live here all year round. I have this one absolutely gorgeous hunk of a man that has taken care of the house for the past few years. The only problem is he's straight and to top that off he's actually getting married tomorrow. What a waste."

"Well that settles it, you'll be back in the city soon," Gerry says. "So tell me about this straight piece of man meat you get to look at all day."

"Gerry, he's actually a really nice guy, you know billboard good looks and very handy. Everyone should have someone like that around."

"Of course we should, honey, but if they're useless in bed then what's the point," Gerry says.

"Oh Gerry you have a one track mind. So I'm not going to tell you about the others."

"Others?"

"Never mind Gerry."

"Oh well, it's good to hear you're still alive," he says.

"Thanks. Sometimes I wonder why I talk to you."

"Because you need me and you care deeply for me," he chuckles.

"Okay, okay, you got me," I respond. "So you have this phone number?"

"Of course I do."

"Good. Just remember it might be a day or so before I return a call."

"Of course Honey." There is a short silence then he says, "Andy, you're sounding good."

"Yeah thanks Gerry, I'm feeling good."

"Well you just keep having fun while you're there and call anytime okay?" he says.

"Of course, I'll talk to you soon. Gerry thanks for just being you."

"Who else would I be Honey?" he chuckles again. A short silence then he asks, "Do you have plans for the fourth?"

"No, there's some sort of town celebrations and fireworks after dark, which I might attend, but I haven't made any concrete plans. I might just sit and watch the stars on the beach at the house who knows."

"You could go to P'town, I'm sure there'll be lots of boys there this weekend," he suggests.

"Well I guess I could." I pause. "I should be going. Gotta clear out my room for the next set of guests. Say hi to everyone for me okay? Bye Gerry."

"Bye Andy," I hear Gerry say as I hang up the phone. Mrs. Belmont is probably sitting out on the back porch. Tim is most likely doing some gardening. The House is booked for the holiday weekend and guests would be arriving in a few hours. Fiona says that this is the start of their busy season. They wouldn't get much rest until after Labour Day. I've packed up all of my belongings and put them in my jeep. I'd miss my mornings with Fiona, with Tim just out of eyesight but still there. I walk through the white door leading to the rear of the house to say my good-bye's to Fiona and Tim, my extended family here in Rocky Beach. The back screen door creaks and groans as I open it and step out onto the back porch. They are just as I pictured them; Fiona is sitting with a big floppy straw hat wearing a flowered summer frock. Tim is working in the garden cursing about some flowers being more trouble than they're worth.

"Andy," Fiona says. "Have a glass of iced tea with us before you leave." She tops up the glass she'd been sipping and then pours two others. "Tim please join us for an iced tea," is all she says. He drops his shovel, comes over and sits on the top step of the porch. Something I'd never seen him do before. Fiona hands me both of the glasses, I hand one to Tim.

He looks into my eyes and says, "Thank you Andy."

"You're welcome Tim." I sit in the chair next to Fiona. Both of us are facing the garden and Tim. "Boy this feels kinda funny."

"How so?" Fiona asks.

"I've only been here less than a week and I feel like I'm leaving home for the very first time." I say.

"Is that a bad thing?" she asks.

I stop and think before I answer her. "No." I pause, "No, it's not. I guess if I feel this way it means that you two mean an awful lot to me."

"Well we've enjoyed having you here," she says. "And I must admit you've been telling us the most interesting stories we've heard in a while." She sips on her iced tea. "And I'm very sure that we'll be seeing you around."

"You talk as If you know something that I don't," I say. Again she just smiles and takes another sip of iced tea. "And I know that if you knew something or felt something you'd never tell me because this is my story. That I know for a fact."

"My, you do learn quickly."

Tim gets up and puts his empty glass on the table in front of us, walks down the stairs back into the garden and picks up his shovel, continuing to work on the project he has given himself.

"Well, I guess I should say good-bye."

"Oh, never say good-bye, say that you'll see us later, it's not so permanent." She smiles at me.

"Well then, I'll be seeing you later." I stand up and so does she. As I wrap my arms around her and hug her I do feel as though it isn't so permanent. I release my hold of Fiona and go to the edge of the porch to yell to Tim, "Hey Tim, I'll see ya around." He looks up from his chore. I wave to him, he waves back at me and then continues his work. I walk out through the back screen door leaving Fiona and Tim in the backyard. I pick up the last of my belongings that I have left by the front door and walk down the flower lined front path to the street. I get into my jeep and drive down Rocky Beach Road thinking that if only life were as simple as this all the time.

Garth checks his watch. Six fifteen. He runs up the stairs of the front porch of his house. He still has a limp from his broken leg so he is still a bit awkward. He tries the door-knob and finds that the door is unlocked. That means that Marcy has made it here as planned. She is helping him set up for the reception dinner. He has decided to make it a buffet rather than a sit down dinner. It would just be a lot easier to do for twenty people. He's borrowed a couple of banquet tables and chairs from Tony's mom's restaurant and has spent last night getting everything set up. He wishes that Joey could have made it here earlier to help him, but at least he'd be here to help clean up.

"Marcy? How are things going?" Garth says as he enters the house.

She comes out into the dining room, dressed in an

apron and oven mitts. "I think that everything will be ready ahead of schedule. I'm just putting together the last plate of hors d'oeuvres and everything else is done."

"So why the oven mitts?" Garth asks.

"Oh I just took the roast out of the oven. Now all you have to do is carve it," she adds. "So how much time have we got before people start to arrive?"

"About an hour," he replies as they both go into the kitchen.

"That should give us plenty of time." She removes the oven mitts from her hands and places them on the counter top. "Garth?"

"Yeah?"

"You're quite close to Tony, do you think..." She stops. "Oh never mind."

"Marcy, what is it you want to know about Tony?"

"Well since he, you know, found out about the baby and all he really hasn't been quite himself, don't you think?"

"Sure, he hasn't been himself. I'm sure any of us if we were in his shoes wouldn't be quite ourselves. Baby, marriage in less than a month. Wow! If you really think about it it's gotta put a lot of stress on a person."

"I guess you're right," she agrees. "I'd probably be a basket case by now if I were him."

"Marcy you're already a..." Before he can finish an oven mitt clips him across the back of the head "Hey I was only joking!" Marcy starts to laugh.

"So what time are you expecting Joey to turn up?" she changes the subject.

"I'm hoping no later than eight, eight-thirty. Dinner will almost be finished but at least he'll be here to help clean up." He begins to carve the roast. Marcy is right he thinks to himself. Tony really hasn't been himself since this entire baby and marriage stuff has come up. And when you want to talk to him to see if anything is bothering him he just passes it off. Even at the rehearsal he wasn't his natural joking self. So maybe he's taking the things in life more serious than he normally would. Tony always said you make your bed you lie in it. He continues with the preparations for this evenings dinner. The guests would be arriving shortly.

Marcy puts out the last plate of food on the banquet table when the front door bell rings. Garth makes his way through the kitchen to answer the front door. He wishes that Joey could have been able to be here earlier, to answer the door and sort of pick up loose ends while he finishes with the dinner. But he has to admit Marcy has been a godsend this last week. She has helped him out enormously with all the food preparation. It's Tony and Elaine with Sara and Tony's mom and Elaine's parents from Boston.

"Hi, come on in." Garth says. "Boy I hope you aren't all that are coming. I've got food for days, we might just have to postpone the wedding until next week so we can eat all this food I've got," he says jokingly. The group chuckles at Garth's humour.

"No, Maria and her tribe are right behind us," Elaine says. Tony remains silent as the first group of people enter the house. Before Garth can close the front door Maria, her husband Joe and the girls pull into the driveway.

Sara says to Garth, "I'll man the door for you." Sara hasn't said much about everything going on around her. Her best friend is getting married and she doesn't seem to be overly excited. Girls, Garth thinks to himself, they can be so weird sometimes.

Within the next fifteen minutes all the guests arrive and are milling about the dining and living rooms. The kids find their way out into the backyard and are noisily playing. The noise level in the rooms has also been elevated. It is getting harder to follow any one conversation. They all seem to run one into another. Garth is finally relaxed enough to put a plate of dinner together for himself. Just as he finishes filling it the front door opens and Joey enters the room. Joey drops his suitcase by the stairs and walks into the dining room. He searches it until he finds Garth by the banquet table with a dinner plate in his hand.

He walks up behind him and says, "So, is that plate for me?"

Garth turns, a big smile on his face. "Great! You made it and in good time. I hope you didn't get a speeding ticket. You know how the cops are on a holiday weekends." You can tell that they'd like to give each other a welcome hug and kiss, but with the mix of people in the room they both think it wise to leave it till later. Garth hands him the plate and picks up another for himself and fills it. The two of them find seats so that they can eat dinner together and give each other a quick update on their lives in the last couple of weeks.

"Oh and one more thing," Joey says.

"Yeah, what's that?" Garth replies.

"I quit work last week."

"You what?" Garth says excitedly. "Does that mean you're moving here?"

"Yup, I figured that it is time. The more time that I spend away from you the more I keep thinking that if I don't do something soon I might lose you." Joey smiles and looks over towards Tony.

Garth slips his hand onto Joey's knee and says in a quiet voice, hoping that no one would overhear them, "You know that there's no one anywhere that could replace you."

"Okay you two have had enough time alone," Marcy says as she approaches the two seated men.

"Joey, let me introduce you to your competition. This is Marcy. I work with her."

She puts her hand out and shakes Joey's hand and smiles at him. "Well, it's good to finally meet the mystery person in Garth's life."

"Hi Marcy," Joey says.

Garth gets up, and takes Joey's empty plate from him. "Would either of you like a drink?" he asks. "Beers?" Both Marcy and Joey agree, as Garth disappears to get a round of beer for them.

"So how have things been going so far?" Joey asks Marcy. Garth has told him that Marcy would be helping him get ready for the dinner so he sort of felt like he knows her.

"Everything's gone smoothly. Garth can sure cook up storm. So if you don't keep him I will." she says jokingly.

"But he's gay," Joey says, smiling at her

"With his cooking skills and looks, I could let him have his 'friends' if you know what I mean. Sex isn't all it's cracked up to be," she jokes.

Garth returns from the bar table he's set up earlier this afternoon, with the three beers. He stops and talks with Tony,

Elaine and Sara.

"Well, this is it," Garth says. "Are we getting excited yet?"

"Lainey was just saying that she'd probably not be able to sleep tonight," Sara says.

"Well she'd better. Tomorrow will probably be a long day," Garth says.

Tony smiles but remains silent.

"We've been talking about baby names," Elaine says. "What do you think about Michael for a boy or Michelle for a girl?"

"Lainey do you really like Michael? It'll get shortened to Mike," Sara says rather disdainfully.

"Oh Sara, you just don't like the name Michael," Elaine says. "Anyway, I don't mind Mike. What do you think Tony?" He'd been silent up until then.

"Oh, I guess Mike will be fine."

"Good input there buddy," Garth says.

"Lainey, I have to go to the washroom. Is there coffee Garth?"

"Yes, it's in the kitchen." He replies to her.

"Lainey are you coming?" Sara asks her. Elaine nods and follows Sara to the washroom. Garth and Tony are still standing where the two women have left them.

"A girl thing," Tony says to Garth.

"Hey, is everything all right Tony?"

"Yeah, I guess I'm just a bit nervous."

"Don't blame you, I'd be too," Garth says to his friend. "Come on over and sit with Marcy, Joey and me." Tony and Garth return to where Marcy and Joey are seated in silence. Joey looks a bit pale.

"Everything all right Joey, you look a bit pale?" Garth asks.

"Yeah everything is fine, I guess it's just been a long day and all," Joey says. He is watching the washroom door where Elaine and Sara have disappeared. "Oh hi Tony. I guess this is quite an exciting day for you?"

Before Tony can reply Marcy says, "Well let's just say he's breaking a lot of hearts in this town right now." Garth and Marcy break out into laughter. Joey watches Tony as he breaks into a pensive smile. Joey also slowly smiles. The two women come out of the washroom and go into the kitchen. The door closes behind them. Lainey, Sara, Lainey, Sara continually runs through Joey's mind. Where had he heard these names together before. He knows he has but he can't quite place it. Then all of a sudden it dawns on him. Lainey and Sara. They were the two women in the truck stop diner four weeks ago talking about babies and the father. He is sure of it now. There can't be too many Lainey's and Sara's here on the Cape. It just has to be them. Shit, if this is them then that means that...holy shit. Joey feels the blood disappear from his face. Garth hands a beer to Marcy and then goes to give one to Joey.

Before he takes it he shakes his head. "Did you offer one to Tony?" he says curtly.

"Are you sure you're all right?" Garth asks. "You're looking even more pale now than you did a few minutes ago."

"Yes, I'm fine." Joey says. "Tony do you want this beer, I think I just need to get some water."

"I'll get it for you Joey," Garth says.

"No! I'll get it. I'll be right back." Joey gets up and makes his way to the kitchen before anyone else can offer.

As soon as he disappears behind the kitchen door Garth says, "Gee, I hope he's not coming down with something?"

Marcy takes a sip of the beer and says, "Probably just from the drive down or maybe the heat. It's been very hot out lately," she states. All three of them are staring at the kitchen door where Joey has disappeared. "Boy that was weird though," Marcy states as she takes another sip of her beer.

The kitchen door swings shut behind Joey as he enters the kitchen. He sees Sara at the kitchen counter pouring two mugs of coffee. Elaine is out in the backyard with the kids. Sara looks up to see who has entered the kitchen.

She turns to him and says, "You must be Joey. I'm Sara. I've heard so much about you from Garth." She continues to prepare the two mugs of coffee.

Joey is sure now. He definitely recognizes Sara's voice as one of the two women sitting behind him at the truck stop restaurant. He says, "I know."

"So Garth has told you about me?" she asks. "Probably because tomorrow I'm his date for the day."

"No, I mean I know," Joey says.

Sara stares at him quite confused. "You know what?"

"I know about Lainey, the baby and Mike."

Sara is about to take a sip of her hot coffee. She stops before it reaches her lips. "You know what about Lainey, the baby and who is Mike?" Sara asks, hoping that what she has heard isn't true or maybe she does hope he knows.

"Mike is the father of Lainey's baby," Joey says so matter of factly.

"Where in the hell did you get such a ridiculous idea?" Sara says. "It's Tony's baby."

"I got the information from the two of you," Joey says.

"Look, I don't know who you think you are...," she starts to say.

"Let's just say I'm a friend, Sara. Do you remember meeting Elaine at the truck stop just about a month ago?" Joey watches Sara as he tells her how he knows about the baby. "I also know that you don't like the fact that she's lying to everyone."

"Look, these aren't my choices, so why don't you just mind your own business and forget what you think you know."

"Sara, I know it was you and Elaine. I just couldn't put it together until you kept calling her Lainey. That's what you called her the whole time you were trying to convince her to either have the baby adopted out or tell Tony the truth." He watches the colour drain from her face. "And just to let you know, I agree with you. Elaine needs to be honest with Tony. If you are any kind of friend you won't let this happen."

"How can you come here and tell me what I should or shouldn't do. Do you know how hard this has been, keeping her secret like this."

"Do you know how hard it is going to be being a part of this lie for the rest of your life?" Joey asks. "I don't think that we have a choice."

"What do you mean we?" she asks.

"Sara, that's exactly what I mean. If you don't say something I will," Joey says. "I think you've always wanted to say something but were too afraid because of your friendship with Elaine." Just as he says that Elaine walks back into the kitchen.

"How's that coffee coming Sara. Oh hi, I'm Elaine," Elaine says. Sara looks at her but doesn't say anything. "What? What's going on?" Again Sara doesn't say anything, so Joey feels that he should fill in the gap.

"Elaine, I'm Joey, Garth's partner."

'Hi, I've heard so much about you...," she starts to say but Joey interrupts her.

"And I know too much about you. Things that you have only shared with Sara," he says.

She looks at both Joey and Sara with a puzzled look on her face. "I don't quite understand. You know me how? And what can you possibly know that I would have told Sara? We've only just met," Elaine says as she reaches for the hot cup of coffee that Sara has prepared for her.

"Oh Lainey, he knows," Sara says.

"He knows what Sara? What have you told him?" Elaine's face is turning red as she turns to her friend.

"She's never told me a thing. You did. At the truck stop diner I overheard the two of you," Joey says.

"It could have been anyone you overheard. You must be delirious if you think that this baby isn't Tony's," Elaine stops.

"You just confirmed it. I never told you what I overheard you two talking or should I say arguing about," Joey says.

Sara is silent throughout the exchange. Silence now comes over the other two as the three of them share the secret of the father of Elaine's baby. Joey finally says, "So what are we going to do?"

"What do you mean what are we going to do?" Elaine says, her voice cold. She's angry. "We'll do nothing. We'll just carry on as if these last ten minutes never happened," she states.

"I can't do that Elaine," Joey says. "I don't have to worry about your friendship to keep me quiet."

"Why you fucking faggot...," Elaine curses Joey.

The door of the kitchen swings open and Garth walks

in. "Gee, I thought you'd only be a few..." He stops mid sentence. He can feel the tension in the kitchen. "Did I walk in on something?" he asks looking at Joey, who hasn't taken his eyes off Elaine. Sara has since turned and is watching the kids play out in the back yard. No one says anything. Garth looks at Elaine, then back to Joey, then over to Sara, who is trying her damnedest to not be noticed. "Elaine? Sara?" he starts. "What's going on?" More silence from all three. Elaine and Joey haven't taken their eyes off one another and Sara continues to stare out the kitchen window. "Joey what the fuck is going on?"

"It's not for me to say, is it Elaine?" his eyes are still locked on hers.

"No Joey it's not, and I really don't think that there is anything that any of us have to say." She puts the hot cup of coffee down on the counter top and walks back out into the dining room. Sara still looks out of the window at the kids.

"What in the hell just happened here?" Garth asks.

"Sara?" Joey asks. "Sara do you want to tell him or am I gonna?"

She turns and looks at both Garth and Joey. There are tears in her eyes when she says, "Look this really doesn't concern any of us so why don't we just forget it and let this just go away."

"How can you be so fucking selfish Sara, isn't Tony your friend also?" Joey asks her, ignoring the fact that Garth is standing next to him.

"Of course he is and so is Elaine. I don't want to see either of them hurts" she says. "And that is all that will happen. They both will get hurt."

"And what about the baby?" Joey asks. "Is it fair to the child when it grows up?"

"Look the two of you, if someone won't tell me what the fuck has been going on in my kitchen..."

"Garth!" both Sara and Joey say in unison. He stops and stares at both of them.

"I don't know what in the hell is going on here and what pray tell has it got to do with Tony, Elaine and their baby!" Garth states.

Both Joey and Sara stare at him, neither of them say

anything for a few moments. Then, before Joey can say anything Sara starts,. "Okay you want to know. I guess it should be me telling you," she pauses.

Another moment of silence goes by. "Well I'm still waiting," Garth says. He sounds irritated.

"This isn't exactly easy," she says. Tears have streaked her face with her makeup. "The baby isn't Tony's."

"What are you talking about? Of course the baby is his," Garth says.

"No, Garth she's telling you the truth. The baby's father is some guy named Mike," Joey says. Sara nods her head in agreement.

"How in the hell do you know this Joey?" Garth asks.

"It's quite a long story. I'll tell you later. The problem now is what do we do?"

Garth pulls up a chair and is sitting in the middle of the kitchen floor between Joey and Sara. "Sara, why didn't she say...why didn't you say anything?" he sounds confused "I still don't understand how it's not Tony's baby?"

"To make things simple Garth, Elaine was screwing around on Tony and obviously not being too careful," Sara states. "And let's just say she told me. Girls do those things, like talk you know."

Silence comes over the kitchen again. "Did she tell you who the father is?"

"Yes, is that really important?" Sara asks.

"We have to do something," Garth says.

"I agree with you," Joey says. Joey and Garth both know that Sara agrees with them that something has to be done.

Garth stands up and starts to walk out of the kitchen, he turns to both Sara and Joey. "Elaine has to tell Tony the truth or I will. I wouldn't be much of a friend to either of them if I weren't honest. But it would be best if Tony found out from Elaine. Sara, you said you know who the father is?"

"Yes I do?" she sounds confused.

"Does he live here in town?" Garth asks.

"Why?" she asks. "Is it really that important?"

"Yes. I have a plan."

"A plan?" Joey asks.

"Yes I do. I want the two of you to go back out there in a few minutes and act as if nothing happened in here. Okay?" Garth says. Both Sara and Joey agree.

"So does he live in town?" Garth asks Sara again.

"Yes, he does. But I don't see..."

"Just let me do the thinking. Call him and make sure that he gets here soon. Can you do that?"

"I still don't..."

"Sara just do it, get him here. My plan is simple we just have to get Elaine to slip up so that the truth comes out."

"Garth that's cruel. I won't have any part of it," Sara protests.

"What's cruel is letting this charade go on. Think of it this way. If you were Tony wouldn't you want the person that you were going to spend the rest of your life with to be honest and trustworthy? And also think of how he'll feel when he finds out that we all knew about this and never said anything. What kind of friends are we? If we were in his shoes we'd expect better from our friends wouldn't we?" Garth stares at Joey and Sara. All three of them know that he is right. Sara walks over to the phone and dials a number. Garth and Joey go back out into the dining room and wait.

"Joey. Why don't you keep an eye on the door. Hopefully Sara can get this guy to show up," Garth says to him. "Just sorta act like nothing has happened. I'm going to mingle."

Before Garth leaves Joey, Sara returnes from the kitchen.

"Well?" Garth asks.

Sara shakes her head. "All I got was his answering machine."

"Boy, what do we do now?" Joey asks.

"Now I'm going over to the bar, okay?" Garth starts. "Then I want you to come to the bar also. Keep your back to that woman. That's Maria, Tony's sister."

"Okay? Then you start telling me about what you know about the baby not being Tony's, okay. Just loud enough for Maria to hear you. That should be enough."

"Okay, ready when you are." Joey says.

"By the way have you met Maria yet?"

"No, she doesn't know me from Adam, why?"

"Good, it'll just make it more believable if you don't know who is overhearing you," Garth says. "Hopefully I can get there without being noticed by her." He starts to make his way across the room to the bar. He glances over to where Tony and Elaine are standing talking to their mothers. Perfect. She's unaware of what's going on. Garth arrives at his intended spot without being noticed by the people he is trying to avoid. A moment later Joey steps up to him. They are standing about four feet from Maria. He has his back to her while Garth is off to one side facing the front door.

"Hi," he says.

"Hi," Garth replies. Silence. "So?"

"So what?" Joey says.

Garth leans over and whispers. "Don't make this anymore difficult than it already is. Just start talking."

"Look, this isn't as easy as it seems," Joey whispers back. "So just give me a minute."

"No, she might leave then we'd be stuck."

"Okay, okay," Joey says. He pauses for a moment then says, "Hey, Garth do you want some dirt on the bride?" He isn't sure whether Maria has heard him, so he decides he might as well turn the old flaming queen act on. So with a lisp and limp wrists flying in the air he starts, "Well Garth dear, I heard the juiciest tidbit of info on the bride the other day. Would you like to hear it?" Garth's eyes get bigger but before he can say anything Joey continues, "Well, I was at this lovely truck stop. You know that one at the intersection of number six and oh you know that other big road, well anyways. Oooh you should have seen all those big burly men! Oh right, enough about that. Anyway, I saw these two women, and guess who they were. Tada! The bride and her maid of honour. Well I just couldn't help but sort of overhearing their conversation. Well, it really wasn't that hard to hear. They were almost yelling at each other." He pauses and gives a look over his shoulder towards Elaine and Tony. He notices that Maria hasn't moved from the bar. He has caught Maria's attention. "So do you want to know what they were arguing about? Well let me tell you. They were arguing about the baby. Can you imagine that, arguing about the baby and it's not even born. Actually it really wasn't the baby they were arguing about but the father. And you're not gonna guess what about the father." Joey pauses again, but only for a second and continues, "He's really not the father. Get it. Oh Garth honey, what I'm trying to tell you is that hunk of a groom isn't really the daddy. Lainey, that's what the other girlie girl called her, said that the baby's real papa is her boss. Oh god these small towns. I think this is where all those big TV companies come to get their story lines for their soap operas." Garth is staring at the production he has just witnessed, hoping that he and Maria were the only ones who've heard it. "Well, I think I'm gonna waltz into the kitchen and get myself a cup of coffee, ooooh and reminisce 'bout all of them truckers." He turns and minces his way to the kitchen. Garth decides that he isn't going to stick around and wait for a reaction from Maria.

Tony and Elaine didn't see what has just taken place. Maria on the other hand, has. She stands there for a moment and then walks into the kitchen after Joey.

Joey is standing at the counter. Instead of a coffee he has opted for a beer. He has almost finished it, when he hears the kitchen door open behind him. He turns hoping that it is Garth. Instead he sees Maria. She is smiling at him.

"Hi, I don't think we've met, I'm Maria, Tony's sister," she says.

Oh, Christ he thinks, I've got to do my act again. So with his lisp and waving limp wrists he says "Why hello, honey, I'm Joey, Garth's better half." He puts out a limp wrist for her to shake.

She quickly shakes his hand and continues to say, "I couldn't help but overhear you talking to Garth in the dining room, and I'm sure you said that Tony wasn't the father of the baby, is that right?"

"Look honey, I don't want to cause any rumours but I was just tellin' my Garth what I heard at that truck stop..."

Maria grabs him by the shirt collar and says, "Look you little fag you're not going to be starting rumours about Tony and Elaine." She pushes him back and Joey bumps a stack of dishes on the counter. They crash to the floor. A moment later Garth and Sara come through the kitchen door.

"What's going on in here? Is anyone hurt?" Garth says. Tony, Elaine and Tony's mom follow just in time to hear Maria say, "This little fag friend of yours is starting rumours about who the father of the baby is. He says that he overheard Elaine and Sara at a truck stop say that Tony isn't the father of the baby."

Shit, Garth thinks, this is getting out of hand. "Joey is this true? Are you starting rumours?" Garth asks.

Joey looks at Garth, then Sara and Elaine and lastly Tony. Sara has moved away from the group of people at the door and has started to pick up the broken dishes that lay on the kitchen floor next to Joey. The sound of Sara picking up the glass pieces from the floor is the only sound in the room.

"Joey?" this time it is Tony's voice.

"Yeah, come on Faggot!" Maria says.

"Maria!" Mama diMarco says as she walks over to where Sara is picking up the broken glass. "He's telling the truth isn't he Sara?" You can tell that Sara has been crying as she picks up the broken glass. She doesn't say anything.

"Mama!" Tony says.

"Tony, be quiet!" Mama diMarco says.

"Oh for Christ sakes do you really think that I'd make this up. Lie about Tony being the father of my baby?" Elaine yells. "I can't believe this! I love your son..."

"Like hell you do Lainey!" It is Sara. "I've had a real hard time keeping your secret for the last month. It has really been bugging the hell out of me. Not being able to look at you or Tony without knowing the truth," she sobs.

"Sara, why are you saying these things?" Elaine says. "I thought you were my friend?" Elaine starts to leave the kitchen.

"I am your friend, and I'm Tony's friend too, that's why I'm saying something now," Sara says.

"Elaine? Is this the truth? Is the baby mine?" Tony asks.

Elaine doesn't say anything. She has her back towards the group of people assembled in the kitchen. "Look Tony, I'd rather not talk about it right now."

"You'd rather not talk about it right now? When would

you like to talk about it? After our wedding, or maybe after the baby is born?" Tony says. His anger is beginning to show in his voice. "Or maybe you'd just like to go on keeping this lie a secret for the rest of our lives? I can't believe you'd do this. How could you be screwing around with someone else?" Tony's face is red, his fists are clenched. "You say you love me, but you go screwing around." She turns and puts her hand on his chest. She opens her mouth to say something. He pushes it away and before she can say anything he says to her, "Don't touch me, you slut!"

"But Tony!" she starts to cry. "I never..."

Tony turns and walks back out into the dining room. The kitchen door hits the wall with the force he pushes it. Everybody just stands and stares at Elaine. The sound of the front door opening and closing follows a moment later. Sara is still picking up the broken glass from the floor. She lets out a sob. Maria is the first person to speak.

"Joey, I'm sorry for my behaviour, I just..."

Joey says, "Look it's okay I understand." The lisp and waving hands are gone.

Elaine faces the door. You can tell she is crying by the way her shoulders are moving. She wipes her face and pushes her way through the kitchen door and walks out into the dining room. It is completely silent in the dining room. She makes her way across the dining room and leaves the house. Her parents follow her out of the house.

Sara finishes picking up the broken glass from the floor. She gets up and looks at Joey and Garth. "You know things will never be the same again, for any of us."

"You don't think what we did tonight was wrong, do you?" Garth asks her.

"No I don't think it was wrong, but we shouldn't have done it like this," Sara says.

"So maybe we should have waited till they were married and then told them?" Garth asks.

"No, that's not what I mean," Sara says "Maybe we could have just sat the two of them down..."

"Sara," says Mama diMarco, "as cruel as this may have been, it was probably the only way that you'd have ever gotten Elaine to be truthful. It was really her responsibility to tell Tony the truth. If she had been honest from the beginning she'd never have slept around, right?" She shakes her head. "Maria, it's time to go home." As she walks out into the dining room she says politely to Garth, "Thank you Garth."

Garth stops her and says, "I'm sorry Mrs. diMarco, I didn't mean for this to happen like this. I only found out about it this evening." Everyone is following Mama diMarco out into the dining room.

"You don't have to explain Garth," Mama diMarco says. "The only one who has any real explaining to do is Elaine, but I doubt that we'll get anything out of her." Again she shakes her head. "They would have made a perfect couple." She is deeply hurt, you can tell. The diMarco family leaves Garth's home, Joey and Sara are standing in the middle of the dining room.

The silence is broken by Joey, "Holy shit, I wonder how Tony is?"

"He's probably pissed at us," Garth says.

"Probably with me more so than with you guys," Sara adds.

"I wouldn't be so sure about that," Garth says. "This whole thing didn't go as I've planned."

"Well, it's not like we meant to really hurt anyone. We just wanted Elaine to be honest with Tony." Joey states. The three friends are trying to justify the way the events of the evening have unfolded.

"Mrs. diMarco is right though," Sara says. "Had Lainey been honest and told the truth when she found out she was pregnant none of this would have ever happened. So I guess if there is anyone to blame for any of this it's Elaine."

All three of them nod in agreement. By placing fault with Elaine, they feel it wiped their slate clean with Tony.

"Well, I think I should be on my way. I guess we've caused enough damage for one day," Sara says as she picks up her purse and walks out of the house.

"I hope he's okay," Garth says as he moves to the living room window and stares out into the driveway. He watches Sara drive away. Tony has taken his mother's station wagon and driven off earlier. "I hope he doesn't do anything stupid."

Joey asks, "Do you think we should go looking for him?"

"Would you want to be found right now?" Garth asks him. "I think he might just want to have some time to himself. He's got a pretty level head. I'm sure he won't do anything stupid." Garth continues to stare out into the driveway. He truly hopes he is right about Tony not doing anything crazy. He thinks that if it had been him, he'd sure as hell be angry and god only knows what he'd do. Going for a drink or two or three wouldn't be a bad idea for starters. Well, he wouldn't have to go far for that. There were a dozen cases of Bud in the back of the station wagon for tomorrow's reception.

Tony walks out into the driveway. He stands there for a moment wondering what he should do. Elaine has been screwing around and the baby she is carrying is not his. Tomorrow is his wedding day. Everything with Elaine is a sham, he thinks to himself. How could she lie like that? Did she really think that she'd be able to keep it a secret forever? How could his friends not say anything to him? How long would it have taken them to be honest with him? He gets into his mother's station wagon, puts the key into the ignition and pulls the station wagon out onto the road. He starts to drive. All he wants to do is get away from her. He doesn't want to see or talk to her. He doesn't even want her to apologize. He doesn't think that he can forgive her. As he is driving down the road he can hear the clanking of the beer in the back of the station wagon. He reaches behind the seat, tears open a case and pulls out a bottle. He knows he shouldn't be doing this but he is feeling a lot stress. It seems like a month ago when he found out that Elaine was pregnant. He wanted it not to be true. He thought then that he never wanted to be a father and it was at that moment that he wasn't even sure if he wanted to get married. He had all these things going through his head. He knew that over the last few weeks he'd been different, especially when it came to the wedding and the baby. He really didn't take much interest in the planning. His mother said that his dad was like that also, so no one paid much attention to him. He takes a long drink on the bottle of beer. It is warm. Tony makes a face. He doesn't care for the taste of it. He continues driving. He has no real destination. Something tells him he should confront Elaine, but he doesn't feel like being lied to again. He thinks about how his mother is taking all this. She must be devastated. He pulls a U turn and heads back to Garth's place. Hopefully she is still there. He puts the half drunk beer back into the case behind the seat. As he drives back to Garth's he feels like a weight has been lifted from his shoulders. He pulls into Garth's driveway. He can see Garth looking out the living room window. He stops the station wagon gets out of the car and runs up the front stairs just as Joey opens the door.

"Tony!" Joey says.

"Is my mother here?" Tony asks.

"No, she left about twenty minutes after you did." Garth says. "Are you okay?"

"Yeah, I'm fine. How was my mom?"

"Actually, she was better than I thought she'd be. She's probably upset but she sure didn't show it," Garth says. Tony walks into the kitchen. Moments later Garth and Joey can hear him talking on the phone. He must be talking to his mother. Later Tony returns to the dining room. He walks over to the bar, grabs a beer from the ice bucket, and drinks the whole bottle. Garth and Joey just watch. Tony gets another from the bucket and cracks it open.

"You guys want one?" he asks them. Both of them walk over and take a beer from the bucket and open them.

"Tony, I'm really sorry for tonight," Garth says.

He doesn't say anything. He empties his second beer and takes a third. "So how come it took you guys so long to tell me? I thought you were my friends?" he says as he puts the third bottle of beer to his mouth and starts to drink.

"It's not how it looks Tony," Joey starts.

"Well, how does it look?" Tony says.

"Well this is how it goes." Joey starts to tell Tony how he figured out just this evening that Elaine isn't carrying his child. As he recounts the afternoon at the truck stop diner Tony continues to open and drink more beer. Garth then explains the events of the last few hours and how everything went wrong. All along Tony continues to drink more beer and say very little. Garth is glad that Tony has come back to the house. At least he knows that Tony isn't out there somewhere doing something irrational. Tony hasn't told Garth and Joey about his feelings. That he really doesn't want to get married and least of all have a child. The sun has long set and the three men sit on the floor close to where the cold beer is in the ice bucket. The mood has lightened, whether from the beer or the fact that Tony hasn't blamed them for handling things the way they did earlier.

"So what's it like?" Tony asks.

"What's what like?" Garth asks.

"You know being gay?"

"Being gay?" Garth asks. "Hey Joey, do you hear that Tony wants to know what it's like being gay!" he giggles.

"Why do you want to know what it's like being gay?" Joey asks.

"I don't know, I just sorta wanta know, I guess," Tony replies. He hangs his head. His hair falls around his face. He is getting drunk.

"Well, I don't know I've always been gay so I don't really know how it feels to be straight, so I guess I don't have anything to compare it to. But for me it's normal," Joey says.

"Okay so, how'd you know that you were gay?" Tony says.

"How'd I know I was gay? Well let me think," Joey says. He is feeling no pain either. The alcohol is running its course through his veins. "I don't know. I guess I've known all my life that I liked guys instead of girls."

"I remember when I figured it out," Garth states. "I was eleven, and I went on a date with this girl. Her name was Cindy. She was ten and had boobs. So I did what every red blooded American boy was supposed to do. I asked her out to a school dance. After the dance I walked her home and we took a short cut through a park and she tried to kiss me and grab my cock."

"Really, at eleven?" Tony says.

"Yes, at eleven, even at eleven I was a hunky kid. So she was grabbing at me and I was feeling her up and I remember that I couldn't get a hard on. Then all of a sudden her older brother shows up from outta nowhere. He grabs her and tells her to go home. And then he just stands there in front of me. I thought that I was in deep shit. He was fourteen. He walked up to me and grabbed my crotch. All of sudden I had a hard on so hard that I thought I was going to burst. He undid my pants and pulled out my cock, he then proceeded to give me a blowjob. My very first. I was so excited by him, that from that moment on I knew that all I wanted was to be with guys. That I wanted to have a dick in my mouth." Garth takes another beer from the bucket, opens it and starts to drink. "I guess what I needed was just to be kick started." All three start to laugh at Garth's story.

"So how'd you know you were straight?" Joey asks Tony as he starts taking a drink of his beer. He starts to laugh and sprays beer over the three of them sitting on the floor. Garth and Joey also start to laugh. Tony doesn't answer the question.

"Isn't that a dumb one?" Garth says.

"Well, no it's not. I've never been straight. How do I know that it's not the same for straight guys as it is for gay guys? You know either through experience or just knowing like I did that helps you decide what you are, gay or straight," Joey says.

"I'm tired. Hey look it's getting light out," Tony says, avoiding the question. He checks his watch. "It's almost four in the morning. I'm supposed to be getting married in less than eight hours. Happy July fourth." He brings his beer up to his mouth and takes a drink. "I think I've had enough to drink." He puts his bottle of beer next to him, gets up from the floor and stumbles over to the sofa to lay down on it. Both Garth and Joey watch him. They help each other up from the floor and go to their room, both know there wouldn't be a wedding today.

Tony lies on the sofa and watches Garth and Joey walk up the stairs. He sees Garth rub his hand down Joey's back and over his round butt cheeks and back up again over his back. They disappear upstairs out of sight. The house is silent. The sound of birds chirping quietly starts outside. Soon Tony has tuned into the soft moaning and the creaking of a bed emanating from the upper floor. That's what he wants to know about, he thinks to himself. What is it like to be with another man? He wishes he could have just been more direct and to the point about it. He sits up. He decides he can't stay here. He got up from the sofa and walked back to the front door. He felt envious of the two men upstairs. He quietly opens the door and walks out onto the front porch. The sky has now lost all it's darkness to the sun. The air is full of the sounds of birds. He knows where he wants to be. He walks down to his mother's station wagon and gets in as quietly as he can. He pulls out on to the road and starts down Rocky Beach Road towards his favourite place.

He pulls the station wagon over to the side of the road, parks it, gets out and locks the doors. He doesn't have the keys to the front gates so he climbs over them. As he reaches the bottom on the other side of the gates he turns and starts his walk down the tree-lined driveway. About five minutes into his walk the house comes into view. It sits so majestically and so perfectly placed. Tony smiles. For some unknown reason he feels like he's coming home. He thinks about its new owner. Tony figures that Andy would understand everything when he talks to him later. Tony takes a quick look at himself as he walks down the path towards the beach. He figures he is pretty drunk. He shouldn't have been driving. He reaches the beach and walks towards the part that is secluded behind the rocks. He starts to take off his shirt so that all he'll be wearing as the sun reaches him is his muscle t-shirt. His arms are brown from the sun. He walks past the large rock outcroppings and out onto the beach behind the rocks.

"Tony?" I say startled. "What are you doing here? You scared the shit out of me."

"I just thought that I'd...," Tony starts to say. I can tell that he is drunk by the way he is slurring his words as he talks. He is weaving a bit as he stands at the entrance to the secluded beach. Tony makes his way over to where I'm sitting up against a log on the beach.

"I'm sorry. I just...I sorta climbed the gates and well, here I am," he says with a big white toothed grin as he parks himself on the beach next to me, so close that his right arm and my left are touching. Now I know he's drunk. I can smell the odour of beer on him.

"Are you okay?" I ask him.

"Sure I'm okay," he slurs. "My life is just taking a big U turn."

I don't know what to say. I really only know him through his work. "Oh?" Is all I can think of to say.

"Yeah, it's okay, Elaine's pregnant, you know?" He looks at me with his big black eyes. "But it's not mine." He hiccups.

"I'm really sorry Tony," I say to him. That explains why he's been drinking. "So you've been out drowning your sorrows, I take it?"

"Either drownin' my sorrows or celebrating, I'm not sure what I want to call it yet."

"So what brings you here?" I ask him really not knowing why he is here.

"Your gonna think I'm crazy," he says.

"Of course I won't," I say.

"Well this place of yours, I've been looking after it for years and it's my favourite place on the planet," he says so matter of factly. He has a big grin on his face. His dark hair is messy and hanging in his face. "No really it is. I used to make excuses just so that I could come here and sometimes just sit and watch the stars or the sailboats." He hiccups again. "You're gonna laugh at me."

"No I won't. This place is great for that, and I can understand why you like it here," I say. It's really true. This place is perfect.

"No, not that. This beach is the perfect place to sunbathe buck naked," he states. He hiccups again, smiles and says, "Oops."

"Do you want a drink?" I ask him, "All I've got is this wine. I was sorta having a toast to my first day here." I hold up an open bottle of wine. "I don't have any glasses..."

"Sure, these hiccups are driving me crazy," he says as he hiccups again. I hand him the bottle, he takes a long swig and then hands me back the bottle. "Your turn," he says with a grin on his face as he runs his hand through his hair. His jaw is dark with the shadow of his beard. His eyes are starting to look glazed as his eyelids get heavy with lack of sleep and over consumption of beer. I take a drink from the bottle as he watches.

"So why are you out here so early?" Tony asks me.

"I decided that since this was my first full day here I was going to toast the dawn," I say as I tip the bottle to him again to take another drink.

"She was fucking around on me and got herself pregnant," he giggles.

"I'm sorry," I try to console him.

"Don't be sorry. She got what she deserves," he says.

Must be the alcohol talking; after he sobers up he'll be either really angry or really depressed.

"I wasn't sure I wanted to get married anyway you know?" he says as he stares into my eyes. "I like your goatee," he adds as he brings up his hand to rub my face. His hand is rough and callused. It feels good to be touched by a man's hand again, even if he's drunk. He lets his hand fall from my face. It lands on my thigh. "I think it's really neat how it's a different colour from your hair." I'm not really sure whether he is actually aware of his touching. He is probably too drunk to realize. He takes off his shoes and rolls up his jeans, like he is preparing to take a stroll in the surf. His feet are as tanned as his arms. I wonder if the rest of his body is as dark. "I've got funny feet," he says out of the blue.

I look at his feet. They don't look out of the ordinary. "They look fine." I feel silly commenting about his feet. I take another swig from the bottle and hand it to Tony, who takes another drink emptying the bottle. After he takes his drink he puts his head back on the log and closes his eyes. He hands me back the bottle with his left hand as his arm stretches across my chest. I follow its length to his hand with the bottle in it. I take the empty bottle from him. His arm stays across my chest after he releases the bottle. My eyes travel back up his arm from his hand. His muscles are well formed. His forearm is covered with light coloured hair that disappears at his elbow. His bicep, which is almost in the centre of my chest, is relaxed but large, about the size of a softball. He lets his arms slide down my chest across my stomach. I feel myself getting hard.

"Boy, I'm getting tired," he says, as he moves his hand and rests his head in it. "I think I'm gonna pay for this later."

"Why don't you come up to the house and sleep it off?" I ask.

"You don't mind?" he says as he starts to stand up. I stand up beside him. I brush the sand from my backside. He tries to do the same but can't get it all. I brush the rest of it off for him. I look at his face. He is staring at me with glazed eyes. His body is weaving as he stands in front of me. If you weren't drunk and straight, I think to myself. This is every gay man's fantasy. He bends over to pick up his shoes and socks and starts to fall over. I grab him by his belt and he swings facing towards me, but the inertia of his body falling knocks us both off balance. As we fall to the soft sandy beach, Tony tries to right himself and brings his body up high enough so that our faces are together. I hit the ground on my back with Tony and all his weight on top of me. We lay there in a tangle of arms and legs. I groan. I can smell Tony's beer breath. His face is so close to mine that he starts to giggle. He rolls off of me and lies beside me still giggling. I start to laugh with him. It would have been a funny thing if anybody had witnessed what just happened. "Sorry," he says in between giggles.

I sit up and look at the man lying next to me, "Why don't we try that again?" I smile at him. "You just stay there until I get everything gathered up." He is still laying on his back on the beach giggling. I get his socks and stuff them inside his shoes, pick up his shirt and the empty wine bottle and make a neat pile on the log. I turn and look at Tony lying on the sand. "God you're a mess," I say to him.

"And you're gay," he blurts out.

I don't say anything. I just walk over and pick him up. He probably won't even remember he said that.

"So?" he slurs.

"So what if I am," I say. He hiccups. "Let's just get you up to the house before you pass out, okay?"

"Okay," he says, as he helps me help him to get to his feet.

I gather up the pile of clothing, the empty wine bottle and tuck them under my left arm. I start to walk up the path. I can hear Tony shuffling along behind me. I turn to see him almost fall. "Just stand still for a moment," I say as I walk back to him. "Here put your left arm over my shoulder, otherwise if you fall I guess I'll have to leave you out here." He puts his arm across my back and his hand grabs my shoulder. I put my arm around his narrow waist and grab hold of his belt. We start to stumble our way up the soft sand path to the house. Tony doesn't say anything as we walk up to the house. His hold on my shoulder relaxes and tightens as we walk towards the stairs. His head rests on my right shoulder. I can feel his beard rub against my skin as we walk. I hope we make it to the house before he passes out. We finally reach the bottom stair and start to climb.

He lifts his head from my shoulder as we reach the top, he drops his arm from my shoulder and I release my hold on his belt. "Thanks Andy. You know you don't have to...," he says as he starts to waver back and forth. "I can just..."

"No, I don't think that it would be a wise thing for you to be going right now. I think you just need to have some sleep, okay?" He nods in agreement. I open the screen door on one of the French doors that lead into the living room. He heads directly for the sofa. He looks at it. There are a couple of cushions missing. "Remember the cushions won't be back until Monday. You'll have to manage the stairs up to the spare bedroom. All I have to do is put some sheets on it." He quietly makes his way to the stairway and starts to climb. He is starting to fade. I walk up behind him. He makes the top of the stairs without incident and stops. I almost walk into him as I reach the top of the stairs myself. I gently push him forward towards the bathroom at the end of the upstairs hall.

"Why don't you go in the bathroom and at least splash some water on your face." I walk him to the bathroom. We both enter the room. "Here," I say to him as I rummage through my bathroom bag, "is a toothbrush and there's the toothpaste. Your breath smells like a brewery." I hand them to him. "No wait." I take them back, undo the lid of the toothpaste, squeeze a straight line of it on the toothbrush and hand it back to him. "There, that'll make it easier," I say to him smiling. "I'll just go and make up the bed for you in the next room." I point to the room next to the bathroom. I close the door and leave Tony standing in front of the bathroom sink. I get the new set of sheets I've bought for that bed from the linen closet. I can hear the water start to run in the bathroom, and then silence, but only for a moment. Then I could hear Tony taking a leak. I could hear the toilet flush and a second later the door opened and Tony walks into the bedroom where I have already gotten the fitted sheet on the bed. He stands in the door way with his belt and the zipper of his pant undone. His muscle t-shirt untucked. His skin tight t-shirt is dirty from the fall on the beach. He shuffles into the room.

"I think you'd better get out of these dirty clothes before you get into this clean bed," I say as I finish tucking the flat sheet under the mattress. I toss a blanket over the bed and proceed to put pillow cases on the pillows. I have my back towards Tony as he undresses. He is very quiet. Everything is probably catching up to him, especially the liquor. I open the window by the bed, to keep the fresh air moving in the room. I turn and see Tony remove his jeans. The covered parts of his body are as dark as his arms and feet. He has a pair of Calvin Klein briefs on. I avert my gaze from his crotch. I figure that I shouldn't take advantage of the situation. I turn the blanket and sheet down on the bed and walk to the door of the bedroom.

"There you go Tony," I say. He walks to the bed and sits on it. He looks at me through his hair that has fallen across his face. He runs his hand through it to pull it out of his eyes.

"Andy, I, ah..."

"Tony, don't worry about anything. Just go to bed. Sleep this off okay?" I say as I lean against the door jamb. "Is there anyone I should let know about where you are?"

"No," he says.

I leave him sitting on the edge of the bed. I walk down to my bedroom collect up a fresh pair of sweat pants and t-shirt. I carry them back out into the hall, open the linen closet to take out fresh towels and bring it all back to the bedroom. I knock before I enter.

"Tony?" I look at the bed where I have left him sitting. He is lying face down on the bed. He isn't under the blankets. I walk to the chair by the open window at Tony's head and put the clothes and towels down. As I turn to leave, Tony stirs and gives a soft moan. My eyes travel down the sleeping body. I look at his shoulders, the way the muscles bulge, the definition of his back, how it tapers to his narrow waist and disappears into his briefs, that snugly hug the round mounds of his butt cheeks. There is a small tuft of dark hair in the small of his back just where the waist band of his jockey's meet his back. It disappears below. The material of his shorts is stretched over the hardness of his butt, pulled tight where his cheeks round and disappear into the crevasse. His dark tanned skin returns from underneath his shorts and continues down his long legs. His thighs are well muscled and strong looking, tapering down to his knees then expanding again in nicely formed calves, lightly covered in hair bleached by the sun. My gaze continues onto his ankles and those feet which he thinks are so funny. A dark tan line circles his feet leaving the souls of his feet a clean pink colour. This is repeated on his hands. It's hard to tell if he's got a tan line under his Calvin Klein's as his skin is dark naturally. He stirs again. He lifts his head and opens his dark eyes. He smiles at me.

"Andy?" he says in a sleepy voice.

"I just brought you some clean clothes and some towels, so when you get up just go ahead and use whatever you can find in the bathroom okay?" I say quietly.

He continues to smile at me. His eyes are searching mine. I almost melt on the spot. I start to walk past him. He reaches up with his hand and grabs my arm firmly.

"I just want to thank you." He pulls himself into a sitting position, then stands beside me. He is still weaving from the beer. He releases my arm, puts his muscled arms around me, pulls my body close to his, and gives me a strong firm hug. His unshaved cheek is in my neck. I can feel his beard rub against my neck as he says, "Thanks for letting me be here." His body feels solid and hard against mine.

I'm lost for words my body temperature rises. I start to sweat. I have now a raging hard on that is straining the front of my shorts and pushing into his crotch. "It's fine Tony," I say as I pull myself gently away from him, hoping that he hasn't noticed my bodies reaction to his hug, "I think you'd better get some sleep okay?"

"Sure, you're probably right," he says as he returns to the bed and crawls under the single sheet on the bed.

I pick up his t-shirt and jeans from the floor and quickly leave his room. As I close the door to the bedroom I wonder if he knows what he's doing. Probably not. It's most likely the alcohol. His clothes have the distinct odour of beer. I decide to wash them. I walk down to the basement and start the washer. I go back upstairs and walk out onto the front veranda and sit in the cushioned rattan lounge. I close my eyes and drift off to sleep.

As I wake up I can feel the heat of the sun as it beats down on the front of the veranda. It is afternoon already. I can hear the sounds of someone in the kitchen. I'm startled. I get up and walk into the living room. I can see into the kitchen through the dining room door. It is Tony. He is dressed in the pair of sweat pants, but not the t-shirt I gave him earlier. I wipe my eyes. So it hasn't been all just a dream. I continue to watch him. He is preparing something to eat. He moves smoothly, like he knows what he's doing. As he moves the muscles of his hairless back contract and relax. He hasn't tied the sweat pants tight around his waist so they are hanging low on his hips. The roundness of his but cheeks is the only thing that keeps them from falling down. I can tell that he isn't wearing his Calvin Klein's under them. I can also tell that he hasn't had much time to suntan buck-naked, as he'd say. There is a distinct tan line at his waist just above where the crack of his butt starts. He still hasn't noticed me so I walk into the kitchen, stop and lean in the doorway.

"I didn't wake you, did I?" he says as he notices me standing there.

"No, it was getting hot out there. I was starting to sweat." I untuck my t-shirt from my shorts and pull it over my head. He watches me take my shirt off and then continues to work on whatever he is preparing.

"I hope you don't mind. I thought I'd make us some sandwiches," Tony says as he continues his working. He sounds better than he did earlier this morning.

"How are you feeling?" I ask. "You were pretty drunk."

"Feeling really good. I think I cheated the gods on this hangover. For the amount I consumed I should be suffering for days but I don't even have a headache," he says as he continues to build the sandwiches. He still has his back towards me. "Andy I want to thank you for letting me stay, the bed, the clean clothes and all."

"No problem, you are lucky that the two of us are about the same size and build," I say to him. He reaches for a couple of plates from the top shelf of the cupboard above where he is working. As he stretches for the plates the sweat pants slide a couple of inches down his backside showing more of the crack of his ass. There the little tuft of sun bleached hair at his waistline turns into a thin little line of hair that disappears between the two globes of his butt cheeks. As he puts the plates on the counter he nonchalantly gives the sweat pants a tug at one hip and pulls them up slightly "And of course the bed, you're lucky that I'd thought that I might get some company from the city and had bought sheets, otherwise you'd have had to share mine."

Tony doesn't comment. He just turns with two plates of sandwiches in his hands and a big grin on his face. "So where do wish to dine?" is all he says. I look at him and start to laugh. He looks rather silly, but mind you if every restaurant that I ever went to had a waiter like him, I'd never have learned to cook. "So? Dining room or veranda?" he asks as he stands there with the plates in his hand. He has a big grin on his tanned face, his eyes, bright and clear. I give him the once over, and smile back at him. His brown chest is almost perfect. Fine hair cover his pectorals, a thin dark line of hair starts just above his belly button travels over his wash board abdomen down towards his crotch and starts to widen just where the sweat pants are hanging showing a lighter shade of skin that hasn't been exposed to the suns rays for some time. There is a definite bulge in the front of the sweats that keep the pants from going any further.

I take a plate from him as he comes up to me, he pulls up the pants and asks, "Something to drink? Beer?"

"You gotta be kidding me!" I say.

"Not for me, I'm just having water," he smiles.

"Water will be fine for me too," I reply.

Tony goes to the refrigerator and gets out two bottles of water. His hands are full and his pants start to slip again. "How about the veranda?" he says. I motion for him to lead the way. He smiles at me as I stand in the doorway of the kitchen.

We eat in silence, staring out over Cape Cod Bay. It is the fourth of July and the bay is full of sailboats.

"Every weekend it'll be like that," Tony says, breaking the silence, pointing out over the bay.

"Let me know if I'm out of place here, but are you okay? Today was supposed to be your wedding day."

"Yeah, I'm fine," he says as he still looks out over the bay. "I should be feeling something like anger or something, but I don't." He looks at me. "I don't know if this is right but I sort of feel relieved." He pauses. "Do you think that's wrong?"

"I don't think so." I stop before I go on about my experience with Rick. I'm not sure he remembers asking whether I'm gay so I figure I should choose my words carefully. "I ended a relationship because of infidelity. I was cheated on and I couldn't justify it nor could I carry on with the relationship without being able to trust. Don't get me wrong. I was hurt emotionally and I was angry, but eventually I did feel relieved. It became obvious that the relationship wasn't meant to be, so yeah, I can say it's not wrong."

"Don't get me wrong. I do feel wronged, but there's just something else, you know..." He stares at me. "I don't quite know how to put it."

I'm not sure what he's talking about and the only advice that I can give him is, "Don't worry about it right now. Take everyday one day at a time." God, I think to myself I sound like a counsellor. "You don't have to make any decisions right away. Take your time and think things out." I'm thinking of Gerry. These were the same words he's used on me. "But don't take too long before you start living again. It's not the end of the world. My friend Gerry told me that after my break up. He was right."

"Good advice, I guess," Tony says.

"It's worked for me," I say. We both fall silent watching the sailboats on Cape Cod Bay. It seems that Tony doesn't or chooses not to remember the events from earlier today on the beach. He hasn't commented about anything except his overindulgence in beer, so maybe he doesn't remember asking me if I was gay. Not that it matters anyway.

"Andy?" Tony brakes the silence again. "Would you mind if I spent a few days here? You know to think and stuff?" he asks. "I've got two weeks vacation and with all this shit going on I don't really want to go back to work quite yet and I don't want to spend it at home with my mom."

I don't want to sound too excited at the prospect of having Tony spend a few days with me. "Sure it'll be good to have some company," I reply. I might have the good fortune of seeing him buck naked while he suntans on the beach.

"I've got my mom's station wagon parked at the gate. I really should get it back to her and pick up a few things," he continues. "I'm going to go into town for a while." He pauses for a moment. I can see the wheels turn as he thinks. "That's going to be the tough part. I'm sure the whole town will know by now about Elaine and I. Do you think people will talk?"

"Sure they'll talk, but what they'll be saying is poor

Tony at worst," I suggest.

"I hate that. I don't like being treated that way. Having people feel sorry for me."

"I don't think you're gonna have much choice, so I guess if you want advice about that the only thing I can tell you is just to carry on and don't use it, the sympathy that is." I add, "The one who's going to be talked about the most is Elaine. Consider this, small town girl screwing around on boyfriend; girl gets pregnant by a lover not the boyfriend. Who's everyone gonna talk about? Not you."

"Yeah, I guess you're right," Tony agrees. He stares back out across the bay. He stands up and stretches. I almost drop my water bottle, as I watch his body stiffens and pump up with his stretch. "I'll just get that t-shirt you lent me and get on my way."

"I'll give you a ride up to the gate," I suggest as I pick up our plates and water bottles and carry them into the kitchen. He follows me. He goes upstairs to get the t-shirt. I grab the keys to my jeep and walk back out onto the veranda to wait for him to return. I hear him run down the stairs. He comes out onto the veranda, I turn and take a look at him. He has put on the white t-shirt. It fits him well. The sweat pants are still untied and sagging on his narrow hips. I start to laugh.

"What?" he says. "What's so funny?"

I can't say anything between the bouts of laughter so I point to his work boots.

"They're all I got!" he starts to laugh with me. "So it looks a bit funny!"

"A bit!"

"Okay a lot!" he laughs. "Let's get going I wanna get back before dark. Your beach is great for watching the fireworks. You can see them perfectly."

"Great, but one thing," I say trying to suppress more laughter.

"What's that?" Tony asks.

"You gotta bring other shoes."

"All right funny man let's go," he says and puts his hand on my shoulder and squeezed. I look him in the eyes quickly not wanting to show him that I really enjoy his touch.

We walk down to my jeep. He gets into the passenger seat. I start up the engine and we drive up the tree lined driveway to the gate. I give him the keys to the wrought iron gates. He quickly runs out to the station wagon and returns carrying a couple of cases of beer and puts them in the back of the jeep.

"We may need some later," he says.

"So you want me to meet you here at the gates later?" I ask him, I don't want it to sound like he may not return. Something out there may change his mind about staying here. I was going to suggest making something for dinner but I don't want to come across as anxious.

"No, I've got my work keys, I'll be able to get in." He pauses as he turns and walks back to the other side of the gates and pulls them closed. The lock clicks shut. He looks through the gate and says; "I'll see you later." As he moves towards the station wagon I can see him adjust the sweat pants as they fall so that they show a bit more of the lighter coloured skin of his butt.

"Sure, later," is all I can think of to say. I give him a small wave and back the jeep back down the driveway. I can hear him start the station wagon, and later I can hear him drive towards town.

Tony drives down Rocky Beach Road towards town and his mother's place. He is sure that she'd be home to-day, especially with the events of yesterday. His thoughts don't linger much on those events, but they do wander back to the house and Andy. Tony can feel himself smile. There is something about Andy that he finds very intriguing. Some-thing he really likes about him. Like the place, Andy makes him feel comfortable. He just wishes that he could really talk to him. The kind of reveal your soul kind of talk. As he drives through town he notices that the town people are starting to gather in City Park. This is where all of the Fourth of July celebrations will be taking place. He waves at some of the people as he drives by. For someone whose whole world has just taken a dump he sure feels good about things. Maybe this is because of the way Andy makes him feel. It doesn't take long before he pulls into his mother's driveway. Only the big white Cape Development truck is parked here. She could be over at Maria's. He gets out of her station wagon, runs up the path and tries the front door. It is unlocked. That means that Mama is home. He walks into the house and down the hall. If anywhere, he would find his mother in the kitchen. Sure enough, there she is just as he suspected, on the phone. She looks up as he enters the room and he hears her say, "Maria, Tony's home. I'll call you back." She hangs up. "Tony! Where have you been? Are you all right? What are you going to do? What's going to happen with you and Elaine? And what about the baby?" Her barrage of questions hit him before he can say anything.

He stands there, looking at her for a moment, then walks up to her and gives her a big hug. "Hi Mama, I'm fine."

"Are you sure? Where have you been? I've been worried," she continues.

"I went out and got drunk and did some thinking and drank some more and thought some more. That's pretty much it."

"Garth has called a hundred times today and so has Sara. They're all worried." She sounds angry. "Maria has been here five times already to see if you had shown up."

"Well I'm here now," he says. "And you know what I'm fine. I'm okay with everything that happened yesterday."

"How could you be fine after just one day?" she asks. "You're just in denial."

"Oh I think I've been in denial but not about what happened last night."

"What are you talking about Tony? I don't understand?" she says.

"Has Elaine called?" he asks her.

"No, but her mother called. She apologized over and over," Mama says. "Why are you so concerned about Elaine after what she did to you."

"Look Mama, as bad as what was she did, I'm sure she had her reasons and you know, as God is our witness, it's not for us to judge."

"Oh don't you go throwing God at me," she starts to say.

"Mama, please listen." He stops her mid sentence. "What I'm trying to tell you is that this whole situation, Elaine, the baby wasn't right. Do you get it?" She has a puzzled look on her face. "What I mean is this is for the best. God obviously didn't want this wedding to happen. Maybe he wanted that baby to be with its real father, but for whatever the reason, I'm actually quite relieved that it's not happening. I've got other things that I've got to deal with."

"What kinda things, Tony?" she asks.

"When I get everything all figured out you'll be the first to know," he says.

His mother steps back and stares at him. She's seen this look before, not on Tony but with her husband. It's the same look he's had many years ago when he was bound and determined that she was going to be his wife. She knew that look, and it was a good look. "You look like your Papa when you talk like that."

"Is that good?" he asks.

"Of course that's good," she smiles. She knows there is no point in standing in his way. He has something to do and she'd be the last person to stand in his way. "So can you give me an idea of what to expect?"

"You know I don't know yet." He checks the clock above the kitchen sink. It reads six o'clock. "I've got to pack a few things." He starts to leave the kitchen and goes up to his room.

"Are you leaving Tony?" He can sense the fear in her voice.

"No Mama, I've got vacation time, so I'm just going to take a few days to figure things out. I'm not leaving Rocky Beach."

"Are you sure?" she asks timidly.

"Oh that I'm sure." He smiles and races up to his room. He pulls the suitcase out from under his bed. It had been his father's. The one he had when he and Mama got married. He quickly packs up some clothes and his personal stuff from the bathroom and closes the suitcase. As he stands there quickly taking stock of what he needs to bring, he sees himself in the full length mirror on the wall. He smiles. Andy is right. He looks funny with his work boots on with these sweat pants and t-shirt. He kicks them off and goes to his closet and puts on a pair of running shoes. He steps back and looks at himself again. Much better he thinks to himself. He knows that if he doesn't get himself out of the house Mama would have Maria here, both of them trying to get him to stay home. He packs up his work boots, grabs his suitcase and goes back downstairs. He places the suitcase and boots by the door and walks back into the kitchen. His mother is on the phone with Maria. Again she hangs up on his sister.

"Maria will be over soon. Why don't we have a tea and wait for her?" she says.

"Look Mama, I don't think there is anything that you or Maria can say to me right now that's gonna make me change my mind. And you have to believe me when I say I'm not leaving Rocky Beach. I'm just gonna be away for a few days like a vacation, okay?" he says.

"So what am I gonna tell people?" she asks him.

"What's to tell? I'm on vacation that's all," he says. He has that look again. She backs off.

"Okay Tony, just remember..."

Before she can finish he says, "I know, and I love you too." He kisses her on the cheek. "I'm not going too far and I'll be in touch, okay?" he says as they both walk to the front door. "Tell that to Garth and Sara, too. I'm sure they'll be calling again." Mama nods. She watches her son pick up his suitcase and work boots and walk to the white Cape Development and Maintenance truck. Tony unlocks the drivers' door, gets in and starts the big truck up. She watches as he backs down the driveway onto the road and drives away.

She is still standing at the door when Maria pulls into the driveway ten minutes later. "Where is he Mama?" Maria says as she walks quickly up the stairs to where her mother is standing. "Has he gone already? How was he?" she asks.

"Oh, he's just fine," she says. There is a tear rolling down her cheek.

"How can he be fine if he makes you cry," Maria says.

"I know he's fine that's why I'm crying. He had that

look," Mama says.

"What look?" Maria asks.

"That same look your papa always had when he did the right thing," Mama says. "He's gonna be just fine. And you know I know that just by that look. He's gonna be happy."

"How can you tell by just a look?"

"I lived with that look for almost thirty years and I know," Mama says matter of factly. "Do you want some tea?" She puts her arm around her daughter's waist and closes the door.

It is six twenty. Tony has been gone for almost two hours. His mother has probably talked him into staying. Can't really blame him. They could be telling him he needs family right now. They're probably right. I take the wet clothes out of the washing machine and put them into the dryer. I walk back towards the stairs leading up to the main floor and notice that I have left the keys to the cabinets that housed my grandfather's kites on the workbench. I pick them up and start to check the locks with the keys. I finally find the right key that opens the doors of the cabinets. They are all empty except one. It contains a number of spools of string, some light doweling and tucked in the back is the bright blue material of a kite. It seems as though Grams had missed a kite when she left. I take it out carefully, in case the material is brittle, but it seems to be fine. I unfold it and place the doweling in the pockets in the blue material. I finish putting it together and lift the finished kite up. It has a long tail, made of bright red and yellow bows that fall to the floor. I can remember this one. It was my grandmother's favourite. Blue was her favourite colour because blue was the colour of the heavens. They'd believed that the angels made this one particular kite fly the highest and do the most spectacular stunts. I smile to myself. It is as if Grams had known that I'd find it. I grab a couple of spools of string and take the kite upstairs. I place the kite on the sofa with the missing cushions and start to tie the loose end of one of the spools of string onto the kite. I just finished tying the knot when I hear the sound of a vehicle coming down the driveway. I set the kite behind the sofa so that it would be out of the way and wouldn't get damaged. I concentrate on the sounds outside. I hear the engine of the vehicle stop, then a door slam shut and then silence for a few moments. It continues with the sound of footsteps climbing up the stairs and walking around on the veranda, followed by a knock on the screen. It is Tony. I don't want to appear overly excited about him being here so I don't go and open the screen door for him. I just call out, "It's open." I hope he doesn't think I don't really care or don't want him here. He puts the suitcase down, opens the screen door, and picks up his suitcase and enters the living room.

"I'm back," he says with a grin. His wavy cheek length black hair is tucked up under a ball cap. He still hasn't tied the strings of the sweat pants. They are hanging low on his hips. He looks down at his feet and says, "Well?"

I follow his gaze down to his feet and see his runners. "Much better," I comment. "I didn't expect you back quite yet. I thought you'd have had to spend some time with your family going over everything that's happened to you in the last twenty four hours." I fiddle with the extra spool of string I have brought up from the basement. He is still standing with his work boots in one hand and his suitcase at his feet. I guess he is waiting for me to welcome him. "Why don't you go and put your stuff up in your room," I suggest.

He has a grin on his face a mile wide. "Sure." He disappears upstairs. His grin, like almost everything else about him makes me melt. I've got to control myself. It only takes him a few minutes and he is back downstairs. "So where'd you get the kite?" he asks looking at the kite tucked behind the sofa.

"I found it in one of the cabinets downstairs. It was one of my grandfather's. He loved to fly kites on the beach when he was alive," I say.

"Looks like it's in good shape."

"Yeah, I was quite surprised at how good a shape it's actually in," I say as I reach behind the sofa and bring it out.

"Do you fly?"

"Kites? No," Tony says. "But I'd give it a try. Do you? Fly kites that is?"

"Not since I was a kid," I say as I hand him the kite. He looks at it and hands it back. "There's a story about flying kites here I'll have to tell you one day."

He nods. "So how old is this one?" he asks.

"Maybe twenty five or so years," I say.

"Wow! It's in great shape," Tony says standing in front of me with his hands on his hips. "So?"

"So?" I say.

"What should we do?" he asks.

"I don't know, what do you want to do?" What a dumb answer I think to myself. I really do know what I'd like to do, but I'm pretty sure that Tony is straight and not into the same kind of stuff. We both stand there, looking at each other. "Ah, why don't we see about making something for dinner?"

"Great!" he says. "Do you like to cook? I was practically raised in a kitchen, but I never really paid much attention to what was going on in it. That doesn't mean I can't cook. I'm just not that good at it." He walks over to the refrigerator and opens the door. I can hear him rustle around inside. He turns around and has two beer in his hand. He cracks the top off one and hands it to me as he opens the second for himself. "How about I make us some pasta. That I can do. Do we have any fresh seafood?"

"Of course we do. We're on Cape Cod. What else would one on the Cape have in the larder?" I say as I take a sip of beer. He raises his beer to me and takes a long guzzle. "So let's get started," I suggest and walk over to where he is standing. I start to get the ingredients needed for dinner out of the refrigerator. After I have everything on the kitchen counter I ask him, "What would you like me to start on?"

"How about getting us another beer and then I'll do the rest," he says. I retrieve another beer for each of us.

"Are you sure you want more beer after last night?" I ask him. "You know you were pretty drunk last night."

"I wasn't that bad," Tony says as he continues to prepare our dinner. "I didn't pass out or anything."

"You probably don't remember a thing from last night," I say jokingly. "Like falling on the beach."

"I do remember that. I fell right on top of you then I rolled off laughing," he says. "By the way I didn't hurt you did I?"

"Of course not, I'm a tough guy," I reply. So he probably does remember a good portion of the events last night, but probably not everything we talked about. "I'll set the table on the front veranda. We'll dine alfresco tonight."

"Sounds great," Tony says.

I open the cupboard and get out two pasta bowls and set them on the counter. Then, I get two wine glasses from another cupboard and ask him, "Do you prefer red or white?"

"Definitely white with the cream sauce," he replies. "Why don't you tell me your story about the kites?" he adds.

"Well okay. It's not like it's very exciting or anything. It's just what we did when we vacationed here when I was a kid," I start to tell him. "My grandfather was an expert kite flyer, if you can imagine that there is such a thing. All us grandchildren loved it when he flew his kites. He could make them do all sorts of tricks and manoeuvres in the sky. He even won a fourth of July kite flying contest in Rocky Beach a long time ago. Grams would pack us a picnic and we'd all go down to the beach between the rocks and set out a blanket and have ourselves a picnic and grandpa would fly kites. When we got a little older, around eight or nine he'd let us hold the string with him and he'd pull and jerk the string we were holding and the kite would do a trick." I pause for a moment. Tony is listening while he continues to work at the stove preparing dinner. "Grandpa would yell at Grams and say look at Andrew or Em or Trish. They're making the kite do tricks. But always at the end of the picnic Grandpa would take over the flying again and do some really technical manoeuvres and then fly the kite as high as he could get it." Again I pause and think back. It is just like it was yesterday when he did that, and not almost two decades since anyone has flown a kite on that beach. "It was at that time when Grams would tell us that when Grandpa flew his kites that high he was flying with angels. Then he'd add that those angels were his brothers who had died in the war. Sometimes he'd let us help him hold the string and he'd ask if we could feel the angels tug on the kite. Of course at nine or ten we didn't know that the higher you go in the sky the stronger the wind was, so when we held onto the string with him, there was definitely a stronger tug on the string. We all believed him. And I think what made us believe even more was the fact that he believed he really was flying with the angels. After he died the kites were never flown again. We never came back to this place for vacations again. We all thought that Grams had sold it years ago. But my mom said that Gram's loved this place so much she could never sell it." As I finish my story I see that Tony is dishing out our dinners. "I'll open the wine," I say.

He hands me my plate, we walk out onto the veranda and sit across from each other at the table. I pour us both a glass of wine and we start to eat dinner. "That's really neat. I mean to have a family story, almost like a tradition. I don't have anything like that in my family. Well, at least none that I know of."

"Think so?" I ask him.

"Yeah I do," he says in between mouthfuls.

"I thought you said you couldn't cook? This is great," I say as I take another mouthful of pasta.

"I'm Italian. I can't go wrong with pasta. I think it's a genetic thing." He smiles at me from across the table.

We both finish two large bowls of pasta and the wine is almost gone. Tony says, "Andy, I want to thank you again for letting me stay here."

"Look enough with the thank you's, you said it a hundred times last night and again earlier this morning." I'm smiling at him. "I told you that it would be fun having someone else here with me for a while."

"Yeah, I remember thanking you a lot last night, but I just want you to know that I'm sincere," he says. "I remember telling you just about everything about me last night, guess that was the beer talking." He takes the wine bottle and splits the remainder between us. "But you didn't tell me anything about yourself."

Shit, I think to myself. Maybe he really does remember what we talked about last night. Hopefully he doesn't remember asking me if I was gay. If he does, I won't lie to him about it. "I think we talked about me. I'm sure we did," I say.

"Look, I was the drunk one last night," Tony says.

"Not much really to tell." I get up from the table and start to clean up. He starts to get up from the table. "No, you cooked. I'll do the clean up." I continue to stack the plates and pick up the cutlery.

"I wasn't gonna help you. I was just gonna get a couple more beer for us," he says teasingly. He gets up and walks into the house. I watch him disappear into the kitchen. I follow him. Maybe he wants me to tell him. I place the dishes in the dishwasher and start the wash cycle. I walk back out of the kitchen. Tony hands me a beer as I walk past him.

"Want to go down to the beach? We'll have the best seats on the Cape for the fireworks. It's almost dark so they'll be getting started pretty soon," he says.

"I'll grab us a few more brews." I get the small cooler I've bought for just such an occasion and fill it with ice and beer. Beer on the beach with a hunk. Life doesn't get any better. I return to the veranda where Tony is standing waiting for me.

"Want me to carry it?" he asks.

"No, I think I can carry it. I work out you know."

"I can tell." He smiles that grin of his, takes his free hand and gives my bicep a squeeze.

"Does Rocky Beach have a good gym?" I ask him.

"Yeah, it's pretty good, not really busy, but it has everything you need," he says. "I've been going there for about eight years."

"I can tell," I comment. "You look like you're in pretty good shape." How dumb I think to myself. Of course he's in great shape, not just pretty good, but I didn't want to sound to over zealous about his body.

"Thanks," he says as we head off towards the beach. Tony falls in behind me as we enter the path, I wish I were following him so that I at least could watch him walk. The movement of his legs, the expanding and contracting of his bubble butt muscles as he takes each step, the swing of his arms and shoulders as they move in harmony with his stride.

Too much to even contemplate. I would have melted.

The sun has set over an hour ago and the sky is almost dark. It is still light enough that we can see the path in the tall beach grasses quite clearly. As I step onto the sand I stop walking. Tony steps up beside me and stares out over Cape Cod Bay.

"It's beautiful. Don't you think?" he asks.

I stare out over the bay and say, "It is isn't it? I can see why you like this spot so much."

"I look after quite a number of homes here, but I have to admit your place has to be one of the best," Tony says.

"You think so?" I ask him. "What makes it so special for you? I know that I have memories and family ties, but what about you?"

"I don't know," he starts. "It's just such a peaceful place. It's also not like many of the others. I guess when your grandfather built this place he took the time and planned it all out. Where the house is situated, how he left a lot of the bush around to keep the privacy, and, I don't know, just the house itself. It's not your typical Cape Cod house." He pauses. "And of course the beach, especially behind the rocks. It's so private. You can't be seen from anywhere, not even the house."

I look back to the house. From where we are standing I can see the whole house, but I know he's right about the secluded beach behind the rocks. Once you go past the first outcrop of rocks the house almost disappears, you can really only see the top floor lights and roof line. As it gets darker, the details of the building seem to disappear leaving only the faint glow of the lights through the windows.

"So where's the best spot to watch the fire works?" I ask.

"Follow me," he says as he starts to walk down the beach towards the rock outcroppings. I follow him in the dark. It is obvious that Tony has spent a lot of time here, even in the dark. He seems to know the path very well. We walk onto the secluded part of the beach and over to the same spot, against the log where we were the night before. I place the small cooler and sit down on the sand beside it. Tony takes a walk down to the waters edge and stands there for a moment, staring out over the bay. I watch him stand there in the failing evening light. He stays only for a few minutes then walks back. He sits down on the opposite side of me, almost as close as we were the night before. It's like he places this sort of safe space between us. The beer I've been carrying is empty so I open the cooler and get myself another.

"Would you like another?" I ask.

"Sure," he says. I hand him the one I just pulled out from the cooler and get myself another. We sit in silence, both of us just staring out across the bay. Faint lights can be seen up and down the beach. There is a cluster of lights that are brighter than the rest. Rocky Beach. I can see now that this is the best place to watch the fireworks.

Tony points to the lights and brakes the silence, "That's where the fireworks will be, but up and down the beach there'll be a lot of smaller shows. A lot of people have their own fireworks for the fourth of July. Tonight will be a good night for them. Clear skies and a full moon just before midnight."

We both fall silent again. I slowly sip on my beer. Tony places his head back on the log.

"You doing okay? I mean with all the shit going on in your life right now," I ask him.

He sighs. "Yeah, I'm okay." He is silent for a moment longer then says, "I knew something was wrong when Elaine told me that she was pregnant. Our sex life hadn't been exactly terrific." He takes a drink of his beer. "I don't think that in all the years we were together that we've ever had sex without a rubber and at that I don't think I ever came insider her. There always seemed to be...," he stops and has another drink of beer. I wait just in case he wants to continue. I don't know whether I should push him to talk about it or just leave it alone. Gerry always said that it was best to talk about things and get it out of the way. That way, with everything said, you can get on with the important things like living the rest of your life. I think he's right.

"There always seemed to be…?" I push him to finish what he's started to say.

Tony takes another sip of his beer. "Something missing, I guess. I mean with me, it's like, you know." He takes another sip of beer. "I'm not so sure about things right now, I guess."

"Oh," is about all I can think of to say, because I'm not quite sure where Tony is going with all this. Is it because of the suspicion he's had with the pregnancy or is he trying to tell me that he is questioning his feelings for Elaine. I'm not sure. He hands me his empty beer. I automatically get him another. Just then the sky lights up. The fireworks have started in Rocky Beach. We both watch and comment about one or another firework that has just been set off in the night sky. The show continues for almost an hour before the grand finale. I take out the last two beers from the cooler. I'm feeling pretty light headed from the beer and wine. I can tell that Tony is feeling no pain either. As the night goes on, smaller fireworks shows can be seen from the private estates along the beach. We can hear muffled explosions as the fireworks erupt in the sky. We continue to talk about the splashes of colour that light up the night sky. Soon the sky is void of the coloured lights, only the stars twinkle above us. We talk with each other in the darkness like we've been friends all our lives. I feels very comfortable in Tony's company. The moon has just started to rise above the horizon and the stars around it start to disappear. Across the bay there is a bright shimmering from the reflection of the moon as it starts its climb across the night sky. I can see Tony's face in the moon light.

"So," Tony says. "Are you gonna answer the question I asked you last night?"

"What question?" I ask.

"You know, are you?" he asks.

"Am I what?"

"You're not really makin' this easy. I don't normally ask people these kind of personal things," he says as he drinks the last of his beer.

I know exactly where he's going with this. He does remember what we talked about last night on the beach. I decide that I'm not going to make it as easy as that. "What kind of personal stuff?" I ask.

"You know, really personal stuff." He looks at me. Even though I can see his face, I can barely make out his eyes.

They blend in with the shadows cast by the moonlight. I can tell he is feeling a little nervous.

"Like?" I push him to be more specific.

"Like, are you, you know gay?" he asks.

"You're right it is rather personal. But does it matter if I am or not?" I ask him as I stare at his face in the dark trying to read it.

"No, of course not," he says. "I'm just curious, that's all. It's just that I thought you might be. I'm fine with it if you are."

I hesitate for a moment. Here I am sitting on a secluded beach after midnight with a stranger who just happens to look like a Roman god talking about my sexuality. It can't get any stranger than this I think to myself. What if he isn't really comfortable with it and goes crazy. It'll be weeks before anyone comes looking for me. I'm still searching his face for any indication that he might get violent if I tell him the truth, but something inside tells me that he is being honest with me and that he is really okay with it. "Yeah, I'm gay," I say.

He smiles at me and says, "I thought so." He lifts his empty beer bottle to his lips and tilts his head as far back as he can. When nothing comes out of his bottle he turns his head back and stares out across the bay. "I think I have this knack of being able to tell if someone is gay. My friend Garth is gay. I knew he was gay before he told me." He sits there staring off into the darkness. He tries again to have a drink from the empty beer bottle. "I've always been sorta...," he stops mid sentence and tries again to take a drink from the empty beer bottle. "Should we have another one?" he says.

"Nah, I think I've had enough, but you go ahead," I suggest to him.

"No, I guess I really don't need it," he replies. "Well, I think that's about it for the fireworks," he states. Both of us just stare off into darkness.

I stand up and start to collect the empty beer bottles and put them into the small cooler. Tony helps me gather up the empties. We walk up the path towards the house. The silence makes me think that what I have just told him about myself really does make a difference. He would probably be leaving in the morning. Oh well, I think to myself, it was fun while it lasted and even if it was only for today. He's good eye candy and good company if nothing else.

As we reach the steps Tony says, "Andy, I guess what I really...," again he stops mid sentence.

"Look Tony, it really doesn't matter okay? It's no big deal. I think it might be best if we leave things just as they are okay?" I say as he opens the French doors and we enter the living room. I carry the small cooler full of empty beer bottles into the kitchen and leave it on the counter by the sink. I've left Tony in the living room by himself. In the kitchen window I see my reflection staring back at me. I feel a little disappointed about how Tony took the information that I am gay. I continue to stare at myself in the window. I guess that subconsciously I was hoping that something might have happened between Tony and myself. Let's face it. It's a gay man's fantasy to have sex with a straight man. How crazy am I? It's obvious that Tony is straight. He just broke up with his fiancée. On the beach he even admitted that they were doing the wild thing, so that sort of proves that he's really not interested in me. I really shouldn't set myself up for anything. I walk back into the living room.

"Well, I think it's time for me to hit the hay. Those beers have made me a bit light headed," I say.

"Light headed or just a bit drunk?" he says.

"I was just trying to pick a nicer way of sayin' that." I smile at him.

"Yeah, I think I'm just this side of being a bit tipsy." He holds up his pointer finger and thumb and holds them about a half inch apart. "And sleep does sound like a good idea."

I walk to the stairs, turn to him and say, "Good night." I walk up the stairs.

"I'll be following you in a sec. I'll just turn off the lights down here."

I get to the top of the stairs and walk into the bathroom. I can hear him walking downstairs as he goes from room to room and turning off lights. I listen to him walk up the stairs and go into his room next to the bathroom. I wash up after I finish taking a leak, brush my teeth and leave the bathroom. I go to my room and close the door. I open the

French doors and turn on a lamp. It casts a low dull light around the room. I undress. I hesitate when I get to my jockey's, but decide to sleep unencumbered tonight. I tell myself I need that feeling of complete freedom. I turn off the lamp. The room is illuminated by the moonlight streaming in from the two French doors. I start to relax and listen to the sounds coming from outside. There are not many, some crickets, the odd croak of a frog and in the distance, the faint sound of the surf. I hear Tony's door open and I look towards my slightly opened door. The bathroom light goes on then disappears as the door is closed. I hear the sounds of Tony taking a leak, the running water in the sink that follows after he flushes the toilet. I close my eyes as I listen to the water stop, the bathroom door opens and the light is being turned off. The top floor is now in darkness other than the light from the moonlight.

"Andy?" I hear Tony say. "Are you asleep?"

"Ah. Not quite," I answer him. I hear my door open and I look towards it. Tony is standing there in the doorway. He has changed into a pair of boxers.

"Can I, ah talk to you for a second?" he asks.

"Sure, I guess I'm not going anywhere." I say.

He walks over to the bed and sits down on the edge. I move over towards the opposite side of the bed and lean on my side. The moonlight from the door behind me illuminates Tony's back. He turns and looks at me. He has one knee up on the bed and is leaning back on one muscled arm. It looks as though he has something to say but doesn't know where to start.

"So what brings this midnight visit?" I ask him, hoping that a little humour might get him talking.

"First, I want to apologize if I've made you uncomfortable talking about things down on the beach," he says. "And secondly, I just want to say that...," he stops again.

"You know you're very good at that, starting to say something and then just not say it."

"What's it like being gay?" he says.

"I don't understand, what you mean by being gay?" I pause while I gather my thoughts. I have never really thought about it. "I've never been asked that question before. I don't know, it's pretty much just being normal to me, I guess."

"How'd you know I mean?" he asks.

"I don't know, I guess I just always was. I've always wanted to be with men." I look at him. He is very attentive. "I never really wanted to be with women, I mean sexually. I found men to be very attractive and very sexy. It's not just a physical thing but an emotional one too."

He runs his fingers through his hair with his free hand. "Oh Shit," he says. "I've wanted to...," He does it again, but this time instead of finishing his sentence he leans over and kisses me gently on my lips. He holds it for a moment, then pulls his face away from mine.

"Tony! Do you..." I start to say. He has taken me by complete surprise

"Don't say anything," he says. "I've wanted to do that for a long time, since I saw you earlier this week when we went through the inspections, I wanted it to be you. Don't ask me why, but I did."

"Tony I think..."

Again he stops me with a kiss. This time I kiss him back. I grab him by his shoulders and push him off, just enough to look into his dark eyes and search his face.

"Tony, do you know what you're doing?" I ask, searching for answers in his eyes.

"Actually I do. For the first time in my life I really do," he says as he presses his lips against mine. I accept his kiss this time and squeezed his muscled shoulders with my hands. He turns his whole body to face me on the bed. I feel him adjust his weight so that he wouldn't roll right on top of me. His right hand caresses my shoulder and runs down my arm, while he leans on his left. I feel him caress my bicep and forearm. I decide to let him lead the way as it was, I suspected, his first time with a man. I can feel his tongue probe into my mouth. I openly kiss him back, taking his tongue deep into my mouth. I can taste the mixture of freshly brushed teeth and beer as his tongue probes my mouth. His hair brushes against my face as he continues to kiss me. His right hand is caressing my arm. Soon his hand finds its way to my face. He rubs it over my jaw and chin as he kisses me. As it goes over my goatee I hear him moan. I wrap my arms around him and pull him close to me. The only thing between us are the bed sheet and his boxers. I run my hands over his back and shoulders, only going as far as the waist band of his boxers. His body is solid and hard. It feels good to be touching a man again. Tony takes his time, slowly moving his hand from my face back to my shoulders. He squeezes them roughly. I let out a quiet moan. Again he squeezes. His hand moves to my back and I can feel the calluses on his hand through the material of the sheet. His hands are strong. He rubs my back and as his hand reaches the small of my back he pulls me closer. Our bodies are now laying side by side on the bed with our arms around each other. From there Tony's hand continues down but instead of stopping at my waist he lets it roam over my butt cheek. I can tell he is nervous. I can feel his breathing quicken and his hand has a slight tremble as it travels over my butt and as far as his arm will reach down my leg. He stops kissing me and pulls his face away.

"I've never done anything like this before," he says.

"Do you want to stop?" I ask. "It's okay if you do."

Instead of answering me he places his lips against mine again. This time opening his mouth he invites my tongue to explore his mouth. I do. He continues to explore the back of my body on top of the sheet with his free hand, running his hand up and down from my head to as far as his arm can reach. With each stroke of his hand he explores the crevasse between my butt cheeks. I continue to keep my hands on his muscled back, but with each stroke of Tony's hand between my cheeks I find my hands exploring past his waist. I stroke the two solid mounds of muscled flesh of his butt on top of his boxers, cupping each globe of butt muscle as my hands reach where they meet his legs. We continue kissing letting each other have turns exploring the other's mouth with our tongues. My hands find their way under the waistband of Tony's boxers and I feel the skin of his butt. It is warm and firm. I continue to caress and knead them. With the movement of my hands over his butt I have worked his boxers down over their roundness. He lifts his butt in the air, and released his hard cock that has been caught in his half pulled off boxers. He presses his body hard against mine.

This time I can feel his hardness against my own. I pull him closer so that he is almost lying on top of me. I find the small tuft of hair in the small of his back and gently play with it. He moans and kisses me harder. Tony pulls his face away from me and turns to sit on the edge of the bed. He stands up and lets his boxers fall to the floor. He turns to face me. As he stands next to the bed I slowly scan the full length of his body. He is just as I imagined he would be naked. I pull back the sheet on the bed and invite him to join me. This time he kneels beside me and starts to caress my body with his hands, searching and exploring, starting with my shoulders and working his way over my chest and abdomen and down my thighs and legs. I close my eyes and enjoy the sensation.

"I've never touched another man before" he says.

"And?" I ask.

"It's good, it feels good."

"Yes it does," I agree.

Time seems to have stopped as we kiss, touch, caress and make love to each other. Tony lies on me pressing the cum and sweat between our bodies and kisses me passionately. I hold him in my arms as we kiss. He rolls off me, gets out of bed and leaves the bedroom for the bathroom. I can hear water running for a few minutes and then he returns to the bedroom. I see he has a wet cloth and a towel. He cleans me up with the wet cloth. I watch him as he does this. God, I think to myself, this man is perfect. After he finishes cleaning me up he crawls back into bed with me, pulls the covers up over both of us, spoons me and wraps his arms around me. We lie here, Tony holding me in the moonlight. He tightens his hold on me. It feels so good. I don't want tonight to end, ever.

"Goodnight Tony," I whisper.

He kisses my neck and tightens his hold on me.

I lie there in his arms listening to the night again. This time the sound of Tony's breathing mixes in with the night sounds. It is as if they belong together. I can feel his chest rise and fall against my back. I can feel his breath exhaling on the back of my neck with every breath he takes. He tucks his knees in closer behind mine. It is as if he is trying to get as close to me as is physically possible. I sigh with satisfaction. I continue to listen to Tony breath. It slows as he falls into a deep sleep. In a few moments I find myself drifting off as well.

The room has gotten lighter as I open my eyes to its brightness. The sunlight is pouring through the open French doors. Tony's arm is still around me. It wasn't all just a wild dream. We hadn't moved from that position all night. Tony's breathing is still shallow. He is in a deep sleep. I slowly lift his arm and slide out of bed. The sheets smell salty from our night of lovemaking. Tony gives a small groan and rolls over. I look at his dark body and again admire how nearly perfect Tony is put together. I walk out of the bedroom and close the door quietly. In the bathroom I wash my face and shave. I quickly take a hot shower, dry myself off and return to the bedroom. Tony is still fast asleep but has thrown the sheet off. He is lying face down in a prone position. I put on a pair of shorts and a muscles shirt. I turn and admire Tony's body once more as he sleeps. His white bubble butt cheeks, his back rising and falling with each breath he takes. I know if I stand here any longer I'd end up back in bed with him. That wouldn't be such a bad thing. But my better judgment gets the best of me. Last night was Tony's first time with a man and I wasn't sure that after what we did he'd be willing to or even want to do it with a man again. This is something that Tony would have to deal with on his own. I leave the bedroom and go downstairs. I quickly clean up the kitchen from the evening before and make myself a pot of coffee as quietly as I can trying not to wake Tony upstairs. I finish the little bit of cleanup as the coffee maker starts to gurgle indicating that it has finished brewing. I pour myself a cup and walk out into the living room. I take my grandfather's kite out from behind the sofa and decide that I'd try flying it. I gather up the two spools of string and walk down to the beach, coffee mug and kite in hand. I make my way to the secluded beach between the rocks where my Grams and Grandfather took us to fly kites many years ago. There is a good breeze off the water today, so it wouldn't be difficult to fly a kite. It takes me a half dozen tries before I actually get the kite high enough in the air to keep it aloft. High enough to feel confident that it isn't going to come crashing down. I let the string roll through my fingers as the kite soars higher. The kite dips a few times, but then catches another up draught and continues its climb in the sky. There is very little string left on the spool when I stop the kite from climbing. That is when I hear footsteps on the beach behind me. I look back at Tony as he emerges from behind the rock outcropping blocking the main beach. He has showered and shaved and is wearing cut offs and a muscle shirt. He is carrying a mug of coffee with him. He approaches me and sits on the big log on the beach.

"Morning," I say.

He smiles and replies, "Morning." He takes a sip of coffee. "About last night...," he starts.

Here it comes, the 'I made a big mistake' talk, I think to myself. I made the right decision when I left him alone in the house this morning.

"About last night?"

"Yeah, well, ah," he stammers. "I don't want you to think that I used you. I mean I really wanted to be with you last night. It felt all too natural. Really comfortable, you know?"

"Yeah, I know what you mean," I agree. Well this wasn't what I was expecting. I watch him as he moves towards me and stands beside me. He looks into my eyes. God, I think if he asks me to stay with him forever right now I think I would say yes.

"I just want you to know that I really like you. It's not like it could have been anyone last night." he says.

"So what are you trying to say, Tony?" I ask, our eyes are now locked.

"It's, well shit, even though you're the only man I've been with I think you're the guy I'm supposed to be with, if you know what I mean?" he says.

I thought back to my short stay with Fiona and Tim, and how she said that I wasn't to say good-bye, that maybe she'd be seeing me around. It's like she had this feeling or maybe she really was psychic and saw things that the average person didn't.

"Are you asking me to stay here in Rocky Beach with

you?" I ask him directly. No point in beating around the bush, I figure.

"Would you?" he asks me. Our eyes are still locked on each other. I know this is really hard for him. I can see that his eyes are searching and waiting for an answer.

I smile at him and say, "Here hold this." I hand him the string of the kite. "Do you think that this tugging is the angels?" He is holding the string in his hands. He looks up to where the blue kite is floating in the sky.

"There sure is a lot of pull on the string," Tony says.

I put my hand on his shoulder squeezing it and say, "Well, if not we'll have a long time to get this old kite flying high enough to make sure that we're really flying with angels."